END
RUN

a novel

HOMER CHARLES HIATT

authorHOUSE®

AuthorHouse™
1663 Liberty Drive
Bloomington, IN 47403
www.authorhouse.com
Phone: 1 (800) 839-8640

Published by AuthorHouse 04/23/2018

ISBN: 978-1-5462-3914-7 (sc)
ISBN: 978-1-5462-3915-4 (hc)
ISBN: 978-1-5462-3913-0 (e)

Library of Congress Control Number: 2018904882

Print information available on the last page.

This book is printed on acid-free paper.

Thank you to my
dear friend
Ellen Hill
for her
careful and patient
editing

For Pat and John

1

Dundee, a staid private neighborhood of central Omaha, featured large old homes typically separated from winding sidewalks and narrow tree-lined streets by hedgerows and iron fences. The Westings lived at 41 Crestwood Lane having purchased the two story brick in 2002 from a cantankerous widow who declared to anyone willing to listen that she was moving to Canada. The old woman had constantly referred to the recent attack on the World Trade Center in New York City, and ended her rants with her wish to spend her remaining days in a country that didn't inspire so much hatred. She moved away ten years ago, and the Westings had no way of knowing if she was still alive. Meanwhile, Warren and Margie established themselves as involved residents of Dundee, consistently voting for neighborhood improvements without much regard for costs. In 2012 the local issue involved mandatory sprinkler systems to water the grass of front lawns and common areas, the expense to be borne by the residents. Most folks knew where the couple at 41 Crestwood stood on the subject.

Warren Westing was a 65-year-old tax attorney for a large law firm in downtown Omaha. A native Midwesterner from a small Nebraska town, he was a rather large man who stood 5 feet 11 inches tall and weighed 230 pounds. He once threw the shot put and discus in high school. He also played one year of football, the year his high school first managed to afford the sport. His position had been fullback and he preferred end runs to smashing into the line. These days his body was more fat than muscle, a paunch pushing his white underbelly forward and his arms and legs just sticks that lacked definition. He retained a handsome head of hair, a longish gray arrangement that enjoyed the attention of a stylist. He shaved every day, even on Sunday and holidays, and he wore contact lens. The clean facial look gave him a boyish appearance, though he worried about wrinkles changing that. Warren knew he was getting old and he didn't like it one bit.

Politically Warren was a Democrat though he had voted for Ronald Reagan during the days of double digit inflation. In general he tended to avoid confrontations, perhaps explaining his preference for tax law instead of the more adversarial branches of his profession. He considered himself to be happily married and appreciated the fact that he and his wife could lead very separate lives and still treat one another amiably when together. He and Margie had been married for 17 years, both for the second time. They both expected and enjoyed their privacies, a situation they both openly admitted to being the secret to their compatibility. As with many middle-age married couples their sex life had tapered dramatically even before Margie was diagnosed with cancer in 2011. At one time Warren considered taking a medication for erectile dysfunction though he really didn't accept the idea that he was impotent. Margie's opposition to the idea surprised him but he never got around to asking why she seemed to lack interest in revitalizing their intimacy. Her illness brought an end to to the matter.

Margie was the same age as Warren and hailed from Texas, though she had lived in Nebraska since her college days. She was a good deal more conservative than her husband both politically and socially which sometimes led to spats between them, some short-lived and some spread over days. She spoke with a southern drawl that she emphasized when she argued. An only child, she had made frequent and extended visits with her parents in San Antonio before their deaths. After that she often visited their graves in Texas, travel that struck Warren as frivolous. It was only out of his respect for her privacy that he never shared this opinion with her.

Margie was petite, standing only five feet two inches and weighing an even 100 pounds. Her movements tended to be quick and sometimes clumsy. Born a blond, she began dying her short-cropped hair white when the first gray hairs showed up. After a career as an purchasing executive for Macy's she took early retirement to do volunteer work at the Lauritzen Botanical Gardens and brought home her acquired skills to adorn their Dundee home with lovely landscapes of shrubs and flowers. Her current daily uniform consisted of a warm-up suit and running shoes. For the last year she wore a bandana on her head, this because she had gone bald due to the chemotherapy she was enduring for non-Hodgkin's lymphoma. When she heard Warren complain about getting old she ripped off her bandana and showed him he had no room to complain. The maneuver always shut him up.

The Westing home was a dark brick. It held two upstairs bedrooms and a guest bedroom on the first floor, two and a half baths, a den, living room, dining room, kitchen, and had an attached garage. The basement was unfinished and housed a dated washer and dryer that sat together in a dank room. A sliding glass door off the kitchen wall led to a stone patio that encircled a small garden pool in which filtered water bubbled. Wrought iron patio furniture sat on the stone surface every day of the year. Beyond the pool lay a rectangle of manicured grass that was regularly watered and mowed by a lawn service. Bordering the lawn were Margie's plants, and behind the plants stood a privacy fence. Both Warren and Margie loved the backyard, occasionally sitting together, weather permitting, on wrought iron chairs and using the round table to hold their drinks and reading material. Warren was a beer drinker. Margie favored margaritas.

Neither Warren nor Margie had children, either from their first marriages or with each other. When first married they had tried to have a child but failed. On the advice of a fertility expert Warren had deposited sperm at the Omaha Fertility Clinic as part of a plan for *in vitro* fertilization. But the Westings were busy people at the time and they simply never got around to embracing the involved project. When they turned 50 they both abandoned the idea. Since then Warren occasionally wondered if there were children running around Omaha who looked like him.

Though there were never children running through the brick home, there was a dog. A Great Dane puppy joined the Westings shortly after the 2002 purchase. His name was Theo and his coat was brindle. Currently he weighed 200 pounds, a burden to his 10-year-old arthritic legs. Because of his affliction he usually avoided climbing the stairs to his masters' bedrooms. These days Theo barked at the foot of the stairs to rouse Warren or Margie for his morning walk. But this day, a warm Saturday in June, his barking did him no good. The old dog struggled up the stairs. He found Warren sitting on the edge of the bed in his bedroom.

"Hey boy," Warren called when he saw Theo. The dog's limp was obvious.

"Margie, did Theo get his pill today?" Warren called. His wife was in the adjacent bedroom. They hadn't shared a bedroom in some time because of his snoring. Since the beginning of Margie's chemotherapy Warren had been grateful for the arrangement. Her vomiting and diarrhea disgusted him, though he had been careful not to remark on her suffering. In fact he made a point of altogether skirting the cancer issue. If Margie felt his lack of support she never said so, and he simply assumed she preferred to keep her illness private. That, he admitted to himself, was the way he wanted it.

"Marge!" Warren called again.

"What in blazes is it?" Margie complained as she appeared at Warren's door. Kneeling, she scratched Theo behind his ears and cooed at the giant. "How is my sugar today?" she said. "Is that bad ol' arthritis botherin' my baby?"

Warren snickered as he gazed on his wife and dog. Theo looked enormous next to Margie. Moving to a full-length mirror Warren donned a white dress shirt, cufflinks included, and slipped on a pair of slacks that belonged to a summer weight navy suit. A leather belt, burgundy suspenders and polished leather shoes came next followed by tie. He chose a subdued club tie. Warren was dressing for a funeral for a work colleague.

"Did Theo get his medication?" Margie asked.

"That's what I asked you," Warren replied.

"Well excuse me for livin'."

"Well, did he?"

"I've been pukin' my guts out this mornin', thank you very much. Haven't had a chance to fetch dog pills."

Warren thought better of continuing this exchange. Instead he donned his suit coat and turned to his wife for her opinion on his choices. It wasn't often that he dressed for a funeral. "How do I look?" he asked.

Groaning as she rose to her feet, Margie walked to face her husband. Her bandana was at the level of his chest. "Just because you're goin' to a funeral doesn't mean you have to look like a friggin' mortician," Margie said as she pulled off his club tie and handed him one with red and white stripes. "Put this on," she demanded.

As usual, Warren followed his wife's advice. When it came to color combinations she had excellent taste. Turning to the mirror he donned the replacement tie. "I can't believe Sanders is dead," he commented.

"Were you two friends?" Margie asked.

"Just acquaintances."

"I'm guessin' all the partners will be in attendance."

"Of course." Warren walked to a window and gazed out over the back yard. It was around 9 a.m. on a Saturday. "Looks like it's going to be a hot one," he called over his shoulder.

"I will not allow you to drive to the church," Margie said. "It's just a block away."

Indeed, the Dundee Methodist Church was the centerpiece of the old neighborhood, situated at the area's understood entrance. A mere six houses separated it from 41 Crestwood. Warren checked his Rolex. "I'd better get moving then," he said. "Don't want to be late." After kissing Margie on the forehead he walked downstairs into the kitchen. Theo followed him. Warren grabbed an amber vial of pills from the window sill above the sink, extracted one, wrapped it in a single slice of American cheese, and fed it to his dog. Theo downed the treat without chewing. "The old lady will walk you this morning," Warren told Theo, who gazed up expectantly. The giant followed his master into the foyer where he grabbed his leash with his massive mouth. Margie met them at the door.

"Come on Sugar," Margie said as she hooked Theo's leash to his studded collar. "Let's have us a lil ol' stroll." In a flash she and Theo were out the door, down the stone walk to the sidewalk where they turned left. Warren followed them. He turned right. He didn't have time for breakfast and he wasn't a coffee drinker, so he walked along on an empty stomach. It didn't take long for perspiration to build up under his suit coat, so he took it off and slung it over his shoulder. As was his habit, he tried to envision what he would experience when he got to his destination. It was a mind game he had played since childhood and it pleased him when his predictions turned out more or less accurate. Stu Gottlieb, his best friend, malpractice attorney and noted early arriver, would sitting in a pew. A bald head on stocky shoulders would indicate his location. The sanctuary would be filled with lawyers, the deceased having been a senior partner in the largest firm in Omaha if not the state of Nebraska. Organ music would fill the sanctuary, which would be hot and stuffy. The eulogy would be long and mostly inaccurate. At the end of the service, Gottlieb would suggest an early lunch at Stogie's, their favorite eatery.

When he reached the old sidewalk leading to the double front doors of the dignified church Warren paused. Gazing up at the double steeples he felt an old distaste well up, a contempt for organized religion that he had carried since boyhood. He recalled the hundreds of hours he sat next to his mother in his home town church. It had been torture for him listening to what he considered to be illogical drivel but his mother gave him no choice. To be sure the unpleasant experience served to keep him away from church. As he headed up the front sidewalk he recalled a pivotal religious discussion he and Margie had shared years ago. More accurately it was an argument. It occurred during their short engagement and almost thwarted the marriage. Margie, who had been raised a Baptist, maintained that regular church attendance helped balance one's life, offered perspective, and provided a certain inner peace. Warren had called her view wishful thinking, naive opinion based on hopelessly twisted dogma and sheer fantasy. At one point Margie had uttered, "I don't see how I can be married to a man like you." Warren had replied, "If it's a bible thumper you want, Omaha is full of them." But somehow the disagreement lost momentum. Their attraction for one another won out. The matter of religion got buried in their private lives and rarely surfaced to spark an argument. If, on any given Sunday morning, Margie left the house she did so without fanfare. And Warren, knowing where she was going, would expect her back before noon.

"Welcome sir," a chipper middle-aged woman said to Warren when he reached the entrance. She was handing out copies of the deceased obituary. Warren recognized her as a secretary at his law firm, though he didn't know her name. He nodded a greeting and scanned the obit as he walked inside. "Christ," he murmured when he got to the year of birth. It was 1946, just a year prior to the year he was born. He had assumed Sanders was much older than he. He was wrong.

Scanning over the seated crowd Warren spotted the bald head and the stocky shoulders he was looking for. Stu Gottlieb was sitting off to the left and toward the front of the sanctuary. As Warren walked toward his friend he listened to the organ music. He didn't recognize the piece, but he didn't expect to. Music was not his forte. Before slipping into the pew next to Stu he put on his suit coat. He had been wrong about the place being hot and stuffy. Air conditioning rendered the church cool, even chilly.

"Move over Gottlieb," Warren said. Stu was busy sending a text message on his cell phone but nevertheless slid to his right to make room for his buddy. He was the same age as Warren, had been his roommate at the University of Nebraska for undergraduate work and for law school, and had even married in the same year as his friend's first nuptial. When Warren divorced, so did Stu. The only break in the pattern came when Stu hit middle-age. That's when his bad luck with women started. Engaged twice, he never made it to a second marriage, suffering two breakups that were not his doing. Currently the man was single.

"All the partners are here," Stu whispered to Warren as he shut off his phone.

"I'd expect nothing less," Warren said in a low voice.

"How did Sanders die?"

"You don't know?"

"I've been on vacation."

"He keeled over from a heart attack right in the middle of a summation."

"Mama mia."

Just then a minister in a black robe walked to a pulpit as the organ music ceased. The eulogy began and in seconds Warren's mind wandered and he began to daydream. His lively imagination, stemming from having grown up in a sleepy rural town, took him back to track meets and football games wherein he embellished certain details. For instance, he half-believed that he won the conference championship in the discus rather than placing third. He scored four touchdowns in the last game of his senior year rather than just one, all on end runs. There had been a University of Nebraska scout in the stands that evening who had come very close to offering him a football scholarship, another example of wishful thinking.

Eventually the hard pew began to numb Warren's legs bringing an end to his fantasy. The drone of the minister's voice tried his patience. His stomach growled with hunger. Irritated, he shifted his weight in an attempt to find a bit of comfort. He turned to his right, his mass supported by one buttock, his legs crossed, an arm draped on the back of the pew. He gaze fell on the open casket that stretched out in front of the podium. What he saw sent chills through his body. Peeking over the purple lining of the coffin at the end nearer him was a tuft of hair, gray hair just like his. For a fleeting second he saw himself lying in place of the senior partner. "Oh God," he whispered. The sound got Stu's attention.

"Are you all right Westing?" Stu asked a bit too loudly, his words drawing glances of irritation from more than one attendee.

Warren just gave Stu a reassuring nod and turned forward, not wishing to look at the coffin and the tuft of gray hair. For additional diversion he pulled out his cell phone and checked his text messages. That proved to be a bad idea.

Vani nisa a ro.

"What the fuck?" Warren said as he stared at the message. His voice was far too loud, prompting an attorney sitting just ahead of him to turn and give him a stern "Shh." Still studying the text, he could see it was clearly a sentence and not an accidental accumulation of random letters. Furthermore, there was no indication of the source of the message.

Taking a deep breath, Warren closed his eyes and tried to compose himself. He came to the conclusion that the text message had been sent to him by mistake. But the tuft of gray hair peeking over the purple lining of the coffin was another matter. No matter how hard he tried he couldn't shake the image.

Mercifully the service finally came to an end and the friends hustled out of the church. Warren, for one, hoped not to have an exchange with colleagues who had heard his outburst. They walked together toward Stu's BMW, though they had not expressly planned to do so.

"So what's going on with you Westing?" Stu asked as they walked.

"I don't want to talk about it," Warren replied.

"Suit yourself," Stu said. It was likely the product of a long friendship that led him to change the subject. "Have you ever been to a Jewish funeral?" he threw out.

"Can't say that I have."

"Well, when I go you'll witness your first."

"What makes you think you'll die before I do?"

Stu sighed. "I don't know. I just do. That bothers me."

The men stared at one another. Warren ran a hand through his hair. Stu stroked his bald scalp. They both hitched up their slacks and took deep breaths. "How about some food?" Stu suggested. "I'll drive."

In no time the friends were motoring toward Omaha's Old Market, an area replete with restaurants and shops. The market was so crowded that Stu had to park his BMW several blocks from Stogies, a popular bar and grill. The late morning was warm and humid, and the men left their suit coats in the car. Still, they looked overdressed compared to the throng that filled the sidewalks. Warren noticed a few stares from baby faced young men who wore their baseball caps backwards. He considered them unworthy of any serious regard beyond wondering why they apparently preferred to look identical to one another. That he and his fellow attorney both sported expensive dress shirts, suspenders, crisply creased slacks and shined leather shoes was lost on him.

When Warren and Stu stepped into Stogies they were told there would be a 30 minute wait before a table opened up. The hostess offered them menus but they declined. Warren always had the half-pound burger, and Stu the pastrami on rye.

"The College World Series crowd, I expect," Warren guessed as he scanned the packed eatery.

"Are you going this year?" Stu asked.

"No way. The Ameritrade stadium doesn't serve beer. At least when the CWS is in town."

"I did not know that."

"I saved you from a disappointing afternoon, didn't I?"

"That you did, Westing. That you did."

Just then a cheer erupted at the back of the restaurant. "Maroooooon!" the voices shouted. "Whiiiite!" other voices screamed back. The exchange continued until it collapsed into laughter and hooting.

"Mississippi State," Warren advised Stu.

Stu grimaced. "Do you want to eat somewhere else?" he asked.

"We're here. Let's tough it out."

A half hour later, the men were shown to a well worn booth. They both ordered pints of a local brew and placed their orders. The restaurant was so noisy that they gave up on conversation. Rather, they toyed with their phones. Warren took another look at that mysterious text message. The more he examined it the more he yearned to know what it meant. He decided he would show it to his secretary at work, a middle aged Hispanic woman whom he had heard speaking Spanish from time to time. Perhaps she could at least offer some incite.

Finished with his cell phone, Warren stared across the table at his long time friend. Stu looked like Don Rickles these days, bald and jowly. It was difficult to accept that he once resembled a young Al Pacino. In fact, Stu was quite the ladies' man when they were in school. Warren knew that the recent failures in courtship bothered his friend far more than he admitted.

Just then the baseball crowd filed out of the bar and grill, suggesting that a ball game in Ameritrade stadium was about to begin. The noise level in Stogie's fell to a civilized din, allowing some small talk between friends.

"So, tell me about a Jewish funeral," Warren said.

Stu snickered. "We don't have the time."

"I take it it's complicated."

"It would be easier for us to wade through the tax code."

"How is the Creighton case coming?" Warren asked, knowing that Stu was heading a major suit against Creighton University Medical Center.

"They're not going to settle."

"You're asking for 40 million dollars. I'm not sure I'd settle either."

"That's chump change these days. The truth is, there's a doctor involved who doesn't like his ego rubbed the wrong way. Speaking of doctors, how is Margie doing?"

"The chemo makes her sick. And she's bald. She hates that."

"I should stop by. I haven't seen her in months. Give her my best, would you?"

The talk was interrupted by the delivery of the hamburger and the pastrami on rye signaling the beginning of a ritual. Stu slathered the mound of cold meat with Dijon mustard. Warren removed the top of the sesame bun along with the tomato slice, pickles, onion and lettuce. He then salted the charred hamburger patty, applied catsup and yellow mustard, and replaced the garnish and bun. The men glanced at one another before ceremoniously cutting their sandwiches in half and digging in. Warren couldn't remember when this ceremony began but knew it had to have been decades ago.

"Did that funeral get to you as much as it got to me?" Warren asked, his mouth full.

"Specify," Stu replied, also with his mouth full.

"I saw myself lying in a coffin."

"Westing, you are one sick fuck."

Warren could see that his friend was right. The funeral was one of those instances where a lively imagination had proved counterproductive.

All he could do was wait for the terrifying image to die away. For now he moved on to another topic

"Any prospects out there for you, curly?" Warren teased.

"You need a new bald joke, Westing."

"What's wrong with this one?"

"You've been using it for 20 years. That's what is wrong."

Warren watched his friend smooth a hand over his baldness. Then Stu grinned in that peculiar way of his. Experience told Warren that his friend had something to reveal. "Don't tell me...you've got a woman lined up," Warren guessed.

Stu took a large bite out of his sandwich and washed it down with a gulp of beer.

"My sister set me up," he said as he wiped his mouth with a paper napkin.

"Your sister the violinist?"

"She's the one. I've got a date with a viola player. The down side is, I've got to sit through a symphony concert first."

"So you've met this woman?"

"Once. She's in her fifties, but she's fit as a fiddle," Stu said as he patted his round abdomen. "I'm not sure we're compatible."

Warren was keenly aware of how out of shape he and his friend had become over the years, particularly recently. They had joined a country club in hopes that playing golf would help them lose a few pounds. Riding around in a cart and then devouring hot dogs and beer had produced the opposite result. The socializing, however, proved to be a good business move for their law firm, as they had made several referrals to colleagues. His mind on golf, Warren thought about the two-man tournament he and Stu had entered.

"Who do we play tomorrow?" Warren asked his friend.

Stu reached into a shirt pocket and pulled out a folded piece of paper. "I've got it right here," he said as he scanned the document. "Oh, boy," he groaned.

"What?"

"We play Billy Bob Richardson and Gar Young."

"Oh no," Warren groaned. Everybody in Omaha knew who Billy Bob Richardson was. He was a chubby loudmouth, a used car salesman whose

TV ads seemed to perpetually run on all the local channels. He dressed like a dime store cowboy and made a point of bragging about his pride in being a devout Christian. There was one word that seemed to pop up at the mention of his name. That word was "obnoxious".

"Have you met the guy?" Stu asked.

"I've seen him at the club. Those cowboy hats make him hard to miss."

"How about his partner?"

"I've never met Gar, but I know his story."

"I'm listening," Stu said.

"One day I happened to watch 'Good Morning Omaha'…"

"You're kidding."

"Margie was sick in bed. I had to wait for a pharmacy delivery."

"No need to explain, Westing. Get on with it."

"Billy Bob and Gar were interviewed. Of course Billy Bob did all the talking. He bragged on Gar for saving his life in Vietnam. He crowed about Gar having a job for life at Billy Bob Motors."

"What did Gar have to say for himself?"

"I don't believe he said a word. He seemed to be sort of a sad sack."

Just then Warren recalled a particular golf tournament rule. Opponents rather than teammates were required to ride together in golf carts during play. "I've got dibs on Gar for a cart mate," Warren declared.

"I'll shoot you for it," Stu said.

The friends then repeated a contest they had used hundreds of times to settle minor disputes. "Evens," Warren said as he presented his fist. Stu copied the move and counted to three, a signal to present fingers.

"Damn," Stu cursed as he looked down at four fingers, two of them his and two of them the winner's.

Warren grinned, saying, "I'll get the tab."

A bit later the duo was in the BMW heading back to the Dundee area where Warren said good-bye to his friend in his driveway. Just before jumping out of the car he intentionally farted. Stu returned the favor. The unsavory exchange had been their signing off gesture for years, though they reserved their juvenile behavior for private moments. As Stu headed his car out of the stately neighborhood and toward his condo on the riverfront, Warren used the garage entrance to enter into the kitchen. Margie was there preparing a smoothie.

"Y'all ate lunch I expect," Margie said as she put blackberries, plain yogurt and crushed ice in a Vitamix blender.

"You know us well," Warren said. He sat on a stool facing a butcher block island counter and watched as the contents of the blender mixed into a bluish thick liquid. When the roar of the gadget subsided, he added, "Stu sends you his best."

"There's a man I haven't seen in a coon's age," Margie observed. She poured the smoothie into two large glass mugs and handed one to her husband.

"He's been tied up with that Creighton suit. And I'm guessing he'll have even less free time if he hits it off with the woman his sister set him up with."

Warren's words seemed to catch Margie by surprise. "Stu is dating again?" she asked.

"Why wouldn't he?"

"You'd think he'd be a little gun shy. It was just a year ago that he had his heart broken for the second time. My goodness gracious."

"Gottlieb is nothing if not persistent," Warren said, knocking back a mouthful of the cold treat. He noticed that Margie put her smoothie aside after just one sip. "Are you sick to your stomach?" he asked.

"Don't worry yourself about little ol' me," Margie murmured. Warren picked up on the sadness in her voice. That, combined with the frightening experience of the funeral of a man his age, threatened to touch what he had come to call over the years as his "soft side." Mathematics and tax law provided him with predictability and safety. He loathed the uncertainty in volatile emotionality. But here he was, suddenly worried about his wife's well being and his mortality.

"I've never told you how sorry I am," Warren muttered.

"About what, Sugar?" Margie said. She seemed to need the counter to steady herself.

"About you having cancer."

Margie gave her husband a long and soulful look. Slowly and purposefully she removed the bandana that covered her bald scalp. He immediately understood that this particular gesture was not to tell him to stop feeling sorry for himself. This time she was asking him to take a good long look at the monster that had taken over her life. She looked so frail. Her eyes were dark and sunken, her cheeks hollowed, her lips cracked. Warren wanted to somehow help but didn't know how. Another feeling seized him, one that he abhorred. He felt helpless.

"I want things to be normal again," Warren blurted.

"And you think I don't?"

"Of course you do. I mean that…"

"I'm going to take a nap," Margie interrupted, replacing her bandana and strolling out of the kitchen.

"Sleep well," Warren called.

Margie raised a hand above her head telling Warren she had heard him. Seconds later he could hear her padding up the staircase. Disappointed in himself, he rinsed his glass and put it in the dish drainer. I'm such an idiot, he thought.

With a relaxing Saturday ahead of him, Warren changed clothes and headed for the back yard and the garden pool, first grabbing a bottle of beer from the fridge on the way. Dressed in a ratty golf shirt and baggy shorts he slipped out of his sandals and sat at poolside to dangle his legs in the tepid water. He disliked how rapidly the chlorinated water heated up in the summer and made a point of regularly replacing the 50 gallons with cooler stuff from an outdoor spigot. This day was no exception. The practice drove up his water bill but having a comfortable pool, however small, was important to him. He drank his beer as he splashed his feet and when done sprang up to drag a garden hose to the edge of the pool. Warm water drained out while cool water flowed in. The chore took 45 minutes.

"You and your pool," Margie said as she joined Warren on the patio. She was carrying a glass of iced tea.

"How was your nap?" Warren asked. He returned to his place at the water's edge. Margie sat on a wrought iron chair.

"Short and sweet. How was the funeral?"

"Very bizarre," Warren admitted. He told Margie about what seeing a man his age lying in a coffin did to him. He skipped the part about the strange text message, satisfied that the thing was just someone's mistake.

"Are you afraid of dyin'?" Margie asked.

"I guess I am Marge," Warren admitted.

"I used to be. Havin' cancer makes you look the grim reaper right in the eye."

Warren nodded his head slowly, as though he understood what Margie had said. The truth was, he simply wanted the topic of conversation to change. They had never shared their views on death and dying before and it made him very uncomfortable. Unfortunately for him his wife wasn't done talking.

"I believe the soul is pure energy, like a beam of light. After you die the energy continues," Margie said. Her voice sounded dreamy and even joyful. Her words stunned Warren. In all the years he had known her he had never heard her talk in such a manner. Then she continued, asking, "What do you think, Sugar?"

Warren could not understand what had happened to his very private spouse. Here she was asking a personal and intimate question, something she almost never did. "Where is all of this coming from, Marge?" he said, almost pleading with her.

Margie didn't respond. Rather she rose to her feet, slipped out of her running shoes, rolled up her sweat pants and joined Warren at the edge of the garden pool. There she dangled her thin legs in the water and threaded an arm around his. "I believe the body recycles into nature," she said. "That's why I want to be cremated. You can scatter my ashes…"

"Don't talk like that," Warren injected.

"Why not?"

"I don't know. I guess it's a little…morbid."

Margie didn't seem to hear Warren's objection. Rather she headed in another direction. "I want you to promise me somethin'," she said.

"Sure."

"I want you to get a check-up."

"Christ. You know how much I hate doctors."

"Promise me."

Warren sighed. "All right, all right," he muttered.

"Thank you," Margie said as she struggled to her feet, grabbed the garden hose and headed for a bed of flowers. Knowing himself well enough not to procrastinate, Warren fetched another beer and carried the Omaha Yellow Pages to a lounge chair on the patio. Theo slipped under the lounger to enjoy the shade. Because of Stu Gottlieb's suit against Creighton Medical Center, Warren perused the list of primary physicians associated with the other major center in Omaha, the University of Nebraska Medical

Center or UNMC. Running a finger down the series of names he stopped at Alvin McHale, M.D. Alvin was a family name, once used by both his father and grandfather. In fact, his middle name was Alvin. "Good enough," he said as he committed the office number to memory. For him ten digits was nothing.

Done with his research, Warren stretched out on the lounger and closed his eyes, intending to nap. In seconds the image of the gray hair peeking over the purple lining of the coffin dominated his mind's eye. With a groan he turned on his left side, pulling up his right knee and stretching out his left leg, and slipping his left hand under a small pillow that he kept on the lounger for napping. It was a sleeping position he had assumed all of his life, and the physical cues did the trick. His mind cleared and he relaxed. Before he nodded off he let three thoughts race through his consciousness. First, he planned to get to the golf course early tomorrow to get in a little practice. Second, he promised himself he would make a doctor's appointment the first thing Monday morning. And third, he imagined he was a beam of light coursing through space. He slept on that lounger for a solid hour.

❚❚

A thunder clap woke Warren early Sunday morning. He checked his digital alarm clock at the side of his bed. It read 5:41. Walking to his bathroom, he flipped on a light and urinated into the commode. The stream produced its expected noise leading to a single deep bark from the first floor. Warren chuckled, pleased that his dog could still hear the signal that promised a walk. Theo is old and arthritic, he thought, but there's nothing wrong with his hearing.

After slipping into a T-shirt, shorts, and flip-flops, Warren strolled down the stair case. Theo was waiting for him, leash in mouth. "Good boy," Warren said, congratulating himself for having taught the Great Dane his trick. Affixing the leash to the dog's collar, he led Theo to the front door and stepped outside. The pre-dawn was warm but the weather threatened, lightning flashing in the distance and bursts of wind rattling the trees. "Let's make it quick, Theo," Warren said.

The giant initially pulled Warren along, but quickly settled into a comfortable pace. They met other dogs and owners who were also getting in their walks before the storm hit. One man said while passing that rain was in the forecast all day. The news made Warren think about today's golf match and Billy Bob Richardson's loud mouth. He admitted that a cancellation wouldn't bother him in the least.

Warren and Theo walked down to the Methodist church, crossed the street and headed home, stopping twice for the dog's eliminations, one of which Warren was obliged to pick up with a baggie. The rain began just as they got to the front door. After toweling off Theo Warren went to the kitchen where he made Margie's coffee in the Cuisinart brewer and poured himself a cold glass of Snapple. His favorite flavor was Mango Madness.

Sitting at the butcher block island he noticed Saturday's mail lying in a pile. He sorted through the bills and magazines, opening a letter addressed to him. It was a statement from the Dundee Retirement Home, the residence of his 91 year old mother, Fern Westing, the woman who used to drag him to church when he was a boy. As usual he winced when he saw the monthly bill of $8500. Though he could afford keeping his demented mother in the upscale facility, he worried that she would live past his targeted retirement age of 70. The woman was physically fit as a fiddle and the possibility of her living past 100 was very real.

The rain intensified and for a brief time hail pelted the neighborhood. The storm and the forecast prompted Warren to call Stu. "What do you think, Gottlieb?" he asked when he heard his friend's groggy voice.

"I think we should be at the club on time ready to play," Stu said.

"I was afraid you'd say that."

"You don't want to forfeit, do you?"

"No, no. What time is our match?"

"Nine sharp."

"I'll see you at 8. I don't know about you but I've got to hit a few balls."

After hanging up, Warren mixed some dry Pedigree with a can of Alpo and offered the bowl to Theo. He then went upstairs to shower and shave, the latter involving lather and a safety razor. When he rinsed his face he paused to examine his skin in the bathroom mirror. Another age spot had turned up, this one on his right cheek. "I hate this," he whispered as he ran a finger over the new blemish, trying in vain to erase the thing.

The next order of business was to decide what to wear. From his walk-in closet Warren chose a pleated pair of black slacks to go with a red golf shirt. Black socks and loafers completed the look. Inspecting his outfit in his full length mirror he laughed at himself. Except for his doughy white skin, his ample girth, and his gray hair, he looked just like Tiger Woods. He peeked in Margie's room before heading out and found her sound asleep. Her repose heartened him. At least she wasn't vomiting. The walk downstairs and to the garage brought him a familiar ache in his left hip as well as a new pain in his lower back, a pain so sharp that when he climbed into his Lexus it stopped him cold. "Ouch!" he cried, massaging his back before easing into the driver's seat. "Old age isn't for sissies," he whispered, repeating the saying that was sewn on one of his mother's decorative pillows in her private room at the nursing home. Until recently he hadn't considered himself old. Pain, it seemed, was changing his mind.

Minutes later, Warren was motoring south through torrents of rain. He was heading to Osage Hills Country Club, a tidy 18 holes about twenty minutes from central Omaha. He and Stu had been members for less than a year, and didn't play enough golf to justify the pricey membership fee. They had entered the two-man tournament in an effort to increase their time on the course and had managed to squeak by the first round of competition. Warren guessed today's match would be much more demanding.

Just as Warren pulled into the club's parking lot the deluge ceased. After parking he crossed the wet asphalt, taking care to avoid the puddles, and entered the humid confines of the men's locker room. There he sat in front of his locker and changed into golf shoes, a pair of black Nikes. Next he gave his name and membership number to a a young attendant who wasted no time delivering his golf clubs on an electric golf cart, the cart toweled off and ready for Warren to drive to the practice range. In no time he arrived at the expanse of wet grass. He was the only one there, largely because there was lightning in the distance. Despite the danger, he grabbed a seven-iron and headed for a neatly stacked pile of practice golf balls. He had hit only two when he heard Stu's voice.

"Are you nuts?" Stu called. He was in a cart of his own, but hadn't brought his clubs to the range.

Warren gave his friend a brief look and then resumed his practice. "You always were a pussy, Gottlieb," he shouted.

"Better a live pussy than a dead idiot."

Warren hit another ball. It was a shank. "Damn it," he cursed.

"You're wasting your time, Westing," Stu called. "Our opponents want to reschedule."

"Well I don't. Not after driving all the way out here."

"Come on, Westing. Don't be as ass. It's supposed to rain all day."

"One more swing," Warren called. Just as he hit the golf ball a clap of thunder shook the area.

"Enough," Stu called. "I'll meet you in the bar."

Warren hopped in his cart and followed Stu to the club house. The friends made their way to the bar lounge and found Billy Bob Richardson strutting around glad-handing anyone he could find. He was a large fleshy man with a red face and a loud voice. He had on a white cowboy hat and a western-style shirt decorated with stitching designed to look like golf clubs. His partner, Gar Young, sat in a corner sipping a vodka-tonic. He was gaunt and stooped, and his long dirty hair, Fu-Man-Chu mustache, and wire rim glasses were throwbacks to the 1960's.

"Well, who do we have here?" Billy Bob yelled when he saw Warren and Stu. "Y'all must be the Yankees who 'er lookin' to get their asses kicked."

Warren made himself smile at the barb, hoping that it had been offered in good-natured fun. He shook Billy Bob's meaty hand, saying, "Mother Nature may have saved our asses today," trying to be self-deprecating.

Billy Bob threw back his large head and laughed. "That's what I like to hear, unswervin' confidence. What's your name, pardner?"

"Warren. Warren Westing."

"Well Warren, over yonder is my partner, Gar. Why don't you go get to know the man while I have a chat with your friend."

Over the years, Warren had come to realize that there were some people on the planet who were naturally unlikable. He saw that Billy Bob Richardson was one of them. But for the sake of sportsmanship and goodwill, Warren followed the man's instructions and walked over to the corner table and extended his hand. "Warren Westing," he said. Gar Young returned the shake but didn't stand up or say a word. He did, however, nod toward a chair. Warren took the gesture as an invitation to sit down. Just before sliding into a padded armchair with wheelers, he glanced back to find Stu. Billy Bob had already corralled his friend at the bar, a heavy arm around Stu's shoulders, his loud voice in Stu's ear. As uncomfortable as he felt sitting next to Gar, Warren was glad he wasn't anywhere near the cowboy who sold used cars on television.

"It looks like we're going to get rained out," Warren offered.

"Maybe," Gar said. He gulped his vodka-tonic and pulled out a pack of Marlboros.

"You can't smoke in here," Warren said.

Gar smirked. "I can get one in before somebody yells," he said as he lit up.

Warren watched Gar make a vicious inhalation, only to slowly exhale a thick, bluish vapor from his nose and mouth. The man's face was pitted and wrinkled, and a scar ran from the edge of an eyebrow to the jaw. A black pearl stud earring adorned his left earlobe. A tattoo covered a forearm, a design that suggested military service.

"I heard you fought in Vietnam," Warren said.

"I don't want to talk about it, man," Gar muttered.

Warren chuckled to himself. It had been a long time since anyone called him "man". "I understand," he replied.

"Were you there?"

"No, I was in school."

"Then ya don't understand."

Warren nodded. He suddenly wished they were playing golf. Anything would be better than this conversation. Just then, a bolt of lightning struck nearby accompanied by a deafening clap of thunder. Warren ducked his head. "Whoa, that was close," he said.

"Waddya afraid of, man?" Gar asked. His tone wasn't at all accusatory. He seemed genuinely interested in an answer.

"I guess I was startled."

"We all got to die, man."

"What?"

"Waddya think would happen to you if you were hit by that lightning out there? I'll tell ya what would happen. Nothin'. You'd stop thinkin', feelin', and bein'. You'd have no pain, no regrets, no wishes. Ya just wouldn't exist. So, there's nothin' to be afraid of, man."

Warren stared at the man wearing a short-sleeve fatigue jacket and an olive drab T-shirt. The outfit was as much in violation of club policy as a lit cigarette. A sly smile formed on Gar's pitted face as he dragged on his smoke. "I'll tell you one thing about fightin' in Nam," he went on. "If ya fight afraid your chances of comin' home in a body bag go way up. I think that's how I made it through. I ain't afraid of dyin'."

Just then a woman's voice called out from behind the bar. "Sir, there's no smoking in here," the voice said. Gar plopped his butt in his finished drink as he flashed Warren a grin, an expression that told the world that he was right about sneaking in a cigarette.

"What was your name again?" Gar asked Warren. "I don't remember so good."

"Warren Westing."

"Lemme buy you a drink Warren."

"Oh no. It's way too early for me."

"It ain't too early for me," Gar said as he stood and headed for the bar. "Talk at you later man."

Suddenly without a conversation, Warren strolled over to join Stu and Billy Bob, guessing that his friend might be in need of a rescue. The blowhard cowboy was shouting in Stu's ear, apparently unconcerned that his voice had made Stu retreat into a cower. When Billy Bob saw Warren approach he swung his girth away from the bar. "You get to know my boy Gar?" the cowboy asked Warren.

"Some," Warren said.

"That's good. That's real good. You two'll be ridin' together next Sunday. Ol' Stu here is gonna teach me what its like to be a Jew."

Warren glanced at Stu, who looked like he was going to be sick. "Shall we go?" Warren proposed. Stu nodded and unceremoniously walked out of the room. Warren shook Billy Bob's hand and then followed his friend.

"Y'all come back now, ya hear," Billy Bob's voice boomed.

In time, Warren and Stu stood at the entrance of the country club gazing up at the stormy sky. "Mama Mia. I can't stand that guy," Stu hissed.

"Ditto," Warren said.

"What's Gar like?"

Warren hesitated. "He's...unique," he said and then told Stu what he had heard Gar say about being hit by lightning.

"So we're up against Hopalong Cassidy and Jean-Paul Sartre," Stu joked.

"Look Gottlieb, I'll ride with Hopalong next Sunday. You shouldn't have to put up with that asshole's bigotry."

"I can hold my own Westing. But thanks for the offer."

The friends farted and parted company. During the drive home Warren's imagination lit up. He put himself in the place of his acquaintance Sanders, the attorney whose funeral he attended the day before. He saw himself delivering a summation to a jury. There would be a brief but severe bout of chest pain before the heart attack killed him. Then there would be nothing, just like Gar suggested. "Waddya afraid of man?" Warren said out loud.

The daydream lasted the entire ride back to 41 Crestwood making the trip feel like it took just minutes. Warren left the Lexus out in the driveway hoping it would rain again and continue to clean his car. The garage door was open so he headed for the kitchen entrance inside the attached garage. He was happy to see Margie's Honda parked in her space. Her recent disclosures regarding life and death had sparked a certain thoughtfulness in him and he now wished to share what he had heard from his golf opponent and philosopher, Gar Young. But when he walked into the kitchen he instantly knew the issue at hand was more urgent than chatting. To his horror he found his wife sitting on the kitchen floor holding a hand over a gash on her forehead.

"Christ, what happened?" Warren asked, quickly grabbing a towel and applying it to Margie's bleeding wound.

"I think I fainted," she said. "I must have hit my head on somethin'."

Taking a closer look at the laceration, Warren said, "You're going to need stitches."

"No stitches. No hospital. Just tape me together."

"Marge..."

"Don't argue. There are band-aides in the cabinet next to the sink."

Warren held the towel on the wound until the bleeding stopped and then cleaned it with fresh water and a sterile gauze. It took two band-aides to close the gash. "Can you stand?" he asked Margie when his work was done.

"We'll see," she said. Warren helped her to her feet. "I'm so dizzy," she added.

"Let's get you to bed," Warren advised. Margie didn't argue. He kept a firm hold on her frail body as he escorted her upstairs. Once in her bedroom, she climbed on her bed and stretched out on her back.

"I hate havin' cancer," Margie said, a hand over her eyes.

"I know you do."

"Did you make a doctor's appointment?"

"I'll call first thing tomorrow."

"Who are you going to see?"

"Alvin somebody. I memorized his number."

Warren gazed at his thin wife. Her face looked pale in contrast to her red bandana and her warm-up suit seemed too large for her limbs. Her eyes were closed but she had more to say.

"Sugar?"

"I'm right here."

"When I'm gone I want you find another woman right away. No mourning. Do you understand?"

"Christ, Marge..."

"Promise me."

Warren knew it was pointless to resist her. "I promise," he said.

"Close the door on the way out. I need a nap."

As Warren closed the bedroom door a wave of heavy rain pelted the roof and a weather siren sounded in the distance. Reason told him he and Margie should get to the basement. He didn't fully understand why he decided against that precaution. Somehow taking shelter seemed like a waste of time. So as the growing storm roared he just walked downstairs and made his way to the refrigerator where he grabbed a Sam Adams Summer Ale, and then to his den where he took comfort in his old leather chair. The heavy relic sported its original brown leather upholstery that had cracked in several places. It had belonged to his grandfather, Alvin Westing, and had been used by his father, Frank Alvin Westing, for many years. It now resided in the home of Warren Alvin Westing and sat in front of a wide screen high definition TV on which Warren intended to watch the ESPN coverage of the College World Series. When he saw that the current game was in a rain delay, he grabbed his check book, wrote a check to the Dundee Retirement Center for $8500, and stowed the check in his wallet. The next day he was to make his weekly visit to the center to see his mother, and intended to personally deliver the monthly fee. Saving the cost of stamp wasn't much but it made him feel like he was doing something to offset the burden of supporting the old girl. The truth was, paying for Fern Westing's stay at the center was something of a sacrifice. Over the years he and Margie could have enjoyed several vacations were it not for this nursing home expense. He sometimes resented the very existence of his demented mother, though he knew full well what his responsibility was.

Warren was on his second beer when the tarp came off the Ameritrade field. The Mississippi State-Oregon State game made it into the third inning before the game was halted because of more rain. Channel surfing,

Warren found a Kansas City Royals game and fourth round coverage of the John Deere Classic. Neither event held his interest. Fetching another brew, he peeked outside through the sliding glass door off the kitchen. He discovered that the wind had knocked down a bird feeder, and despite the rain he rushed to return the thing to its place on a tree limb just off a kitchen window. Back inside, he walked to the kitchen sink and gazed out that window. It pleased him that a bright red cardinal had already found the supply of sunflower seeds, and that Margie would surely enjoy her birds the next morning.

"You don't worry about lightning, do you my crimson friend?" Warren said as he swilled his beer, very much enjoying his beer buzz. "Hell, you don't worry about anything, not even cancer."

Emboldened by alcohol Warren strolled into his back yard, a foolish thing to do considering the amount of lightning in the area. The rain was misty now and the sky was dark. Pant legs rolled up, he sat at the edge of the garden pool and kicked his legs through the water. Thunder rumbled and lightning lit up the horizon. "What are you afraid of man?" he asked himself.

The last of the beer went down easily. Warren thought of the promises he had made his sick wife. "Another woman?" he slurred. "I don't want another woman. And I sure as hell don't want a check-up."

Just then lightning flashed across the sky followed by a loud clap of thunder. Startled, Warren didn't move. Heavy rain returned but he stayed at poolside. It was only when lightning struck somewhere near and he felt the electrical charge in the pool water that he retreated to the interior of the house. "You win," he yelled as he entered the kitchen dripping wet. A brief wave of fear made him lock the sliding glass door.

III

Because of the nature of his work as a tax attorney, Warren had the luxury of determining his own hours at his law firm. This Monday morning he called his secretary, a matronly Hispanic woman by the name of Gabriela Hernandez, and told her he would be in at 1p.m. Gabriela reminded him that the firm's first quarter revenues were available to him today, a detail he had forgotten. He reassured her that he would work as late as necessary to process the data, and further assured her that her day would end at 5 p.m. as usual. She said something in Spanish, words that came out so quickly that Warren wasn't sure what he had heard. But when the woman hung up, he guessed that an understanding had been reached.

Dressed for work, Warren found Margie in the kitchen loading the Vitamix blender. She wore a blue bandana and a gray warm-up suit, telling him she had been up long enough to shower and change clothes.

"Feeling better?" Warren asked.

"I am right as rain. I didn't drink 'nuf water yesterday is all," Margie said.

After pouring himself a glass of Snapple, Warren took a look at his wife's forehead wound. The bandaids were still in place. The surrounding tissue showed a mix of colors, the red of a recent injury and the black and blue of a blow. "Chemo today?" he asked.

"Monday, Wednesday, and Friday of this week. Then I get a cottin-pickin' rest."

"Be sure to show someone your nasty gash."

Margie didn't respond. Rather, she flipped on the blender filling the kitchen with a roar. A minute later, she poured a thick purple liquid into two tumblers. "What's on your plate today?" she asked.

"I'm going to visit my mother before work," Warren said.

"How is old Fern these days?"

"The same as always. A picture of health except for her lost mind."

Margie just sighed. Warren could tell she resented having to support the old woman as much as he did. Kissing her on the cheek he said, "I've got to go."

"Drink your smoothie first," Margie advised.

"I'll drink it on the way to the nursing home."

"Don't spill it on your suit. I guarantee it'll stain it somethin' awful."

Smoothie in hand, Warren drove to the Dundee Retirement Center, a sprawling building in western Omaha that offered apartments for independent living, areas for partial assistance, and complete nursing home care. Fern Westing lost the ability to live in an apartment years ago. Warren remembered the day well. His mother had trapped herself in her bathroom, having forgotten that she had locked the door. No amount of coaching from the outside could get her to simply turn the lock handle. She had screamed and slammed the door with her fists. A janitor had to unhinge the door, this witnessed by a nurse supervisor. Fern was relocated to the area for the mentally challenged that very day.

The day was sunny and warm, and Warren left his suit coat in his car when he parked in the home's lot. He entered through the automatic sliding glass front doors after announcing his presence into an intercom receiver. Nodding greetings to the overly friendly staff he passed by the dining area where he saw a few elderly folk lingering over breakfast. Then it was on to Green Acres, a closed off living area whose doors could only be opened by entering a four-digit code. Warren punched in the numbers, once again reminded that his mother would never be able to remember the means to escape her ward should she ever desire to do so.

Looking around the central visiting area, Warren spotted faces that had become familiar to him, though he didn't know any of the residents' names. He saw Fern sitting in front of a large flat-screen TV. She was still in her bathrobe. He walked up to her and patted her on the back. "Hello mom," he said.

"Look what the cat dragged in," Fern said, her eyes off the screen for a fraction of a second. Warren pulled up a chair and sat next to her. "What are you watching?" he asked.

"See for yourself."

Warren watched Kathy Lee Gifford talk to a chef about ways to prepare quick meals. "Are you learning anything?" he asked his mother, knowing his words wouldn't stay with her for long.

"A lot of baloney if you ask me," Fern said.

Just then, a staff member approached. "Good morning Mr. Westing," the young black woman said. "Remember me? I'm Takisha."

"Oh sure, Takisha. Nice to see you."

"I need to talk to you about your mother."

"Oh?"

"In private."

Warren grimaced. "This sounds serious," he said.

"It is."

"Tell you what. Let's have our chat after my visit with Fern. Say around 12:30."

The young woman nodded in agreement and walked away. Warren could see she was angry.

"I don't like 'em you know," Fern growled.

"You don't say," Warren snarked, well acquainted with his mother's long-standing racism.

"They steal."

"Stop it right now."

Fern shifted her weight in her chair. "Your father didn't like 'em either, bless his soul."

"That is not true and you know it," Warren protested. His mother's cruel remark turned his memory to his deceased father, Frank Alvin Westing. Warren had been close to the man, fishing together for bluegills on lakes nearby their hometown of Prairie Center, Nebraska and often camping out on lake shores. His father usually was present for his son's track meets and didn't miss a football game. Frank Westing had been a kind-hearted soul and his friends and acquaintances knew he didn't have a racist bone in his body. The fact that he stayed married to Fern for so many years was a mystery to everyone.

"When did Frank die again?" Fern asked Warren.

"Dad died in 1990."

"Is that a long time ago?"

"That was 22 years ago, Mom."

Fern began to moan. "I should've gone with him," she wailed, now rocking back and forth as she talked.

Warren didn't say a thing, but admitted that he wished that had been the case.

"I'm going to die here. I'm never getting out of this place," Fern yelled.

"Keep your voice down, Mom," Warren urged.

"Don't tell me what to do. I'm your mother."

"How well I know."

"Do you go to church?"

"Yes, Mom," Warren lied.

"Don't lie to me."

"I'm not lying."

Suddenly, Fern's agitation vanished. "So, how are your children?" she asked.

"I don't have children."

"You don't?"

It's Steven who has the kids."

"Oh. I guess I knew that."

Warren watched his mother's face turn expressionless as she gazed at the vapid morning television fodder. He thought on his younger brother, Steven Westing, who was a Unitarian minister in St. Louis. Steven was two years younger, and the brothers had never been close. The man had always been quite extroverted in contrast to Warren's reserved and cautious manner, and was slim and fit as opposed to Warren's tendency to stay portly. It had been years since they last saw one another. They communicated by e-mail from time to time. When Steven's children were young Margie had made sure to send them cards and money for their birthdays. These days, Warren didn't know their ages or what they did for a living. He guessed that Margie had lost track of them as well.

"Do you want to use the exercise room, Mom?" Warren asked.

"There's an exercise room?"

"Right down the hall. Unless they moved it."

"Don't get smart with me, young man. I'm your mother."

"Come on. I'll help you get dressed."

A while later, Warren helped Fern stand on a treadmill. The old woman held on for dear life as the belt began to move under her feet. "I'm going to fall!" she yelled.

"Move your feet, Mom," Warren coached. "Walk along. You've done this dozens of times."

"I'm going to fall!"

"For God's sake," Warren cursed. He pulled his mother from the slow moving treadmill. "I guess it's a walk day," he said.

"Why do you try to make me fall?" Fern spit.

Warren didn't offer any explanation or try to reason with her. Rather, he took her arm and led her to the main hallway where they walked until they reached the exit doors.

"Are we leaving?" Fern asked.

"You can't leave, Mom."

"Why not?"

"You just can't," Warren said as he turned his mother to walk in the opposite direction. He had learned that just changing what Fern was looking at instantly changed what was going through her mind. He wasn't surprise by her next question.

"So, how are your children?"

"Steven has the children."

"So, how are his children?"

"They're fine."

"Elizabeth, Judith and Brian," Fern recited.

This time his mother surprised Warren. "I do believe you're right, Mom. Very good."

Fern cackled. "I'm not dead yet."

After the walk, Warren and Fern played a game of checkers. As the pieces mixed, Fern had difficulty remembering if she was red or black. Later, they watched a taped movie, "Raiders of the Lost Ark". At noon, they ate lunch together. The day's fare was a grilled cheese sandwich and tomato soup. Then it was time for Fern's nap. Warren led her to her room and saw to it that she was covered by an afghan.

"See you next week," Warren said as he patted his mother on the shoulder.

"If the creek don't rise," Fern said.

His duty done, Warren headed for the exit. As he was punching in the exit code he remembered that he was to hear what Takisha had to say about his mother. Turning around he was surprised to find her standing right behind him. "So what is this all about?" he asked her.

"Your mother has started using the "N" word," Takisha said.

"Oh Christ."

"I know she's old and demented but I'm not taking that."

"You're right of course."

"What are you going to do about it?"

Warren's mind raced. The truth was, he hadn't a clue what could be done about his mother's racism. It took him some time to offer a possible solution. "I'll call her doctor," he threw out. "Maybe her medication could be changed. Maybe that will help."

"You'd better hope so. If Fern keeps it up I'm filing a complaint."

Warren had no response to the threat, but he knew he should be very concerned. If his mother were booted from this home on the grounds that she was using racist slurs she might not find another suitable place to live. "I'll make the call today," Warren said. Looking at the skepticism on the young woman's face he could see that he needed to act quickly. With nothing more to say he exited the area and soon was out in the heat of the day. The interior of the Lexus was very warm but the air conditioner remedied that. As Warren drove to work his mind drifted from the problem at hand to general memories of his childhood. This reflection was common after a visit with his mother, and though its theme varied from week to week the characters naturally remained the same. This day he remembered how Fern had tried to make Sunday dinners special, how she wanted the family to eat together right after church. She liked to serve roast beef and new potatoes. They sat at an oval wooden kitchen table in their home in Prairie Center, and they all had designated seats. Frank sat at the east end, Fern at the west, Steven on the south side, he on the north. Insisting on saying grace before eating, Fern expected all to bow their heads in prayer. Warren never listened to her words, and his father often showed his contempt for the ritual by playfully and secretly kicking him on his shoe. The prank made Warren want to giggle, but he knew he had to restrain himself or endure the wrath of his mother. After the prayer,

Steven usually asked his mother questions about what she had just said, as though the words held a mysterious meaning. He would ask, for example, why she wanted God to bless the food, and how God would go about it. Warren remembered the questions as the first indication that his brother would one day become a minister. The memory led Warren to envision the Prairie Center Congregational Church. He could feel how the hard pew cut into his small legs as he sat out a long hour, week after week and month after month, next to his mother. The fact that his younger brother came away with such a different experience was hard for Warren to believe. He wondered how Steven could have found anything of value in that religious drivel. As for himself, Warren had gravitated toward mathematics and had gone on to major in math at the University of Nebraska. Working with numbers had always made him feel safe and secure. Tax law was an extension of that skill and discipline.

Eventually, Warren pulled into the underground parking garage of the building that housed his law firm. He parked his Lexus in a spot reserved for the employees of SL&T, which stood for Sanders, Litchfield and Tannenbaum, the huge law firm that occupied the entire 12th floor in the tallest building in the state of Nebraska. Out of his car, he strolled to the first floor lobby and snuck in an elevator just as the door was about to close. There were several people in the cab returning from lunch, one of whom was Stu Gottlieb.

"Wish me luck, Westing," Stu whispered to Warren.

"What for?"

"I've got a date with that violist tonight."

"Right. Your sister's friend."

"I'm taking her to see 'Wicked'."

"Well, good luck Curly. You'll need it."

"New joke, Westing. You need a new joke."

Warren stared at the elevator monitor. In time it read, "12" and the friends exited. Walking to his office, Warren reminded himself to call his mother's physician. He also remembered that he was to make a doctor' appointment for himself.

"Good afternoon Gabriela," Warren called as he approached his secretary. She was sitting at her desk just in front of his office door staring at her computer screen. She was square-shouldered but shy of being heavy set.

Her hair was black with streaks of gray and was always piled high, kept in place with an ornate silver and turquoise hair pin. She wore girlish dresses, open at the top to show the cleavage of her ample bosoms and just long enough to show off her shapely though stocky legs. Two-inch heels usually adorned her feet. Her personality came with three gears that could shift from one to another in a heartbeat. Her happiness included a warm smile and a lighthearted approach to life. Her work mode brought thoughtfulness and focus. But when angered she characteristically furrowed her face into a deep squint as her patience ran thin. Today, as Warren noticed, the woman was smiling.

"The revenue data is on your desk, Boss" she told Warren. "And there is something else waiting for you."

"Really."

"It's just a bowl of beans and rice. I couldn't eat it all."

"Frijoles y arroz," Warren said.

Gabriela squinted. "That's not necessary," she said.

"Hey, I need the practice," Warren explained as he pulled out his cell phone and brought up the mysterious text message he had received two days before. Showing Gabriela the text he said, "Do you have any idea what this means?"

"Actually, I do," she said as she viewed the phone screen. "It's in Mixtec. It means 'You did well.'"

Warren stared at the message. "Vani nisa a ro," he mouthed. The mere repetition of the words made him feel dreamy, a state of mind he found strange and pleasant. It was much like a beer buzz without the alcohol. It also reminded him of smoking marijuana during his college years. He wasn't aware of the silly grin he wore as his eyes remained fixed on his phone.

"Are you okay, Boss?" Gabriela asked.

Warren quickly closed his cell phone and put it in a coat pocket. "I'm fine," he answered. "You know me. I tend to day dream. So tell me, what is Mixtec?"

"It's a native Mexican language. I spoke it as a child."

"Mixtec," Warren repeated. "How odd."

"I would say so," Gabriela said in agreement. "Who would send you such a text?"

"Beats me," Warren said as he headed for his office door. Just before entering his work space he took the time to try more Spanish. "Gracias por los frijoles y arroz," he said to his secretary. As he closed his door to begin a long day of tax work he heard Gabriela utter her well worn expression of exasperation. She muttered, "Ay-yi-yi."

IV

Two weeks later Warren sat in the waiting room of his doctor's office with a half-dozen other patients, all adults with somber expressions. They were waiting to be seen by Dr. Alvin McHale, a practitioner of Internal Medicine who worked alone in an office adjacent to the UNMC. Warren knew nothing of the man other than he bore a Westing family name. He had considered doing some investigation prior to his appointment but decided that a mere check-up didn't merit the effort. Looking around the waiting room he sensed that most of these people were less than healthy, and he hated to think that he might join their ranks. That possibility meant that he should have learned something about the physician he was about to face. His uncertainty almost made him cancel his appointment. Just then a translucent glass window slid open and a woman's voice boomed, "Warren Westing."

Too late now, Warren thought as he stood and walked toward the window. Peering in, he saw a sour looking hag. "Step through the door to your right," she ordered without looking up. "A nurse will be right with you."

Warren did what he was told, entering a hallway that led to exam rooms. Seconds later a nurse emerged from one of those rooms and sauntered toward him. "Wow," he whispered. She was young with a sexy figure. Her pretty face bore a Hispanic complexion, her almond eyes and full lips accented with mascara and red lipstick. She wore a crisp white uniform that had a name tag pinned on a lapel. Her name was Gabriela.

"Mr. Westing?" she asked as she stopped at a door to grab a chart from its file holder.

"In the flesh," Warren joked.

"Come on in. I'll take your vitals."

Warren was soon sitting on the edge of an exam table having been weighed seconds before. He stared at the upright scale as the nurse took his pulse, temperature and blood pressure. The fact that his mass now exceeded 235 pounds embarrassed him. He knew it was too much for a man of five feet, eleven inches. He was certain the young nurse knew it as well.

"You have a lovely name," Warren commented, hoping he didn't sound flirtatious.

"Thank you," the nurse said. "I was named after my aunt."

"My secretary's name is Gabriela."

"Is that so? What's her last name?"

"Hernandez."

The nurse stopped in her tracks with a look of disbelief on her face. "Middle aged Latina, wears her hair up, kind of stocky?" she asked, gesturing as to outline an invisible body.

"She's the one."

"Mr. Westing, your secretary is my aunt."

Warren couldn't believe his good fortune. The connection might well mean he would be seeing more of the gorgeous creature who stood before him. He knew, of course, that his marital status and his age prohibited a relationship. But he enjoyed his fantasies and this nurse was an ideal subject.

"Omaha is an oversized cow town," Warren said. "We shouldn't be all that surprised at this."

The nurse didn't seem to hear Warren's attempt to explain the odd situation, saying, "I love my tia so much."

It was then that Warren had an idea borne out of curiosity. "Do you have any photos of your aunt when she was, say, in her twenties?" he asked.

The nurse had turned toward a computer and was entering Warren's vitals into his cyberchart. "I'll look through my mother's family album," she said, distracted. Finished, she said, "Dr. McHale will be right in," and then hustled out of the room.

Alone now, Warren looked around the room. There were colorful models of body parts, charts, and framed diplomas everywhere. One document said that Alvin McHale, M.D. was board certified in Internal Medicine. That, Warren figured, was a good thing.

Just then the exam room door opened with so much force that it startled Warren. A wiry, slightly built man in a short white coat appeared. A buzz cut cropped his gray hair. He wore thick glasses and a bow tie. "McHale," he said as he offered his hand for a shake.

"Westing," Warren said in parody. His humor seemed to go unnoticed. The doctor raced to the computer and scanned the screen. He started talking, reading off questions to his patient. Warren listened as carefully as he could, answering questions about his health history, work, family, allergies, medications, and even his general mental state. The interview took 15 minutes.

"Well, that's not so bad," McHale said as he turned to Warren. "You're a little overweight, the pain in your hip and back is probably arthritis that should improve with weight loss, your mother's dementia is an issue, and your wife's lymphoma is surely a source of anxiety. Am I on track?"

The quick talking physician made Warren smile. The guy was fast but efficient. What was more important, he was likable. "You're on track, doc," the patient said.

"Ready for your physical?"

"Not really."

"Well said," McHale said as he handed Warren a gown. "Strip and put this on. I'll be back in a jiffy."

McHale rushed out of the room and Warren undressed, slipping into the paper gown. He had never felt so vulnerable in his life. As promised, the physician promptly returned and proceeded to examine Warren from head to toe. When done, he said, "Nothing amiss here," as he entered his findings into the computer. In conclusion he handed Warren a laboratory form that indicated tests to be run. "Take this form to the lab on your way out," McHale ordered. "I'll mail you the results. Any questions?"

"What if there's something...abnormal..."

"I'll handle any and all eventualities. Okay?"

"I guess."

"You worry too much. That reminds me, would you like a tranquilizer to help deal with your wife's illness?"

The question surprised Warren. "No, I'm fine," he answered, perhaps a little too quickly.

"Suit yourself," McHale said, once again extending his hand for a shake. "Nice meeting you...Westing."

Warren grinned as he watched the frenetic man scurry out of the room. He realized that his doctor had picked up on his attempt at humor, which told Warren that McHale was sharper than he thought. After dressing he made his way to a medical laboratory down the hall from his doctor's office. There he submitted a urine sample and allowed a technician to draw several tubes of blood from his arm. He had no idea what he was being tested for but figured McHale knew what he was doing. What bothered him was his sense of foreboding. All that blood meant many tests. Many tests increased the probability of finding something abnormal. It was the way a mathematician thought.

An hour later Warren walked in his law firm carrying a quarter pounder with cheese and small fries he intended to eat for lunch. Gabriela was waiting for him at her desk with a big smile on her face. "My niece just texted me," she said.

"Oh yeah?" Warren said, pulling a few fries from the bag and stuffing them in his mouth. He was starving.

"She is so excited that you are my boss."

"It's a small world."

Gabriela reached into her purse and pulled out her wallet. She flipped open the wallet and showed Warren an old, cracked Polaroid that was stuck behind clouded plastic. "Is this what you wanted to see?" she said. He could make out the image of a young woman leaning against a car, a 1962 Ford Fairlane, the same make and model he drove when he was in high school. The girl wore a mini-skirt, go-go boots, and a tight sweater. Her dark hair was in a bubble cut. Her smile gave her away. It was a young Gabriela Hernandez.

"Wow. You were pretty," Warren said, immediately recognizing his mistake. "I mean you were as pretty then as you are now," he said in retreat.

"Ay-yi-yi," Gabriela said as she put her wallet back in her purse. "You hombres are all alike."

Deciding that he had said enough, Warren took refuge in his office. As he ate his lunch he lingered on the old photo he just saw. Gabriela really was an attractive woman those many years ago. He guessed that she saw him in a similar light, too old to be good looking. He yearned for his youth, for his Ford, for the chance to drive that girl in the mini-skirt and go-go boots to the local McDonalds for a 15 cent burger.

Just as he finished his lunch Stu walked in. Warren could see that his friend had a lot on his mind as he was stroking his bald head and hitching his pants at the same time. "We're on for Sunday again," Stu said as he sat in a leather chair.

"Christ," Warren groaned. The golf match with Billy Bob Richardson and Gar Young had been rained out for three consecutive Sundays. Warren, for one, was getting tired of anticipating what was certain to be a miserable outing.

"The good news is, the violist and I hit it off," Stu announced, beaming.

Warren started to remind Stu about his bad luck with women but could see that his friend, a hopeless romantic, was in a happy frame of mind. "What's her name?" he asked.

"Her name is Gloria. Gloria Chase. She's 55..."

"Isn't she a little young for you, Gottlieb?"

"We're not in high school, Westing."

"Sorry. Go on."

"She's 55, divorced, has two grown daughters, plays second viola in our symphony, and get this...she runs marathons."

"Twenty-six miles?"

"Yep."

"Jesus."

"Two years ago she ran the Omaha marathon in four hours and twenty-two minutes."

"Very impressive."

"There's more. She's got me jogging."

"You? You used to say the best way to handle exercise was to lie down until you forgot about it."

"Not any more. You're looking at the new Stu Gottlieb."

"Just be careful, Gottlieb. You're no spring chicken."

"I want you and Margie to meet Gloria."

"I think you'd better slow down," Warren said, unable resist giving a little advice. "Remember your last two girlfriends."

Warren's words seemed to freeze Stu. The man's posture stiffened and his expression turned serious. "It's not like she'll be meeting my parents," he countered.

"Your parents are dead."

"It's an expression, Westing."

Warren sat back in his swivel chair and put his hands behind his head. "Okay Gottlieb have it your way. Bring Gloria over this Saturday."

Stu grinned again, jumping to his feet, saying, "You'll love her."

"No doubt," Warren said, farting. Stu returned the favor and left the room. We are children, Warren thought.

A couple hours later, Warren called it a day. As he walked out of his office, he paused at his secretary's desk. "Is your niece married, Gabriela?" he asked.

Gabriela swiveled from her computer and toward Warren, her hands folded in her lap. Her expression was sad. "She is divorced," she said.

"Oh?"

"She can't get pregnant. She and her husband tried and tried. After five years of marriage he left her."

"Lord, who would leave a woman like that? She's beautiful."

"The man wanted children. That's all I can say."

"Did they try the Omaha Fertility Clinic?"

"Funny you said that. I suggested that very thing."

"And?"

"He would have nothing to do with it. He insisted on things being natural."

"He sounds like a sweetie."

"I never liked him, but my niece loved him. He broke her heart when he left."

On a whim, Warren changed the topic. "Let me see that photo again, Gabriela," he said.

"So you can make fun of me?" turning back to her desktop.

"Come on. Miniskirts were always a favorite of mine."

"No way. I shouldn't have showed you my picture in the first place."

Gabriela returned to her typing and Warren understood that he would never again lay his eyes on the girl leaning against the Ford. To show he meant no harm, he walked up behind his secretary and leaned over to whisper in her ear. "You were a foxy lady back in the day," he said, an innocent compliment that made her giggle. To add to the humor he composed a jingle right on the spot: "I'm Chiquita Banana and I'm here to say, Bonita Sobrina has made my day."

"I'll pass that along to my niece," Gabriela said.

"So I got the sobrina part right?"

"Yes you did Boss. But Boss…"

"Yes?"

"Your Spanish still stinks."

Warren headed for the elevator, calling out "Hasta la vista" over his shoulder. He listened for Gabriela's trademark expression but when he didn't hear it he glanced back at her. She was smiling. It was then that he realized he had learned more about her on this day than in the ten years they had worked together.

When Warren got home he changed into shorts and a Hawaiian shirt and headed for his garden pool and a beer. Margie wasn't home yet. He guessed she was delayed at her busy oncologist's office. When he heard his wife drive into the garage he braced himself for the news.

"There you are, Sugar," Margie called when she slid open the glass door to the back patio. "It's such a nice evenin'. I think I'll open up the house."

"Want some help?"

"I can handle it. How about a pitcher of margaritas?"

"Sure," Warren replied. The news is going to be good, he thought. Swilling the last of his pale ale, he heard the air conditioner condenser shut off and several windows open. A short time later Margie appeared holding a glass pitcher of the icy yellow beverage and two martini glasses. Theo followed her outside and found his customary spot under the lounger.

"So, let's have it," Warren said as he took over the job of pouring the drinks. He sat opposite his wife at a wrought iron patio table. As usual, she wore a bandana and a warm-up suit. He couldn't tell much from her expression.

"The lymphoma seems to be regressing," Margie began. "But my blood work isn't good enough for another round of chemo."

"What does that mean?"

"It means we're in a holding pattern, which is fine with me. I'd rather hold a rattler by the tail than go through all that sickness again."

"Spoken like a true Texan."

"How did your doctor's appointment go?"

"Very well. I like the guy. He's thorough, fast, and he's got a sense of humor."

"Did you pass muster?"

"So far. I'm supposed to get my blood test results in the mail."

The couple sat back and enjoyed the mild weather and the margaritas. Warren, for one, felt satisfied with the state of affairs. He was healthy enough and Margie seemed to be improving. Glancing over at his sleeping old dog, he hoped the arthritis medication was affording him adequate pain relief. It was then that he remembered the conversation he had with Stu at the office.

"Stu is bringing Gloria over on Saturday," Warren announced.

"I assume you mean his new gal."

"Who else?"

"I wish you'd give me a heads up once in a while. This place is a pig sty."

"First off, I just did give you a heads up. Second, the place is not a pig sty."

"I swear, you could live in a barn."

"You're the one who fired the cleaning lady."

"She was a longhorn steer in a china shop."

"I'm guessing you haven't hired a new one."

"I've been busy. Or haven't you noticed."

Warren knew where this exchange was headed. If its course wasn't altered, they would end up in an argument. He remembered the last one. They had been watching a documentary entitled "The Men who Built America." He had made the off-hand comment that America may well have been built on genocide, slavery, and greed. His words had struck Margie as not only inaccurate but unpatriotic. The ensuing argument was conducted in shouts and lasted, off and on, for days, a near reenactment of the Civil War. But on this day, luck was on their side. A text message signal rang on Warren's cell phone. It was from his brother Steven, and it provided the diversion the Westings needed.

Hey bro. I'll be in Omaha next week for a Unitarian convention at the Doubletree. Awesome if I could see you and Margie.

"Oh wow," Warren muttered.

"What?" Margie asked.

"Steven is coming to town next week."

"I know."

"You know? How do you know? I just got the text."

"He mentioned it in his last e-mail," Margie said, massaging her calves. "These friggin' cramps," she cursed.

"Hold on," Warren interjected. "You and Steven exchange e-mails? Since when?"

"Since I got cancer. His counsel has been a great comfort to me."

Warren wasn't one to anger easily, but hearing that his wife had been communicating with his brother for a year without his knowledge lit his fuse. "Why didn't you tell me?" he started.

"You don't need to know everything I do, Darlin'," Margie said.

"What else have you kept from me?"

"Wouldn't you like to know."

Warren glared at Margie. Respecting one another's privacy had been the mainstay of their marriage but when he inadvertently learned a secret of hers it always infuriated him. It was though her life was somehow richer than his simply because he kept no secrets of his own. It didn't seem fair.

Margie continued to knead her calf muscles. Then, suddenly, she stood up. "I'm going to take a hot bath," she said.

"You do that," Warren spit.

"Don't drink the whole pitcher."

"Don't worry about me."

"No friggin' problem," Margie said as she went inside.

Warren poured another margarita, slipped off his flip-flops, and found his favorite spot to relax, the edge of his garden pool. The water was too warm but this day he did nothing to correct it. Adding to his discomfort was his feeling that things were going on behind his back. "What's wrong with my advice?" he said to no one. He was starting to feel buzzed and his irritation with his wife mounted. Knowing that he had no right to his anger, that he was a willing participant in a marital agreement based on privacy, just made things worse. "What's so special about my dumb-ass brother?" he muttered.

As he kicked his legs through the tepid water Warren looked back on other junctures in his life with Margie that had struck a nerve. About ten years ago he discovered that she had a secret bank account containing a substantial amount of cash, money that, as a tax attorney, he should have managed. They argued about that matter for weeks. Two years ago he found out that she had not traveled to Texas to visit her parents graves but had vacationed in Mexico. He had questioned her on the need for deception. She had dismissed his inquiry, calling her trip a last minute change of plans and, most importantly, none of his business. There had been other conflicts but Warren's memory was rapidly fading with the steady increase in blood alcohol. He grabbed the half-empty pitcher of margarita and headed for the den. Theo trailed behind.

Plopping into his old chair Warren began channel surfing. As always he was amazed that despite having hundreds of channel at his disposal he couldn't find a show or a movie that interested him. He settled for a old rerun of "Bonanza." Ben Cartright was in love with an attractive widow. His sons were delighted. Warren was certain that a tragic turn of events would sabotage the promising relationship. "Things don't even work out on TV," he directed at Theo, who was now lying at his feet. A half hour later Warren's prediction came true, a sad climax that coincided with his emptying of the pitcher. The last thing he thought of before he nodded off in his chair was Margie's answer to his last question. She had said, "Wouldn't you like to know."

"Yeah, I would like to know," Warren mumbled as his eyes closed. When he woke the room was dark and he stumbled off to bed.

V

The next morning around 4 a.m. Warren was awakened by the ringing of his land line phone. This phone rang so infrequently these days that he was confused for a few seconds as to what the noise was. Stumbling out of bed he groped through the dark to a corner desk in his bedroom, promising himself that he would cancel this phone service, though as he picked up the receiver he knew that was something he would never do.

"Hello," Warren croaked.

"Warren, it's me Steven."

"Steven? Christ, is something wrong?"

"I just had a dream, a very vivid dream."

For a second or two, Warren found himself at a loss for words. "You called me at four in the morning because you had a dream?" he finally asked.

"I dreamt that Margie melted, like the witch in The Wizard of Oz."

Again, Warren couldn't speak for a short while. My brother has lost his mind, he thought. "This couldn't wait?" he said in a tired voice.

"I take my dreams very seriously."

"Evidently."

"Is she okay?"

"Margie is fine, all things considered."

"Put her on, would you?"

"I will not. She's asleep."

"I need to hear her voice."

"You'll be here next week. You can talk to her then."

Warren heard his brother's raspy breathing and wet coughs. He recalled a funeral for an uncle he attended in St. Louis several years before

45

where he witnessed the Steven's capacity to smoke cigarettes. He chain smoked unfiltered Camels back then and Warren guessed he was still at it. Before Steven spoke again, he sent the sounds of a coughing spasm over the phone, an attack that lasted a full thirty seconds. When done he said, "That was a doozy."

"Steven, you sound awful," Warren said.

"It's nothing. Say, could you pick me up at the airport on Monday? I'm coming in on Southwest around 11 a.m."

"Sure."

"Warren, I'm really worried about Margie."

"Why don't you e-mail her your concern?"

For an instant there was silence on the line. "I guess Margie told you about our correspondence," Steven said.

"She did."

"Good. That's good. It means she's shedding some of her fear."

"What?"

"I'll fill you in next week. Are you sure you won't put Margie on the line?"

"I'm sure."

"And you say she's doing well."

"I'll fill you in next week."

"Funny guy. Okay, later," Steven said before hanging up.

Yawning, Warren crept back in bed, flabbergasted that anyone could take a dream so seriously that he would make a phone call at such an ungodly hour. He fluffed his pillow and assumed his customary left sided sleeping position, right knee up, left leg extended, left hand under the pillow. He was asleep in minutes. His dream began some time later. The Indian was an old man with leathery wrinkled skin. He wore no shirt. A turquoise and silver necklace hung over his chest, and earrings of a similar design were on both ears. He was sitting at a camp fire. It was night. The old man spoke in a soft but distinct voice. "Vani nisa a ro," he directed to Warren, who sat on the opposite side of the fire. "Vani nisa a ro," the old Indian repeated.

Warren awoke to morning light that had flooded his room. He couldn't remember feeling more rested, even peaceful. The image of the old man was still fresh, though he couldn't remember the words in the dream. But the details of his experience weren't important or so he decided. What mattered to him was the delightful exhilaration he was enjoying, a state of affairs he felt he owed to a sound sleep and a stimulating dream. Indeed, he didn't want to get out of bed, but because he wished to get in a little practice at the golf range before the weekend match he forced himself out from under the covers. When his feet hit the floor a sharp pain arose from his lower back.

"Ouch!" Warren cried. The pain caused him to stoop forward and then drop to one knee. He reached for the small of his back, a futile effort to ease his discomfort. "What the fuck," he mumbled. "It's getting worse." For lack of anything better to do he waited, still on one knee and still massaging his back. Gradually the pain ebbed allowing him to stand and walk to his bathroom. The episode fouled his mood. As he showered all he could think about was the secret correspondence between his wife and brother. He nicked himself twice when he shaved.

After dressing Warren walked Theo. After the walk he stood at the foot of the stairs as he contemplated looking in on Margie. He decided against it. His irritation with her got in the way. Instead headed for Osage Hills CC. to practice his golf game. Eventually he stood at the practice range, his bag of clubs propped up next to him. Because it was a Saturday the range was crowded and Warren was lucky to have found a practice spot. Grateful for the distraction from the recent domestic upset, he unwisely skipped the stretching exercises a pro had taught him and started right in with the lofted irons, gradually making his way to the long irons, the fairway metals and finally his favorite club, his Titleist driver. Luckily his back withstood the swinging. Initially his shots were erratic but in the short period of time that he was at the range he gained some consistency. This he attributed to his natural athletic ability. To be sure, he was overweight and out of shape, but he still had better than average coordination. When he hit a superb drive he decided it was time to work on his putting. He toted his clubs to a golf cart intending to head for the practice green, but before he got under way his path was blocked by a gaudy red vehicle, a cart clearly not owned by the country club. A large set of a bull's horns adorned the front of the cart. Its driver was Billy Bob Richardson.

"Ya'll are wastin' your time Yankee," Billy Bob shouted.

Warren groaned. The last thing he wanted to do was talk to Omaha's biggest blowhard. "It's you who are wasting my time," Warren countered.

Billy Bob babbled on. "There's no way on God's green earth that you and the Jew can beat Gar and me. No way."

"We'll see about that."

"I done prayed on it."

"What?"

"Ask and ye shall receive. Says so right in the Bible. That's all I need to know and that's what I've done. The match is ours."

Warren couldn't believe his ears. The loudmouth was using his Christian fundamentalism as a propaganda tool. His breathtaking arrogance left Warren speechless.

"You received Jesus, Yankee?" Billy Bob went on.

"Can't say that I have," Warren muttered.

"Ya need to. Know where the First Baptist Church is on West Dodge?"

"Vaguely."

"Come join us. But not tomorrow. Tomorrow is your ass whippin'."

Billy Bob drove off, honking an obnoxious sounding horn as he did so. The experience left Warren more determined than ever to prepare for the golf match. When he got to the practice putting green he called Stu.

"Gottlieb, get your fat ass to the golf course and get in some practice," Warren urged over the phone. "We've got to beat these guys tomorrow."

"I don't know, Westing. I'm kind of tired," Stu said. "I just ran three miles."

"Christ. I forgot about your new life style."

"You should try it."

"I'll stick to golf."

"You could stand to lose a few pounds."

Warren patted his paunch. "I'll think about it," he said.

"What time do you want Gloria and me?"

"How about 5 o'clock for poolside cocktails?"

"We'll be there."

"I'm looking forward to meeting your new girl."

"She may be the one, Westing."

Stu's words made Warren grimace. He prayed his best friend's heart wouldn't be broken for a third time. "See you later Gottlieb," Warren said before hanging up. Minutes later he was bent over his putter stroking one golf ball after another on the practice green. Try as he might he couldn't concentrate on his form. His mind on his friend, Warren picked a hole about thirty feet away and made a bet with himself. If this goes in, he thought, Gottlieb will finally have some luck. The stroke was solid and the ball rolled true. When it reached the hole it ran in like a varmint seeking shelter. "Attaboy," Warren murmured. Then his thoughts turned to Billy Bob Richardson. Another bet, another putt, another make. Grinning, Warren decided that he had practiced enough. He jumped in his cart and drove to the clubhouse. "Pray on that you fat ass," he shouted as he sped away.

*   *   *

Saturday evening was overcast and the humidity was low, ideal weather for a get together around the Westing garden pool. Stu and Gloria were due in minutes, and Margie raced to throw together a cheese and cracker plate for the guests. She wore a silk bandana and a simple dress in an effort to doll up for the party. When Warren joined her in the back yard she scolded him for his casual attire, saying, "Your knobby knees are showin', Sugar."

Warren glanced down at his shorts and his legs. "You think my knees are knobby?"

"Go put on a pair of slacks," Margie said, not bothering to answer Warren's question.

"Christ. It's just Gottlieb and his girlfriend."

"Whom you've never met. It's just common courtesy…"

Just then the front doorbell rang. Warren hustled to the foyer and opened the door. Standing before him was an extraordinarily physically mismatched couple. Stu stood five-six and was round in appearance. Warren judged his date to be at least five-nine and was as slim as a reed. She wore her salt-and-pepper hair very short and this evening donned a black short-sleeved blouse that hung on her thin frame, and Capri plants that hugged her sleek legs. "Gloria Chase," the woman said as she extended a hand to Warren. Clearly she wasn't waiting for an introduction from Stu. During the handshake Warren's eyes fell on a blemish on her neck, a dark, crusty, cigar-shaped mark about two inches in length and a half inch in width that ran horizontally. It didn't look like a birth mark to Warren. He wondered if she had recently sustained some sort of injury. No matter its cause he couldn't take his eyes off the thing.

"It's from my viola," Gloria explained, apparently noting Warren's stare.

"I'm sorry. I didn't mean..."

"No apology necessary. Everybody stares."

"Come on Westing, show us the booze," Stu chided. Always the good host, Warren ushered the couple toward the backyard patio, stepping aside at the glass door to allow them to step outside first. It was then that he had a good look at Gloria's calves. For a thin woman she was well muscled, at least in her legs. Warren was reminded that she ran marathons in addition to playing in the Omaha Symphony.

"Stu Gottlieb!" Margie cried when she spotted the man. "It's been a coon's age." She embraced him and then turned to Gloria, who had already positioned herself for a handshake.

"Gloria Chase," she said, addressing Margie. Warren could see that Margie was staring at Gloria's neck blemish. "It's from my viola," Gloria added.

After some chit-chat the four sat around the wrought iron patio table. Margie and Gloria sipped on white wine. Warren and Stu drank beer. Early on Warren asked Gloria about her marathoning.

"I just ran one," Gloria admitted. "Twenty-six miles is just too long for me. I don't have enough time to train for that distance."

"But we're going to run a 10 K together, right babe?" Stu added.

Warren did the math. "That's just over 6 miles, Gottlieb. You'll never make it," he said.

"Don't be too sure," Gloria cautioned. "Stu's running is steadily improving."

His girlfriend's compliment made Stu smile self-consciously. He ran a hand over his bald scalp and hitched the belt on his Bermuda shorts. Warren could see that his friend was a little embarrassed. Gloria took Stu's hand, likely wanting to offer some reassurance and comfort. They looked into one another's eyes, giving the impression that some degree of love existed in their relationship. It was enough for Warren to believe that they might just make it.

The afternoon passed quickly, the conversation touching on Margie's health, Stu's multimillion dollar law suit against Creighton Medical Center, arthritis in large dogs, and the fact that everyone in Omaha knew who Billy Bob Richardson was. All parties were on their third or fourth drinks when Warren asked Gloria about her neck blemish.

"It's an occupational hazard," Gloria started. "I steady my viola against my neck. Over time repeated rubbing breaks down the skin and turns it dark."

"Can't you put something between your neck and your viola? A piece of cloth for instance?" Warren asked.

"Some can. I cannot. I need to feel the vibration of my instrument."

Stu stood and made his way to Gloria where he arranged himself behind her and massaged her shoulders. "Isn't she something, Westing?" he gushed.

"Indeed," Warren said, happy to see his friend so taken.

"We should go," Stu said in Gloria's ear. "We've got to get up early if we want to get in our run before Westing and I have to play golf."

The four said their final goodbyes in the foyer. Then Warren helped Margie clean up. "What did you think of Gloria?" he asked her as he carried a snack tray to the kitchen.

"She's a bronc, that one. Strong, sassy, says what she thinks. I like 'er."

"She's perfect for Gottlieb," Warren said. "He could use a little direction in his life right now." Just then he spotted a pile of mail on the butcher block island. He stopped his cleaning for a moment to sort through the stack. There he found a letter addressed to him. The return address read "Alvin McHale, M.D."

"Oh, oh," Warren muttered, holding the envelope up to the light as though he could gather advanced information before opening it. He started to rip open the letter but was interrupted by a loud thump at the kitchen sink window. He knew exactly what had happened. Racing outside he found a bright red cardinal lying on the ground under the bird feeder. He wasted no time gathering the bird in his palm, stroking its crest and encouraging it to stand. When it peeped he placed it on a low branch, making sure it had its balance before stepping back. A minute passed, and the cloudy appearance in the bird's eyes gradually disappeared. The bird gave Warren a quick look before flying off.

"What are you doin' Sugar?" Margie called from the sliding door.

"Another bird almost bit the dust," Warren said as he walked back inside. "We've got to move that damn feeder."

"Then move it. I ain't stoppin' you. Are you hungry?"

"Not a lick."

"Then I'm going to lie down a spell. There's a frozen pizza in the freezer if you change your mind."

As he watched Margie slowly climb the stairs to her room Warren grabbed Theo's leash from the coat rack in the foyer and rattled it. It was all it took to summon the dog's presence. After leashing the Great Dane, Warren walked it to the front walk and then to the Dundee sidewalk. It was dusk now and the evening was cool. As they walked along he reviewed the long day. It had started with Steven's early morning phone call. There had been that strange dream of the old Indian man. Billy Bob Richardson had invited him to church. He had met Stu's new love. But he had no way of knowing that the day was far from over. Just as he and Theo stepped from the sidewalk to cross the street and head home the sound of breaking wood filled the air. Tree debris rained downward and then a crash thundered behind them causing Warren to recoil and Theo to yelp in fear.

He spun around and saw what had happened. An enormous tree limb from one of Dundee's towering oaks had broken away from a trunk and smashed on the sidewalk below. Had this rare event happened seconds before, a man and his dog would have been killed.

"Jesus fucking Christ," Warren uttered. "What the hell is going on?"

Shaken, Warren walked his dog home. More accurately, Theo pulled Warren home. He was still unsettled when he reached the kitchen and finished tidying up after the get together. It was then that he saw his doctor's letter waiting for him. Perhaps it was out of a need for self-preservation that he postponed reading it. He felt too scattered to handle bad news, if that what was what the letter held. "Tomorrow," he said as he placed the letter in a rack on the wall reserved for important documents.

Flipping off the kitchen light Warren trudged upstairs knowing that he was too unnerved for sleep. Down to his silk boxers he slid under the sheets and propped up the book he had been reading these last months, "Truman" by David McCullough. Try as he might he couldn't concentrate. His mind raced from lightning bolts to crashing tree limbs to an old Indian man to that tuft of gray hair peeking over the purple lining of a coffin. Eventually he just heaved a great sigh, turned off the bedside lamp, closed his book and then his eyes. Mercifully the move brought him some peace. His mind's eye brought him his red cardinal. He imagined it nestled in a pine tree still spinning from its injury. But Warren believed the bird would heal. The beautiful creature was just gathering its energy for the coming dawn.

VI

The next morning Warren showered, shaved, and donned the Tiger Wood's Sunday colors in preparation for the 10 a.m. golf match. On the way down stairs he looked in on Margie. She was asleep, her chest moving quietly under a sheet. It struck Warren that she usually was up by this time but he saw no reason to disturb her. Before leaving he spotted her lap top computer on a desk near the south window and saw a chance to see for himself what kind of exchanges she had been having with his brother Steven. Quietly, he walked to the laptop and gave it a tap. An e-mail came up.

> Your last letter tells me you're in a good place, M. Talking about death is a positive step. We've taken death out of the darkness and brought it into the light. The taboo has been broken. By the way, I dreamt that you melted. I don't know what that means but I'm thinking on it. See you soon. S

Warren's face turned red with anger after reading the message. He felt ignored, passed over because his wife valued his brother's advice over his. An urge to shake Margie awake gripped him. He wanted to demand that she quit this secret correspondence, this death counseling. It was only because she was ill that he swallowed his outrage, quietly closed the laptop and crept out of the bedroom.

Still fuming as he walked downstairs, Warren headed for the kitchen and a glass of Snapple. He paced as he drank but the irritation he felt toward his wife and brother wouldn't abate. It was then that his eyes fell on the letter from his doctor. With an angry, rapid swipe of his hand he grabbed the letter from the rack on the wall, ripped open the envelope and began to read.

Dear Mr Westing:

> *Two values in your blood tests came back abnormally high and demand further investigation into your state of health. It would be best if we discussed this matter in person. Please schedule an appointment at your earliest convenience. I suggest no delay as there may be some urgency here.*
>
> *Sincerely,*
> *Alvin McHale, M.D.*

"What the fuck?" Warren muttered. "I don't need this."

He now understood why he was reluctant to open the letter. Somehow he knew there was bad news inside. Suddenly the pain in his lower back and left hip that he had endured for several years, took on an ominous significance. Am I ill, he asked himself? Do I have diabetes, liver or kidney problems, some sort of anemia? Do I have cancer?

Glancing at the clock on the microwave, Warren saw that it was time to head for the golf course. He carefully tucked the letter back in its envelope and returned it to the rack on the wall, vowing to make his appointment the next day. A short time later he was motoring toward Osage Hills CC. He drove too fast and wrung the life out of the steering wheel. A former athlete, he recognized body tension. "Hang on Sloopy, Sloopy hang on," Warren sang at the top of his lungs. It was an old trick he used to relax his muscles. "Sloopy let your hair down girl, let it hang down on me, yeah...." Gradually his tension eased, his irritation with his brother and wife temporarily receded, and his worry about his health ebbed. By the time he got to the golf course his muscles were loose and his mind was clear.

"Time to kick some butt," Warren said as he got of his Lexus and walked to the locker room. Minutes later he drove to the practice range to warm up. Billy Bob Richardson and Gar Young were already there standing over their piles of practice golf balls.

"Hey Gar, here's your Yankee," Billy Bob shouted. Gar's head came up, a cigarette dangling from his lips. He gave a subtle nod and returned to his swinging. "Where's the Jew boy?" Billy Bob asked.

"His name is Stuart," Warren said.

"Ooh, ain't we high and mighty."

Warren decided to ignore the blowhard. He grabbed his Titlest driver and a seven-iron and walked to the far end of the range to put as much space as possible between the cowboy and himself. Fifteen minutes later he had worked up a sweat. The good news was that he was hitting good shots. The bad news was, Stu hadn't arrived and the match was to begin in 10 minutes. Returning to his cart, Warren pulled his cell phone out of his golf bag and called his friend. A woman's voice answered.

"Who is this?" Warren asked. He had no trouble hearing the distress in the woman's voice.

"This is Gloria," she said, her voice trembling.

"Where is Gottlieb?"

"Is this Warren?"

"It is."

"Oh Warren. Stu had a heart attack."

Warren slid into the cart seat, fearing his knees would buckle. "What? What are you saying?"

"We're at the emergency room. They carted Stu off somewhere."

"Creighton or UNMC?"

"The latter. Could you come? I could use the support."

"Sure, sure. I'll be right there."

Without hesitation Warren jammed his golf clubs in his bag and got behind the wheel of the cart. His behavior caught Gar's attention. "We concede," Warren called to Gar, who nodded his head and returned to his practice.

"Yippee. Hear that Gar?" Billy Bob yelled. "Ask and ye shall receive."

"Ass hole," Warren mumbled as he drove off. After changing shoes and storing his clubs, he headed for the University of Nebraska Medical Center. His stomach turned a bit as he thought about his best friend in jeopardy. It added to the weight of unpleasantries he had suffered lately. Indeed, he felt his life was beginning to spiral out of control. He hummed "Hang On Sloopy" over and over. When he came to a notoriously long red light he decided to text Margie to tell her he was heading to the hospital. The words that appeared on the screen of his cell phone were: *Vani nisa a ro*. He stared at the sentence for a long while, trying to remember his secretary's translation. In the end, he gave up.

After texting Margie he drove off, dreading what he would find at the UNMC emergency room.

Warren found Gloria pacing in a waiting room. She was in a jogging outfit of shorts, a singlet, and brightly colored running shoes. When she spotted him she rushed to embrace him. He could feel her trembling. "It was awful," she cried. Leading her to a bench, he held her hands as they sat. She launched into her story. "We were jogging on the foot bridge over the Missouri River," she continued. "Do you know the one?"

"I do."

"Stu grabbed his chest and went to his knees. I though he was going to die."

"Jesus Christ."

"I flagged down a cyclist. Luckily he had a phone and called 911. The ambulance got there in minutes."

"And that's how you got here?"

"The EMTs let me ride in the ambulance. I told them I was Stu's wife."

"Clever."

"They gave him a shot which seemed to give Stu some relief."

"I hear they're miracle workers."

"They told me Stu had a myocardial infarction. Warren, this is all my fault."

"Nonsense."

Gloria began to cry. "If my Stuie dies..." she sobbed.

Warren let Gloria rest her head on his shoulder. He got a close up view of that ugly brown blemish on her neck and figured she had recently played her viola, as the mark showed a crust of blood. His first impulse was to ask her if the thing hurt, but he held his tongue. Stu's heart attack was the focus, not his girlfriend's neck sore.

Once Gloria regained her composure Warren volunteered to go to the hospital cafeteria for doughnuts and coffee. They sat together picking away at their food waiting for news of Stu. Warren offered his coffee to Gloria seeing that he never developed a taste for the stuff. Two hours crept by. Finally, a physician in scrubs approached.

"Mrs. Gottlieb?" the man asked Gloria.

Gloria leapt to her feet and faced the doctor. Warren supported her by holding her arm. After clearing his throat, the doctor began. "The short story is, the cardiac cath shows three 90% obstructions in addition to the 100% lesion that led to the MI. Your husband needs quadruple bypass surgery."

Warren could feel Gloria reel. "But he's going to be all right?" she squeaked.

"We need to go step by step. I'll be back in about 4 hours and give you an update."

"Oh God," Gloria mumbled. "I have to sit down." The doctor put a hand on her shoulder, offered a few words of assurance and then walked away leaving the couple alone in the cheerless waiting room. Gloria sat upright on a hard plastic bench, the back of her head against the dingy wall. It was as though she had begun a vigil with her posture intended to send strength to Stu. Warren spread out his bulk, his arms along the back edge of the bench and his legs crossed. In no time pain grew in his left hip which caused him to reposition his legs. The discomfort made him think of the letter from his doctor. No telling what I'm carrying around, he thought. For a diversion he asked Gloria a question.

"How long are you going to pretend you're married to Stu?" he asked.

"As long as necessary," Gloria said. Her eyes were focused somewhere in middle-space, her face expressionless. "I was going to move in with him. Now I don't know what to do."

Warren could see her point. If Stu made it through his surgery there would surely be a lengthy recovery, hardly a romantic situation for a live-in girlfriend. The possibility that his old friend might die was too terrible to contemplate. "I feel absolutely helpless," he said to himself.

"Did you say something?" Gloria asked.

"Just talking to myself. Bad habit of mine."

Sighing, Gloria continued her vigil. But after several minutes of silence she invited a conversation. "Tell me about Stu," she said to Warren. "What was he like when he was young?"

Warren welcomed the invitation. "Stu had a full head of hair in college," he started, grinning. "It was black and curly, so thick he could wear it in an afro."

"Really," Gloria exclaimed. Now she was grinning.

"He wasn't nearly as heavy as he is now. In fact, he was a decent shortstop. He almost made the 1971 Nebraska squad."

"I never would've guessed."

"He majored in Philosophy. He was quite the Existentialist."

"Another surprise."

"You'll like this. Stu was a lady's man."

Warren's words made Gloria chuckle. He decided to elaborate. "I can't remember a semester when he didn't have a girlfriend. Sometimes he'd string two along. In law school he shacked up with a professor for a time. Lord, I can't believe it. I forgot her name."

Gloria was beaming now. "He was a lover in training," she said, massaging her bare legs. "I have to say, he's the most aggressive man I've ever been with."

"I'm not surprised."

"He's the opposite of my ex-husband."

"How so?" Warren asked, recalling that Gloria was divorced with two grown daughters.

"My ex was very meek. He was a Buddhist. The guy drove me crazy with all that detachment rhetoric. He meditated more than he slept."

"What happened to him?"

"He drowned a year ago. He was scuba diving off the California coast. Nobody could say what led to the accident. If it was an accident."

"You're saying he might have killed himself?"

Gloria shrugged her shoulders. "What do you do after you reach Enlightenment?" she said, half joking. "I can't imagine life offering a more suitable encore."

Warren fell silent as he mulled over what he had just heard. He had always considered suicide to be the result of misery. For the first time he pictured it an end to a successful religious journey. He imagined himself underwater in a state of perfect contentment. How easy it would be to dive deeper and deeper until the surface was out of reach.

"Warren?" Gloria said. Her voice brought him out of his trance.

"Sorry. I daydream a lot. Another bad habit." Standing and stretching, Warren paid close attention to the pain in his lower back. He was certain it was getting worse. "Would you like some coffee?" he asked Gloria.

"Cream and sugar please," she advised. In no time Warren returned with two paper cups, coffee for Gloria and water for himself. They sat next to one another and sipped. Warren searched for another topic of conversation.

"Tell me about your daughters," Warren asked of Gloria. The request put a grimace on the woman's face. She had to hold her coffee with two hands to keep from dropping the cup.

"I don't want to talk about my daughters," Gloria said. Her cold tone told Warren to drop the subject, so he moved on to the next thing that popped into his mind.

"Did Stu tell you he was involved with a couple women relatively recently?" Warren asked Gloria.

"He did. There was the attorney two years ago and the CPA a year ago. They both broke it off because he moved too fast."

"And you don't object to that?"

"I like a man who can make up his mind. When he asked me to move in with him I jumped at the chance. At our age we shouldn't dawdle."

"You're 55?"

"I am. And except for his sorry lack of fitness, Stu matches me in every way despite being 10 years older. He took up jogging to get in shape. Now look where we are."

Warren felt the conversation slipping away. Indeed, he and Gloria assumed the positions they took at the beginning of the long wait and only occasionally shared some small talk. At one point they were joined by a mother who had brought her son in for stitches. Her wait was only an hour. Then, as promised, the doctor who had talked to them four hours earlier appeared.

"Well Mrs. Gottlieb I've got mostly good news," the man said as he approached. As before, Gloria stood and Warren held her arm. "The bypass surgery went without a hitch and your husband is in stable condition."

"But?" Gloria said.

The doctor shifted his weight. "We had difficulty getting him off the bypass machine. That's not a good thing."

Gloria heaved a big sigh. "But you say Stu is okay."

"Yes ma'am."

"Can I see him?"

"He's heavily sedated. I suggest you come back in the morning. You can talk with him then."

Warren gave Gloria a little tug, saying, "Come on, I'll give you a lift home." After thanking the doctor for his update, they made their way to

Warren's car and motored to her condo. She lived on the second floor of the same building that housed Stu's place, though his condo was on the 12th floor. They hadn't known one another until Stu's sister introduced them, but did recall spotting each other from time to time. It was mid afternoon when they reached the towering place, a new construction on the banks of the Missouri River. Gloria invited Warren up for a beer. He accepted.

A bit later Warren relaxed on a sofa that afforded a grand view of the river. Gloria took a shower while Warren drank his Michelob Ultra. The stuff tasted like water to him. He preferred stouter brews. Studying the label on the bottle he understood why a woman runner would drink this brand. The limited calorie/carb pitch made him think of Stu's name for this kind of beverage. He called it "Chick Beer."

Finished with her shower, Gloria joined her guest. Her short salt-and-pepper hair was still wet and she wore an old sweat shirt and baggy shorts. Warren noticed her bare feet and her bunions.

"So, how is your health, Warren?" Gloria asked as she opened her beer and plopped on a chair opposite him.

The question gave Warren pause. Prior to opening that letter he would've answered her in positive, or at least neutral terms. A little overweight, a little arthritis, a little near-sightedness. Nothing serious. Now, though, things were different. "I have some kind of blood abnormality," he admitted.

"Oh my. I'm sorry. What kind of abnormality, if you don't mind me asking?"

"I don't know. I have to go back to my doctor and find out."

"Hmm," Gloria muttered. Swilling her beer, she crossed her legs and leaned forward. "That must put an extra burden on your wife. Now she has you to worry about along with her cancer."

"Actually Margie doesn't know yet."

"But she will."

"Of course."

Gloria drank some more, abruptly rose to her feet and walked to the balcony door where she gazed outside. "I'm sorry. I tend to pry," she said over her shoulder.

Warren didn't say a thing. He watched as the woman's head bowed and her shoulders began to heave. A soft cry filled the room. At a loss for what to do, he spoke the first thing that came to him. "Stu is going to be fine," he called.

Returning to her chair, Gloria wiped her eyes with a sleeve of her sweat shirt. "We were doing so well," she said, her voice cracking. "And now this."

"Things have a way of working out," Warren said, not really believing what he said.

"I suppose."

A silence developed, Warren looking on as Gloria tried to compose herself. Minutes later, satisfied that his host had found some stability, he said, "I guess I should go."

Without ceremony, Gloria showed Warren the door, saying, "I'll probably see you tomorrow." Warren nodded and headed out.

As he drove toward home, Warren remembered a superstition that he and Stu shared. They believed that bad things came in threes. The day had brought him discouraging medical news and Stu's heart attack. He grimaced as he anticipated the third calamity, praying that it would be something less than devastating. As he pulled in his garage he spotted a puddle of oil under Margie's Honda. "That's it," he said, relieved that the final part of the evil trio was just an oil leak.

He was wrong.

Warren knew there was something amiss the moment he walked in the house. The place felt unused, devoid of the smell of food and the litter of human activity. He crept up the stairs and looked into Margie's bedroom. She was still in bed, motionless under a sheet. "Oh no," he whispered. Afternoon light gave the room an eerie look, something like a church sanctuary. Warren walked to the bedside and looked down on Margie's pale face. Her head rested on a pillow, her frail body absolutely still. "Margie?" he called as he nudged her shoulder. He hoped she would moan or move a little. He got nothing. He put a hand close to her open mouth. He felt nothing. He swallowed hard, knowing that his wife was dead.

An autopsy done a day later would reveal that Margie Westing died of an intracerebral bleed caused by low platelets resulting from the chemotherapy meant to treat her lymphoma. For now, the cause of her death didn't matter to Warren. He sat next to her, removing her bandana and stroking her bald scalp. She felt cold. "You slipped away from me, Marge," he said. "I'm sorry I didn't keep up. I'm sorry you had to turn to Steven."

Warren remained at Margie's side for over thirty minutes, trying his best to remember the good times. Then, with a sigh, he patted her on the shoulder and called 911. The dispatcher told him an ambulance would arrive shortly to transport his wife to a hospital where she would be pronounced DOA. An autopsy would be done in accordance with state law. Then she would be taken to the funeral home of his choice. Once again, Warren felt inadequate. He had no idea what funeral home Margie would have preferred.

After the short conversation with the dispatcher, Warren started for the bedroom door. Before leaving, he walked to Margie's open lap top and brought it to life. He saw Steven's e-mail about bringing death into the light. And there was a new message, this one from Margie to his brother.

There is nothing so sweet as a Texas rain in high summer. I can smell it and feel it at this moment. It's so dark in here. I'm so tired. Go Cowboys.

Warren chuckled at the last sentence despite realizing that what he just read was the last thing Margie wrote and one of the last thoughts she formed. He shut off the computer and walked out of the bedroom, quietly closing the door behind him as if Margie needed the privacy. A loud and deep bark echoed from below. Theo needed his medication, his food and a walk. And after that, Warren needed to scan the Yellow Pages for funeral homes.

As he walked downstairs, his lower back and left hip aching, Warren remembered that Steven was flying in the very next day. He also remembered that he needed to made a doctor's appointment. Theo was turning in circles, having been neglected all day. His best friend was in the hospital. His wife lay dead.

"I fucking hate this," Warren cursed, sure that this day was his worst in memory.

VII

The next morning, a Monday, Warren lay in bed awake, his will weighed down by his inability to grasp his situation. Theo aside, he was alone in his home for the first time. That fact alone made the moment hazy and the future uncertain. He had a headache and his thoughts ran everywhere. He could have been the cardinal that flew into the kitchen window.

Margie had been swept away the evening before and was now in some funeral home the name of which he could not recall at the moment. He had talked with the director on the phone and relayed Margie's wish for cremation. He wasn't sure when that would occur or what the next step would be but guessed the details would come his way soon enough. Stumbling into the bathroom Warren took a long hot shower. Even such a mundane act felt odd to him, almost as though he was showering for the first time in his life. When he toweled off the effort seemed to last longer than ever before. This day he didn't dress for work, instead slipping on a golf shirt, shorts and sandals. He checked the time. It was too early to call Gabriela to tell her why he wouldn't be in. Christ, I hate this, he thought.

Ambling downstairs, Warren let Theo out into the back yard after offering an apology for skipping the morning walk. He just wasn't up for walking. In the kitchen he stared at the Vitamix blender. I need a smoothie, he thought. Yogurt, blueberries, crushed ice. Get it done.

Minutes later Warren watched the blender do its magic. The blue swirling liquid and the roar of the machine made him think of Margie. He could see her patiently waiting for her favorite treat, an image he wished to extinguish. Distracted, he clumsily turned off the blender before its work was done. The smoothie looked distinctly unappetizing. Not one to waste food he did his best to pour off the ice into the sink and put the rest in

Theo's food bowl. "Here boy," he called from the sliding glass door. The Great Dane slowly entered the kitchen and promptly walked to his food bowl. The dog lapped at the slop and then gave Warren a puzzled look. "You don't like it?" Warren asked. Theo gave the blue mixture a second look but didn't touch it. Rather, he stood still, a clear sign that he expected to be fed a proper breakfast. "Okay, okay," Warren said as he went about throwing the ill-fated smoothie in the sink and filling the bowl with dog food. "You're getting fussy in your old age," he told his dog as he offered the new dish to his beloved pet.

What to eat, Warren thought? A quick inspection in the refrigerator didn't produce any ideas. Glancing in a cabinet he spotted a jar of peanut butter. This led him to toast a piece of whole wheat bread. In time he was munching on peanut butter toast, a favorite of his when he was a boy. As he ate he walked through the house, leaving the kitchen for the living room, the dining room and finally the den. What am I going to do with this place, he asked himself? It's too big for just one person. Dammit Marge, why did you have to die?

As he slumped into his chair Warren admitted that trying to avoid thinking about his dead wife was hopeless. Seventeen years was a long time to spend with another person. He searched his memory for special times they had spent together. There weren't many. Supporting his mother had precluded most vacations. They attended his firm's Christmas parties and the botanical garden fund raisers. That was about it. The more he reflected on Margie the more he realized that there was likely a great deal he didn't know about her. Sure, they had shared drinks at poolside but their conversations were rarely more than polite banter or meaningless arguments. They had given each other birthday and Christmas gifts but both admitted to not really knowing what the other one liked. As he had told himself many times before, he and Margie were private people. It had been cancer that brought up some genuine feelings between the two of them. But now she was gone. He regretted that deeply.

Just then a phone rang. The sound came from Margie's bedroom. Warren hustled upstairs and found Margie's cell phone connected to a charger. He answered but the person on the line hung up without a word. "That's weird," he murmured. After disconnecting the phone from the charger he pocketed it. He understood that this phone was the first of many of Margie's possessions that would require some kind of disposition. Then, before he left the bedroom, the phone rang again. And again, he answered it.

"Mr. Westing I presume?" the voice queried.

"Who is this?" Warren asked.

"This is Doris from Gundaker Realty."

"Who?"

The woman laughed, saying "I've always done business with Margie. Is she home?"

The question caught Warren by surprise. Margie's death was so recent he lacked appropriate words to announce it. "Margie is not home," he simply said. "What is this all about?"

"Well, the two-year lease on your apartment is up July 1st. I need to know if you wish to renew."

Warren held his breath for a second, completely at a loss for words. Befuddled, he forged ahead with an effort to understand what he was hearing. "Ma'am I'm not aware of entering into an apartment lease agreement," he said.

"I don't understand. Margie was the sole signer on the apartment but she listed you as a co-user."

"That's news to me."

This time there was silence on the other end of the line. Finally Doris spoke. "I'm confused," she said in a sheepish voice.

"Have we met?" Warren asked, sensing that he was near an understanding.

"You don't remember? You and Margie were at the apartment complex's pool party last year," the woman said. "I hosted it for Gundaker."

Warren pursed his lips and gritted his teeth. He hated to put this woman on the spot but he had to get to the bottom of this riddle. "I'd like to ask you to describe me."

"What? Why?"

"Just amuse an old man," Warren suggested.

"Well, let's see. I remember your black hair and beard. You made Margie's white hair look like snow. You two made a handsome couple."

"Christ. I don't believe this," Warren muttered.

"Excuse me?"

"Look. Doris. There will be no renewal of the lease. Okay?"

"But what about your furniture?"

"Tell the guy with the black beard to move it. Good day."

After hanging up Warren slowly descended the stairs, his eyes unfocused and head spinning. It was all he could do not to trip and tumble down to the first floor. His imagination told him that the guy with the black beard had been the first caller. Perhaps he wanted to discuss the love nest. Did he know how sick Margie was? How long had this affair been going on? Did her cancer put an end to it? He struggled to remember the sex life he had, or didn't have, with his wife. Naturally her illness rendered sex unattractive. But the realtor said the lease was for two years. Margie's diagnosis was made just a year ago. And there was no telling how many times that lease had been renewed. "Jesus H. Christ," Warren whispered.

As always, discovering one of Margie's secrets made Warren angry, but this one was particularly hurtful. He felt betrayed, inadequate, helpless and foolish all at the same time. This enraged him. A bit earlier he had been struggling with the loss of his wife. Now, suddenly, he was glad she was out of his life. He wasn't one to wish death on anyone but, that aside, he was happy to have avoided the confrontation that might have developed had he discovered Margie's infidelity. He had heard horror stories from colleagues at work that centered on messy divorces involving prolonged legal battles over sizable estates. He wasn't a rich man but he owned his home and had a considerable nest egg socked away. No worries now, he thought.

Becoming aware of Margie's cheating had an effect on Warren he didn't expect. His hazy thinking was replaced by focused anger toward his deceased wife. He made himself another piece of peanut butter toast and toured his home again. This time he saw his place as his castle. There was no way he would sell it. Passing the stair well he gazed up at Margie's bedroom and felt an impulse to collect her things and toss them out a window. It was only a pain in his lower back, a sudden stab that came with his first step upwards, that prevented him from doing just that.

Another phone call came in, this time on Warren's cell. It was the funeral director with the message that Mrs. Westing's cremation was completed. The man asked Warren if he wished the memorial service to be at his funeral parlor. The question caught Warren off guard.

"I have to think about that," Warren told the director.

"I ask that you give me an answer within a week," the director said.

Warren snorted with contempt. "Just so you know, there may not be a memorial service at all," he said. His words silenced the director, who simply hung up.

Shortly before 11a.m. Warren headed for Eppley Field to meet his brother's flight. As he drove he wondered if Steven's so-called counseling to Margie had touched on her extramarital relationship. By the time Warren spotted Steven emerging from a concourse he had decided to bring up the matter first thing.

"Hey bro," Steven called as he approached Warren. Six feet tall and thin, Steven sported a thin light brown mustache and had his brown hair in a small pony tail. He wore a white cotton shirt, jeans and leather sandals. There was a pack of cigarettes in his breast pocket. When the brothers embraced Warren could smell cigarette smoke. "Awesome seeing you, bro. Just awesome," the man went on. "I've got to hit the head. Be right back. Watch my backpack will you bro?"

Remembering that he had not talked to his secretary all morning Warren used the wait to call Gabriela. The woman sounded as though she expected him to take the day off. "Mr. Gottlieb's heart attack is the talk of the firm," she said. "I'm sure you're at his side."

"There's more, Gabriela," Warren said.

"Oh?"

"My wife died yesterday."

"Ay-yi-yi. How terrible. Oh you poor man. Is there anything I can do?"

"I need a few days off…"

"Of course. I'll arrange everything. Don't worry about a thing."

"Has the new Nebraska tax code arrived?"

"It got here today."

"Will you send it to my home? I'd like to look it over ASAP."

"Will do Boss. And I'll send you some food."

"Frijitos y arroz?"

"Good bye Boss."

Just then Steven returned from the bathroom. Warren noticed a small wet spot on his brother's jeans. The scourge of old men, Warren thought. "I got some bad news," Warren started.

"Margie died," Steven said in a matter-of-fact tone.

"How did you know?"

"Her last e-mail told me she was about to die."

"That's horse shit."

"A visceral memory, an honest assessment of one's physical condition, and a bit of light hearted humor. It was all there, bro."

"If you were so sure why didn't you alert somebody? Me for instance."

"It was Margie's time. We'd been preparing for it for weeks."

"Did she tell you she was having an affair?"

"She mentioned it. It didn't seem like a central part of her life. She was far more concerned with dying."

Warren handed the backpack to Steven and the brothers headed toward short-term parking. Warren felt his anger surge. "This whole thing really pisses me off," he spit.

"How so?" Steven asked.

"It's the secrets I can't stand. You should have told me about the e-mails and Margie's indiscretions."

"My correspondence with Margie was confidential. She told you about our exchanges. That was a good thing. Did she tell you about Jeff?"

"His name is Jeff? What's his last name?"

"She never told me. Like I said, I got the impression the guy wasn't all that important to her."

By the time the men reached the Lexus Warren's mood had simmered to a mild irritation, but he had more to say. "I know you're a minister and you deal with death and dying, but I can't understand why Margie didn't share her concerns with me," he said.

"She told me you weren't interested in her illness."

"That's not true," Warren said half-heartedly.

"That's the way she saw it. And that's all that counted."

"We were beginning to talk about things…at the end."

Steven had no reply to this. The brothers climbed into the car. Steven had his Bic lighter and an unfiltered Camel at the ready. "Mind if I smoke?" he asked.

"Go ahead," Warren said, figuring that a few burning cigarettes wouldn't stink up his car that badly. Driving off, he fell back on small talk. "How are the kids?" he asked his brother.

"Elizabeth is a nanny for a family in Florence, Italy, which is helping her Italian in a big way," Steven began. "Judith is a chef in a major eatery in downtown St. Louis. And Brian is a third-year law student at Wash. U."

"And your ex?"

"She's engaged. I'm happy for her. She does better with a man in her life."

"What's this meeting all about at the Doubletree?"

"Unitarian epistemology."

"What?"

Steven laughed. "Think of it as an excuse for people like me to get together and talk for a week. You know the old joke, right?"

"Joke?"

"If a Unitarian dies and on the way to heaven comes to a crossroad that bears two signs, heaven to the right and a discussion group about heaven to the left, he will go left every time."

"You find that funny?"

"Don't you?"

Warren didn't answer Steven. Rather, he made a suggestion. "Why don't we go see Mom?" he posed.

"Awesome idea," Steven said.

On the way to the Dundee Retirement Center, Warren recalled the funeral director's question about a memorial service for Margie. The woman had no living relatives but had many friends at the botanical garden. She also had several old chums from her days at Macys. Sitting in the car was a minister. The timing seemed perfect.

"Would you say a few words at a memorial service for Margie?" Warren asked.

"Awesome idea, bro. I'm there." Suddenly Steven leaned forward and began a long series of hacking coughs. His face turned red and the veins in his neck stood out. After what seemed to Warren a very long time, Steven sat back and took several deep breaths. "Whew, that was a doozy," he said.

"How long have you been smoking?" Warren asked.

"Since I was 15."

"Forty-eight years," Warren said.

"I guess so."

"Why don't you quit?"

"It's too late for me. Emphysema is irreversible. I might as well enjoy my smokes while I can."

Eventually the men reached the retirement center and walked toward the front doors, large panes of shiny glass held by aluminum frames. Warren spoke into an intercom receiver to identify himself, and as he and his brother waited to be allowed entry he had a chance to compare his ample girth to Steven's slender build, their reflections in the glass as clear as day.

"I've got to lose some weight," Warren said as he sucked in his belly and pulled up his shorts.

Steven snickered. "It might be too late for you as well, bro," he said.

In time they found their way to the area of the center where the demented lived. "I gather Mom is no better," Steven commented as Warren punched in the 4-digit entry code.

"She started using the "N" word," Warren said. "Her medication had to be increased."

"Racism dies hard."

"If ever."

In time the brothers found their mother Fern in her usual place in front of the wide screen TV. She was in her bathrobe.

"Hello Mom," Steven said. His words got Fern to take her eyes off the screen for a fleeting moment.

"Look what the cat dragged in" the woman said. She slurred her words and there was drool on her bathrobe.

"Mom, it's me, Steven."

"I know who you are," Fern said as she watched the local news. A commercial featured Billy Bob Richardson yelling something about a used Buick.

Warren positioned himself in front of his mother. Because he obstructed her view of the TV, he expected a reaction. He wasn't disappointed.

"Son, get the hell out of the way," Fern shouted.

"Mom, Steven is here for a visit."

"Elizabeth, Judith, and Brian," Fern shouted. "That's what you came for, ain't it?"

Warren glanced at his brother, who took his place in front of the old woman. "Would you take a walk with me, Mom?" Steven asked.

Fern looked up at her younger son's face and burst into laughter. "You look just like your father did when he got old," she blurted.

Steven returned a smile and gently aided his mother out of her chair. The couple started down a hall. Warren decided to stay put and give them a chance to visit. Takisha joined him, saying, "It must be hard for you to see your mother like this."

"I wish she weren't so sedated, if that's what you mean."

"But did you see how she perked up when you and your friend walked in?"

"He's my brother."

"Really? I guess he's from out of town."

"He is."

"Anyway, I just wanted to thank you for talking with Fern's doctor. She's...behaving herself."

"Glad to be of help."

"I'm sorry about all of this, Mr. Westing. I really am," Takisha said.

"So am I, Takisha. So am I."

Turning his attention to the hallway, he saw that Steven and Fern were making their return trip. They seemed to be talking up a storm as they continued their walk. Takisha moved off, leaving Warren alone in front of the TV. He watched the last of the local news, a human interest story featuring a local hot air balloon race. A young woman reporter flitted from one balloon to the next swooning over the bright colors as the envelopes filled with hot air. She focused on one entrant, a red, white, and blue balloon whose basket displayed large words in bold script. On one side of the basket the words *Billy Bob Motors* hung for all to see. On the opposite side was the name *Jesus*.

"Christ, the guy is everywhere," Warren said to himself.

The reporter stopped to talk to a man standing near this balloon festooned with the colors of the USA. He was a gaunt individual in an army fatigue jacket. He wore a Fu Man Chu mustache and smoked a cigarette. Warren found the remote and turned up the volume, actually interested in what Gar Young would have to say.

"Aren't you a little afraid to be heading a balloon so high up in the sky?" the young woman asked Gar.

After a deep drag on his cigarette, Gar tilted his head and stared at the woman. His contempt for her and her question filled the screen. "What's there to be afraid of, lady?" he mumbled.

The reporter turned to the camera and smiled. "This guy is one brave dude," she said. Turning back to Gar, she asked, "Mind if I go along?"

Gar crushed his cigarette under a shoe heel and turned away. His voice barely made the television audio. "Hop in," he said.

Giggling, the reporter playfully waved goodbye to the camera as the coverage returned to the studio. Warren snapped off the TV. He wondered if the unsuspecting woman would get an earful of Gar's take on sudden death and Vietnam as they rode together for hours in the confines of a hot air balloon. He chuckled to himself, guessing the poor girl may well end up thinking about jumping.

"Mom says it's time for lunch," Steven said as he walked toward his brother. Fern was already seated at a table starting in on a cup of vegetable soup. Before they joined her, Steven spoke in a muted voice, saying, "I had no idea Mom was so out of it."

"I guess you have to see it for yourself to believe it," Warren said.

"What does this place cost you?"

"$8500 a month."

"My Lord," Steven said as he rubbed his chin. "I tell you what. The day Brian graduates from law school, I'll start sending you money."

"You don't have to do that."

"I want to, bro. This whole thing isn't fair to you."

"Steve, I can handle the expense. Now that Margie is gone..."

"There's one less mouth to feed?" Steven chimed.

Truth be told Warren didn't know what he was about to say, but he found his brother's preachy interruption callous and thoughtless. "What a shitty thing to say," Warren yelled, his voice so loud it drew the attention of those seated at nearby tables.

"Oh, lighten up, bro," Steven said.

"Lighten up? My wife just died," Warren said. He tried to project some indignation in his words but he suddenly realized that his brother's suggestion had some merit.

"You don't act all that broken up about her death, bro."

"Now you're going to tell me what my marriage was like?"

"If the shoe fits..."

"You are one arrogant prick. And stop calling me 'bro'."

Steven snickered. "I'm going outside for a smoke," he said as he started for the door.

"You do that," Warren said. Fuming, he joined his mother at the table and watched her spoon her soup. "What a jerk," he said under his breath.

"You two never got along," Fern said, her attention on her soup.

"That's the truth," Warren mumbled. His mother's comment lent him immediate perspective. She was demented but she knew her sons. Warren and Steven Westing were opposites in almost every regard. And as outraged as he was at Margie's infidelity, Warren remained almost equally angry with her for having sought advice from his impetuous brother. "How did he get to be such a nitwit?" he asked his mother.

"Alvin always liked you better than Steven," Fern said. "It hurt your brother somethin' awful. Turned him to God is what it did."

"His head is in the clouds."

"Maybe. This soup is too salty," Fern said as she sat back and yawned.

"Time for a nap, Mom," Warren said. He led his mother to her room where she stretched out on her single bed. "See you next week," he said as he covered her with an afghan.

"If the creek don't rise," Fern said.

Leaving the retirement center, Warren found Steven leaning against the Lexus smoking a cigarette. Warren walked to the driver's side, unlocked the doors with a push of a remote and climbed in behind the wheel. His brother got in the car as well, cigarette in hand.

"Get rid of the cigarette," Warren demanded.

"Whoa. Sudden change in policy," Steven chided as he flipped the burning cigarette out the window onto the parking lot asphalt.

"Get your stupid ass out of the car, pick up your cigarette, and carry it to the front entrance where you'll find a sand ashtray," Warren shouted. Glaring at Warren, Steven did as he was told. When he returned to the car he had a scowl on his face. The brothers drove to the Doubletree Hotel in silence. The moment the Lexus came to a halt in front of the hotel Warren had more to say. "I don't buy that bull shit about you knowing that Margie died," he said.

"Whatever."

"And I decided not to hold a memorial service for her."

"Man. You must really hate her."

"You can't hate someone who is dead."

"Sure you can, bro. And you better deal with it or your hate will ruin what's left of your life."

"All right. That's it. No more preaching."

"Fine," Steven said as he reached for his backpack and got out of the car. "I'll check in from time to time," he said before he closed the door. Warren didn't get a chance to tell him not to bother.

Still irritated, Warren gunned his car back into traffic. The hasty and reckless move proved to be a mistake as an Omaha police officer had to hit his brakes to avoid colliding with the Lexus. The flashing lights of the police cruiser told Warren he needed to pull to the curb. Minutes later he surrendered his driver's license and proof of insurance to a female officer. "Very careless driving, sir," she said before returning to her cruiser for a computer search. A short time later she stood at Warren's car window. "Your record is clean, sir, so I'm giving you a warning," she said as she handed Warren his documents.

"My wife died yesterday," Warren offered, though the minute he spoke he regretted his words.

"Sorry to hear that, sir. Maybe you shouldn't be driving."

"I'm fine."

"Where do you live?"

"In Dundee."

"I'll follow you home."

"But I have to get to the hospital."

"Why is that?"

Warren hesitated. Telling her that his friend was hospitalized would give her more reason to escort him home. "I have a doctor's appointment," he lied. "Please officer, I've been waiting for this appointment for months."

"I'll follow you there then," the policewoman said. "Which center are you using?"

"UNMC."

"Okay. You head out. I'll be right behind you. And be careful."

As Warren eased into traffic, he had to admire how closely the officer tailed him. He also congratulated himself for coming up with a good lie. Lying was never a strong suit of his. It was then that he understood something about Margie. His wife must have been an excellent liar.

By the time they arrived at the hospital Warren's irritation with his brother had disappeared. He waved at the police officer who waited in her car until he entered the front door of UNMC. Negotiating the elevators and hallways of the enormous center he made his way to Stu Gottlieb's private room where he found Gloria sitting on a metal chair reading a magazine. Stu, heavily bandaged, was asleep in his bed. When Gloria spotted Warren she gestured her wish to have their conversation outside of the room. They talked just outside a closed door.

"Dentyne?" Gloria asked Warren as she popped a piece of gum in her mouth.

"No thanks. How is Stu doing?"

"The doctors say he's stable. But they keep talking about that bypass machine and how much time it took to get him off the thing. Apparently his heart problems aren't over."

"Christ. It's always something," Warren said. He took a big breath and held it, telling himself that the next thing he would do is tell Gloria about Margie. She would get the news before Stu, a sequence Warren didn't like. But some things couldn't be helped. After exhaling Warren spilled the beans. "Margie died yesterday," he blurted.

"What?"

"I found her dead in bed."

"Oh my God. I am so sorry," Gloria cried. She covered her face briefly with both hands and turned away. "I'm sorry, I need a moment," she said as she walked toward a row of hallway chairs. She sat, her head bowed. Warren looked on. The woman, clad in her usual running outfit, seemed to fall into a state of contemplation. Warren guessed she was trying to make sense of all the calamity that had touched her life. He knew he was. In time she returned to his side. "I only met her once you know," she said.

"I know."

"But I can't imagine what you must be going through. If my Stuie died…"

Just then a nurse showed up. "Your husband hit his call button," she explained to Gloria. "He must be awake. Shall we see?"

The threesome walked to Stu's bedside. Warren had never seen his friend is such bad shape. He was pale and had a film of sweat on his round face. After telling the nurse he needed a pain pill Stu gazed at Warren. "Well Westing, what do you think?"

"You look like shit Gottlieb," Warren said. He wished he were lying.

"Don't sugar coat it, Westing."

"Actually, for a guy who just had bypass surgery, I'm guessing you look pretty good."

"I'll take that as a compliment."

"So tell me, Gottlieb. What's been the best and the worst of your experience?" Warren asked. It was a common question the friends passed between them when one asked the other to share what had happened to him.

Stu glanced at Gloria. "Sweetie, would you get me today's Wall Street Journal?"

"Sure Stuie," Gloria said. "I'll be right back." After she left the room Warren waited for his friend's answer to his question. He knew his buddy well enough to guess that it wasn't for his girlfriend's ears.

"The best are the back rubs," Stu confessed. "These nurses are pros, especially that blond number who works the night shift."

"And the worst?"

"The surgeons. I just don't buy what they're telling me."

"Which is?"

"They say I'm going to have to take a ton of medication to keep my heart going."

"Why don't you get a second opinion?"

"Where? I'm first chair in a law suit against Creighton."

"There's a medical center in Des Moines. And there's always Mayo Clinic."

"That seems like a lot of trouble."

"Then stop your bellyaching and take your pills. Christ, Gottlieb, sometimes you can be one obstinate fucker."

Warren's comment silenced Stu for a moment. It was the window for the news about Margie's death. But before Warren summoned the words a nurse arrived with several pills and capsules that she insisted her patient swallow. There were so many that she had to refill the glass of water twice. After Stu consumed his medications the nurse told Warren that visiting hours were over and he had to leave. At the same time Stu rolled to his side, saying, "I'm going to take a nap Westing. See you tomorrow." The events happened so quickly and smoothly that it seemed to Warren as though he was watching a stage play. He thought about asking for a private moment with his friend but the nurse, a rather large and stern woman, indicated with her body language that she meant what she said. Visiting hours were over.

"Talk to you tomorrow, Gottlieb," Warren said as he left the room. He couldn't believe that he missed the chance to tell Stu about Margie. But as he walked the halls of the massive medical center he shrugged his shoulders and sighed. Dead is dead, he thought. What difference does a day make?

After the hospital visit, Warren drove to the funeral home and picked up Margie's ashes. He told the director there would be no memorial service, news that seemed to surprise the man. Indeed, the director acted indignant. "We've held very small services," the man advised as Warren wrote him a $2500 check for the cremation. "Just last week a widower honored his wife's passing by himself. He played a tune on a harmonica in her memory. It was rather touching."

"I think I can manage without you," Warren said as carried the box of ashes toward the exit. He realized he had been short with the director but he was exhausted. It had been a long two days.

At long last, Warren got home. Theo was waiting at the door, his leash in his mouth. After a quick walk, Warren grabbed a Sam Adams Summer Ale and headed upstairs for a nap. Without thinking he grabbed the box of ashes. When he walked by Margie's bedroom he peeked in, gazing at the bed, the dresser, and the clothes in the walk-in closet. What am I going to do with all this stuff, he wondered? It was then that he spotted a purse on a bedside table. The thing was large and made of red leather. Curious, he put the beer aside, set the box of ashes on the bed, and spilled the purse's contents next to the box. Out fell a pen, a box of Tic-Tacs, a wad of used tissue, a nail clipper, a tube of lipstick, a collection of credit cards, and a wallet. Opening the wallet Warren found Margie's driver's license, a membership card to the Lauritzen Botanical Gardens, and thirty-seven dollars. He also found a bank statement that indicated Margie had several hundred dollars in a checking account. The only name on the account was Margaret Westing. It was one more hurdle he would have to overcome, the withdrawal of money from an account that wasn't his. To be thorough Warren examined the inside of the purse and found a side pouch that was zippered shut. Inside was a single key. The apartment, he thought. "Margie's secret life," he murmured. He wondered when and if Jeff of the black beard would find out she was dead.

Aside from the cash, the items that lay before Warren were of no use to him. He pocketed the thirty-seven dollars and then put the odd assortment of objects back in the purse, even the key to the zippered inner side pouch. The box of ashes and the red purse rested next to one another on a bed sheet that just a day before covered his dying wife. Lifting the two items, he walked to the closet and placed them one-by-one on a top shelf. Then he took a moment to gaze up at their resting place. It much like looking at someone's gravestone. "Rest in peace," he whispered. And with that Margie's memorial service ended.

VIII

During the few days off work Warren had time to give serious thought to Margie, her private life, her affair, her cancer, and the lonely way she curled up and died. There was no question in his mind that he preferred their marital arrangement, the separate way they conducted their affairs. Why, then, was he so easily angered when he stumbled on something Margie was trying to keep to herself, he wondered? Why was he surprised to find that she sought sex from another man? After all she spent her last days exchanging e-mails with his brother that surely were more intimate than any roll in the hay with the Jeff of the black beard. Why was he so repelled by her cancer, her vomiting, loss of hair and muscle wasting? Was he afraid the same would happen to him one day? And what was it like for her to send a last message and then crawl into bed to spend her last hours? Why wasn't he there? Why didn't she summon him? Many of these questions would never be answered. But those that involved him might offer a little insight on his life if he paid attention. After all, his doctor's letter implied that something was amiss. He might turn into the very person he found so repugnant.

To pass the time he took inventory of Margie's belongings. She owned a Honda, had a large closet full of clothes, and then there was that bank account. He rifled through a desk in her bedroom and found only a checkbook and personal letters. It astounded him that she apparently had no will, a situation that embarrassed him. After all he was a partner in a large law firm and should have taken care of that basic necessity. This discovery led him to re-examine his own state of affairs. One afternoon he sat in his den going over his will, trust, IRA, deed to his home, and bank accounts. Because of Margie's death they all required changes. This would take some doing but he knew the right attorneys to ask for help.

Thinking about his estate and about what to do with his wealth once he was dead had an understandably sobering affect on Warren. He had always assumed Margie would outlive him. She had been the healthy one while he was miserably overweight and out of shape. Now he needed a new heir. His mother was too old, his brother too irritating, and his nieces and nephew too distant. His best friend Gottlieb came to mind but the man certainly didn't need more money. He thought of a charity but hadn't been involved in any humanitarian cause. Then he thought of his dog Theo. Omaha's Humane Society was the perfect fit. Pulling out the White Pages he found the society's telephone number and memorized it, planning to inquire about its contribution policy the first chance he got. But for now, he wished to go to UNMC to visit Gottlieb. Nearing discharge, his friend had become very impatient with his care-givers. The man apparently needed his friends to deflect his spite.

A half-an-hour later Warren walked into Stu's private hospital room. As always Gloria was there. The elaborate IV apparatus was gone. Stu was no longer in a hospital gown, instead wearing a cotton warm-up suit. He was lying on top of the sheets, arms folded across his chest and a scowl on his face. When he saw Warren he had a few words for him. "I can't believe you didn't tell me about Margie," Stu shouted as he waved a dated obituary page in the air.

"I didn't have a chance..."

"That's bullshit Westing. You could've called or texted. Instead I had to hear the news from Gloria. Some friend you are."

Warren glanced at Gloria who just shrugged her shoulders and proceeded to leave the room, saying, "I'll leave you two boys to your tiff." Her departure created an awkward silence between the men. Finally Warren spoke.

"I'm sorry Gottlieb. I should have been more forthcoming. But there's more to the story than Margie's passing."

"What more could there be?" Stu asked. His tone was biting and accusatory. But when he heard Warren's account of the secret apartment and the black-bearded Jeff he mellowed. "Mama mia," he murmured after the tale sunk in. "Man, I'm sorry Westing. I truly am."

"Yeah, me too."

"Did you have any idea..."

"Not a clue."

Picking up the obituary page Stu studied Margie's obit, saying, "I thought she was younger than us."

"She was born in 1947, just like you and me," Warren said. "She would've been 65 in December."

"It says here she was cremated."

"I have her ashes at home."

"I've got to hand it to you Westing, you're more generous than I would've been."

"How's that?"

"I would've dumped her ashes in the river."

"I hope that's your stitches talking."

Stu sneered. "My stitches are the least of my problems," he said as he handed Warren a list of medications. "Feast your eyes on this," he told of his friend.

Scanning the list, Warren's mouth dropped open. "Eleven medications?" he uttered. "Why so many?"

"They tell me my heart is no good. They say I will eventually need a new one."

"A heart transplant? Jesus H. Christ."

"There's more, Westing. They want me to retire."

This news set Warren back on his heels. He and Gottlieb had been side by side since college. Not having his best friend at work was unthinkable. Fortunately Stu's stubborn streak came to the rescue. "I say fuck them," Stu growled.

"I'm with you Gottlieb. When do you get out of here?"

"Tomorrow," Gloria chimed as she entered the room. She was carrying the latest Wall Street Journal which she handed to Stu.

"The first thing I'm going to do is treat myself to a pastrami on rye," Stu declared.

"I'm pretty sure that's not on your diet," Gloria said.

"Like I said, fuck them."

With a snicker Warren headed for the door, saying, "This time the tiff is yours."

* * *

After a few days, Warren dressed for work. Though he had been off work for just a week his summer weight suit felt oddly constricting. He snapped his suspenders, hitched his belt and took a last look at his smooth face and hair before heading downstairs. Theo was waiting for him. "Just a quick walk today," Warren said. "I've got a doctor's appointment."

Walking down the sidewalks of Dundee, Warren watched his brindled giant walk along. Theo was on a new medication for arthritis and had improved after just one day, his limp barely detectable. As for Warren, he continued to have pain in his lower back and left hip. Within an hour he guessed he would learn more about its cause.

At 8 o'clock sharp Warren walked into Dr. Alvin McHale's office. He was glad to see he was the only one in the waiting room. He intended to be at his firm by 10 a.m., knowing that he would be facing a back log of tax work. The receptionist directed him straight back to the inner hall of the office where he was met by the lovely niece of his secretary, the young Gabriela.

"Right on time," the nurse said. The woman was shorter and shapelier than Warren remembered her. Her white uniform hugged her waist and thighs, and contrasted nicely with her Hispanic skin tone. As on his first visit, Warren laughed at himself for leering at her, and at the same time congratulated himself for having the wherewithal to feel the attraction.

"Light day?" Warren asked as he followed the nurse into an exam room.

"Dr. McHale announced his retirement last week," Gabriela said. "Many of his patients have already found new doctors."

"Retirement? He doesn't look that old."

"He's 75."

"Really. He runs around like a teenager."

Gabriela took Warren's vital signs all of which were within normal limits. His weight came next. "Ouch," he said when he read the result. He was up to 239. Expecting a comment from the nurse, he glanced to his right only to find her grimacing and running a hand through her long dark hair as she faced the computer. She looked worried. "Something wrong?" he asked.

"It's nothing," she said.

Stepping off the scale, Warren took a seat on the edge of the exam table. "Come on Gabriela, I've known your aunt for years. You and I are practically related."

"It's just that I have to find a new job," Gabriela said. "Nursing positions are hard to come by in Omaha these days."

Before Warren could offer words of support Gabriela turned from the computer and showed him a little smile. "My aunt said she showed you her old picture," she said, grinning.

"She was a cutie," Warren said.

"I think she's beautiful."

Warren held his tongue. Calling his secretary beautiful was a stretch. In his opinion a handsome middle-aged woman was a more accurate description. Gabriela had more to say. "I hope you don't find this inappropriate Mr. Westing," she began, her smile replaced by a cautious look. Warren stared at her, at a loss as to what she was getting at. "My aunt told me about the passing of your wife," she went on. Warren waited. "If you should ever find yourself...looking for another woman..." she said.

Suddenly Warren understood. His secretary's husband had died several years ago. She was single. Now he was single. Searching for the words for a tactful yet honest answer, he hesitated. His response never materialized because at that moment Dr. McHale burst into the room.

"How are you Westing?" the doctor asked, offering a handshake and then scurrying to the computer. He wasted no time bringing up Warren's recent blood tests. "Ah, here we are," the slight man murmured as he scanned the screen.

Gabriela looked dour as she left the room giving Warren the impression that she regretted what she had just suggested. He wished he had a chance to tell her he appreciated her thoughtfulness but his doctor began to talk, words flying from him like gun fire.

"We've got trouble here," McHale started. "Your PSA is sky high and an enzyme called alkaline phosphatase is also elevated."

"English please."

"You probably have prostate cancer. And it may have already spread to your bones."

Warren reeled at the news. "I've got cancer?"

"We'll know for sure after more tests," McHale said. He faced his patient, fiddling with his bow tie, wiping the lens of his glasses with a paper towel, and then crossing his arms. "You will need a prostate biopsy and a bone scan to begin with," he recited. "Are you with me, Westing?"

Warren stared at the frenetic physician. The man couldn't have weighed 130 pounds. His hair was gray but his face was young and alive with expression. "I can't believe this," Warren said, hoping against hope that this little doctor was dead wrong.

"My nurse has probably told you about my retirement..."

"No. Please Dr. McHale, you can't leave me like this," Warren begged.

"I have plans, Westing. Besides, this office is closing as of today..."

"I'm begging you. I need you to see me through. I don't know another doctor. I can't find one on such short notice," Warren said. He was close to shouting. Inside he was trembling. Luckily for him his manner seemed to have an impact on McHale. The physician put his glasses back on and then gave Warren a long look before he spoke.

"I tell you what I'll do," McHale began. "I'll keep you on as my only patient. We can meet at UNMC's out patient facility. Fair enough?"

"Thank you sir," Warren said, immensely relieved. Finding out that he might have a spread cancer was bad enough. Putting his trust in someone he never met would've been unbearable, or so he feared.

Nodding, the doctor returned to the computer. A short time later Warren held a document listing his scheduled tests including an out-patient prostate biopsy at UNMC. "I'll get you the results as they come in," McHale said before hustling out of the room. Warren checked the time. It was only 8:30. After leaving the medical building he headed for an IHOP. There he treated himself to a stack of pancakes with a side of bacon. As he ate he thought about his weight. Then he thought about possibly of having cancer, followed by the memory of Margie's struggles with nausea and vomiting. Weight, he thought, might turn out to be the least of my problems. Accordingly he finished the breakfast with a tall glass of creamy chocolate milk. The treat did little to ease his worry but when he eventually got to work his mood improved when he saw Gabriela charging toward him with open arms. It was the first time the two had seen one another in a week.

"I am so sorry for your loss Warren," the woman gushed as she enveloped him in her strong arms. Accepting the hug, Warren put his arms around her, surprised at the feel of her substantial girth. Her back was firm, her waist thick, her breasts ample, her head heavy on his shoulder. Yet when she stepped back from the embrace she looked trim enough in her dress. It was a trick Warren had to admire.

"How back logged are we?" Warren asked as he headed for his office.

"Not too bad," Gabriela said. "You'll catch up in no time."

Taking off his coat, Warren entered his office and sat down at his desk prepared to dive into his work. Within fifteen minutes his lower back and left hip began to ache causing his mind to drift. He recalled that one of the tests he was to have was a bone scan. That had to mean McHale was looking for cancer in his bones. That meant that all this time his pain might have been caused by cancer. "I hate this," Warren whispered. His first day back on the job saw little accomplished.

Around 4 p.m. Warren decided to call it a day. Slinging his suit coat over his shoulder he left his office only to spot Gabriela packing up as well. Her enormous purse sat on her desk, a black leather bag that usually held several small Tupperware containers. This day was no exception.

"I see you still eat at your desk from time to time," Warren said as he pulled one of the containers out of the purse, lifted the lid and smelled the contents. "Porko?"

Gabriela chuckled. "Your Spanish stinks," she said.

"So does my cooking. How about rustling up a little extra tomorrow so I can join you for lunch?"

"I'd be happy to. Cooking for two is easier than cooking for one."

Warren put the plastic container back in the purse and headed for the elevator. "Hasta proximo tiempo," he called, listening for the famous "Ay-yi-yi." She didn't fail him.

Hours later Warren sat in his chair watching the History Channel. His stomach was full of pizza and beer, and he tended to doze off during the lengthy commercials. Around 9 he decided to read in bed. After a dozen or so pages of "Truman" he snapped off the bedside lamp, turned on his left side with his right knee flexed and left leg extended, put a hand under the pillow and fell asleep. After some time he began to dream. His dream put him on an ocean beach. It was daytime and sunny. A man walking in the surf approached him. It was the old Indian. "Vani nisa a ro," the old man said to Warren.

"What does that mean?" Warren asked in his dream. Before he had an answer he looked out over the ocean and spotted a giant wave. Somehow he knew the tidal wave would cover him if he didn't run. He jumped to his feet and raced away from the sea, almost falling as he struggled for traction in the sand. He looked back once and saw that the old man was waving to him. He also saw that the wave was very near shore. Running hard now he heard a roar behind him and felt the sunlight disappear. He understood that he had been caught. Falling on his belly he sank his hands in the sand and held his breath. Water crashed down on his back. He lay submerged. He desperately needed air, and could no longer hold his breath. That was when he woke, gasping.

"Jesus Christ," Warren said as he sat up in bed breathing heavily. Sweat covered his face. In time he was breathing normally but was not the least bit sleepy. The digital alarm read 3:17. Swinging out of bed he inched through the dark to his bathroom, flipped on the light, and urinated. Theo's deep bark resounded from below.

"Go back to bed Theo," Warren called. It was no use. The dog was awake and wanted his walk. What the hell, Warren thought. I'm up. He donned a lightweight bathrobe and slippers and headed downstairs. Theo was in the foyer holding his leash in his mouth. "Do you know what time it is, boy?" Warren asked. The Great Dane didn't seem to care.

Strolling the sidewalks of Dundee in the middle of the night proved to be a pleasant experience. The decorative streetlights provided ample light on this warm evening. As Warren walked he pondered his dream. He had experienced the same tidal wave nightmare before and had always associated it with times of stress in his life. The dream had presented itself at a predictable juncture. The old Indian man, though, was something he could not explain, nor could he remember the words the man spoke. It was something he once would've mentioned to Margie.

Warren spent the rest of the night watching a movie "Casablanca.," s movie he owned. Theo lay at his feet. The sun rose just after 6 a.m. He decided to ready himself for work and go to the office to get a head start on the day. By 7 he was at his desk. Gabriela came in at 9. "My my, look at the early bird," she chirped when she peeked in his office.

"Couldn't sleep," Warren explained.

"I brought in my beef burritos. They're a specialty of mine."

"Can't wait. Is 11 too early for you?"

"It's a date," Gabriela said as she closed the door.

That last remark got Warren's attention. He knew his secretary was a proper and modest woman who would give the death of his wife all the respect it deserved. But the words of Dr. McHale's nurse stuck in his head. He and Gabriela were two single individuals who had every right to eventually entertain a relationship. He had to admit that he found the idea attractive.

Just before 11 a.m. Gabriela waltzed into Warren's office with a large Tupperware and two plastic plates and forks. He cleared off his desk and she served up the steaming burritos along with rice and refried beans. "Everything you see here is homemade," Gabriela bragged. "Except for this," she added as she produced a bottle of water.

"This looks delicious," Warren said. He was practically drooling and wasted no time digging in, devouring the food on his plate before Gabriela was half done with her meal.

"You must have been hungry," the woman observed, sitting on a chair with her plate of food balanced on her lap.

Warren smiled. "Eating has always been my favorite pastime," he said.

"I should've made more."

"No, no. This is fine," Warren said. He leaned back in his swivel chair and rubbed his full belly, watching his secretary daintily consume her lunch. He judged her movements to be more graceful than he would've expected from a woman her size, but instantly realized he had no reason to hold that prejudice. After all, he was a large individual and was reasonably coordinated. Gabriela, it seemed, shared that asset. He noticed more about her, the straight spine and the comfortable way she crossed her legs. At she ate she glanced at him a few times.

"You're making me self-conscious," Gabriela complained at one point.

"Sorry. I was just thinking. This is the first time in ten years that we've shared a lunch in my office."

"I'm sure you're right. Maybe we should do this more often," Gabriela said. Her voice lilted, her eyes softened, her smile was warm.

"Do you know what your niece said to me?"

"I do. And I apologize. She was out of line."

"You don't think we'd make a good pair?"

"It's too soon for us, Warren. It's way too soon."

That Gabriela called him "Warren" and not "Boss" was not lost on him. He had to admit that starting a relationship with her at this juncture would be in poor taste and would likely generate a good deal of gossip in the firm. But he could imagine their future together. It was then that he decided to lay his cards on the table. He leaned forward and rested his arms on his desk. "I've got something to tell you," he said.

"Oh?"

"I hate to burden you with this but you're going to have to do the scheduling and all…"

"What is it, Warren?"

Warren took a deep breath and then gave Gabriela the news. "There's a chance I have cancer."

The admission froze Gabriela. She stopped eating and stared at Warren. At first her dark eyes showed fear, but slowly began to express compassion. "I am truly sorry for you," she finally said. "When will you know for sure?" Warren handed her the document listing the dates and times of the bone scan and prostate biopsy. She seemed to understand what needed to be done. "I'll take care it, Boss," she said. It was then that she did something Warren didn't expect. Putting her plate aside she walked around the desk to Warren's side. There she embraced him, an awkward move that pulled the side of his head to her breasts and the point of his shoulder to her abdomen. Even from a sitting position and separated from the woman by the arm of his chair, Warren felt the strength in her arms. Her dress smelled of spices and perfume. He heard a soft sound coming from above. At first he thought Gabriela was crying. She was not. She was humming a song.

After a minute or so into the embrace, Warren thought it appropriate to hug back. Still sitting and pressed against Gabriela's body he put an arm around her waist and gave her a gentle pull. Her humming changed to words. Listening carefully, he didn't recognize the language. He wanted to ask about her song but dared not. The moment felt special and he didn't want to spoil it.

At long last Gabriela released Warren and began gathering the remains of the lunch. He watched her work, wishing he knew what she was thinking. He started to say something but she spoke first. "My husband died of cancer," she said.

"I didn't know," Warren returned.

"I used to sing to him like I sang to you."

"I thought it was...nice. Thank you."

"If you have cancer you will need help. I should be the one to help you. I know all about it."

"Well let's wait and see," Warren suggested, unnerved by the notion that he might someday be in need of someone's help.

Gabriela opened the door but before she exited Warren called to her. "What language were you singing in?" he asked.

"Mixtec."

"Oh yes. I remember. The language of your youth."

It was then that Gabriela opened her heart. "I cannot lose another loved one to cancer," she said. "Do you understand?" Not knowing how to respond to this confession, Warren just repeated what he had said before.

"Let's wait and see," Warren said. Gabriela nodded and left his office.

By 4 p.m. Warren's lower back and left hip were aching as never before. He couldn't avoid imagining masses of cancer cells eating away at his skeleton. When he headed home Gabriela handed him a work schedule that allowed for his upcoming tests. Her warm smile and soft eyes had vanished. She was his secretary again. He was the Boss.

IX

The date was July 13, 2012. Warren was sitting in the private office of Dr. Alvin McHale. The rest of the office was empty. All of Warren's testing was complete including a prostate biopsy that had left him sore and peeing blood. While he waited he looked around the office. The large wooden desk looked like an antique. The rug was Persian. Framed photos sat on bookcase shelves and told stories about the doctor. He had been in the Marines. He once caught a marlin. He came from a large family. One of his grandchildren was or had been in the Peace Corp.

Suddenly McHale burst in holding several pieces of paper. "Good day Westing," he said as he sat behind his desk.

"McHale," Warren returned, trying to sound positive.

"I've got bad news. You do indeed have prostatic adenocarcinoma metastatic to your left femur, the fourth lumbar vertebra, the eighth left rib anteriorly and your right parietal lobe.

"I'm not familiar with the last..."

"Your brain."

"Jesus H. Christ."

"I recommend chemotherapy and radiation."

"Chemotherapy killed my wife."

"That can happen."

Warren stared past the doctor at a gold clock that sat on a table under a window. The clock was covered by a glass dome. A pendulum rotated underneath the face, first clockwise, then counterclockwise, and then back again. It seemed to him that its rate was picking up while he looked on as though time was accelerating.

"Are you with me Westing?" McHale asked, snapping his finger to get his patient's attention.

Warren's eyes returned to the man in the white jacket and bow tie. "This is a little hard to accept," he admitted. Truth be told he was terrified but was too proud to show it.

"No doubt," McHale said as he texted a message. "I've taken the liberty of handing your case over to our oncology board. UNMC takes pride in offering a coordinated treatment plan when it comes to cancer, though your ultimate treatment is decided by the primary physician, namely me. I'm sending the board the results of the final path report as we speak."

"So you're keeping your promise?" Warren asked. "I'm still your patient?"

McHale grinned. "As of today you're my only patient. Otherwise I am retired."

"A doctor with one patient. That's got to be a first."

"Not at all. Consider Michael Jackson and Elvis Presley. Both had physicians whose practices had a single individual."

"I'm hardly in their financial league."

"Don't worry about me," McHale said. "I've got plenty of money."

Warren's eyes fell on the picture of the giant marlin. McHale was standing next to the hanging fish with a smile on his face. The catch was twice his size. "I feel like I'm keeping you from your life," Warren said.

McHale followed Warren's line of vision. "I'll be fishing soon enough," he said. Warren felt that the good doctor could have chosen his words more carefully. He sounded as though he was counting on his patient's imminent demise. But Warren judged that he had no time to waste on paranoia. Rather he turned his focus to the matter at hand.

"When do I start treatment?" Warren asked.

"After a review of your case and my recommendations, the board will contact you by e-mail. Treatment schedules and information about side effects will be included. I will provide your follow-up at the UNMC out-patient facility."

Warren nodded. "No sense keeping an office open for one patient," he said. "Do you happen to know if your pretty nurse found another position?"

"Gabriela? I'm happy to report that she now works at the Omaha Fertility Clinic, a first-rate operation. I'm sure she'll be happy there."

"Good for her. She's my secretary's niece you know."

"I didn't know that," McHale said as he handed Warren a prescription.

"What's this?" Warren asked.

"It's a pain pill. Oxycontin."

Staring at the scribbled note Warren mouthed what he read. The word was so strangely contrived. He wondered if he would end up with a list of medications like his friend Gottlieb. "I'm not in that much pain," he insisted.

"It's best to be prepared for the worst," McHale said.

"Are there any side effects?" Warren asked, hoping that an intelligent question would mask his terror.

"Your pharmacist will tell you all about it, trust me."

Warren folded the prescription and put it in his shirt pocket. Standing he accepted a handshake from the doctor. "Good luck to you sir," McHale said.

"Why don't you call me Warren?"

"Only if you call me Alvin."

"Your first name was the reason I chose you for my doctor."

McHale smiled as he ushered Warren out the door of his private office and toward the general exit. "I'm grateful for the glowing recommendation," McHale joked.

As the men walked their steps echoed in the empty hallway and waiting room. Absent were nurses, receptionists and patients. "Maybe I should think about retiring," Warren said.

"That will depend on your insurance coverage," McHale said. Warren hadn't given a thought to what the cost of his treatment would be. As he left the office he felt a pat on his shoulder, a gesture that signaled a degree of finality. When he got to his car he suddenly felt quite alone. When he started the Lexus he wondered if it would be the last auto he would own. Looking out on the bright day brought a fear that he would not see another summer. A cough caused his lower back to hurt.

"I have cancer," Warren said slowly and deliberately. "I have fucking cancer. Jesus H. Christ." As he drove home he sensed that his body was no longer his. Some malevolent force had seized it and was transforming it into tissue that was of no use to him. In time he would be unrecognizable. Then he would die.

Later that afternoon Warren sat near his garden pool drinking a Snapple. The memory of Margie's suffering had made him take a cautiously aggressive position. He decided, even before beginning cancer treatment, to give himself every advantage. He vowed to eat well, take regular walks, avoid alcohol, take naps, work fewer hours, and to try to maintain a cautious optimism. Margie had lost her battle, but he just might win his. He was strong while she was frail. He was once an accomplished athlete while she planted shrubs. He was a realist while she was a dreamer. The truth was, they were very different people. This fact gave Warren hope. Despite having a dreaded disease that had spread to his bones and even to his brain, he just might beat it. He had always avoided confrontation but now he had no choice if he wanted to live. He had to perform, to take the ball and run with it, this time into the line and not around the end.

Gradually Warren's thoughts turned to more practical matters. His colleagues at his law firm would need to know his situation. Gabriela would need access to his treatment schedule. Stu and Gloria had to be told immediately. He would, of course, tell his mother he had cancer though he doubted she would retain the news. Then there was his brother Steven and his family. Because he wished to avoid a diatribe on death and dying, Warren decided not to involve his younger sibling. But just then his cell phone rang.

"Hey bro," the voice rang. Of course it was Steven.

"What can I do for you?" Warren said, hoping to keep the conversation short.

"I had a dream. I just had to call. Bro, you died. A dragon swallowed you."

"Jesus," Warren muttered.

"Well?"

"Well what?"

"Are you dying?"

"We're all dying."

"You know what I mean."

Warren hesitated. Instead of revealing his plight to his brother he chose an alternate subject. "Look Steven, we have to talk about Mom."

The remark silenced his brother. Warren continued. "There's a good chance she'll outlive me. If that happens you'll have to take over her support."

"I knew it," Steven said.

Warren groaned. He realized he had just told Steven what he wanted to know. Just before he got around to the cancer he heard his brother begin a protracted wet cough. "You might go before I do," Warren jibed after the spell ceased, referring to his brother's advanced emphysema.

"That's a distinct possibility. I'm ready though."

"Oh Christ, here we go."

"Bring death out of the darkness and into the light. Break the taboo..."

"I've got to go," Warren lied, ending the call. It was all he could do not to throw his phone in the garden pool. He couldn't believe Margie had once taken comfort in Steven's bullshit. If he had been in her place he would've asked how that Unitarian mumbo-jumbo applied to being hit by a bolt of lightning or crushed by a giant tree limb.

The next day at work Warren sat in a large conference room with the other partners of his law firm. The meeting covered routine matters and was headed for an early adjournment. Just as the attorneys started to leave Warren called for their attention. In a slow and steady voice he told his colleagues of his cancer. It was a short speech.

"That's a damn shame," one man said.

"You'll beat it Westing. You're a bull," another remarked.

The only non-attorney in the room, a school marm of a woman who was the head of Human Resources, said, "Mr. Westing if you could stop by my office at your convenience I'd like to go over your retirement plans and pension with you." Her request was met by angry stares. Warren could see the bewilderment on the woman's face. He knew she was just trying to be helpful. He was also beginning to understand that cancer was a touchy subject. Nothing smelled of death like cancer.

A bit later Warren sat at his desk. When Gabriela strolled in carrying a stack of paperwork he told her of his diagnosis. She took the news like she was listening to a weather report. "You're going to need a lot of help Boss," she said, repeating her earlier advice. "Do you have your treatment schedules?"

"Not yet," Warren said.

"I'll need them ASAP. We have a few time-sensitive tax issues to work around."

Warren gazed at her. She looked youthful in her light-weight beige dress and matching heels. "Exactly how old are you Gabriela?" he asked.

"Ay-yi-yi. You never ask a woman her age," she complained.

"Would I be wrong if I guessed you were…say…59?"

Gabriela smiled. "You'd be close," she said before leaving the office. On the way out she brushed by Stu Gottlieb who barged in wearing a Hawaiian shirt and shorts.

"We have a dress code in this firm Gottlieb," Warren joked.

"I don't return to work until tomorrow," Stu said.

"Then what are you doing here?"

"I was just down in Human Resources collecting my paid leave check. The hag who runs the place said you have cancer. What the fuck, Westing?"

Warren sighed as he gestured toward a chair. "Have a seat Gottlieb. I'll tell you all about it."

The friends sat together for a good length of time. Warren described the spread of his disease and the planned chemotherapy and radiation. Stu raised his shirt and revealed his surgical scar. The sutures had been removed but the wound still looked angry and painful. He also complained about bleeding. The slightest knick of a razor would produce a flow of blood that would refuse to stop for what seemed to him a very long time, this the result of a potent blood thinner that he needed to take indefinitely. At one point the men stared at one another without speaking. Warren became acutely aware of their mortality. He was sure Stu had similar thoughts.

"We're a pair, aren't we Gottlieb?" Warren observed.

"First class protoplasm," Stu said. "Oh, I almost forgot. Gloria wants to introduce you to someone."

"What?"

"Her name is Naomi…something. She plays viola in the symphony. She sits next to Gloria. I've seen her plenty of times though I haven't actually met her…"

"Gottlieb! Hold your horses. My wife just died, I'm an overweight middle-aged lawyer and I, as you now know, have cancer. What woman in her right mind would be interested in me?"

"Gloria says that woman would be Naomi…something."

Warren shook his head. "This is a bad idea," he said, though he had to admit he was intrigued. Then he thought about Margie and her affair. In some perverse way getting involved with a woman seemed fair. He found himself wishing that Margie was around to see it.

"I've already made reservations at Anthony's Steak House for the four of us," Stu went on as he handed Warren a note listing the date and time of the dinner.

"Why so late?" Warren asked as he read the note.

"We're going to a symphony concert first."

"Oh no."

"Come on Westing. You can sit through one concert."

Warren sat back in his swivel chair and ran a hand through his hair. "Let me get this straight," he began in summation. "You want me to go on a blind date with a violist to one of the most expensive restaurants in Omaha after sitting through a couple hours of music that has always put me to sleep?"

"I've always admired your ability to comprehend the obvious," Stu joked. The smile on Stu's face told Warren they were headed for mischief. It was a signal that, over the years, almost always meant good times.

"Okay, for the sake of argument let's say I agree to join you. Can you at least tell me something about this Naomi?" Warren pleaded. As he spoke he could feel himself falling for his friend's proposal. Gottlieb could get him to go along with just about anything.

"As I said, I haven't met her," Stu began. "I know she's about Gloria's age and that she's supposed to be one hell of a musician."

"That's not telling me much."

"Come on, Westing. We'll have fun. What have you got to lose?"

The question was a good one, Warren had to admit. His health may fail him at any time. He should enjoy himself while he had the chance. "All right Gottlieb, you win. As usual," he said.

Stu jumped to his feet, clapped his hands once and farted. Warren farted back. "I'll meet you at the symphony hall," Stu said as he handed Warren a symphony ticket and then headed for the door. "Don't be late." Warren glanced at the ticket. The double date was set. As he watched his old friend leave the office he wondered how many times they had ventured out with girls on their arms.

When done with his day, Warren stopped by a Walgreens on the way home and picked up two frozen pizzas and a six-pack of Coke. His vow to eat healthier stood fresh in his mind, but he was starving and decided to settle on a quick meal just this once. He bought a Snickers candy bar on an impulse as he was checking out, intending to freeze the candy when he got home the way he used to do it as a teenager. Just as he was about to exit the store he remembered the prescription for the pain medication. He reversed direction and headed for the pharmacy. Once there he handed the Oxycontin script to a pharmacist, a young woman with a serious case of acne. She smiled when she saw him but her smile vanished when she read the prescription. "One moment sir," she said as she turned and walked to the interior of the shop. Minutes later another pharmacist appeared. He was older and looked dead serious.

"Could I see some ID?" the man demanded of Warren.

"Is there a problem?" Warren asked as he produced his driver's license.

The pharmacist didn't offer a reply. Rather, he studied the license, gazing at the photo ID and then at Warren. He did this several times. "What's your address?" he finally asked.

"41 Crestwood lane Omaha, Nebraska," Warren said. "What's this all about?"

Handing the license back to Warren, the man continued his questioning. "Do you know what Oxycontin is?" he asked next.

"I'm told it's a pain pill."

"It's a narcotic. It's highly addictive and it carries a substantial street value."

The pharmacist's attitude started to rub Warren the wrong way. "Just give me my medication and I'll be on my way," Warren growled.

"Why do you need Oxycontin?" was the next question.

"That's none of your goddamn business," Warren shot back, fuming now.

The pharmacist took another look at the prescription. "I'll have to call your physician," he said.

"Jesus H. Christ."

"I'll ask you to watch your mouth sir."

"Just make the goddamn call," Warren spit as he reluctantly took a seat on one of two metal chairs obviously meant for waiting customers like himself. As he sat he listened to the sound of a radio sitting inside the pharmacy. The vapid tune that carried over the counter sounded to him like elevator music. When the music ended a voice identified the station as the local source for "Christian Harmonies." When a commercial aired Warren wasn't surprised to hear Billy Bob Richardson's booming voice urging the faithful to visit his car lot for righteous deals. Another piece began, this one a choir singing a standard hymn. The music came and went. Billy Bob's voice returned twice. A full 30 minutes went by. At long last the pharmacist reappeared at the window.

"Sir, your medication," the man called. Warren rose and walked to the counter where he handed the pharmacist a credit card. The cost of the medicine was substantial, adding to Warren's irritation. After putting the amber plastic vial of pills in the bag with the pizzas, coke and Snickers, he signed the credit card receipt. As he did so he had a question for the pharmacist.

"How do you stand that crap?" Warren asked as he pointed to the radio.

"Christian music is all I listen to," the pharmacist said. "And I resent your attitude."

"Not as much as I resent you, you arrogant prick," Warren shot back. Wheeling on his heels he stormed out of Walgreens, certain that his pizzas had begun to thaw and the Coke had warmed. As he drove home he realized that he his confrontation with the pharmacist had arisen without a shred of reluctance or anxiety on his part. His patience with bullshit was running out. Margie once said that having cancer made you think. For Warren it was not so much thinking as saying what was on his mind. That was the only positive thing about the mess he had found for himself. He was learning how to confront his world. That was something.

X

A week later a lengthy e-mail arrived on Warren's lap top. It was from the UNMC oncology board with an endorsement from Alvin McHale M.D. First the general theories behind radiation and chemotherapy were set forth along with a list of their side effects. Next came the dates and times of treatments. Radiation to the brain would begin first followed by attention to the left femur, fourth lumbar vertebra, and finally the 8th left rib. During one of these visits a port would be surgically implanted in a simple out-patient procedure. The message explained that a port was a durable site for intravenous medication to be delivered repetitively and would most likely be located just under a clavicle or collar bone. Once placed, the port would allow chemotherapy to begin. The chemo treatment schedule was long and involved hours of sitting in what was called the "Chemo Room". Reading material and computer activity were recommended to help pass the time. Food was discouraged because of the gastrointestinal distress common among patients in the treatment room. Nurses would assure hydration with frequent offers of bottled water.

The e-mail turned personal, predicting the specific side-effects likely to befall Warren Westing. Hair loss, fatigue, and chronic nausea headed the list. As Warren scanned the message he got the distinct feeling that these side-effects weren't possibilities. They were certainties. He wondered why Dr. McHale, or Alvin, hadn't discussed these eventualities with him. He had a pain pill in his possession but hadn't been prepared to lose his hair, suffer fatigue or feel constant nausea. But he was a rookie in the cancer game and decided to let the veterans show him the ropes.

One change in his health showed Warren that McHale knew his stuff. As of late, the pain in his lower back had substantially increased. Warren feared his imagination was responsible for this, that the mere thought of cancer lurking in his bones augmented the constant throb in his spine. Real or not, he had to deal with the pain and Oxycontin was the answer. The narcotic worked and he was thankful to have a supply.

After showering, shaving, and dressing for work Warren walked his dog. As he strolled he reflected on the coming week as being the last one before the dreaded treatment began. On the weekend he was to meet his blind date, the woman called Naomi, and he felt grateful that he would not yet be fatigued, bald and sick to his stomach. The word "date" struck him as oddly ill-suited for a man his age, particularly because he was a widower with cancer. He began his mind-game, trying to imagine what the "date" would entail. Because he had only Gloria Chase as a model he saw Naomi as a woman with a similar build and manner. She would have salt-and-pepper hair and a pleasant smile. Like Gloria she would be a good conversationalist. Turning his attention on himself he thought it wise to get a haircut before the date. His dark blue suit would be his choice for the evening. He would offer to pay for the dinner, as would Stu. The men would split the bill as was their custom.

Later at work, Warren gave Gabriela the lengthy treatment schedules. Sitting in front of her computer she scanned the documents with a serious expression on her face. When done she swiveled on her chair to look at Warren. "I'll have to start grocery shopping and cooking for you, Boss," she said.

"What? No, no. That won't be necessary."

"Trust me. You will need to eat well and get as much rest as you can."

Warren swallowed hard. He knew Gabriela made sense. What she said next hit him even harder. "Maybe you should take a leave of absence," she advised.

"It's going to be that bad?" Warren squeaked. His meekness betrayed his dread. He watched Gabriela's eyes enter into a deep squint, an expression she made when she was determined or angry. He had seen the squint many times before and he braced himself for what was to come.

"You're not going on vacation, Boss. Next week won't be a picnic. You're in for a fight. You need to focus and pay attention to your body. Things are going to get confusing. You're going to feel sick and become very tired. I will help you but you have to do what you can to help yourself."

Warren recalled what he had read on the e-mail from the oncology board. Hearing the same information from a human being carried much more weight, especially from a woman who had cared for a victim of cancer. Without hesitation he wrote down a 6 digit number on a post-it and handed it to Gabriela. "This is the entry code for my burglar alarm," he said. "I'll leave a key under the mat."

Gabriela stuck the note in her purse. "Shall I start the leave of absence paperwork?" she asked.

"Let's see how things go," Warren said. Again, his voice dripped with uncertainty.

"You're the boss, Boss."

*　　*　　*

The next evening Warren drove his Lexus to the Holland Performing Arts Center. Stu was waiting for him at the entrance. "You're late Westing," Stu said.

"So what?" Warren said with a shrug.

"Once the symphony begins playing they won't seat anybody. That's what."

Warren just shook his head and followed his friend into the hall. He and Margie had been to the ornate place a few times, usually for benefit concerts. The walls and ceiling were richly decorated and the seats were plush, making for an enjoyable experience. It was classical music that he found boring. When they reached their seats he dutifully glanced through the playbill. The music was to be an all-Beethoven presentation with one intermission. Warren yawned. So did Stu.

Toward the back of the pamphlet was the list of symphony members. Warren found Gloria Chase in the viola section. There was a Naomi at the head of this section. Her full name was Naomi Zcycz. "Jesus," Warren muttered.

"Something the matter Westing?" Stu asked.

"How do you pronounce Naomi's last name?"

"Beats me."

At that moment the orchestra members began to take the stage. Warren spotted Gloria right away. She was in a full length black dress. In time she took her seat. Next to her sat a smaller woman, also in a black dress. This woman wore her salt-and-pepper hair in a long braided ponytail. When the music started the women sat bolt upright with their violas braced firmly against their necks. Warren couldn't take his eyes off of them, impressed with the power and enthusiasm of their playing. He was so taken with the sight that the first half of the concert flew by for him. At the intermission he ascertained from Stu that the woman with the ponytail was Naomi, and at concert end he was so moved by the violists that he joined the enthusiastic crowd in a standing ovation. "Bravo," Warren yelled. "Bravo."

"I thought you didn't like classical music," Stu commented as the men walked to a stage door.

"I've never had anyone to keep my eyes on," Warren said. "It makes all the difference."

A short time later, Gloria and Naomi emerged from backstage. They had changed clothes, Gloria in a knee-length black dress and heels and Naomi in a wrinkled sweater, faded corduroy skirt, dark knee socks and flats. Warren had been right about the salt-and-pepper hair, but wrong about the woman's stature. She was short, round, and apparently had little regard for what she wore. When introduced to his "date", Warren spotted the tell-tale blemish of a viola player, the ovoid ugly brownish wound on Naomi's neck. He couldn't avoid staring.

"It's from my instrument," Naomi said as she shook Warren's hand. Her voice was very soft and carried a thick Eastern European accent.

"I've heard all about it from Gloria," Warren said, trying to avert his stare.

"Indeed," the woman replied. At least that's what Warren thought he heard. He hoped he wouldn't spend the evening struggling to understand her.

Stu led the party to his BMW and in no time they arrived at Anthony's Steak House where Stu handed over his car to a valet parking attendant. Inside they were seated at a table sporting a white table cloth, crystal, artfully folded cloth napkins and shining tableware. As a young man in black poured water, Warren started off the conversation. "What is your nationality?" he asked Naomi.

"I was born in Hungary. But I have been in this country for many years. I became a citizen the year I graduated from Juilliard."

"Naomi is one of the finest violists in the U.S. if not the world," Gloria added.

"Please," Naomi said. As soft spoken as she was she left no doubt that she considered her friend's remark out of place.

The conversation continued over wine and ultimately a fine meal. Stu and Gloria had filets and Warren ordered a New York Strip. Naomi worked with the server to come up with a vegetarian plate, an uncommon request for the steak house. Somewhere in the middle of the dinner Stu raised his wine glass for a toast. "To my beautiful fiancee," he said gazing at Gloria. It was then that Warren noticed her engagement ring.

"You old dog Gottlieb," Warren clinking his glass against his friend's.

"Congratulations to the love birds," Naomi said. She raised her glass but didn't drink her wine. It occurred to Warren that she might not drink alcohol.

"Have you set a date? Warren asked.

"We're thinking about next June," Gloria replied. Warren had to wonder if he would be alive to see the wedding. His back and hip had been aching since the concert and the pain was increasing as the evening wore on. He retrieved an Oxycontin and downed it with a sip of water while the amber pill vial balanced on a butter dish.

"Oh my," Naomi said as she read the label on the vial. "You are on OxyContin. Are you ill Warren?"

Sighing, Warren ran a hand through his hair. He had told several people about his cancer, but the confession wasn't getting any easier. "I've got cancer," he said, watching Naomi's expression. She had a plain face with no make-up, but she showed a certain youthfulness. Her serene blue eyes looked back at him with kindness. She grabbed her long pony tail and draped it forward over a shoulder.

"What kind?" she asked in a soft and even tone.

"Prostate."

"I had colon cancer. It's been 5 years now since my surgery."

"Oh Naomi, I didn't know that," Gloria said as she put a hand on her friend's forearm. "Why didn't you tell me."

"It's water around the bridge as they say in Hungary," Naomi said, turning back to Warren. "Have you had surgery?" she asked him.

"I start radiation and chemo next week," Warren answered.

"I see," Naomi said as she brushed her pony tail with the palm of her hand. She seemed to fall into a short deliberation, her eyes downcast. Finally, she said, "Perhaps if we become friends I could be a help to you."

The unusual and generous offer took Warren back to Margie's reluctance to talk about her illness. He now understood that reluctance. The last thing a person with cancer wants to talk about is cancer. "I wouldn't want to drag you..."

"I know I can help you if you let me," Naomi interrupted.

"Westing, don't be a jerk," Stu said. "You're going to need all the help you can get."

Warren instantly thought of Gabriela and her dire prediction. On the spot he decided to add to the number of people in his corner. "All right. Let's see where things take us," he said.

"We will start with a meal at my home," Naomi said. "I will prepare an eggplant casserole to go with my homemade hummus and pita bread. How does next Saturday sound?"

Raising his wine glass in assent, Warren said, "Here's to a momentous evening." This time Naomi sipped her wine. Warren limited himself to one glass.

* * *

The next Monday Warren rose early to prepare for his first day of treatment. Understanding that he was to abstain from food prior to the surgical placement of his port he skipped his customary glass of Snapple. By 10 a.m. he had his port, a plastic gizmo about the size of a quarter that involved a canula leading to a deep vein. Situated just under his right collarbone, it would now permit repeated needle insertions involved in his chemotherapy and avoid damage to his arm veins. His first infusion was scheduled for the following day. At 11 o'clock he was lying on his back on a table in UNMC's department of radiotherapy. A technician marked his head with temporary ink and then aimed the device that was to irradiate Warren's metastatic locus in his right parietal lobe of his brain. A short time later he walked out, but not before the technician reminded him of the next day's treatment again scheduled for 11 a.m.

Done with the day's medical affairs, Warren went to work. He was surprised that things had gone so smoothly, that he felt reasonably well, that he had yet to suffer the side effects he had been warned about. Of course he knew he had many days of treatment ahead of him, but he was grateful for a comfortable first day. He had promised himself to stay positive. That was what he was trying to do.

After pulling into his parking spot at SL&T Warren jumped out of his Lexus and headed for the elevator. He ran into Stu who wasted no time bringing up their double date. "What did you think of Naomi?" he asked Warren as they rode the elevator together.

"She's interesting. I can't believe she wants to get involved with my illness."

"Gloria said Naomi didn't bat an eye when she heard you just lost your wife," Stu added.

"She's a horse of a different color."

"She marches to the beat of a different drummer."

"She's one in a million."

"She's as rare as hens' teeth."

"They broke the mold when they made her."

The competition ended when the elevator reached the 12th floor. Just before the elevator door opened the friends took advantage of the absence of others and said farewell in their traditional manner, leaving a foul odor in the cab.

Gabriela was on her cell phone when Warren reached his office. She hung up when she saw him approach. "No need to stop your chat on my account," Warren said.

"My niece and I talk every day. We needn't talk long."

Warren thought back on the pretty nurse, regretting that he would no longer get a look at her now that McHale closed his office. "I understand she's working at the fertility clinic," he said.

"That's correct. She's bored out of her mind."

"She's overtrained I expect."

"Si," Gabriela muttered as she swiveled to face her desk top.

"The next time you talk to your niece ask her to check on my... donation."

"You gave money to the Omaha Fertility Clinic?" Gabriela asked over her shoulder.

"I deposited my sperm there seventeen years ago."

"Ay-yi-yi. Too much information."

Warren snuck up behind Gabriela and whispered in her ear. "Just think. One of my offspring may be ready for college." The woman's broad shoulders shook as she giggled, telling him his comment was in reasonable taste.

The rest of Warren's medical week went smoothly. He continued his brain irradiation and started chemotherapy, the latter requiring that he arrive at the chemo room at 7 a.m. to be done by 11a.m. By Friday he was starting to feel the side effects of his treatment. He was slightly nauseated most of the time and his appetite fell off. Patches of hair started to fall from his head. Most of all he was dead tired. As far as pain went the ache in his lower back and left left hip had increased some but was nicely controlled by Oxycontin. He wondered if his rib would start to hurt. As it was he couldn't even remember if the cancer was in his left or right side of his rib cage.

On Saturday Warren slept in. Theo's insistent barking roused him from sleep. It was after 10 a.m. Groggy, he stumbled into the bathroom and urinated. It was then that a wave of nausea hit him unlike anything he had ever experienced. Bending over the commode he vomited. There was little in the way of food in the vomitus. Rather it was a thick yellow material that burned his throat. "Jesus, this is terrible," he muttered when the attack was over. As he rinsed his mouth he realized he had become just like his deceased wife. He was a card-carrying cancer patient.

Slowly Warren gathered himself to shower, shave and dress. After taking Theo for a short walk he tried to eat some of the breakfast burrito that Gabriela had crafted and insisted that he eat. One bite sickened him. He decided to put a call into Dr. McHale's exchange, admitting that he needed a medication to fend off his nausea. While waiting for his doctor's call he remembered that he was to have dinner with Naomi that evening and thought it best to cancel the event. He didn't wish to be a guest in her home only to vomit in her presence. He brought up her number on his cell phone and touched the pad. A soft voice with a thick accent answered. He explained his situation.

"I can help with the nausea," Naomi said after listening to Warren's tale of woe.

"You have medicine?"

"I have something better than medicine."

Curious, Warren waited for an explanation. None came.

"You can come to my home now if you wish," Naomi said.

"I'd appreciate that."

"I live at 235 Penguin Lane. It's across from the zoo entrance."

Warren wasted no time heading to Naomi's home, and after a short drive south he pulled up in front of a tiny bungalow with a small front yard, a few stone steps and a heavy wooden front door. Out of his car he was hit by the pleasant smell of hay and manure that wafted from the zoo across the quiet street. He heard the roar of a lion and the calls of birds. The experience struck him as particularly unusual, fitting the woman he was about to visit. He walked up the front steps and knocked on the door. When the door opened another aroma hit him. He recognized it from his college days. It was marijuana.

XI

"I am sure you know what this is," Naomi said as she handed a burning joint to Warren.

Warren laughed, saying, "Lady, I went to college in the 60's."

"Come then. We shall share."

Naomi led her guest to a sofa in her tiny living room. There they shared the pot and in minutes Warren was stoned. He had to believe that Naomi was in the same shape. Unable to speak intelligently, he looked around. He saw dozens, even hundreds, of small ceramic figurines occupying virtually every nook and cranny of the living room. A dirty fireplace lent a sooty smell to the space. A rocking chair dominated a far corner. On the coffee table before him lay a large hardbound book entitled "Cathedrals of Europe." Then there was the music. Soft piano strains seemed to rise from everywhere though he saw no speakers.

"Are you fond of Chopin?" Naomi asked Warren as she offered him another toke on marijuana. He waved off the joint. He wanted to comment on the extraordinary potency of the marijuana but simple couldn't put words together. What he did manage to do was get a good look at Naomi's profile while she smoked. Her face was bathed in a soft light that streamed in through a front window giving her an angelic glow. Her nose was small and round, her brow gently angled up to her thick head of hair. Her lips were narrow and her full chin slid into a middle-aged wattle. As always her heavy braided pony tail hung down to the small of her back. She sat straight up the way she did when she played her viola. Done with her smoking, Naomi placed the joint in an ash tray. "Do you like my angels? she asked as she gestured toward the many ceramic figurines. "I collect them," she added. Warren just nodded. Then she asked, "Would you like to eat?"

The question gave Warren pause. He realized, happily, that not only was his nausea gone but that he was ravenous with hunger. He smiled at Naomi, hoping he was answering her. She stood and took his hand. "Come," she said. He followed her into her kitchen.

The kitchen was also very small. In its center was a wooden table that Naomi set with two plates, two forks, and two cloth napkins. A casserole came out of an oven, a bowl of hummus came from the refrigerator, and a stack of pita bread came from a bread box. In no time the couple sat across from one another munching away. Warren had never tasted anything so delicious.

"Eggplant?" Warren asked after he had regained some speaking ability.

"Yes. It's my mother's casserole recipe."

"Are your parents..."

"They were killed in the war. My grandmother raised me."

"So you're alone."

"Like you."

Warren remembered what Stu had told him about this intriguing woman, that she was apparently unconcerned that he had recently lost his wife. She also seemed comfortable with his cancer. As he ate his meal he glanced at Naomi, who appeared to be relishing each bite of food. She ate with a purpose, a focus. It was as though what she was doing at that moment was the most important thing in her life. At one point she rose to fetch two glasses of tap water, one of which she set before her guest. They both had second helpings of the eggplant casserole and ate all of the hummus. At the end of the meal there was one piece of pita bread left that Naomi tore in half to share with Warren.

"That was great food," Warren said. Naomi didn't respond. Rather, she cleared the table and washed the dishes. When done she produced a fresh unlit joint and handed it to Warren.

"This is for you," she said. "It will help you through your ordeal."

"So marijuana is your answer to nausea."

"When I went through my chemotherapy I used marijuana every day," Naomi confessed. "I advise you to do the same."

"One joint isn't going to cut it."

Naomi grinned. "You will find some more. Just be careful with whom you deal. Now if you will excuse me I must practice my solo."

It took Warren a minute to understand that the visit was over. Standing, he put his napkin on the kitchen table and tucked the joint in his shirt pocket. Naomi walked to the front door and he followed her. Facing her, he towered over the woman. He noticed that she had a small bald spot on the top of her head. She looked up at him with a caring and concerned expression on her plain face. "Are you able to drive, Warren?" she asked.

It was a valid question, Warren admitted. He tilted his head to and fro, raised and lowered his arms, and did a quick knee bend. "I think so," he said, satisfied with his coordination. He had always trusted his coordination.

Naomi stood on her toes and kissed Warren on the cheek. Then she whispered, "I would like to have sex next time." He couldn't believe how natural that suggestion sounded. At a loss for words he returned the buss and headed out of the house. A cool breeze hit Warren in the face and had a soothing and sobering effect on him. He sniffed the air for smells of the zoo and detected a faint scent of hay. In his car he assessed his ability to drive. He felt alert and satisfied, no longer dulled by the marijuana but not quite free from its influence. When the Lexus came to life he decided, playfully, to let his car show its stuff. A minute later he was heading toward downtown Omaha at 70 mph. It took the flashing lights of a police cruiser to bring him to a stop.

"License and proof of insurance sir," the officer demanded at the driver window. Warren produced what was needed. The policeman took the information to his vehicle and after a short time returned. "Have you been drinking sir?" he asked.

"I don't drink," Warren said, which of late happened to be true.

"I'm going to ask you to get out of the car," the officer said.

"Christ," Warren muttered.

"What was that?"

"Nothing. Nothing at all," Warren said as he open his door and stood in front of the policeman. After taking a breathalyzer test he performed a series of balance exercises. He had to be careful not to allow the joint to spill out of his shirt pocket.

"It's my opinion you have operated your vehicle while impaired," the cop said.

"That's bull shit," Warren said. The second the words were out of his mouth he regretted saying them.

"I can smell marijuana on your clothes and you look unsteady. That's enough for me," the officer said as he began to write a ticket.

Gradually Warren gathered his wits. Even if he were given a DUI it would be easy for an attorney at his firm to have it amended. He leaned against his car waiting for the cop to finish his work. Finally, he was handed a ticket.

"Where are you headed sir?" the policeman asked.

"Dundee."

"I'll follow you home."

"Fine."

A short time later Warren pulled into his garage. He watched the squad car pull away and then walked into his kitchen. Getting a ticket had put an end to his fun. Checking the time he was surprised that it wasn't even noon. It seemed like he and Naomi had spent hours together. For lack of anything better to do he sought the lounge chair next to the garden pool and tried to take a nap. Sleep eluded him. Sounds seemed augmented, the chirping of cicadas and the bubbling of the pool pounding his ears. This he blamed on pot. Marijuana, he discovered, wasn't the drug it used to be.

Gradually Warren's high ebbed. What he was left with was extreme fatigue, a nearly debilitating weakness that he had come to expect from his cancer treatment. Because of a threatening sky he decided he would be better off in his bed, as he didn't know how long he would be asleep and wished to avoid being caught in the rain. He struggled to his feet and headed for the bedroom. His bed was unmade and his sheets were so dirty they felt oily. Nevertheless, he took off his shoes and climbed in. He was asleep in minutes.

He was in the huddle. He was the fullback. The play called for him to carry the ball just off left tackle. He hit the line and was tackled. Another play, another smash into the line, another tackle. Again and again. He asked for an end run. He started out wide to his left. The greater his effort the slower he ran. He could hear his pursuers and waited for the crushing.

"Boss?" Gabriela called from the foot of the stairs. Her voice woke Warren.

"Up here," Warren called back. Sitting up he found his fatigue to be just as severe as when he started his nap.

"There you are," Gabriela said, looking in the bedroom from the door. Warren gazed at her outline. She looked immense to him. He watched her run a hand over his sheets. "These are filthy," she said. "Up you go."

With a groan Warren climbed off the bed and stood. He felt lightheaded and sick to his stomach. As he watched Gabriela strip the bed he lit the joint that Naomi had given him. His nausea promptly passed.

"Why didn't you tell me you used pot?" Gabriela asked, her arms full of sheets.

"We were just introduced," Warren joked.

"Marijuana is easy to get in my neighborhood. I can get you some if you like."

Warren knew that Gabriela lived in what was known as Omaha's Latino Village. He felt a little ashamed over never having been to her home. "How much for...a big bag?"

Gabriela laughed. "Give me $200 and we'll see what we get."

The next Monday at 8 a.m. Warren had more radiation, this time to his lumbar spine. At 10 he walked into the UNMC chemotherapy room for his second week of treatment. He had learned to delay putting on his dress shirt until the infusion was over, wearing just a t-shirt under a light weight jacket. He also learned to bring his lap top. Video games, e-mailing and getting a little tax work done made the four hours more bearable.

This day Warren slid into a padded chair and a technician stuck an IV needle through his port. Above hung a chemotherapeutic solution that dripped to the port through a plastic line. Settling in for the session, Warren placed his computer on his lap and began reading his mail. Most of the messages were from his law firm announcing meeting times and other mundane items. He was about to bring up a game of Sudoku when a man plopped down on the chair next to his.

"Name's Gordon. Jim Gordon," the man said as he reached over to Warren for a handshake. He appeared to be at least 70 and was very thin with sallow skin and a few strands of white hair. "Whatcha in for Bub?" he asked before Warren could tell him his name.

"Prostate cancer," Warren answered, guessing that was what this Jim Gordon wanted to know.

"Well, it's nice to have a new chemo pal. My old one just bought the farm."

Warren was struck by the man's callousness. And he wasn't at all sure he wanted to be this guy's "chemo pal."

"What's your name Bub?" Jim asked.

"Warren."

"Well Warren what you see before you is a man in his third year of chemo for some bad ass type of leukemia. The sucker has a long name that I can't ever remember."

"Three years?" Warren repeated. He couldn't imagine enduring chemotherapy for that long.

"What's your five year survival rate?" Jim asked. Warren hadn't a clue what his chemo pal was talking about. Apparently Jim saw Warren's empty expression. "How many of you guys with prostate cancer are alive after five years percentage wise?" the old man clarified.

"I'll get back to you on that," Warren said. It was hard for him to accept that had fallen into a statistical group and slowly acknowledged that he had to be at the low end of the survival pool--percentage wise.

"The Big C is a bitch, ain't it," Jim growled as he pulled an amber vial of pills from his shirt pocket. "These here are my Oxys," he said before downing four pills.

"Good God," Warren uttered in disbelief. His reaction made Jim smile.

"Don't you take pain pills?" Jim asked.

"Yes, but..."

"They'll grow on ya, Bub. Hard to say if they stop workin' so good or you're just gettin' sicker. Know what I mean?"

As Warren gazed on his new acquaintance he realized that he just might be looking at an image of himself three years in the future. The possibility of his medications losing their efficacy disturbed him. He included marijuana in this group. Fortunately the opportunity to share his worries presented itself. Dr. McHale showed up.

"Hello Warren," McHale said as he walked up and inspected the label on the IV bag. He wore his usual bow tie and short white jacket.

"Alvin," Warren returned.

"How are things going?" McHale asked as he produced a stethoscope and began listening to his patient's heart and lungs.

"I guess I could be worse."

"Agreed. Is the Oxycontin controlling your pain?"

"For now."

"What do you mean by that?"

Warren glanced over at Jim Gordon who had fallen asleep. Then, addressing his doctor, he said, "I'm given to believe pain pills stop working."

McHale snickered. "I can keep ahead of your pain, trust me," he said. "I see you've lost some hair."

Warren ran a hand through his once thick mane. He came away with a tuft. "I'm thinking of shaving my head," he muttered.

"Not a bad idea. Any nausea?"

"I'm glad you mentioned that. Marijuana knocks it out completely. I even have an appetite when I smoke pot."

McHale nodded, saying "I'll try to get you approved for medical marijuana. It'll take some time so I advise you to stay with the illegal stuff." Then, as an addendum, he said, "You didn't hear that from me."

After writing a few orders McHale scurried out of the room. Warren wondered why the frenetic man was in such a hurry, seeing that he had only one patient. To help pass the time Warren returned to his lap top and played a few games of Sudoku. It was 11a.m. when the infusion ended. Jim Gordon had slept the entire time. Disconnected from his IV, Warren slipped out of his seat as quietly as he could. His chemo pal looked so serene in his slumber that Warren gave serious thought to taking four Oxys next session.

Warren got to his office around noon. There was a mountain of tax work waiting on his desk. Before starting in he ate the ham and cheese sandwich that Gabriela had prepared for him, his nausea quelled by a quick toke of pot in his car minutes before. While he was eating Gabriela brought him a bottled water. She also took the time to massage his shoulders. He could see that she was becoming indispensable to him. He also admitted that he had feelings for her, perhaps like a patient's attachment to his nurse. Of late he had been paying attention to what she wore and how she looked at him. It was a silly thing to do, he knew. He had cancer. But he found a welcome distraction in the attraction. It took his mind off his troubles, and it helped ease his loneliness.

Done for the day at 4:30, Warren visited the partners' bathroom, a space that required a key for entry. It was there that he took a long look at himself in a mirror. His boyish appearance was slowly disappearing. His eyes betrayed his fatigue, his hair was not only falling out but lacked its old luster. As he stood there over a sink he became nauseated and feared he would vomit. Then he did just that. When done, he quickly rinsed out the sink, afraid a partner would walk in and see the disgusting material in the basin.

On the drive home Warren took a hit on his joint, which was now down to a stub. Gabriela had procured some more marijuana which she had left at his home but which he had yet to try. A block away from Dundee he passed a police car. He waved to the officer, smiling as he did so. His ticket for a DUI had disappeared, courtesy of a colleague's connection with certain people at traffic court. Working at SL&T law firm did indeed have its advantages.

The next morning Warren got up an hour early in order to visit his mother at the Dundee Retirement Center. He had yet to tell Fern about his illness, their last meeting thwarted by the severe drowsiness induced by a new medication for her dementia. He hoped there had been a change, that the staff had notified her physician of this unacceptable side effect. When he found his mother sitting in front of the wide screen television in the area reserved for the severely demented, he was happy to see that she was fully clothed.

"Hi Mom," Warren said as he took a seat next to his mother on a sofa.

"Look what the cat dragged in," Fern said, flashing her eyes on her son before returning to her program. Her clear sentence added to Warren's optimism. He decided that now was the time to give his mother the bad news.

"Mom, I've got something to tell you," Warren began.

"What is it now?" Fern spit.

"I've got cancer."

Fern turned to Warren but said nothing. Her eyes scanned her son's face the way Warren remembered her doing when she thought he was telling a lie. Eventually she appeared to have something to say, her droll mouth quivering but not producing words. Her shoulders heaved as she took a deep breath. What she said came out loud and clear.

"A child should not die before his mother," Fern said. Her words stunned Warren. His mother had actually thought something through. She had become more lucid than she had been in years. Just then a woman approached, a mousy individual in her thirties who wore a name tag that read, "A. Herbert, Nurse Supervisor."

"Don't you think Fern is better off this way?" the woman asked Warren.

"What way?" Warren asked as he stood to face the supervisor.

"Her physician stopped her medications. I think she's much improved mentally."

The first person Warren thought of was Takisha, the black aide who threatened to make a formal complaint about his mother's tendency to use racial slurs. "What about..." he started.

"The "N" word business? Your mother has proved to be a reasonable person in that regard."

"So she's...behaving herself?"

"She is, thank goodness."

Breathing a sigh of relief, Warren gave Fern a congratulatory squeeze on her thin shoulder. Next he eyed the supervisor's name tag, saying "I can't tell you how relieved I am Ms. Herbert."

"As are we all Mr. Westing," the woman replied. "I'll leave you two alone for your visit."

Warren sat back down next to his mother. "So, you were over-medicated," he said. Fern didn't take her eyes off the TV, nor did she say anything. Wanting to discover more about Fern's state of mind, he asked a question. "Do you remember what year you and Dad were married?"

"Of course I do. December 28, 1941. War just started. Frank joined the army and fought in Italy. Lost a kidney."

"I remember him telling me all about getting shot."

"I believe that wound had something to do with him dying so young."

"He was 70. That's not so young."

"I miss him."

"I miss him too, Mom." It was then that Fern reached for Warren's hand and held it. At first he thought it was her attempt to show some affection. But her next question told him she wanted some information.

"What's wrong with me, son?" Fern asked. "Why am I in this place?"

Warren hesitated. It was the first time his mother had openly wondered why she lived in a ward for the demented. "Your memory isn't what it should be," he finally said.

"That's all? That's why I'm locked up?"

"I'm afraid so."

Pulling her hand away, Fern folded her arms across her chest. "Ain't right," she muttered. The scene weighed heavily on Warren. He had given little attention to the understanding of her situation mainly because he had blindly accepted her diagnosis. Now, for the first time, he had to accept that her disability wasn't as dire as commonly regarded, that if she had not been improperly medicated her expensive care may have assumed a different look both in cost and location.

"Steven in the one with the children," Fern went on. She was staring at the TV, her eyes bright and her jaw set.

"That's correct Mom," Warren said.

"Elizabeth, Judith and Brian."

"Right again."

Turning to face Warren for just a second Fern resumed gazing at the TV before her next question. "Why didn't you have kids?"

"Margie and I tried," Warren said. "I guess we got too old to keep it up."

"How is Margie?" The question made Warren deeply ashamed. Because of his assumption that his mother wouldn't retain the news of Margie's death he had simply avoided telling Fern of his wife's passing.

"She's fine," Warren lied.

"Bring her the next time you visit. I'd like to see her."

"I will. Say, how about a walk on the treadmill?"

Mother and son spent the rest of the visit in a rather routine manner, a little exercise, a game of checkers, a movie and finally lunch. Before he left Warren walked Fern to her bed and covered her with an Afghan. It was then that she grabbed his wrist and held it as she spoke what would be her last words to him. "I'm sorry you have cancer, son," she said. Releasing her grip she rolled away from him, pulled her knees to her waist, and shut her eyes.

XII

A week before Thanksgiving Warren and Stu met at Stogie's for lunch. They had not socialized for months, Warren busy with his cancer treatments and Stu in endless evaluations of his slowly failing heart. They sat in a booth, ordered their usual fare and drank a local brew. Because he was finished with chemotherapy, at least for the present, Warren was drinking alcohol again. He had also decided to deal with his hair loss by having his head professionally shaved. The two bald guys looked like cue balls with faces.

"I'm assuming the wedding plans are in full swing," Warren said as he prepared his half-pound burger, removing the lettuce, onion, tomato and pickles before applying the catsup, mustard salt and pepper. After reassembling his sandwich he cut it in half.

"We've hit a snag," Stu replied. "Both of Gloria's daughters said they're not coming."

"Not coming to their own mother's wedding?"

Stu cut his pastrami on rye in half and took his first bite. "They're both bitches," he said with a full mouth.

Warren recalled that Gloria once refused to talk about her daughters. He was just beginning to understand why this was so. But he judged the matter none of his business so he moved on. "Are you still on the transplant list?" he asked his friend.

"As soon as UNMC finds a match, I get a new heart."

"What about retirement?"

"No way. I'd go bat-shit crazy sitting around my condo all day long," Stu said. Just then a small rivulet of blood streamed down his cheek and hit his upper lip. "Mama mia," he cursed as he wiped the blood with a paper napkin and then produced a cosmetic mirror that he used to examine his face. "There you are you little sucker," he muttered as he pressed a bit of napkin against a cut on his cheek.

"What gives, Gottlieb?" Warren asked.

"I'm on a goddamn blood thinner. I cut myself shaving and this happens. I'm telling you, Westing, sometimes I think I'd be better off dead."

Warren didn't respond but he admitted that over the past months he had similar thoughts. The chemotherapy and radiation had devastated his energy and morale. For the first time in his adult life his weight was under 200 pounds. Worst of all his work had suffered, not only because he had trouble putting in the necessary hours but because his mental acuity had dropped off. At times he felt like a failure and considered retiring. On one occasion he mentioned his concerns to Gabriela. It was her response that kept him working. She had said, "If you retire I'm out of a job." Warren knew she spoke the truth. No one at his firm would take on a middle-aged secretary when a pool of cuties asking for starting salaries was available.

"How about your treatment, Westing?" Stu asked.

I'm done with chemo. Three metastatic sites have been radiated. One to go," Warren answered, pointing to a rib.

Stu shook his head. "We're a pair aren't we," he said. He wasn't smiling.

"What are you doing for Thanksgiving?" Warren asked, looking for a brighter topic.

"Gloria is cooking the turkey. You know she's moved in with me, right?"

"I didn't know that. Congratulations."

"What about you?"

"Gabriela is cooking dinner at my home," Warren said. "We're having her niece over."

"Oh yeah? You've told me about the niece. At your age the excitement might not be such a good idea."

"I'm not that old."

Stu looked his old buddy in the eye and spoke as only a best friend can. "You look it, Westing."

Warren knew Stu spoke the truth but rather than admit to his wretched appearance Warren decided to concentrate on his hamburger. He chewed each bite carefully and thoroughly, searching for texture and taste. The thought of losing the joy in eating was unbearable to him. It's coming back, he thought. It's got to come back.

"You know, I'm surprised you're not having Thanksgiving dinner with Naomi," Stu went on. "I know you've been to her home several times."

Warren smiled. "How do you know that?"

"Naomi and Gloria are friends. Apparently they share…secrets."

Warren was mortified to hear that his sex life was fodder for conversation between two women. The more he thought about it the more irritated he became. "That really pisses me off, Gottlieb," he growled.

"I wouldn't worry too much about it, Westing. The girls are nothing if not discrete."

"Call me old-fashioned but I believe intimate matters should remain private," Warren insisted.

"I'm pretty sure Naomi doesn't share your opinion," Stu said.

Of course Stu was right, Warren admitted. After sharing Naomi's bed several times over the last several months he came to understand how carefree she was about sex. To her making love was like eating a fine meal. She was capable of thoroughly enjoying herself without becoming emotionally involved. What's more she adapted herself to his weakened state, asking for oral sex when he suffered from drug induced impotency and showing patience when he fell asleep from exhaustion. On one occasion he woke to the sound of Naomi's viola. She had played her instrument naked at the bedside. He had to admit that it was one of the most thoughtful gestures he had ever enjoyed. "I guess I shouldn't complain," Warren concluded. "Naomi's been very kind to me." At that moment Stu grinned, telling Warren that he had a confession to make.

"What is it, Gottlieb," Warren demanded.

"Gloria and I call Naomi's place the 'Sugar Shack'," Stu blurted.

"Christ that is so juvenile."

"We think it's cute."

"Gottlieb you're turning into a woman."

"Then you can pay for lunch."

The friends finished their meals and then headed back to work at the SL&T law firm. Once again they rode up to the 12th floor alone in an elevator cab and parted company with their traditional odorous sign-off.

When Warren got to his office Gabriela handed him a memo. All it said was, "Call Naomi."

"Who is Naomi?" Gabriela demanded. She was squinting. He stared at the memo and then at his secretary, at a loss as to why the moment felt so tense.

"A friend of a friend," Warren said. His explanation did little to change Gabriela's expression. "She introduced me to marijuana," he said. "Why are you upset?"

"I'm the one who takes care of you Boss," she declared, still squinting. "I don't want anyone else meddling in our affairs."

Gabriela's words took Warren by surprise. He had no idea she had so much invested in the help she was offering him. "Naomi probably wants to know if I need more pot," he offered. He had no clue why he needed to lie to his secretary.

"I supply your pot," Gabriela reminded Warren.

"So you do," he said. "So you do." Crushing the memo in his fist Warren retreated into the sanctuary of his office grateful to have a load of tax work on his desk. Women, he thought. If I live to be a hundred....The expression caught him short. Not likely, he mused. Then he got to work.

* * *

On Thanksgiving day the kitchen at 41 Crestwood was alive with rich aromas. Gabriela was outdoing herself with a mixture of traditional Mexican dishes and the standards of turkey, dressing, cranberry sauce and pumpkin pie. Clad in a blue dress, she scurried from oven to stove, from refrigerator to pantry, from kitchen to dining room, energized by the spirit of the day. Warren had carefully shaved both scalp and face, and had donned the same green sweater he always wore on this particular holiday. Margie had given him the sweater on their first Christmas together. If she were still alive, and had he not discovered her cheating, it would've been their eighteenth holiday season. But knowing that she once had a lover did a lot to lessen his nostalgia.

The front doorbell rang and Warren hustled to open the door. There she was, the young and beautiful Gabriela beaming with a smile. "Hello Mr. Westing," she said.

"There'll be none of that young lady," Warren scolded as he ushered the stunning Latina inside and took her coat. "I am Warren to you. Comprende?"

Gabriela smiled. "Yo comprendo," she said.

Suddenly the older Gabriela appeared, gushing, "My Gaby." The namesakes embraced as Warren looked on.

"Gaby?" Warren repeated.

"She's been 'Gaby' since she was a little nina," Gabriela explained, now standing next to her niece with an arm draped over the young woman's shoulder. The pose gave Warren the chance to compare the two, the square shouldered bulky aunt contrasting with the shapely petite niece. He could see a resemblance in their dark eyes and perhaps their cheekbones. Suddenly he became aware that they were eyeing him as well, a man ravaged by cancer and its treatment. For the first time in his adult life he felt self-conscious.

"Let's eat," Warren said. "I'm famished."

Some time later the trio sat at the dining room table, part of a set of furniture that he and Margie had purchased together at an auction. The wood was cherry. There were six chairs, a cupboard with glass doors, and a buffet. The table included a leaf that could expand its size, but this day it remained in its smaller form. Warren sat at the head of the table and his guests sat on either side. Bowls and plates of food covered the surface, and Warren started to serve himself.

"Would you say grace, Warren?" Gabriela asked. The request surprised him. He couldn't remember the last time he had even heard someone say grace. Perhaps he had once listened to his numskull brother do the honors. Maybe it had been his mother way back in his childhood in Prairie Center. The point was, he wasn't about to act the hypocrite just because it was Thanksgiving.

"I'd appreciate it if you'd handle it, Gabriela," Warren said. He watched her eyes squint. Then she bowed her head and began to speak. In Spanish. Sentences flew by as did the minutes. Occasionally Gaby added a word of support, also in Spanish. Warren had never endured such a long prayer.

"Amen," Gabriela concluded.

"Amen," Gaby said.

The women crossed themselves telling Warren that they were Catholics.

The demonstration didn't surprise him in the least, nor did it hold any meaning for him. Cultural behavior was predictable, or at least that's how he saw things. For all he was concerned they could've bowed to Mecca.

Finally it was time to eat. Despite his blunted taste buds Warren piled hot food on his plate and soon enjoyed how the spicy corn casserole set off the turkey and dressing. He slathered butter on Gabriela's home made flour tortillas, using them to corral runaway peas. He had made sure there was a white and red wine for the occasion and had a glass of each. Dessert was a delicate pastry stuffed with minced dates. The conversation was light and pleasant. Even at the dinner's end Warren could tell that Gabriela was still miffed at his refusal to say a prayer, but he could also tell that she didn't want to spoil Gaby's day with a critical remark. At one point the chatter turned to Gaby's work at Omaha's Fertility Clinic.

"I am so bored there," Gaby complained. "All I do is paper work."

"Did your aunt tell you that I have a deposit of sperm at your place?" Warren asked.

"Warren, we're eating," Gabriela said. She was squinting again. Gaby had no such reaction.

"Is your sample for general distribution for private use?" Gaby asked.

"I honestly don't remember. I donated a long time ago."

"Would you like me to look it up for you?" the nurse asked.

"Sure," Warren said with a smirk on his face. He glanced at Gabriela who looked like she wanted to box his ears.

Done with the excellent dinner, the three of them pitched in to clear the table, put the leftovers in the refrigerator and load the dishwasher. As Warren worked he felt sharp twinges of pain in his left rib cage. Naturally he worried about the cancer in his left anterior 8th rib. It hadn't received radiation yet. He hoped he could hold out. It was just after Gaby said her goodbye at the front door, hugging her aunt and kissing Warren on the cheek before that he made a foolish move. It involved Theo. The lying giant seemed to be having difficulty getting up to his feet. Warren straddled his dog's rump and pulled up. The snap in his rib cage came first, the lightning bolt of pain next.

"Owww!" Warren cried. He slumped to his left holding a hand over his rib. Each breath triggered a sharp and searing pain. He could feel a crunch as his chest moved.

"What's wrong Boss?" Gabriela asked as she grabbed his right arm in an effort to support him.

"Don't pull on me!" Warren pleaded.

"What happened to you?" Gabriela asked, backing off.

Warren had broken a rib once before as a child when he fell off his bicycle. The pain was unmistakable, though simply lifting a dog hardly qualified as a violent injury. Nevertheless he offered his opinion. It turned out he guessed correctly. "I think I broke a rib," he said.

"Ay-yi-yi."

"Could you help me to my bed?"

"Of course," Gabriela said as she once again grabbed Warren's right arm, this time taking care not to jostle the slumping man. "Ready?" she asked.

"Let's go."

Slowly the couple climbed the stairs, Warren bent at the waist, his left arm pressed against his chest. Gabriela instinctively timed each of her steps to match Warren's, who had to pause on each stair tread before moving upward. He felt the agony in every step and every breath. After a tortuous effort he reached his bed. Cautiously, after sitting, he wedged off his shoes, swung his legs onto the bed and curled up on his right side. Experimenting with subtle changes in position he settled on angles that minimized the movement of his broken rib. Shallow breathing also helped control the pain, which despite his best efforts regularly penetrated his chest like a red hot poker.

"All I did was try to lift Theo," Warren grumbled.

"I hate to say it but I think your cancer is behind this," Gabriela said. Warren thought the same thing but he didn't say so. "I'll go get your pain pills," she said as she left the room. Alone now, he remembered what his chemo pal Jim Gordon had said about the "Big C." He said it could be a bear. He was right. Moments later Gabriela returned with the Oxycontin and a glass of water. She managed to get a pill into Warren's mouth followed by a sip of fluid.

"Give me two," Warren directed. He got his wish.

"I'm going to call your doctor," Gabriela said.

"It's Thanksgiving. Give the guy a break. Besides, what can he do for me?"

"You can't know unless we make the call," Gabriela reasoned. Warren got her point. He grunted his assent and she used his phone to call Dr. McHale's exchange. Five minutes later she had a short conversation with the man and then gave Warren the unexpected news that McHale was on his way to 41 Crestwood.

"Alvin is coming here? On Thanksgiving no less?" Warren said, surprised.

"He said to tell you not to move. He said lying on your right side was the correct thing to do."

"A house call in the the 21st century. That's got to be a first," Warren mumbled.

An hour later McHale finished what he called a nerve block, a technique that numbed Warren's 8th left intercostal nerve and gave complete relief from the pain stemming from what the doctor called a pathological fracture. To gain access to his patient's thorax while avoiding the struggle involved in shedding clothing he had to cut away Warren's green sweater and shirt. The shredded clothing lay on the floor.

"An X-ray will confirm my diagnosis and radiation will begin asap," McHale said when done with his work. "Until then you must remain as immobile as possible. We don't want that rib puncturing a lung."

"I can't thank you enough, Alvin," Warren said, elated to be free from the excruciating pain.

"Think nothing of it,"

"To make a house call on a holiday…"

"I'm old school, Warren. Besides, I don't like turkey. Oh, and sorry about your sweater and shirt. Couldn't be helped."

Gabriela showed McHale to the door where they had a short conversation. Meanwhile Warren took two more Oxycontins just to play it safe. By the time she returned to the bedroom he was asleep. When he awoke it was dark. He found himself covered by a blanket. Thinking about rolling over he remembered McHale's advise and remained on his right side. But he had to urinate. And despite the feast earlier in the day he was hungry. Luckily Gabriela chose that time to check on him. She turned on a bedside lamp and sat on the edge of the bed near his knees. "How are you doing Boss?" she asked.

"I've got to pee," Warren said.

"Okay. Up we go," she said gently hoisting him to a sitting position and then to his feet. "From here on out you're on your own," she joked. Warren ambled to his bathroom. As always the sound of his urine stream hitting the commode water brought a deep bark from the first floor. To cover his bare chest he slipped into a silk bathrobe and then returned to bed. Gabriela was waiting for him.

"Would you mind walking Theo?" Warren asked her.

"Sure thing. How about some warmed up turkey and gravy?"

"That sounds great," Warren said as he fluffed two pillows and reclined on the bed. "And Gabriela?"

"Si?"

"Um...gracias por todos."

"Boss you need lessons," Gabriela said as she left the room.

A while later Warren devoured an evening snack while he sat quietly on his bed. Gabriela sat on the edge of the bed balancing her plate of leftovers on her lap. "I've got something to ask you Boss," she said.

"Shoot."

"What are you going to do with Margie's car?"

"Sell it I guess."

"For how much?"

"I haven't a clue."

"Well I'm interested. My old Honda is falling apart."

"Then name your price and Margie's car is yours."

"Are you serious?"

"Sure. Just getting rid of the thing would be a load off my shoulders."

Gabriela fell silent for a moment or two. Then she asked another question. "Do you miss Margie?"

Warren hesitated. His friend Stu was the only person who knew of Margie's affair. But he decided he needn't be careful with the secrets of someone who was dead. "I don't miss her as much as I should," he told Gabriela. "There's a reason for that."

"Oh?"

"She cheated on me."

"Ay-yi-yi. I never would've guessed."

"Yeah well, that's water around the bridge," Warren said.

"You mean under the bridge."

"Of course," Warren admitted, amused that he had just used Naomi's old Hungarian expression.

"Narcotics are making mush of your brain. I've seen it happen many times."

Gabriela was correct. Warren's head was spinning, the four OxyContins rendering his thoughts difficult to keep in order. For that reason he decided to bow out of the conversation. "I think I'll go back to sleep," he said. Putting his food aside and closing his eyes he did his best to allow slumber to take over. But that didn't happen. Rather he listened to Gabriela munch on her food. Occasionally he felt her shift her weight, the mattress moving under her. Minutes passed. Other than the sound of Gabriela's chewing the room fell silent. More time went by. When Warren heard Gabriela's voice he thought at first he was dreaming.

"Who is Naomi?" the voice asked. Warren didn't respond. "Tell me who she is, Boss. I have a right to know," the voice continued. Again, Warren remained silent. He heard Gabriela sigh and then slip off the edge of the bed. He listened as she gathered the food plates. He guessed she was near the door when she spoke again. "I'm going home for a few things but I'll be back," she said. "I'd better stay the night."

Feigning sleep Warren stayed quiet. He heard the disappointment in Gabriela's voice when she said, "Goodnight Boss."

What a day and what a life, Warren thought. The last thing that entered his mind before he nodded off was Margie and her secrets. He grunted as he admitted to himself that he was now behaving in much the same way, keeping a lover secret from someone in his everyday life. "I'll cut you some sh-lack Margie," he slurred. Then he fell asleep.

XIII

Christmas was fast approaching. For the first time the Westing household stood devoid of decoration. Margie had been the one for that, insisting on a real tree adorned with traditional ornaments, strategically placed scented candles, and an abundance of greenery. Hot cider was often on the stove and she seemed to be wearing something red and green all through the season. Her favorite had been a festive head band that used to set off her pretty white hair before she lost her tresses to chemotherapy. As for Warren, decorating for any season was something he simply didn't do. This year he ignored the boxes of Christmas supplies stored in the garage and instead bought a small artificial tree that came with tiny white lights. He placed the thing on a living room table so passers-by could see it through the front window. Its lonesome existence spoke volumes about the change at 41 Crestwood. It's likely neighbors felt sorry for Warren regarding the loss of his wife. If so their sorrow was misplaced. The only issue negatively impacting him was his cancer.

Fortunately Warren was enjoying an excellent response to his treatments. Scans showed a marked diminution in the sizes of the metastases and the blood tests returned to normal. Dr. McHale cautioned against too much optimism and advised frequent surveys for the return of disease. Subjectively Warren felt better than he had in months. His back and hip didn't hurt, his appetite was as vigorous as ever, and his weight was holding steady at a respectable 200 pounds. It pleased him that he needed to buy new clothes to accommodate his slimmed body, one unexpected positive feature of having a malignancy.

Gabriela bought Margie's Honda, which took a burden off Warren's shoulders. She kept shopping and cooking for him, work he greatly appreciated. She also continued supplying him with marijuana though she disapproved of his recreational use. It was only Warren's insistence that pot augmented his appetite that got her grudging approval. But she drew the line at narcotics. Often pointing out that her deceased husband had died a narcotics addict, she scolded Warren when he took an OxyContin for a mere twinge of pain. He objected to her admonishments, citing that a person with cancer had every right to his pain pills. Narcotics became a bone of contention between them and it appeared that neither was likely to back down.

On Christmas morning Warren slipped into a pair of dark green corduroy slacks, a white button-down shirt and an old wool sweater he had owned since law school. He had to cinch his belt tightly to hold up his pants but was surprised to find that the sweater fit nicely. He guessed he had weighed close to 200 pounds while in school, not the portly 235 he had carried until recently. After donning socks and shoes he stood in front of the full-length mirror. His shaved scalp glistened like an ornament. His cheeks were not as full as they once were. But he looked trim and fit, very unlike a man with cancer.

Just then the doorbell rang. Warren knew it was Gabriela whom he had invited over for a gift exchange, a tradition they had honored over the ten years of working together. He guessed it was the formality of the day that prompted her to ring the doorbell rather than use her key. When he opened the front door he discovered the reason for her timidity. There were two Latinas standing before him.

"Gaby," Warren said. "What a nice surprise. Come in."

Stepping back to let the women in the foyer Warren took a large wrapped package from Gabriela to allow her to take off her heavy winter coat. She hung her coat on a coat tree and Gaby did the same with her wrap. "May I use your bathroom Mr. Westing?" Gaby asked.

"Hey. What did I tell you about…"

"Sorry. Warren," Gaby said.

"That's better. Go through the den and find a hall. The john is to your left."

When Gaby was out of hearing range Gabriela offered an explanation for her niece's presence, saying "The poor thing had an argument with her mother last night. She came to me for support."

Warren handed the Christmas gift back to Gabriela. "What did they argue about?" he asked.

"Gaby's work at the fertility clinic. My sister thinks the *in vitro* process amounts to a disregard for life."

Warren had heard of this argument before, Pro-life advocates calling the discarding of embryos murder. He hadn't given much thought to the dispute, but this day he was glad it existed. It had led a lovely young woman to his doorstep. "I'm guessing Gaby is pretty upset," he said.

"She's devastated," Gabriela said. "Her own mother called her a baby killer."

"Christ."

"My sister can be bull-headed."

Warren snorted saying, "Families can be complicated. I've got a brother who drives me up a wall."

Just then Gaby joined Warren and her aunt in the foyer. Her hair was pulled back and she wore no makeup, a combination that made her look like a little girl. Sadness was all over her face, an expression that compelled Warren to get busy playing the host. "Do you like egg nog, Gaby?" he asked.

"Sure," the young woman answered.

"Good. Why don't you and your aunt have a seat in the living room while I get us some." The two Latinas moved from the foyer to the living room and found places on stuffed chairs that framed a rarely used fireplace. In the kitchen Warren filled three mugs with chilled egg nog he bought at a grocery store. In previous years Margie had made her own egg nog. Hope this measures up, he thought.

In no time Warren and his guests sat together sipping their holiday drinks. He got a kick out of Gabriela's hair pin, reindeer led by Rudolph with his red nose. Her face was filled with the joy of the season, though each time she glanced at her niece she squinted. At one point she offered the young woman her hand, which Gaby took. "Your mother didn't mean what she said to you," Gabriela insisted.

Gaby squeezed her aunt's hand. "Do you think I should quit my job?" she asked.

"That's up to you, Gaby."

Sighing, Gaby dropped her hold on Gabriela's hand and rubbed her eyes. "At first I was very bored at the fertility clinic. But lately I've enjoyed with the work. And nursing positions are so hard to find in this city."

"Then stay with it," Gabriela advised. "Your mother will survive."

"Hmm," Gaby muttered. Suddenly her eyes lit up. "Mr. Westing. I mean Warren. I looked up your sperm donation."

"And?" Warren prompted.

"You specified that your sperm was for private use only."

"So there are no Warren Westing look a-likes running around Omaha?"

"Nope."

Warren chuckled. "Maybe I should change the specs on my sperm."

"You'll have to do that in writing," she said.

"Do you think I'm still viable?"

"Sure." For the first time that morning Gaby smiled.

It was then that Gabriela picked up her present for Warren and handed it to him. "Enough of the sperm talk," she said. "This is Christmas."

Knowing that Gabriela liked to reuse wrapping paper, Warren carefully removed the red ribbon and white paper that covered a large cardboard box. In the box was a green v-neck sweater. It was a medium-large. "No more extra-large clothes for me," Warren commented as he pulled the sweater from the box and held it to his torso.

"Looks like I guessed the right size," Gabriela said.

"Thank you so much, Gabriela," Warren said. "You were there when my doctor cut my old green sweater in half."

Giggling, Gabriela said, "I bought you a new sweater the very next day. Merry Christmas."

Warren reached into his pants pockets and produced a small wrapped present that he handed to Gabriela. "Right back at you," he said. He watched as his secretary opened her gift. When she saw the ring she gasped.

"Oh Boss. It's beautiful," Gabriela gushed. She slid the turquoise and silver ring on a middle finger. It pleased Warren that it closely matched her earrings and necklace.

"It's to go with your favorite jewelry."

"You noticed?"

"You sound surprised."

"Well, you are an hombre. So, Boss, what are your plans for the day?"

"I'm having dinner with Stu and his fiancee," Warren answered. He didn't mention that Naomi would be there. "How about you?" he asked Gabriela.

"My sister is having the family over for the traditional feast."

Gaby shook her head, saying, "I wonder if I'm invited."

"Don't you worry your pretty head," Gabriela said. "I can handle your mother."

Warren and the Latinas chatted for a while and finally adjourned to the foyer where they said their good-byes. It was there that he checked his Rolex and judged that he had enough time to visit his mother before driving to Gottlieb's condo. Before leaving for the retirement home he gave Theo his Christmas present, an enormous rawhide bone. The giant accepted his gift graciously and carried it to his dog pillow in the den. Warren noticed that Theo's limp had worsened and gave him an extra dose of arthritis medication. No sense being in pain if you can avoid it, Warren thought.

Later, when Warren entered the retirement home's facility for the demented he looked for his mother at her favorite place in front of the wide screen television. She wasn't there. Checking in Fern's room he found the nurse supervisor standing next to his mother, who was lying on her back in bed. The supervisor wasn't wearing her name tag and Warren couldn't remember her name. So he winged it. "What's going on?" he asked her.

"Oh. Mr. Westing. I was just about to call you," the woman said as she closed Fern's chart. "You missed your mother's doctor by only a few minutes."

"My mother's doctor was here?"

"He thinks your mother had a small stroke," the woman said. "She's lost the ability to speak." The news shocked Warren. He had always believed his demented mother had many years ahead of her, that something like a stroke just wasn't something worth considering. The supervisor went on, saying "It's a shame when you think about it. Just when Fern was regaining some of her mental faculties she had a stroke. Life is so cruel sometimes."

Gazing down on his mother Warren could see that she was asleep. "Should I wake her up?" he asked the supervisor.

"She's sedated," the woman said. "Why don't you visit tomorrow."

Warren leaned over and kissed his mother on the forehead. He felt eerily content with this state of affairs. After all, the old girl had to die of something. This seemed to him a pleasant way to go. "Merry Christmas Mom," he whispered. He then nodded at the supervisor and left the room.

Because of the foreshortened visit with his mother Warren arrived at Stu and Gloria's condo building early. He rode the elevator to the 12th floor and let himself into the couple's living space. He could see that Gloria was in the kitchen putting together a dish of lasagna. He had tasted her lasagna. The noodles had been overcooked, the ricotta cheese soupy, and the ground meat tasteless. Stu was preparing a tossed salad. Naomi huddled next to the flames of the gas fireplace. She wore her winter garb, a wool sweater, corduroy skirt, heavy knee socks and clogs.

"Winter is getting harder for me every year," Naomi said when Warren joined her. Her accent was as thick as ever. He chuckled when he saw the jolly elf figure on the end of her pony tail. His amusement ended when he noticed that her dark blemish on her neck was bleeding.

"Christ, what happened to you?" Warren asked the violist.

At first Naomi looked puzzled by the question, but apparently could follow the train of Warren's sight. She placed a finger on the ugly mark on her neck. "We played a concert last night," she explained. "Sometimes my neck sore oozes blood."

"Hot toddy?" Gloria asked as she approached holding two steaming mugs. Warren focused on her neck mark. Gloria noticed. "No I am not bleeding," she told him. "Naomi had the solos. And, I might add, she was brilliant."

Warren nodded in understanding, recalling the first time he watched the two violists play for the Omaha Symphony. He had been back twice for a concert. Both times he had been greatly impressed with the skill of the women before him. He accepted the toddy, as did Naomi, and the two clinked mugs before sipping the holiday drink.

"I can tell Gottlieb made the toddys," Warren said after a taste. "Too much sugar, not enough bourbon." He offered his opinion in a loud enough voice to reach Stu. His friend flashed a middle finger to convey his contempt.

Gloria reached for Warren's mug saying, "I'll put a little more wallop in yours if you like."

"It's fine, Gloria," Warren said. "I just like to give Gottlieb grief."

"I've noticed."

Warren could hear the mothering in Gloria's voice, the protection she shed on her fiancé. Occasionally Stu complained about her sometimes overbearing and bossy tendencies, but he insisted she was the one for him.

"Have you run any races lately?" Warren asked Gloria, referring to her love of jogging.

"Not since last October."

Waiting for some elaboration, Warren quickly saw that none was coming. He asked the first thing that came to mind, blurting, "I understand your daughters are presenting a problem regarding your wedding plans."

"Fuck you Warren," Gloria said before storming off into a bedroom and slamming the door.

"What did you do Westing?" Stu demanded, rushing to the scene of the exchange.

"I mentioned her daughters..."

"Mama mia," Stu shouted as he ran to the bedroom. In seconds Warren and Naomi were alone.

"I guess I hit a nerve," Warren told Naomi, who said nothing. Rather she fetched a framed black and white portrait of two young women. Both were blond and thin. One was standing with a hand on the shoulder of the other, who was sitting with her hands folded on her lap. The photograph was beautifully lighted, or so Warren thought as he gazed at the photo. "I'm guessing these are the daughters," he said.

"Yes," Naomi said. "They are a problem."

"I've gathered that. What's the deal?"

"It is complicated."

Warren looked at the closed bedroom door. "Something tells me we've got time for the story," he said.

Naomi placed the photo on the mantel and turned to Warren, her arms behind her back as she stayed near the gas flames. "They blame Gloria for the death of their father," she said.

"The Buddhist? I thought he drowned."

"They insist that if Gloria had not asked for a divorce, he would not have moved to California, taken up scuba diving and died in that accident."

"That's a stretch."

"I agree. Gloria has been trying to reason with her daughters for years. She thinks they hate her."

"Do they?"

"I do not know. It is complicated. Would you hold me?"

Surprised by the request, Warren took Naomi in his arms. It had been a while since they had sex, and he could feel his stirring. She pulled him close, nestling the side of her head against his chest. "I am so cold," she murmured. A suggestive comment entered Warren's consciousness but not wanting to make another verbal blunder he held his tongue. A minute or two went by. Finally the couple separated and returned to their toddys. As Naomi sipped her drink she gazed in Warren's general direction. "Oh no," she stammered as she pointed to the front of his green sweater. Looking downward Warren saw the fresh blot of blood on the fabric.

"This isn't something you see every day," Warren joked.

"I am so sorry," Naomi said. "I should have been more careful."

"Don't worry about it. Dry cleaning will take care of the blood stain. But I've got to say, playing an instrument until you bleed seems excessive."

"Passion does not recognize caution," Naomi answered.

Just then Stu emerged from the bedroom. "I'm going to L.A. and talk some sense into those bitches," he announced. "Why don't you come with me Westing? We could rent a car and get in a round of golf at Pebble Beach."

"I've got too much work to do, Gottlieb," Warren said. The truth was, he feared that the force involved in swinging a golf club would snap a cancerous bone. In fact a subtle dread arose with practically every move he made these days, whether it was taking out the garbage, walking down the stairs, or bending over to tie his shoes. His illness carried more than physical consequences. A constant trepidation, he was learning, was something he had to live with.

Stu gave Warren that look that over the years had come to mean he accepted his friend's decision and would simply let it be. As for Warren he truly regretted having to pass on what would have been a memorable trip with his buddy. But as they stood together in tacit understanding Stu suddenly became short of breath. "Excuse me, Westing," he said as he headed for the bedroom. "Time for some extra medication."

"Is it his heart do you think?" Naomi asked Warren.

"No doubt," Warren said, abundantly aware that his friend was still waiting for a new heart.

"Life can be complicated," Naomi said.

"I couldn't agree more," Warren said as he sipped his toddy. Then, carefully, he eased himself onto a sofa while making sure his moves were calculated and safe. Naomi stayed near the fire.

Ten minutes later Gloria emerged from the bedroom and approached Warren. "I'm sorry." she began as she dabbed at her tears with a tissue. "I had no right…"

"No need to apologize," Warren interjected. "We've all got our problems."

Next Stu appeared. His breathing looked fairly normal. "Lets eat," he chimed. "We've got lasagna."

The four sat at a dining table made of heavy glass and chrome. Conversation touched on Stu's myriad of medications, Warren's good fortune on the cancer front, Naomi's recent offer to join the Boston Philharmonic, an opportunity she was seriously considering, and Gloria's plan to run a half-marathon in the spring. Warren and Stu reminisced on memorable Christmas gifts they once exchanged. Years ago Warren hired two strippers to dance for his friend in the privacy of his apartment. Not to be outdone, Stu went to the trouble of finding the beat up discus that Warren once threw for Prairie Center High School, a relic that now sat in a glass display case in Warren's den.

The hour became late and the foursome got sleepy. After the goodbyes Warren walked out with Naomi and stood with her at the side of her old Volvo. She was wrapped in a heavy coat and a wool stocking cap covered her head.

"The only thing that keeps me from taking the Boston position is the weather. Winters are terrible in Massachusetts," Naomi said. Her hands were shoved in the front pockets of Warren's winter coat.

"I'm sure you'll make the right decision," Warren said.

"I am sorry about your sweater."

"Don't worry about it."

"Would you like to come over?"

"I'd love to. But I can't stay long. I've got a lame dog at home who needs to be walked."

"I will do my best to get you home on time."

Warren chuckled. "I'll follow you," he said. Soon he was cruising in his

Lexus through Omaha, the streets clear of traffic on this Christmas night. "Hang on Sloopy, Sloopy hang on," he sang as he drove. It hit him that he was singing the song usually reserved for his tense and nervous moments. He had nothing to feel nervous about, or so he thought. But the truth won out. There were plenty of troubles in his life ranging from the obstinance of Gloria's daughters through Stu's heart disease to the ever present problem of cancer. He thought back to a simpler time, when singing a song prepared him for the single challenge of a track meet or football game. Life can be complicated, he thought, using Naomi's exact words.

When he pulled up in front of the "Sugar Shack" he took the time to inspect the blood stain on his green sweater. It was deep and by now almost black. It was hard to believe that it was caused by a violist's bleeding blemish. He knew the sweater, Gabriela's Christmas gift to him, would need a prompt cleaning so he could wear it throughout the Holidays. An explanation of how the stain came to be was something he wished to avoid.

"Hang on Sloopy," Warren sang as he jumped out of his car and headed for Naomi's bungalow. It was just a few yards to her door and he left his winter coat in the car. When his lover greeted him at the open threshold he rushed in and took her in his arms. It might have been the cold that led him to do this. More likely he needed some immediate comfort.

XIV

Stu made a quick visit to the west coast to try to persuade Gloria's daughters to change their attitudes toward their mother and to attend the upcoming June wedding. He was known for his persuasiveness. After all his expertise in medical malpractice law placed him in front of juries. Indeed, he recently won a $40,000,000 judgment against Creighton Medical Center. But the young women proved to be stubborn, much like their mother. They promised to give the matter due consideration, but when Stu got back to Omaha he told his fiancee not to get her hopes up.

These days Stu took thirteen different types of medications all meant to forestall heart failure. A heart transplant was his only hope and he and Gloria led anxious lives as they waited for news from UNMC that a match had been found. Despite his poor health Stu continued to work though he wisely stepped away from courtroom argument. He acted as a kind of professor emeritus to his department, and it was commonly acknowledged at SL&T that his input was invaluable to the firm.

On a snowy day in late February the friends met for lunch at Stogie's. Both were bald, Warren having decided to continue to keep his scalp smoothly shaved and Stu having lost his hair years ago. Warren's weight was still holding at 200 pounds but his back pain had returned. Stu looked gaunt and pale. Dried blood of shaving nicks dotted his face, Drinking their ales in a booth, they gave their lunch orders to a waitress.

"I'll have the half-pound burger with tomato, pickles, onion, and lettuce," Warren told the woman.

"The Caesar salad for me," Stu said.

"No pastrami on rye?" Warren asked.

"Doctor's orders."

"Since when did you follow their orders?"

"Since Gloria threatened to walk out on me."

"You're kidding."

Stu frowned, saying, "I don't want to go 0 for 3. So I decided to toe the line."

Warren sipped his beer and took a good look at his friend. Stu was no longer the stocky man of yore. In fact he was quite frail, and the dried spots of blood on his face made him look like a voodoo doll. "So what's the latest news about the new heart?" Warren asked.

"We're still waiting," Stu said. "Waiting is the hardest part. It sours our wedding plans. If I get a new heart this Spring I'm guessing the June wedding will have to wait. How is your health, Westing?"

Warren grimaced as he pulled an amber vial of pills from a pants pocket. "I'm back on daily Oxycontin," he said as he popped a pill in his mouth. "My back hurts all the time."

"Cancer?"

"Could be. Alvin ordered an MRI."

"Alvin?"

"Dr. McHale."

"You call your doctor 'Alvin'?"

"Why not? He calls me 'Warren'."

Stu snickered as he sipped his beer. "Maybe if I called my doctors by their first names they'd find me a heart sooner rather than later."

Just then the Caesar salad arrived along with a small metal container of house dressing. Stu dumped all of the dressing on the salad, sprinkled heavy amounts of salt and pepper on his meal, and dug in. "I really miss my pastrami," he muttered.

Minutes later Warren had his burger that he treated in his traditional way. As he cut his meal in half he thought about Naomi, who was currently in Boston as a guest performer for the city's symphony. "Has Gloria heard from Naomi," he asked Stu.

"She has. Apparently all Naomi talks about is how cold Boston is."

"Let me ask you something, Gottlieb," Warren said, his lover uppermost in his mind.

"I'm all ears."

"I was married to Margie for 17 years. In all that time I never strayed. And as you know opportunities abound in a large law firm like ours."

"What's your point, Westing?"

"My point is, if I had known Naomi while I was married to Margie I…"

"You're kidding me. You were so pissed off when you found out about Margie's cheating. Now you're telling me that you would've done the same thing if the right woman had been available. That's a tad hypocritical Westing."

"Maybe so. But Gottlieb, the woman is amazing," Warren continued. I mean look at me. I could be wracked with cancer. Naomi doesn't care."

"Perhaps that's because she's a cancer survivor."

"Maybe that's part of it. But there's more to it than that. It's as though evil doesn't exist for her."

Stu guffawed, his mouth full of salad. "Better leave the philosophy to me," he managed.

"I'm serious. I've never met anyone so carefree. She waltzes through life without a worry. When I'm with her I begin to feel the same way."

"Is there question in here somewhere?"

Warren took a bite of burger and then wiped a drip of catsup from his mouth. "Do you think I should ask Naomi to marry me?" he said through a mouth full of food.

Stu nearly choked on his salad. "You can't be serious," he finally said. "Margie's only been gone…what…eight months now. I'm no expert on etiquette but I think you should wait awhile before getting hitched again."

"I may not have a whole lot of time," Warren said.

"I'll give you that. But on the other hand you might live for years."

"A chemo pal of mine once asked me what my 5 year survival rate was so I did a Google search."

"And?"

"I have a 28% chance of living 5 years," Warren said. The grim statistic made him swallow hard. "That's why time is so important to me."

"It's just numbers pal. You of all people should know that."

"Granted. But that doesn't change the fact that I want Naomi in my life."

Stu pushed his salad aside having eaten very little of it. He drank some ale and then smoothed a hand over his baldness. Then he spoke as only a best friend could. "Look Westing, I think you're being a bit selfish here," he said.

"Selfish?"

"Contrast your proposal with my situation. I need a new heart. That may never happen. To be fair to Gloria I offered her a chance to cancel our wedding plans until such time as a new ticker is beating inside me."

"What did she say to that idea?"

"She turned it down. But the point is she had a chance to avoid marrying a man who might be dead in a year. Now you say that Naomi has no problem with your cancer. But do you expect her to marry you and your shitty outlook?"

Warren shifted his weight on the hard bench. His back was killing him. "I see your point, Gottlieb," he said. "I'll wait until I get the results of the new scans. But if I'm cancer-free I'm going to pop the question."

Stu called for the waitress telling Warren that the discussion was over. "Bring me a pastrami on rye," he told her. Then he grinned at his friend saying, "I'll eat healthier in my next life."

* * *

A few days later Warren had his MRI. The very next day, a Friday, he was at his desk hard at work when his cell phone rang. It was Dr. McHale.

"The good news is that your original metastatic sites have resolved. The bad news is you've got several new metastatic foci in several vertebral bodies," McHale began.

Warren grimaced as he smoothed a hand over his scalp. "That doesn't sound good," he said. McHale went on.

"The disease is too wide spread for radiation. I recommend another round of chemotherapy."

"Oh shit," Warren spit.

"I know. There's more nausea and vomiting ahead. But it's your best shot."

"I'm guessing I'll need marijuana. Any progress on the approved stuff?"

"Not yet, Warren. Be patient. I'll e-mail you your chemo schedule after I have a chat with the oncology board. Any questions?"

Warren hesitated. Then he asked the question he should have started with months before. "How long do I have Alvin?"

"I honestly don't know. Let's see how you respond to the second tier drug."

"I'm in the minor leagues now?"

The doctor chuckled. "You could say that," he said. It was then that Warren heard his doctor say something indicative of his sole patient's true situation. "You've had a good life, Warren," he said. "That's something to be grateful for."

When the conversation ended Warren stared at the piles of paperwork on his desk. He couldn't focus on tax law. He grew restless, loosening his tie and shoving the padded swivel chair he sat in away from the desk. Spinning around to face a bookcase full of law books he closed his eyes. He imagined himself to be Tom Hanks in the movie "Castaway", alone on a small island in the Pacific ocean. He felt precisely like that character, alone, desperate and determined to change his fate.

"Que pasa Boss?" Gabriela asked. She had just entered his office with an armful of paperwork. Warren swung his chair around to face her and told her the bad news. "Ay-yi-yi. More cancer and more chemo," she said. "I'd better get you some pot." She looked on as Warren swallowed two OxyContins with a mouthful of water. "My worst nightmare is coming true," she murmured.

"What's that?"

"You're becoming an addict just like my poor dead husband."

"Gabriela, we've been over this..."

"Suit yourself," Gabriela said as she threw up her arms in exasperation, her face in a squint. "You're the boss."

"I'll get you the chemo schedule ASAP."

"Why don't you take a leave of absence?" Gabriela suggested "You're going to be high all the time anyway." Her sarcastic tone wasn't lost on Warren.

"Hey, I could use a little support here," Warren complained.

"Oh I'll support you. I'll cook and run your errands as always. I only ask that you take my opinions seriously."

For the first time since their differences over the use of pain pills surfaced Warren started to see that Gabriela might have a valid point.

"Are narcotics that bad?" he asked. He felt like a child asking a teacher a question.

"They are the worst, Boss. And addiction is a bad disease. Why would you want to add it to your cancer?"

Warren sat in his chair holding the amber vial of pills in his hand. Gabriela walked behind him and began massaging his shoulders. "We'll get through this," she said. And then she began to sing. Her soft voice and strong hands instantly soothed him. Listening carefully to the strange words of the song he remembered that it was in Mixtec, the language of Gabriela's youth. As the massage and the singing continued Warren's thoughts drifted. He knew he should give up the notion of asking Naomi to marry him, that the return of cancer demanded that. But here was Gabriela Hernandez. She seemed to be what he needed. He had become dependent on her much like he relied on his pain pills. He wondered if she could act as a substitute for the medication he held in his hand.

"Allow me to propose a hypothetical," Warren said. He waited for a response from Gabriela but none came. He went on. "Suppose I figured out a way to retire. Would you be willing to come to work for me on a full-time basis?"

"As what?"

"As a cook and housekeeper."

Gabriela stopped her massage and walked to a chair that faced Warren's desk. She took a seat and looked him straight in the eye. "Boss, I need my salary and my benefits," she said.

"What if I matched your salary and provided, at minimum, a catastrophic health care plan?"

"How could you afford all that?"

"As I said, it's a hypothetical. Well, what do you say?"

Gabriela rubbed her forehead, obviously falling into deep thought. A full minute went by before she spoke. "I have to say, the offer is tempting," she finally said. "But I would add something to my job description."

"Which is?"

"Health care manager."

Warren grinned. "Done," he said.

"When will you get past the hypothetical?"

"I have to call my brother to see if he can assume our mother's nursing home expense. If he is willing to do that I believe I can both afford to retire and hire you."

"That's a big 'if'."

"Steven has made the offer. The trouble is, we're not on the best of terms."

At that moment Gabriela's mouth puckered and a tear ran down her cheek. Clearly something had saddened her. "Gabriela?" Warren said. "What's wrong?" Wiping at her tear she took a deep breath and sat up straight.

"Sorry Boss," she said. "I hate to say this…"

"Yes?"

"What if you…die? I'll be out in the cold."

For reasons Warren didn't fully understand he hadn't given that eventuality a thought. But the solution to that situation came easily to him. "I'll change my will and my estate trust," he said without hesitating. "Believe me, you'll be taken care of."

"You would do that for me?"

"I've got no one else except a brother I don't like and his three kids whom I haven't seen in years. Yes, I would do that for you."

It was then that Gabriela broke down and cried. Her broad shoulders shook as she buried her face in her hands. Her sobbing went on for some time and Warren looked on helplessly and without a clue as to why she had fallen into such a state. But an explanation came when she eventually composed herself. "Just knowing that you would leave your estate to me touches my heart," she said. "Thank you so much, Boss." Warren just nodded. Women, he thought.

That evening Warren did some arithmetic. His pension and social security would support his retirement. Medicare and a supplement would cover most of his medical bills. If need be he could draw from his IRA. All he needed to do was get out from under the $8500/month nursing home bill. It was then he did something he loathed doing. He called his brother.

"Steven Westing speaking," the voice on the phone said.

"This is Warren."

"Bro! How's it hangin'?"

"I'll make this short. If you recall you offered to pay for Mom's nursing care."

"I did?"

"You did. I'd like you to keep your word."

A silence fell on the phone. "Well, my son finishes law school in May," Steven finally said. "I could start contributing then."

"I'm not talking about contributions. I want you to pay the whole amount."

Another silence occurred. "Why the sudden shift?" Steven eventually asked. Guessing that he would have to offer a valid explanation for his request Warren gritted his teeth and spoke.

"I have cancer, okay? I want to retire and…"

"That explains my dream," Steven said. "You were eaten from the inside out by a swarm of gnats."

"Jesus H. Christ. Will you just give me a simple answer. Will you…"

"Have you faced your death, bro? Margie did such a good job on that score."

Warren, who was sitting in his old leather chair in his den, became so annoyed with his brother that he almost threw his cell phone at the TV screen. "Yes or no on Mom's bills, you moron!" he screamed.

"Calm down, bro. I bet you're in the anger phase of dying."

I'll give him 10 seconds, Warren thought. Then I'm hanging up.

"Warren? Are you there?"

"A simple yes or no. That's all I'm asking," Warren hissed.

"Okay, okay. But I'll have to move her to St. Louis. The Unitarian Churches run a nursing home. I get a discount."

"Fine. When will that happen?"

"As I said, I'll have extra coin starting in May."

Warren had his answer. He would retire on May 1, 2013. "Thank you," he said. "We'll talk later."

"But what about your death. We should talk now," Steven said. That was the last of the conversation. Warren hung up.

XV

At 8 a.m sharp the next Monday Warren showed up at the UNMC chemotherapy room. There were only three chemo chairs prepared for patients and Jim Gordon was in the middle one. "Mornin' Warren," the man called.

"Gordo," Warren replied as he slid into his padded chair. "I didn't think I'd see you so soon."

"It's a bitch ain't it. Your cancer came back I'm guessin'."

"It did. How about you."

"Hell my leukemia never goes away. The Docs say they just keep it under control."

Just then a man walked into the chemo room and took the third chair. Warren had never seen him before and assumed he was new to the world of chemotherapy. He looked no older than 40, was tall and thin, and wore thick horned rim glasses. His skin was very pale and his expression was sullen. He wasted no time opening his lap top, and when Gordo asked what he was being treated for he didn't respond. Warren and Gordo's eyes met, communicating their confusion over the newcomer's unfriendliness. It was then that Warren decided not to introduce himself.

In no time all three patients were hooked up to intravenous lines and the hours of chemo began. Gordo took four Oxy's and fell sound asleep. Warren checked his lap top for e-mails and then played a few games of Sudoku. Occasionally he glanced over at the new guy who looked engrossed in whatever was on his computer. Two hours went by and Warren's back began to throb. He recalled Gabriela's warning about narcotics but decided to take a pain pill anyway. I'm not retired yet and she's not yet my nurse, he thought.

Just then Dr. McHale walked in. To Warren's surprise Alvin walked up to the new patient and said hello. "Professor, it's nice to see you again," he said. The new guy raised his head briefly and then returned his attention to his work. Warren watched his doctor's expression expecting some degree of annoyance. He saw the opposite. McHale beamed a smile and then shifted over to Warren. "How are you this fine day?" he asked his only patient as he busied himself checking Warren's heart and lungs.

"Alvin," Warren whispered.

"Yes?"

Warren pointed a finger at the newcomer. "Who is he?"

McHale finished his exam and then stood back and spoke in a voice he didn't bother to control. "That man is Clark Seehausen, professor of theoretical physics at Creighton University. He is a consultant to the Department of Defense, NASA, and practically every think tank in Washington. He won the esteemed J.J. Sakuri award for outstanding work in the field of theoretical physics. And, I might add, he is the youngest individual in the history of the United States to achieve full professorship in any field of higher learning. Have I left anything out, Professor Seehausen?" McHale called.

Seehausen glanced at McHale. "It was difficult finding another physician," was all he had to say.

"Sorry about that. Your myeloma was diagnosed after I retired."

"If you're retired why are you here?"

"If you must know, because of an odd turn of events I have one patient," McHale explained as he gestured toward Warren. "This is Warren Westing."

Warren's eyes met the professor's for a brief moment. Warren nodded a greeting. Seehausen nodded back and then returned to his computer. Warren glanced at Gordo who was snoring away. This is going to be a long day, he thought.

After writing orders and double checking the concentration of Warren's infusion McHale had a bit more information to impart. "This new drug is easier on the GI tract but with respect to efficacy has a poorer track record than the one you took the first time around," he told Warren. Hearing this, Warren said nothing. He was getting used to bad news, but learning that he might not be puking his guts out for weeks on end was something to lean on. But then he remembered Gabriela's concern about narcotics.

"Alvin, a friend of mine is worried that I'll become addicted to my pain pills," Warren posed.

"So what?" McHale said.

"That doesn't concern you?"

"Look Warren, you have stage 4 prostate cancer. If anyone is entitled to pain pills it's you. Narcotics are great at controlling pain. And by the way, addiction is irrelevant in your case. I'll supply you with all the pain medication you need so you should never feel a craving or any other addictive symptom. Sure, you might find your thinking a little muddled from time to time and you probably will have to deal with constipation. But in my opinion these things are better than suffering chronic pain. Are you with me?"

"I guess so," Warren mumbled, though as he spoke he could see a serious conflict in his future. Gabriela expected him to avoid narcotics while his physician planned to keep him well supplied. He needed to decide what path to follow but at this point saw good and bad aspects in each approach. Gabriela's way was healthier, McHale's was effective. Gabriela was asking him to deal with pain, McHale told him to ignore addiction. It was then an understanding came to him. The decision might not be a rational one. Cancer might decide for him.

McHale bade Warren and Seehausen a cheery good bye and left the chemo room, leaving the patients with their computers. Warren was about to return to a game of Sudoku when he heard Seehausen slam shut his lap top. "Idiots," the professor grumbled.

"Something wrong?" Warren asked.

"It's nothing."

"Come on professor. We've got a lot of infusion time left."

"It's my department. You'd think physicists would show some sense. It's money, money, money with those morons."

Warren didn't have much interest in the financial woes of a physics department but he also didn't want the conversation to end. "What did you get that award for?" he asked. To his surprise Seehausen angled his body toward him and took off his glasses, holding them in front of him as he began what proved to be a lively lecture.

"There is nothing colder than absolute zero and nothing faster than the speed of light," the professor began. "I contend that there exists a fraction of time that cannot be further reduced. I call it a Seehausen Second or SS. It follows that a finite number of events occur within an SS. Furthermore, there is a finite number of Seehausen Seconds in the universe. Think of existence as a reel of film with each cell representing an SS. Now the events in each SS are connected to events in contiguous SSs. That means that there are billions upon billions of possible pathways or outcomes, but the important thing to remember is that the number is finite, not infinite. Each outcome is predetermined, but as individuals we are free to choose our paths. That means that free will and predestination coexist. It also means that time within the confines of an SS does not exist."

"Wow," Warren swooned. "You know its funny but that makes perfect sense to me."

"It should. It's the truth. And I have the physics to back it up. That got me the Sakuri prize."

"Very impressive."

"Thank you. But it's really very basic stuff. Now if you will excuse me I have work to do." Seehausen put on his glasses, turned forward, opened his lap top and stared at the screen. As for Warren he googled the word Dr. McHale had used when referring to the professor's illness, myeloma. His reading told him that his new chemo-pal was in as much trouble as he was.

At long last Warren's infusion ended. He was the first to finish, Gordo still asleep and Seehausen still at his computer. As he drove to his law firm where he intended to put in an afternoon of tax work he amused himself by imagining various routes from the hospital to his downtown building, all pre-set by the principles set forth by the professor and yet all available for his choosing. He thought of Gar Young and his take on being struck by lightning, of Margie and her belief that the soul is a beam of energy, of that crashing tree limb that nearly killed him and his dog, of Steven and his dreams, and even of that loud-mouth Billy Bob Richardson and his fundamentalist clap-trap. He saw that there was logical room for everyone in Clark Seehausen's universe. Then, as he pulled into the SL&T underground parking area it occurred to him that he might have chosen to have cancer. That thought was anything but entertaining.

Just out of the elevator on the 12th floor Warren picked up the latest

SL&T newsletter from a stack in the lobby. He read that Stuart Gottlieb, a member of the medical malpractice division, had officially taken on a role of consultant to the firm. He also read that Warren Westing, a tax attorney for the firm, was on a six week leave of absence.

"Wow. That was fast," Warren said as he looked around for an audience. A young man who Warren guessed was an intern stopped to listen. Warren obliged, saying, "The firm put me on leave and didn't tell me."

The intern smiled. "I know how you feel, sir," he said. "Nobody tells me anything around here." The comment took Warren back to his days in law school. He remembered the contempt his professors showed the students and guessed the lawyers in his firm were treating this individual with similar disregard.

"Hang in there, son. Things will get better," Warren advised.

"When?"

"When you pass the bar."

"I hear the Nebraska bar exam is a bear."

"It's not easy. But I'm sure you'll do fine."

Nodding and helping himself to a newsletter, the young man started to walk away. "I've got to go, sir. Thank you for your kind words," he told Warren.

"My pleasure," Warren said. He watched the intern merge into the busy lobby crowd, envying the man his youth and bright future. He thought back on his law school days, remembering that he never gave his health a second thought. Those were the days, he thought.

When Warren got to Gabriela's desk he put the newsletter in front of her. Rather than offer an explanation for why he wasn't told about the leave of absence she had a question for him. "What are you doing here?" she asked as she looked up from her desktop.

"Nobody told me..."

"I-YI-YI! I forgot to send you an e-mail. I'm so sorry Boss."

"No worries. I had chemo this morning so I was out and about."

"I put you down for the maximum time off. You can return to work earlier if it suits you."

Gazing at his efficient and thoughtful secretary Warren understood more than ever how lucky he was to have her help. And there was something else. The Latina looked.... He couldn't find the words. Then they tumbled out of his mouth.

"You look lovely today, Gabriela," he said. The instant the sentence materialized he recalled the yearly lectures the entire firm was required to attend. They often centered on office conduct. Sexual harassment was a frequent topic. Studying his secretary's expression he was happy to see that she wasn't squinting.

"Gracias," Gabriela said. Her tone sounded measured, as though she wished to keep her feelings to herself. Warren kept staring at her. For reasons he didn't understand he suddenly found her captivating. She was a large woman but she was nicely proportioned. Her coal black hair shimmered, her dark eyes sparkled...

"Boss?" Gabriela said, perhaps as an attempt to snap Warren out of his altered state.

Warren took a step back and rubbed his eyes. I'm an idiot, he said to himself. Gradually he regained his bearings and searched for a way to act the lawyer and not the suitor. "Maybe I'll work half a day," he said as he headed for his office.

"There's no work for you," Gabriela said. "Go home. You're making me nervous."

Nodding in agreement, Warren started to walk away. But again, for reasons he didn't understand, he needed to say one more thing. From several feet away he turned and faced his secretary. He smoothed a hand over his baldness and hooked a thumb under a suspender strap. "What am I going to do for six weeks?" he asked.

"You're going to begin taking care of your health," Gabriela replied. "I'll bring you some food this evening. We'll go over things then."

*   *   *

True to her word Gabriela showed up at 41 Crestwood at 6 p.m. She carried two filled plastic bags and a covered casserole. Warren was in the kitchen trying to to tolerate a slug of Maalox. After only one day of chemo his stomach was in a turmoil. "Having troubles already Boss?" Gabriela said when she joined him.

"My doctor said I'd have an easier time of it this go around," Warren said.

"Doctors. What do they know?" Gabriela said as she put her load on the butcher block island counter. She reached in a bag and pulled out a baggie of marijuana that she tossed to Warren. "Remember, pot is only for the nausea," she cautioned.

"Oh God thank you," Warren gushed. Without hesitation he loaded with a small pipe with marijuana and lit up. Two minutes later he felt much better. "By the way I have good news," he told Gabriela, rushing his words because his high threatened to impair his speech.

"Let me guess. Your brother is going to pay for your mother's care."

"Correcto."

"And now you can afford to hire me on a full time basis."

"Correcto."

It was then that Gabriela began to unload her plastic bags. Warren took a seat on a kitchen stool and looked on. Basically she produced large vials of capsules and jars of what turned out to be protein powder. In addition there was a set of compact discs entitled "Beginning Yoga." "If I'm going to be your cook and health care manager you're going to have to do things my way," she said.

Warren listened to Gabriela as carefully as he could but was distracted by the aroma wafting from the covered casserole. His stomach problems controlled, he was famished. "Whatever you say," he mumbled. "What's in the covered dish?"

"Huachinango," Gabriela said. "Red snapper."

"Yummy. Let's eat."

In no time the couple sat in front of their fish chowing down. Though Warren's sense of taste was blunted the pot held his nausea in check. Furthermore he had mastered the art of speaking when high on marijuana. "I wish to retire on May 1st of this year," he told Gabriela.

"I'll draft your resignation papers tomorrow Boss."

"I assume all of these supplements you dumped on the counter are part of your plans for me," Warren guessed.

"They are. You are going to eat whole foods, take vitamins and extra protein, and learn yoga."

"Yoga?"

Gabriela picked up the CD set labelled "Beginning Yoga Disc 1" and showed it to Warren. "This will get you started," she advised.

Warren snickered at himself. Once a football player now a swami, he thought.

"And one more thing," Gabriela added. "You must allow me control of your pain pills. If we're careful with their use we can keep you out of trouble."

"How do you know all this stuff?"

"I told you. My husband had cancer. And he did quite well for a time. To this day I believe he died of a drug addiction."

The meal finished, Gabriela cleared the counter while Warren took another hit of pot. This didn't escape his nurse's eye and she gave him a nasty squint. He rubbed his abdomen to indicate gastric distress. The ruse worked. No scolding came his way.

It was then that Theo ambled into the kitchen with his leash in his mouth. "How about a walk Gabriela?" Warren suggested.

"Sure Boss. Let me get my coat."

Minutes later the trio was walking down the pleasantly lit sidewalks of Dundee. The dusk was cool and the humans wore coats. The Great Dane didn't seem to mind the chill. Warren broached a subject that from time to time teased him. He gathered his thoughts and let the words spill out. "Personal question," he slurred.

Gabriela groaned. "See what drugs do?" she said. "All right. Ask your question. If you can."

"Before the cancer…did you…see me differently?"

"I didn't think you noticed. I admit I hoped for a future with you."

"But cancer changed that?"

Boss, I just can't go through losing another loved one. That's why I can't get close to you. I'm sorry but that's the way I'm put together."

Warren didn't reply. He remembered Stu's advice pertaining to Naomi, suggesting avoiding a serious relationship with her if his illness returned. Now it sounded like the advice also applied to Gabriela. Sighing, Warren admitted that it was time to see himself in a clear light. He was a dying man.

When the walk ended Warren showed Gabriela the courtesy of seeing her to her car. The clear cold air had freshened his mind but his back was throbbing. He couldn't wait to get inside and take an Oxy. "I can't give you control of my pain pills just yet," Warren told her. "Our retirement is two months away."

"I'll have to trust you Boss. I'll prepare the food, you take your supplements, and we'll work on the yoga together. But come May 1st I will have the time to dole out the narcotics. Is it a deal?"

"Thank you for everything," Warren said. Standing next to the Honda, Margie's old car, they embraced, a tacit understanding that they had entered into a partnership. Then Gabriela climbed in to her car but promptly rolled down her window. "I forgot to tell you that Gaby found a man she really likes," she told Warren.

"Good for her. What's his name?"

"Edgar Channing. He's a financial advisor for Bank of America."

"Well if it turns out to be serious let's have them over for dinner."

"When is your chemo finished?"

"Six weeks from now."

Gabriela nodded. "That'll give the lovebirds enough time to see if it's for real. Buenas noches Boss." Warren watched as the Honda drove off. Then he hustled inside and took a pain pill. Before he retired for the night he took another.

*   *   *

The six weeks of chemo hit Warren hard. Contrary to Dr. McHale's predictions the GI side effects were devastating. Even marijuana began to lose its effectiveness in controlling Warren's nausea. As a result he lost a lot of weight, ending up at 181 at the end of treatment. Fatigue and weakness were daily factors and Warren saw that Gabriela's intuition was sound in putting off inviting Gaby and Edgar for dinner until the poison was gone from his body. He was just beginning to regain some sense of well-being when he met with Dr. McHale to get the results of the latest tests. He got good news.

"I don't believe this," McHale exclaimed as he gazed at the scan print outs. He and Warren were in a small out-patient room of UNMC. "A second tier drug doesn't normally get such good results," the doctor went on. "Warren I am happy to report that there is no trace of a malignancy anywhere."

Warren couldn't believe his ears. For the first time in months he let himself believe he just might beat cancer. "That's great news Alvin," he said.

"Great news? It's incredible news. This means you might be entering into a remission. At any rate it's a cause to celebrate."

Warren sat quietly as he watched his physician write two prescriptions. He reflected on the facts that his back had ceased to hurt and his appetite had returned, fortunate changes consistent with the results of his recent tests. He was surprised, then, when McHale handed him the two scripts. "You've been approved for medical marijuana so I'm prescribing a hefty supply for you," McHale said. "Of course you'll always have your OxyContin."

Gazing at the scribbling on the two paper rectangles Warren had to wonder why McHale felt it necessary to supply him with drugs. It made him think that his doctor expected the cancer to return. "Do you think I need these?" he asked.

"Not at the moment," McHale replied. "Let's just say we like to be prepared."

"Oh," Warren murmured. It was the only sobering moment in his talk with Alvin.

The next day Warren made his weekly visit to the Dundee Retirement Center to visit his mother. Over the six weeks of chemo he had seen Fern just twice, his ill health keeping him at home. Since her stroke Fern had rapidly deteriorated, though it was difficult for Warren to decide exactly what other faculties she had lost. The stroke robbed her of the ability to speak, but there was more to her decline than that. She looked very dejected and depressed. Her eyes had turned dull. She rarely watched television. She had no interest in checkers or watching movies. In sum, Warren feared she had decided to die.

"Hello Mom," Warren called. Fern was sitting at an empty dining table in the area for the demented. She was in a bathrobe. If she heard her son's greeting she didn't respond to it. "How about a walk?" Warren suggested. His mother acted as though he wasn't there. Just then a woman approached, the one wearing the name tag reading "A. Herbert, nurse supervisor."

"I'm afraid your mother hasn't improved with speech therapy," the supervisor told Warren. "But there's another problem. She has to be fed. That means she'll have to be transferred to a full care wing."

"If things work out the way I hope they do my mother will be moving to St. Louis," Warren said

"Oh really."

"Really."

"And when would that be?"

"Maybe in a couple weeks."

The supervisor rubbed her chin in thought. "Have you found our care unsatisfactory in some way?" she asked

"It's nothing like that," Warren answered. "My brother is going to see our mother's care from now on."

"Well, it wouldn't make sense to transfer your mother to another area for just two weeks, would it?"

"I wouldn't know."

Glancing at Fern the supervisor grabbed a paper napkin and wiped spittle from the old woman's chin. "I'll ask you to keep us abreast of your plans for your mother," she directed to Warren.

"Of course."

As the supervisor walked off Warren gazed at his mother. He remembered being concerned that she would outlive him, even before his cancer diagnosis. Now he saw that old age had a way of rather suddenly ending a life, that old age was just as treacherous as the big C. He once resented supporting Fern. Now he pitied her. She didn't look like she was in any pain, but he had to wonder if she harbored any feelings, any regrets, any wish to be somewhere else. After patting her on the shoulder Warren left the nursing home. It was the last time he saw her alive.

* * *

A few weeks later, his formal retirement from law rapidly approaching, Warren dressed for a brunch that Gabriela had arranged at his home. In turned out that Gaby and her new boyfriend Edgar had hit it off. The new couple was to join him and his soon-to-be full time employee for an informal gathering featuring tacos and beer. After donning a golf shirt and slacks in his bedroom Warren slid into his bathroom and checked his weight on a digital scale. It read 187, an improvement. Then he gazed at his face in the mirror. Still bald he wondered if he could grow back some hair. If so, he considered a mustache. He had worn one for a brief time in law school. The thought made him feel young.

When he heard the doorbell ring Warren walked downstairs to the foyer. As he walked he recalled how that simple act sometimes sent bolts of pain from his back to his legs. That was a situation he desperately wished not to revisit.

"Come in, come in," Gabriela cried. She had been busy in the kitchen preparing food. Gaby entered first. The young woman carried a deep dish covered with foil. She kissed her aunt and then bussed Warren on his cheek. Then Edgar walked in.

"My lord in heaven," Warren gasped when he laid eyes on the man. "You're me when I was your age." The unexpected comment produced a short-lived silence. "I'm sorry," Warren finally said as he extended his hand for a shake. "You must be Edgar."

"That I am," Edgar said as he shook Warren's hand. "And you must be the dude who's going to hire my girl's aunt."

Before Warren could respond Gabriela spoke up. "Everybody in the kitchen," she said. "The tacos are lonely."

Warren found the brunch delicious, which included the corn casserole Gaby provided. It amused him to find that Gabriela, Gaby and Edgar all drank Michelob Ultra or "Chick Beer." As they ate Warren had a chance to have a good look at Edgar. The man was around 5 feet 11 inches tall, had light brown hair and a round, rosy baby face, and carried a small paunch under his belt. He could have easily passed for a 40-year-old Warren Westing.

But as the brunch continued Warren found himself increasingly annoyed with Edgar. The young man was far too egocentric for Warren's taste. The man bragged about his job at Bank of America and the handsome salary he drew, he insisted that his home town of Chicago was the best city on Earth, he made frequent references to Yale, his alma mater, and he didn't hesitate to voice his opinions on politics, religion, women's rights, and sports. As the meal drew to a close Warren was sure he didn't like the guy, placing him in a category with Billy Bob Richardson, people on the planet who were unlikable.

The visit, however, did not end with the meal. Gabriela suggested that the men retire to the den while she and her niece cleaned up. Reluctantly, Warren led Edgar to his den where the young man instantly spotted the old discus in its glass display case. "Is that yours?" Edgar gushed as he lifted the display up to his eyes for a closer look.

"Careful with that," Warren demanded. "A friend of mine gave me that for Christmas years ago."

"This is so cool, dude," Edgar said as he placed the glass case back on a table. "Did you throw the discus?"

"I did."

"So did I. I was second in the Ivy League my senior year."

"You don't say."

It was then that Edgar opened a photo album that lay next to the discus. Warren had been leafing through the album the night before and had neglected to return it to its shelf. He couldn't believe that anyone would look through such a personal item without the permission of its owner. But Edgar apparently had no such boundary. "Is this your fam?" Edgar asked.

"It is," Warren muttered.

"Oh wow. There I am in your family album," Edgar joked. Warren joined in the perusal. He could see that Edgar was looking at a picture of a young Warren Westing. Except for the longish hair and the bell bottoms the guy in the photo very much resembled Edgar, who joked, "Maybe I'll go for the disco look," a weak reference to men's clothing style of the 70's.

"All right, that's enough," Warren said as he grabbed the family album from Edgar.

"What's your problem dude?" Edgar said, hands in the air as though surrendering something.

For the second time that morning Gabriela's voice interrupted the men's exchange. "Gaby has to get to work," she called from the foyer. The men joined the women. Warren carried his album in an irrational act to protect his privacy. Polite gestures were swapped ending with a power handshake between Warren and Edgar. Giving it his all Warren nevertheless secretly conceded that the younger man had the firmer grip. He and Gabriela watched from the doorway as Gaby and Edgar climbed into a late model Mercedes. As he backed out of the driveway Edgar tooted his horn twice, a stunt Warren found childish. The guy is an idiot, Warren thought.

"That was a nice visit," Gabriela commented as she shut the front door. Warren had nothing to say and Gabriela noticed. "You didn't think so?" she asked him.

Warren sighed. "I just don't like the guy," he confessed.

"Well Gaby does. That's all that matters."

Shrugging his shoulders Warren walked back to the den where he started to put the family album in its traditional place in a rear bookshelf. But before doing so he opened the album to a random page. One of the photos showed his father, Alvin Westing, kneeling behind a pile of bluegills. Warren remembered that day. He and his dad had spent the afternoon fishing from an old wooden john boat. His father rowed. He sat in the rear. They had used worms as bait. Both caught at least a dozen keepers. They shared the chore of cleaning them and his mother pan fried them in butter. That was a good day, Warren thought.

A short time later Gabriela announced that she was leaving to run some errands. She reminded Warren to take his vitamins and protein supplements, do his yoga exercises, and suggested that he take a nap. When alone he opted for another course of action. He smoked the last of the marijuana that was supposed to be used for nausea and took an OxyContin that was supposed to be for pain. But he did take that nap.

XVI

Back to work for the two weeks between his leave of absence and his retirement, Warren found the experience bittersweet. He had been a tax attorney with SL&T for over thirty years and had made many friends. Retirement was unknown territory for him, a contrast to the certainty that came with a position in a prestigious law firm. He knew he would miss the work and the camaraderie. But there was more. Leaving his career seemed like he was admitting that cancer ruled his life, a concession that made him feel defeated despite his apparent remission.

On his last day the firm honored him and his best friend Stu Gottlieb with cake and champagne, Stu finally having retired weeks before. "We must seem like Bert and Ernie to these folk," Stu quipped to Warren as they stood in the lobby among colleagues, paralegals, secretaries, interns and even the janitorial staff.

"Laurel and Hardy would be more accurate," Warren said.

"Martin and Lewis."

"Simon and Garfunkle."

"Abbot and Costello."

"Amos and Andy."

"Penn and Teller."

"Bacon and eggs."

Stu laughed. "You went off-task," he claimed. "Victory is mine."

Before Warren had a chance to object Gabriela approached the men, and Warren took the opportunity to give his secretary her due. He tinked his champagne glass with a fork and got the crowd's attention. "Ladies and gentlemen I would be remiss if I didn't announce the retirement of my long-time secretary and good friend Gabriela Hernandez. She's been at my side for over 10 years and, believe me, I would've been lost without her. So please join me in a toast to this wonderful woman."

The attendees raised their glasses and drank. Gabriela looked embarrassed. "Boss, that wasn't necessary," she whispered to Warren.

"Nonsense," Warren said. "You deserve as much recognition as we do. In fact, I'd like to take you out to dinner to kick off our new...partnership. What do you say?"

"I'd like that."

"Excellent."

"Don't forget the dinner you promised Gloria and me," Stu reminded Warren.

"Your wedding present will be a feast at Anthony's Steak House," Warren said. And a week later he kept his word. After Stu Gottlieb and Gloria Chase were married in a judge's chamber on a warm May afternoon with Warren and Naomi as witnesses, he drove them to the noted restaurant where they dined as they had the first time the four of them gathered there months before. Gloria looked great in her yellow dress and matching heels. Still the long-distance runner, her sleek figure belied the fact that she was in her mid-fifties. It was only her short salt-and-pepper hair that gave her away. As always Naomi appeared rather frumpy and disheveled. Though the day was warm she wore a light black sweater over a wrinkled white blouse. Her long dark skirt had a stain on its front from what she said was spilled tomato sauce. Her trademark braided ponytail hung down to the small of her back.

After being seated and served wine, Warren raised his glass in a toast. "To my great and long-time friend Stu Gottlieb and his new bride Gloria Chase. May you live many years together in peace and happiness," he said. All clinked glasses and sipped the Chardonnay. After the toast Naomi wasted no time making her announcement.

"I have accepted the first viola chair in the Boston Symphony," Naomi said.

"Oh no," Gloria cried. "You can't."

"I must. The opportunity is too attractive to pass up."

The violists stared at one another, their neck sores badges of distinction. Warren thought of the dark ovals as merit badges. "What are we going to do without you, Naomi?" Gloria murmured.

"I am just one person," Naomi said, her words barely audible and difficult to understand. "The Omaha Symphony will go on without me. I am sure of that."

Gloria turned to Stu, saying, "Such sadness on such a happy day." Acting the good husband, he took her hand and gave it a reassuring squeeze.

Warren had suspected that Naomi was planning the move. She had acted as carefree and playful as ever during their recent sex romps but otherwise had been less engaging, less interested in him. It was though she was already in Boston. Warren couldn't help feeling annoyed at being so easily dismissed but tried to act like an adult. He imitated her coolness, her dispassion. But now, hearing the official word, the public announcement that meant the end of the fun at the "Sugar Shack", he felt compelled to speak his mind.

"I think you should have told me about your decision before now, Naomi," Warren said. He had tried to sound even-tempered but feared he had not succeeded. Naomi stared at him as did Stu and Gloria. My big mouth, Warren thought.

"I have hurt your feelings," Naomi said. She pulled her ponytail to the front of a shoulder, something Warren had learned was a sign of more to come.

"No, no..." Warren stammered in retreat.

"There is nothing wrong in admitting that you have feelings, Warren," Naomi added.

Warren felt mortified and to disguise this he wiped his mouth with his cloth napkin. The last thing he wanted to do was draw attention to the fact that he was fonder of Naomi than he wished to show. Indeed, it was only his cancer that prevented him from proposing marriage to her. He could feel her eyes on him and eventually returned her gaze. Naomi mouthed the words, "I am sorry." He believed her.

Just then the appetizers arrived, the steak house's famous oysters on the half shell. "I could eat these things every day," Stu raved as he covered his oysters with lemon juice and fresh black pepper. Gloria and Naomi dug in as well. Not a fan of oysters Warren stuck to bread and butter. From that moment on the dinner proceeded without a hitch. Stu and Gloria shared a New York strip for two. Warren ate a rib eye. Naomi once again troubled the chef for a vegetarian dish. The meal was over in an hour and the newlyweds had the hostess call them a cab. They were off to Eppley Field for a flight to San Francisco and a short honeymoon. On the way home they planned to drop down to Los Angeles to visit Gloria's daughters. Even if the bitches didn't come to the wedding, Stu had said, we're going to them.

After seeing the couple off, he drove Naomi home. It was near the summer solstice and there was plenty of daylight though it was after 8 p.m. when the Lexus pulled up in front of the "Sugar Shack." Naomi had found a classical station on the radio and sat enrapt in the music. Suddenly she announced, "This is the Minute Waltz." As she hummed she reached for Warren's zipper. Deftly, she coaxed his penis out into the open and quickly had her mouth over the stiffening thing. While she was performing the oral sex, a man and his dog walked by on the adjacent sidewalk. The man gave a thumbs up to Warren, who returned a sheepish grin. One minute later Warren climaxed. It would occur to him the next day that Naomi had probably timed the performance.

"I shall miss you Warren," Naomi said when the sex was over. "You have been a fine companion."

"Likewise," was all Warren had to say. Naomi gave him a peck on the cheek and then got out of the car. He watched as she disappeared into her little bungalow so near the Omaha Zoo. He hoped to see her again but knew it was a long shot.

*   *   *

The next day Warren met Dr. McHale at an out-patient clinic area at UNMC. McHale had the latest scans and blood test results. His smile told Warren that he had good news.

"Warren, you are going to live forever," McHale said tugging on his bow tie.

"I doubt that Alvin."

"Okay, that's an exaggeration. But your scans remain clear and your blood tests have normalized. Warren, you are officially in remission."

Warren couldn't believe his ears. His cancer was officially gone. It was too good to be true. "What's my outlook now?" he asked.

"I can tell you that your chances of being a five year survivor are very good."

"Better that 28%?"

"I'd put it at 75%."

"Wow. I just might make it to 70."

McHale scoffed. "Curb your enthusiasm, Warren. Being that old isn't that great."

"How old are you, if you don't mind me asking?"

"I'm 75."

"I think I knew that," Warren said as he looked at the wiry man in his short white coat and bow tie. "But I never would've guessed."

"How are you fixed for meds?" McHale asked. Warren didn't want to admit that he was now taking OxyContin to relax and for a sleep aid. So far he had kept this development a secret from Gabriela who, in addition to advocating her health regimen of supplements, rest and yoga, remained steadfastly opposed to the use of narcotics.

"I could use a refill," Warren said. It astonished him how willingly McHale supplied him with pain pills though it had been weeks since he had experienced any discomfort. Prescription in hand Warren agreed to go through another series of tests in two months. He said goodbye to his physician and headed home. On the way he absentmindedly drove toward his office and had to make a U-turn. I guess I'm getting old, cancer or no, he thought.

Once home Warren collected his mail that lay on the hardwood floor of the foyer. Flipping through the envelopes he found a bill from the Dundee Retirement Center, which reminded him that this was the month that his brother Steven was to assume the care of their mother Fern. It was obvious to him that Steven had yet to take on this responsibility. Once again he made the dreaded call to his preachy brother.

"What's up bro?" Steven chimed when he answered his phone.

"I'm calling about Mom," Warren said.

"What about her?"

"You were supposed to pay her bill. And you said something about moving her to St. Louis."

"Not necessary, bro. She's going to die soon."

"Don't start with that Unitarian mumbo-jumbo."

"I had a long talk with Ms. Herbert the nursing supervisor. Mom is showing all the signs of death preparation. She'll be gone in a week or two. Speaking of dying how is your end-of-life work coming along?"

"Christ you are an idiot," Warren cursed. Enraged, he closed his cell phone. Seconds later he regretted doing so. He was a retired man and couldn't afford shelling out $8500/month for his mother's care. He thought about calling back his brother to try to reason with him, to beg him for his help if necessary. A call on his land line put the matter to rest.

"Mr. Westing?"

"Speaking."

"This is Anita Herbert the nurse supervisor at Dundee Retirement Center."

"Yes?"

"I'm sorry to tell you that your mother passed away. She died in her sleep and likely experienced no discomfort. You have my sympathies."

"Holy crap," Warren mumbled.

"Excuse me?" the supervisor asked.

"I was just talking to myself," Warren said. Truth be told his thoughts were on his brother and his claim regarding predicting death. Steven had been right about Margie's passing and now he apparently saw the approach of the end of their mother's life. Lucky call, he thought. "I suppose there is some paperwork I'll need to attend to," Warren said after clearing his head.

"Yes sir. The sooner the better."

"I'm retired. I'll be right over."

Thirty minutes later Warren stood at his mother's bedside. Fern looked peaceful enough lying on her back, her arms folded on top of her frail body. The supervisor handed him a clip board that held the routine forms that a next of kin was required to sign. Included was the designated site of burial. That was easy. Warren indicated that Fern Westing was to be buried in the cemetery of the Prairie Center Congregational Church next to her husband Alvin Westing. Done with the paperwork Warren looked at his mother for the last time. I wish you had been more like Dad, he thought.

On the way out of the nursing home Warren was stopped by Takisha, the black aide who once threatened to file a complaint about his mother's racist remarks. Warren was under the impression that the issue had been resolved but by the look on the young woman's face he could see that something had riled her. Sure enough, she produced a single piece of paper and handed it to Warren. "Take a look at this shit," she spit.

Scanning the document Warren could see that it was a certificate of membership. Fern Westing had been a member of the Ku Klux Klan. "Jesus H. Christ," he sighed.

"I found that when I boxed your mother's belongings," Takisha said.

"I had no idea…"

"Yeah, right."

"I swear I didn't know. I mean I knew my mother was a racist but I knew nothing of her ties with the Klan."

"Well I'm glad she's gone."

"Hey. Show some respect for the dead."

"Don't talk to me about respect," the woman yelled. She wheeled on her heels and stomped off. As Warren watched her march away he thought it ironic that he sort of agreed with her. He, in a way, was also glad his mother was gone.

* * *

A few days later, with his mother's funeral scheduled and his brother notified, Warren made good on his promise to take Gabriela out for dinner. He drove to a hispanic neighborhood in south Omaha, an area informally known as Latino Village, and found her home on a quiet street lined with modest homes most of which boasted lavish displays of flowers. Warren jumped out of his Lexus and strolled up a neatly trimmed sidewalk to a set of wooden stairs that creaked under his weight. Standing at the front door he glanced to his right and spotted a gliding swing meant for two people. Potted pansies hung above and to the rear of the swing. He imagined that Gabriela spent a lot of time on her front porch gliding to and fro. And he felt a little ashamed for never having visited her home before.

Warren pushed a doorbell button but didn't hear a ring. He knocked and soon heard footsteps. The door opened and Gabriela appeared. "Wow," Warren swooned. "You look great." This evening she wore her hair down, her thick tresses falling on a maroon dress that had short sleeves and a buttoned front. Her heels were higher than the ones she wore to work. From a few feet away Warren could smell her perfume.

"Thank you Boss," Gabriela said. "You look good, too. You're wearing my favorite suit." Just as she started to close her front door a small yippy dog emerged from the house, scolding Warren for his very existence. The dog stopped short of attacking the trespasser but barked menacingly until Gabriela told him to stop. "Pedro!" she shouted. "Kennel up." Instantly, Pedro fell quiet and disappeared into the house.

"Now that's a well trained mutt," Warren said.

"He's old and blind, but I love him so," Gabriela said as she locked her door.

"How does he make it to his kennel if he's blind? Warren asked.

"Taking care of a blind dog is easier than most people think," Gabriela said.

"Is that so," Warren said as he offered Gabriela his arm and walked her to the car. He waited for her to elaborate on the care of her pet. None came.

"I made reservations at La Palapa," she advised, signaling Warren that dog training was not on her agenda.

"I haven't heard of it," Warren admitted.

"If you like my cooking you'll love this place."

Warren's mouth watered. Gabriela truly was a fine cook. Good food was part of her health regimen, a program that was in direct opposition to his rather careless use of narcotics. He feared she would discover his secret, see his behavior as a betrayal and abandon him. Careful big boy, he told himself. Loose lips sink ships.

Five minutes later the couple reached their destination. From the outside the restaurant didn't look like much. But when they walked in the place they were greeted by a distinguished looking gentleman in a tuxedo, and Warren judged that this evening he would be spending a tidy sum.

In short order Warren and Gabriela were sitting at a table for two. Muted music drifted their way as did soft chatter from neighboring tables. A young man poured their waters in crystal glasses. Then a waiter who identified himself as Alfonso offered menus and proceeded to describe the specialty of the day, quail with hominy and roasted chilis.

"Um, that sounds good," Gabriela swooned.

"Make it two, Alfonso," Warren said. "And I'd like to see your wine list."

As the waiter moved off Warren turned his attention to his companion. "So tell me Gabriela, where were you born?"

"Mexico City. I came to the U.S. when I was 14."

"So you went to high school in the U.S.?"

"I did. It was very difficult for me to learn English but I managed."

"Did you play a sport or an instrument?"

Gabriela took a sip of water. "You'll think I'm bragging," she said.

"Promise I won't."

"I played tennis. A lot of tennis. By the time I was 20 I was ranked 211th in the world."

"Are you serious?"

"I lost in the 1972 U.S. Open quarter-finals to Billy Jean King."

"Wow. I am impressed."

"She beat me in straight sets."

"Still, what you did was a real accomplishment."

Just then the waiter returned with the wine list. Warren ordered a 2008 Simi Cabernet despite its listed price of $180. He then turned back to Gabriela, who was becoming more fascinating with every question. "How long did you play tennis at that level?" he asked.

"I quit at 25. That's when I met my late husband."

"You said he died of cancer."

"Prostate cancer."

"Yikes. That's too close for comfort," Warren said. "But I have good news. My doctor says I'm in remission."

Gabriela surprised Warren with her lack of enthusiasm over the report. She didn't hesitate to explain why that was so. "I don't trust that word 'remission'," she said. "It builds up your hope, which makes it all the worse when bad news comes. I'm sorry. I've been hurt before. That's hard to forget."

The wine arrived and the couple started in on a fine Cabernet. Warren decided to quit the cancer talk and move on to a lighter subject. "I should've guessed you were an athlete," he began. "You have a certain grace about you."

"Did you play sports, Boss?"

"I threw the discus. And I played one year of football."

"Soccer or North American football?"

Warren chuckled. A timeless cultural impasse, he thought. "The latter," he said. "I was a fullback. Every time I got the chance I'd make an end run to avoid those bruising defensive linemen."

Alfonso delivered the entrees and refilled the wine glasses. There were two quail on each plate surrounded by hominy and roasted chili peppers. Warren made a point of combining the three tastes in his first bite. Despite his dulled taste buds, a casualty of chemo, the highly seasoned food gave him a rare savory treat. "My this is good," he told Gabriela. "I think I'll start putting Tabasco sauce on my food."

"No need Boss. I can spice up your meals. Just say the word."

As Warren enjoyed his entree he gazed at his old friend and partner. A wave of gratitude swept over him. What a help she's been to me, he thought. I'm a lucky guy. It was then that an idea popped into his heat. "Why don't you move in with me?" he proposed.

"Ay-yi-yi. You'd better not have any more wine Boss."

"I'm serious. You could use the downstairs bedroom. Living with me would save the commute and cut down on the wear and tear on your car. You could sell your home and put some extra money in your pocket. What do you say?"

"You've already been too good to me. I'm very happy as it is."

"You could be happier. And if I should die, and I don't intend to any time soon, my trust now names you as heir to my estate including my home. So if it's a question of a place to live…"

It's not that, Boss."

"What is it then?"

Gabriela sipped her wine and wiped her lips with her cloth napkin. "I'm afraid," she confessed.

"Afraid of what?"

After a deep breath Gabriela ran a hand through her thick hair while her expression turned serious. "I'm afraid of having…feelings for you," she murmured. "When I go home it's like putting a distance between us. That helps me keep my control. But if I lived with you, if my habits mingled with yours, I think I would…"

Fall in love with me?" Warren suggested.

"Yes. And you know how I feel about that."

"I'm willing to take that chance. If having had cancer taught me anything it's that a whole lot of living can be crammed into a very short period of time," Warren said as he reached across the table and took Gabriela's hand. "Love or no love, let's live out the time we have left together."

As she did in Warren's office when she learned of his offer to make her his sole heir, Gabriela broke into a quiet sob. After wiping her tears away she spoke a few words, saying, "Let me think about it Boss."

Warren straightened up and returned to his meal. "Of course," he answered. The couple at in silence, Warren, for one, surprised for having expressed himself so intimately. He hoped he hadn't put Gabriela on the spot and felt reassured when she finally moved the conversation to a lighter topic.

"My niece tells me she and Edgar are talking marriage," Gabriela said.

"That seems quick," Warren opined.

"I told her to slow down. But Gaby has always been headstrong and impatient."

"Unlike her aunt," Warren joked.

"I am not impatient," Gabriela insisted, cleverly omitting the other adjective. Warren appreciated the humor.

"I'm not fond of Edgar," Warren reminded Gabriela.

"I remember. Maybe that's because he looks like you when you were younger."

"Spare me the psychobabble. I get enough of that from my brother."

"Sorry Boss," Gabriela said, finishing her meal. "Dessert?" she asked Warren.

"I think I'll have a brandy."

"I'm going to have their flan."

"Oh, so you've been here before?"

"I have. My sister treated me for my 50th birthday."

"How many years ago was that?"

Gabriela laughed. "You are a persistent man Boss."

After paying the hefty tab, Warren escorted Gabriela to his Lexus. On the way to her home she scanned for a Hispanic radio channel and filled the car with rhythmic soulful music rich with brass harmonies and runs of an accordion. Warren listened carefully to the Spanish but as usual couldn't understand much. "What is the guy saying?" he asked Gabriela.

"My love for you is like the sea. It is vast, deep, and cannot be truly understood."

"Ay-yi-yi," Warren joked. Again, Gabriela laughed.

Once home Gabriela unlocked her front door, kissed Warren on the cheek and headed inside. Then, in a soft voice that carried both sadness and hope she said, "Margie has been gone for a year now, no?" It was more a statement than a question.

"That's right. One year."

Nodding her head she started to close the door. "Buenas noches, Warren. And thank you so much for dinner." They were her last words of the evening. It wasn't lost on him that she didn't call him "Boss".

XVII

Fern Westing was laid to rest next to her husband Alvin in a small cemetery behind the Prairie Center Congregational Church. Besides the minister there were only two people at the funeral, Warren and Steven Westing. The brothers ended up standing alone at the gravesite. A stiff warm wind blew from the west making it difficult for Steven to light his cigarettes. On one occasion Warren offered his cupped hands as a windbreak, a rare gesture of kindness toward a brother he found irritating at best.

"I'll miss the old girl," Steven said between wet coughs.

"Miss her?" Warren objected. "You've only seen her once since I put her in the nursing home."

"Bro, I had every intention of spending time with Mom after moving her to St. Louis."

"Lucky for you she never got there."

Steven pulled on his cigarette and gazed upward, saying, "I think I could've purged Mom of her racism."

Groaning, Warren picked up a small stone and flung it into space. "The high opinion you carry of yourself never ceases to amaze me," he said.

"I called Mom's death, did I not?"

"The woman was 90 and had a stroke. That nurse supervisor may have told you any number of things…"

"What about Margie?"

"Again, the woman was sick. A foreshortened e-mail may have tipped you off."

"Bro, you've got to start having a little faith in people."

Warren picked up another stone and threw it, this time with more effort. "I've got plenty of faith," he muttered. "I just don't believe in witchcraft."

"Is that what you think of me?" Steven asked. "You think I'm a witch doctor?"

"If the shoe fits…"

"A lack of faith and bitter as well. An unhealthy combination."

"Don't start with the preaching," Warren warned.

"Why are you so adverse to my counsel? You got angry when you found out I was helping Margie, you refuse my advice when it comes to your cancer, and now you won't address your feelings toward our dead mother."

Looking around for another stone to throw Warren noticed a sizable flat rock about the size of a discus. Despite his concern over a bone breaking as a result of sudden exertion, he hefted it and then flung it in the style of a track and field star. "I admit to being pissed off about the secret messaging between you and Margie," he started. "As far as Mom goes I'm happy that she didn't outlive me. As for myself I don't need any help from you. So save your bull shit for someone who asks for it."

"Everything is bull shit to you…"

By throwing up his hands and walking away Warren cut short his brother's lecture. "You can handle the funeral expenses," he called over his shoulder. "It's the least you can do."

"You're in denial bro," Steven called. Hearing this prompted Warren to give his brother the finger. A minute later he drove away from the church in his Lexus feeling fortunate that his brother had rented a car and would not need a ride to Omaha to catch his flight back to St. Louis. Before heading home Warren toured the town of his youth. His high school had expanded but the track where he had thrown the discus was as he remembered it, as was the football field where he played fullback. The frame house where he was raised was gone and an apartment building stood in its place. Main Street seemed empty, not nearly as bustling as it once was decades ago. Unchanged were the community hall, the volunteer fire department garage, and the post office. After the short tour he left Prairie Center. The moment was bittersweet, as he couldn't think of a reason why he would ever return. Indeed, somewhere out on the four-lane highway in the two hour drive to Omaha he guessed he would never lay his eyes on the little town again.

When he reached Dundee and pulled into his drive at 41 Crestwood Lane he jumped out of his car and stretched. Before being told of his remission he would have never made this move. Now he dared his body to fail him. With the spryness of a man half his age he trotted upstairs, shed his clothes and donned a velour warm-up suit. In his bathroom he inspected his hair growth. He had stopped shaving his scalp, and a fine coat of bristles had already sprouted. The new hairs looked finer and lighter than he remembered them.

Just then Warren heard a stirring in the kitchen. He had become used to Gabriela's comings and goings and assumed she was the one making the noise. But when he heard a dog's yelp he thought otherwise. Hastily, he walked downstairs. He found Theo stumbling into kitchen cabinets, apparently having having lost the ability to navigate.

"Jesus H. Christ. What is going on," Warren moaned as he grabbed the Great Dane's collar and steadied his dog. Theo's eyes were dilated and cloudy, and his legs were trembling. "Dammit, it's your eyes," Warren muttered. "We're going to the vet." Leading his pet to the front door he clipped the leash to the dog's collar and slowly led Theo to the Lexus where he lifted him into the back seat. The effort reminded Warren on the day his rib snapped. This day he had better luck.

An hour later Warren left the vet's office. Theo was indeed blind, a victim of sudden retinal degeneration. He was to stay the night and receive high doses of cortisone. The prognosis was not good. As he drove home, Warren feared having to euthanize his beloved dog. He felt worse over possibly losing Theo than losing Margie. Warren felt some shame in admitting this, but it was the truth. After all she had cheated on him. His dog was a true companion.

The next day around noon Warren called Gabriela's cell phone, remembering that she had a blind dog. He got her voice mail and left a message describing Theo's disability. An hour later she returned his call. "My mama died," she blurted. Warren could tell she was crying.

"I'm sorry, Gabriela," Warren said.

"I have to fly to Mexico City."

"Of course."

"I'll be gone for a while."

"How long?"

"Maybe a month."

"A month? Why so long?"

"My father is still alive but he's an invalid. Now that mama is gone I will need to find papa a nursing home or a live-in caretaker," she explained.

"Does it have to be you?" Warren asked. "Don't you have siblings, cousins, aunts, uncles?" There was a short silence on the line. He knew what her answer would be.

"It's my responsibility," Gabriela said. Warren could hear the firmness in her voice. "Now when I'm gone I want you to eat well and take your vitamins. And don't forget your yoga."

"But I'm in remission," Warren objected. His words produced another silence. He knew it was pointless to counter the woman's wishes. "Okay, I'll be a good boy," he said. "Say, do you have any information about blind dogs?"

"Sure. I'll have Gaby bring them to you." After another silence Gabriela began muttering, saying, "I need a plane ticket. I need to cancel the meeting with the realtor…"

"Whoa. I heard that," Warren interjected. "I hope that means you're seriously thinking of moving in with me."

"I'm still thinking about it," she said.

Warren took that as good news. But what he heard next was even better.

"I'll call you when I get to Mexico City," Gabriela said.

"Please do."

"I'll miss you."

"I'll miss you too," Warren said. He realized he wasn't just being polite. He meant what he said.

A minute after Warren ended his talk with Gabriela another call came in. It was the vet with the bad news of Theo's persistent blindness. The man asked for Warren's view on euthanasia, implying that putting the dog down might be the right thing to do.

"I'd like to bring Theo home," Warren said. "I'm given to believe that caring for a blind dog is manageable." He was surprised by the vet's quick agreement. They arranged a pick-up time and that was that. I'm going to need those books today, Warren thought after hanging up. It was then that a third call arrived. It was Gaby who promised to bring by her aunt's dog books during her lunch break. She kept her promise, showing up at 41 Crestwood at 12:30. When Warren let her in he was, as always, struck by her natural beauty. Though he was old enough to be her father he had to admit he was jealous of Edgar. It was unfair that such an unlikable man possessed such a lovely woman, or so he thought.

"My aunt told me your dog went blind," Gaby said as she followed Warren into the kitchen.

"Unfortunately."

"Well if he does as well as little Pedro he'll be fine," the woman said as she handed Warren three books on the management of blind dogs. He instantly began leaving through their pages and rapidly assimilated the information, understanding the need for strict consistency in Theo's future world. His dog would need a large wire kennel that would never be moved. His feeding bowls would always sit to the same side of the kennel. Textured floor runners would lead him from one first floor room to another. A harness would replace his collar and the new leash would be much shorter than the old one to give him the sense that his master was close during walks. The tips went on, and as he read them Warren became ever more convinced that his dog would be able to enjoy a few more years. It took Gaby's voice to get his eyes off the pages.

"Warren?" Gaby cooed. When he looked up he saw that she was holding up her left hand with its backside facing him. The engagement ring was easy to spot.

"Oh my God," Warren said. Putting down the reading material he strode to Gaby and gave her a paternal hug. "Congratulations, Gaby," he murmured. "This calls for a toast," he added when he stepped back. "I think there's some champagne in the fridge."

"I gave up alcohol," Gaby said. "Edgar and I are going for a pregnancy right away."

The way Gaby phrased the plan struck Warren as odd. He recalled Gabriela telling him that Gaby's first husband left her because she couldn't get pregnant. Then there was the coincidence that Gaby worked as a nurse at the Omaha Fertility Center. He wondered just how determined she was to get pregnant, if she would go to extraordinary lengths to achieve her end. Suddenly he was glad he wasn't in Edgar's shoes. "Well I wish both of you the best," was all he had to say.

"Thank you. We're going to need it," Gaby said. Warren just nodded, but suspected that this pregnancy thing was likely far more complicated than he knew.

"Have you set a wedding date?" Warren asked.

"When my aunt gets back from Mexico we'll all sit down and pick a Saturday."

"And the place?"

"Our Lady of Guadalupe of course."

Warren was familiar with the church. It was a monstrous edifice in central Omaha capable of seating hundreds of attendees. "Are you going to need a place that large?" he asked.

Gaby giggled. "My family could fill that church twice over."

Theo's pick-up time approached so Warren thanked Gaby for the reading material and showed her to the door. It was dusk when man and dog arrived home. Before guiding Theo inside, Warren unloaded a wire cage and set it up in the den next to his leather chair. Then he gently led his dog into his new sleeping quarters and shut the wire door. "I'll get up early and we'll start training," Warren whispered to Theo. The giant turned around once brushing his head against the wire walls, and then curled up for a good night's sleep.

Warren warmed up a piece of cold pizza and washed it down with a beer. His hunger satisfied and his dog bedded for the night, he headed for his bedroom for some slumber of his own. As he climbed the stairs he played a little game he occasionally found entertaining as a child. He closed his eyes and pretended he was blind. Negotiating the stairs was slow going. When he reached the top he took an elevated step where it wasn't necessary and almost fell. His foolishness brought him to his senses and reminded him that a fall could spoil his regained state of good health. Cancer may well have left him more fragile than he thought, and a broken bone meant certain pain. Eyes open, he turned on every light near him. I'm an idiot, he thought. I'd be better off in a cage.

Just a week later, exposed to two training sessions a day, Theo was ready to be re-introduced to his home. Each day Warren rose early to teach his blind dog how to negotiate the rooms and hallways of the first floor and to feel comfortable on leashed walks. He felt proud of himself and his dog, and felt lucky to know a woman who supplied him with just the right information. The situation felt predetermined, yet he had clearly made a good choice in caring for a blind dog. Seehausen Seconds were at work. His chemo-pal had taught him that. Cancer had paved the way. Believing he was beginning to get a grasp on his life, Warren also began to believe he was happy. One hot day in July changed that.

It was a Sunday. Stu and Gloria had invited Warren to their condo for grilled steaks. Warren wore a Hawaiian shirt, white cotton slacks and sandals. His gray hair was just long enough to comb to the side. Before heading out he checked his weight. It was 195, twenty pounds more than his lowest point. He felt good.

What he saw in front of a liquor store that day should have gained Warren's attention. He had stopped to buy a bottle of wine, a chewy Cabernet to complement the porterhouse steaks waiting at the condo. When he jumped out of the Lexus he spotted a rusty pick-up truck. In the bed of the truck sat an old man. He looked Native American, was shirtless, and seemed to be looking in Warren's direction. Fascinated, Warren took a few steps toward the old man. The Indian had dark leathery skin. Silver and turquoise earrings hung from each ear and a matching necklace draped from his wrinkled neck. About five feet from the truck Warren stopped.

"Do I know you?" Warren asked. He realized he was acting like a fool, but he couldn't resist the question.

The old man's piercing eyes seemed to glisten in the sun. A warm smile exposed several gaps in his teeth. He gave no sign that he heard or understood Warren's query. Then he used a hand to make a slow wave in front of his chest, as though he was canceling any connection between himself and his questioner. Warren somehow understood that the short interaction was over and so with a little nod of his head he retreated. His mind spinning with memory flashes, Warren entered the liquor store and made his purchase. When he exited he found that the pick-up had driven off. Or disappeared. The experience seemed to him something of a warning, but other than that he had no clue as to why it meant so much to him. By the time he got to Stu's condo building he had almost forgotten it. He took the elevator to the 12th floor and, as was his custom, walked in the apartment without knocking. Gloria was in the kitchen tossing a salad. She called her greeting while pointing to the balcony. Stu was out there presiding over his gas grill and talking on his cell phone. Warren joined him.

"Today?" Stu asked. "Can't it wait until tomorrow?" As he talked he handed a long bar-b-que tong to Warren, who understood that he was now in charge of the steaks on the grill. "Can I at least enjoy a steak with my friend and wife?" Stu continued. The man looked exasperated. "Fine. I'll be there in an hour," he said before hanging up.

"What's up Gottlieb?" Warren asked.

"They've got a heart for me. They want to do the transplant today."

"Christ. Why the rush?"

"Beats me. Anyway, I've got to meet a team of surgeons at UNMC in an hour. And get this: no steak for me."

Warren looked at the three hearty cuts of meat that sizzled on the grill, flipping the one that appeared to need it. Just then Gloria joined the men on the balcony and heard the news. She gave her husband a quick kiss and a reassuring hug and then turned to Warren saying, "Help yourself to a steak and salad, but please be a friend and put our steaks in the fridge after they cool."

"You're not going to eat?" Warren asked.

"I'm going to the hospital with Stu," Gloria said as she retreated into the condo. "I've got to change clothes," she told Stu. "Won't take but a minute."

Gloria's exit left the old friends alone. Their eyes met and an understanding rose out of shared trepidation, the same insight that had preceded pivotal exams and interviews for positions throughout their lives together. Warren spoke first. "You'll breeze through this, Gottlieb," he said.

"Do you think they know what I used to do for a living?" Stu joked.

Warren laughed. "What better way to deal with the cold heart of a medical malpractice attorney than to replace it," he said. He extended a hand for a shake, the men farted, and that was that. They were ready for the next test.

A while later Warren found himself alone in the condo. As he sat at the chrome and glass dining table feasting on the porterhouse he surveyed the cozy place. When Margie died he had considered selling his Dundee home and buying a space like the one he sat in. Cancer had put a hold on that plan. Now a blind dog held him back. Theo required his environment to be exactly as he remembered it to be. A change would devastate him.

The bottle of Cabernet was nearly empty at the end of the meal and Warren thought it prudent to take a nap before heading to the hospital to check up on his old friend. The thought of a DUI brought back a memory of driving under the influence of marijuana. The experience seemed to belong to another lifetime. As he stretched out on a sofa he thought of Naomi. She also belonged in that other lifetime. He fell asleep in a minute. Eventually he began to dream. The old Indian was back in the truck.

"I do know you," Warren said in his dream. He walked up to the bed of the rusty pick-up truck and stared at the old man, whose appearance was unchanged from the encounter at the liquor store. The Indian again waved a hand in front of his bare chest but this time spoke.

"I am sorry. Your cancer has returned," the old man told Warren.

"What? No. My tests..."

"I am sorry. Vani nisa a ro."

Warren spotted a funnel cloud in the distance. There was no question it was headed straight for them. The wind picked up. The tornado was on them in an instant, sweeping the truck and the Indian into the stormy sky. Warren was left standing alone. When he awoke he had a headache. When he stood there was a twinge of pain in his back, something he had not suffered for weeks. When he drove to the hospital he tried to remember his dream. He failed.

XVIII

The clock in the UNMC waiting room, an old fashioned analog, read 17 past 2. That it was a morning hour was painfully obvious to those sitting in the stuffy space. Warren and Gloria sat next to one another on hard plastic chairs waiting for news of Stu and his heart transplant. Ten hours had passed since he went under the knife. There was no telling how much longer they would have to wait.

Warren's back was killing him. He reasoned that the pain was to be expected, seeing that the chair was hard and bare and that he was no spring chicken. To pass the time he walked the halls of UNMC, an exercise that gave temporary relief from the backache. He visited the cafeteria to buy two coffees and doughnuts. He had never liked coffee and this particular purchase reminded him why.

The long wait gave Warren a chance to reflect on the past year of his life. Ever since that funeral at the Dundee Methodist Church, the ceremony where he was haunted by the tuft of gray hair peeking over the purple lining of a coffin, and where he received an indecipherable text message in an ancient language, the pace of his life had accelerated. Margie died, his cancer showed up, he enjoyed his first sexual fling, he retired, his beloved dog went blind, and his best friend had a heart attack, retired from the practice of law, had married, and was now getting a new heart. What was next, he wondered?

As he sat next to Gloria he glanced several times at the ugly skin blemish on her neck. Lacking anything else to talk about he focused on the brown cigar shaped sore that he had learned was the result of the viola rubbing on her skin. "I've had a lot of cancer lore dumped on me recently," he began.

"I expect you have," Gloria commented. She wore an odd cap over her salt-and-pepper hair, a lightweight green thing with a small bill and yellow racing stripes. She also had on a cotton jacket, yoga pants and running shoes.

"I've been told that chronic irritation can cause cancer."

"What's your point?"

Warren pointed to Gloria's disfigurement. She understood instantly. "I'd rather die of cancer than lose the ability to play a decent viola," she said.

"Does Naomi feel the same way?"

"I'm sure she does."

"Have you heard from her since she moved to Boston?"

"We text each other."

"So, what does she have to say for herself?"

Gloria stood up and began a series of stretches. She was very fit for a middle-aged woman. Warren was particularly impressed with the definition in her calves. "As you know Naomi isn't one for small talk," she said as she flexed her torso over a raised leg.

"Does she mention me?" Warren asked. He knew he sounded a bit self-centered but it was two-thirty in the morning. He felt he could give in to a little self-indulgence.

"Actually, she did."

"And?"

"She asked about your health."

"And what did you tell her?"

"Just what Stu has told me about you. You're in remission, right?"

Warren was about to launch into the details of his illness, the onset, the spread, the treatments, and the unexpected resolution of his metastatic lesions. He felt as though he was referring to a terrible summer at camp, bad memories that thankfully were of things long past. But before he got started a surgeon suddenly appeared.

"Mrs. Gottlieb?" the man began. He was in sweat-stained scrubs.

"I'm Gloria Chase, Stuart Gottlieb's wife," Gloria insisted.

"Oh. I apologize."

"How is my husband?"

The surgeon sighed and shifted his weight. "I'm afraid I've got some bad news," he said.

Hearing this prompted Warren to stand at Gloria's side and place a supporting arm around her shoulders. He could feel her trembling. Truth be told he wished there was someone to steady him. The surgeon went on with his account.

"The transplant went well, but when we converted from bypass support to the new heart Mr. Gottlieb's neuro signs crashed."

"What are you saying?" Gloria asked. Warren pulled her closer. He was afraid she might faint.

"Mr. Gottlieb has suffered an intracranial bleed. I'm afraid it was a massive bleed. I'm sorry."

"Is he alive?" Warren asked.

"He is. But there's little chance of a recovery."

"Christ," Warren murmured. The surgeon's words brought back a bitter memory, the autopsy findings on Margie that also showed bleeding in her brain. He understood that her chemo was to blame for this, but Stu's case involved no such medication. "What caused the bleeding?" he asked the physician.

"We're trying to find that out," the surgeon said.

"May we see him?" Gloria asked just before she broke out in tears.

"Of course. Follow me."

Minutes later Warren and Gloria stood at Stu's bedside. He was unconscious and his breathing depended on a respirator. Tubes ran everywhere. There was nothing to be done but stare at the man. Gloria cried. Warren fought back tears, though several made their way down his cheeks. Just then the surgeon approached. "Does Mr. Gottlieb have an advanced directive?" he asked.

I know for a fact that he does," Warren answered. "We had ours drawn up on the same day."

"So he's declared what he wants done in the event of a catastrophic health event?"

"We both specified that we do not want life support."

Gloria reached over the side rail of the hospital bed and smoothed a hand over Stu's bald head. "You poor man," she whimpered. As Warren looked on he felt grateful that she at least would be spared having to make the horrible decision to pull the plug on her husband.

"Are you going to turn off the respirator?" Warren asked the doctor.

"We're obliged to run a couple tests first. If they confirm brain death we'll stop life support."

Warren nodded, shook the surgeon's hand and joined Gloria at the bedrail. Stu's face was swollen, his eyes were taped shut, and there was saliva running out of the edge of his mouth. He looked ready to die. "Goodbye old friend," Warren whispered. He felt as though his insides had been tied in knots.

When it was time to leave Warren kept a close eye on Gloria. She had stopped crying but looked very unsteady. Without speaking they made it to the parking garage and stood together for a moment next to Stu's BMW. "Warren. I'm lost," Gloria said. He had no words to match hers but admitted to himself that his world had suddenly been reduced to shambles. Crying again, Gloria tacitly asked for Warren's shoulder. As he held her he felt ashamed in worrying if her neck sore would stain his Hawaiian shirt. It was a silly moment he normally would've shared with Gottlieb over lunch. That his best friend was gone was nearly too much to bear.

In time Gloria regained some composure. "I guess I'll go home," she said as she pulled the car keys from a small purse. With a push of a button she unlocked the BMW but before she got in she had a question for Warren.

"You've been through this," she began. "What the hell do I do now?"

"You keep living," Warren said. "What else is there to do?"

*   *   *

A week later Warren went to Gloria's condo at her invitation. Stu Gottlieb's obituary lay on the dining table, a reminder that his funeral was two days before. Warren remembered the day his friend had asked him if he had ever been to a Jewish funeral and then declared that he would be the first to die. Lucky guess Gottlieb, Warren thought.

Naomi, who had flown in from Boston to console her fellow violist, was busy preparing her eggplant casserole. It was she who requested Warren's presence, a fact that both pleased and worried him. He felt honored that she still found him desirable but a misgiving pestered him. Though in remission from cancer he feared that the mere history of harboring that disease would render him impotent. Naturally he remembered how Naomi had made adjustments around his debilitated states when undergoing cancer treatments, but now that he was back on his feet he wished to do his part when it came to sex. "Wonderful to see you again, Naomi," Warren said as they traded a kiss.

"Please give me some time to prepare dinner," Naomi said. Her stern words surprised Warren. They were hardly what he expected from his old lover. But to be accommodating he decided to join Gloria who was out on the balcony. On the way he grabbed a beer from the fridge, disappointed that "chick beer" was the only option.

"One of Stu's heart surgeons called me this morning," Gloria told Warren the instant they were together. The mighty Missouri River flowed in the near distance. Gloria held a glass of white wine. Warren took a swig of his Michelob Ultra.

"I trust he found out what happened to Stu," Warren said.

"He called it an intraoperative miscalculation."

"There's a world class euphemism."

"He said too much blood thinner was given. The bleeding happened before they caught the mistake."

"UNMC heart surgeons are the last people I'd expect to make a mistake," Warren said.

"Poor Stu," Gloria muttered.

"Are you going to file suit?"

"No way. Life is too short. And suing somebody wouldn't bring my Stu back."

Gazing at the river water and then out over Iowa farmland, Warren was seized, once again, by the cold fact that his long-time best friend was dead and gone. Memories flooded in, such as Stu in his college afro or watching him devour a pastrami on rye in Stogies. It was then that Warren gave out a subtle but unmistakable laugh. "Did Stu ever tell you how we said goodbye to one another?"

"Let me guess. You had a secret handshake."

"We farted."

"Oh for God's sake. I could've gone a life time without knowing that."

Gloria and Warren exchanged a few stories about their lives with Stu, but eventually their visit was cut short by Naomi's voice which carried from inside the condo. As always, it was soft and thickly accented. Warren believed she said that dinner was ready. A minute later the trio sat at the glass and chrome dining table on which sat a steaming casserole, a dish of hummus and a stack of pita bread. It was the same meal Naomi once prepared for Warren the first time he visited the "Sugar Shack."

"I am very sorry for the loss you two have suffered," Naomi began. "I hope this food will offer a small measure of comfort."

"Thank you for taking the trouble to be here, Naomi," Gloria said. "It means a lot to me."

"And how is your health Warren?" Naomi asked. She was already into her plate of casserole.

"I just had a fresh batch of tests. I should hear from my doctor any day now."

"I hope you get good news," Naomi said.

"You're not the only one," Warren replied. Somewhere inside he knew the news would be rotten.

"How are you finding Boston?" Warren asked, seeking a change of subject.

"It is cold. And the symphony conductor is a stick-in-the-mud."

"Really?" Gloria reacted.

"It is so," Naomi said. Her mouth was full of food. "It is enough to make me want to return to your side, Gloria." Then, suddenly, Naomi stood. "I wish to show both of you something," she said as she grabbed the bottom hem of her blouse and the belt line of her skirt and pulled them apart. Exposed was a plastic bag that appeared attached to the left side of her abdomen.

"What is that?" Gloria asked.

"It is what is known as a colostomy bag," Naomi explained. "You see, my colon cancer returned and…"

"Oh Naomi. Why didn't you tell me?" Gloria cried.

"Your husband was ill. I didn't want to trouble you."

As for Warren, he was beginning to believe all his dear friends were destined to die before his cancer did him in. "Christ, Naomi. Not you too," he said.

Returning to her meal Naomi began eating with gusto. "Death is part of living. Do not grieve for me," she said. "Gloria, do you have any grated Parmesan?" she added.

An hour later the trio had consumed three and a half bottles of decent Chardonnays. Warren couldn't believe how care free he felt. He expected Stu's passing and hearing of Naomi's cancer to put him in the dumps. But he remembered that just being in Naomi's presence usually lightened his heart. This afternoon was no exception. "I've been dying to ash you something, Naomi," he slurred, instantly realizing that he had downed too much wine.

"Yes?" Naomi said.

"It's kind of...personal."

"I share my life with my friend Gloria. You may ask me anything in her presence."

"Well, you remember the day we were in my Lexus in front of your home. It was evening but there was plenty of daylight. You gave me...how should I put this?"

"I gave you a blow job," Naomi said.

"Exactly. And as I remember a classical tune was on the radio."

"The Minute Waltz."

"Exactly. So my question to you is: did you time your performance to last one minute?"

Gloria spit a little wine before erupting into a belly laugh. "God, that is so you, Naomi," she said. Naomi began laughing as well. They held hands as they guffawed together. For Warren he felt just as excluded as when Gabriela and Gaby spoke Spanish in his presence. But he knew one thing for certain: Naomi Zycyz was easily the most unique individual he had ever known.

* * *

The next day Warren sat next to his garden pool nursing a hangover. The fact that his back ached as much as his head disturbed him. He was lying on the lounger when his cell phone rang. "Warren, we've got problems," Dr. McHale began.

"I knew it," Warren whispered.

"What's that?"

"Nothing. Give me the bad news."

"You've got metastasis to your brain, vertebral column and liver. Dammit Warren I thought we had this thing licked."

Warren swallowed hard. "My liver?" he squeaked. Somehow he understood that having cancer in the liver was a very bad thing.

"I have to pass your case along to the oncology board but I know you're in for more radiation and chemotherapy."

"Christ Alvin, I don't know if I can go through that shit again."

"Then don't."

Warren was stunned by his doctor's words. Was McHale giving up on him he wondered? The death of Warren Westing meant the retirement of Alvin McHale. Foregoing treatment made sense. For one of them.

"I'm not sure what you mean," Warren finally said.

"Narcotics will keep you comfortable. I'll add two medications to prevent the mets in your brain from causing mischief. And UNMC has an excellent hospice service."

"Hospice. That's for the terminally ill," Warren said almost shouting. This time it was McHale's turn to hold his tongue. "Isn't it?" Warren added, expecting a reply. None came. Warren went on. "Look Doc, I'm not ready to throw in the towel just yet."

"Fine," McHale said. "You know the drill. Your treatment schedules will be sent to you by email. How are you fixed for pain pills?"

Warren began to feel irritated at his physician's casual attitude toward his illness. The more he thought about McHale's suggestion that they give up cancer treatment for mere comfort measures the more betrayed and isolated he felt. "Did you used to abandon all your patients?" he blurted.

"Look Warren, we have to be realistic here. Your chances of living another year are not good."

"Then you better get me some more Oxys."

"Will do. And I'll meet you in the chemo room when you get your first infusion."

After the grim conversation ended Warren lay back on the lounger and reached under it to pet Theo who had assumed his traditional shaded spot. "Want to trade places boy?" Warren asked. "You can be the man with cancer for awhile and I'll be the blind dog." Theo whimpered. Then Warren fell asleep. He was wakened an hour later by a familiar voice.

"Boss? Wake up Boss," Gabriela urged. "You've had too much sun."

As Warren's eyes popped open he saw Gabriela's outline standing over him. She had purposely blocked the July sun from hitting his face. A bolt of pain flashed from his back when he tried to sit up. "Let me help you," Gabriela offered as she wrapped her strong arms around his torso and pulled him to a sitting position.

"I'm glad to see you," Warren confessed. "How was Mexico City?"

"Mama's funeral was very nice. Most of the family was there. And my father is now in a clean nursing home."

"An affordable one I hope."

"My whole family will chip in. There shouldn't be a problem keeping him there."

Warren rose to his feet. "I just got some bad news," he told Gabriela.

"Your cancer is back?"

"Big time."

"I am so sorry Boss. I thought you were out of the woods."

"Me too."

"Well now it's doubly important to eat well, take your supplements and exercise."

"I'm going to need more pot. I've got to go through more chemo." he said.

"I'll get you some. And Boss, I've decided to move in with you, if the offer is still open."

"It sure is," Warren said. Struggling to his feet, he faced Gabriela. They embraced. It was as natural as the sunlight. As they held each other, Gabriela began to sing softly. Once again she sang in Mixtec, the language of her childhood. And once again Warren enjoyed her smells, her strong arms, and her ample bosom. It was the best thing that had happened to him all day.

IXX

Gabriela moved into 41 Crestwood without a hitch. Warren received his treatment schedule and was set to begin radiation to his brain and a third round of chemotherapy. He prepared himself to lose his hair again, suffer more fatigue and nausea, and generally feel awful. Fortunately he had a substantial supply of marijuana that Gabriela provided. He didn't share with her that he had been approved for medical marijuana because he preferred the real stuff. He also didn't tell her that he had a stash of OxyContin. If she was suspicious about his use of narcotics she didn't say so, though Warren got the distinct impression that she was staying vigilant regarding narcotic side effects, particularly diminished mental acuity. To hide his use of Oxys Warren made a point of speaking clearly and carefully focusing on conversational points. This effort was as exhausting as enduring cancer treatment but he considered it necessary. After all he was as dependent on Gabriela as he was on his pain pills.

It was mid-August when Warren began brain radiation and chemotherapy. The morning he returned to the chemo room he found his old chemo pal Jim Gordon hooked up to an IV. "Hey Warren," the old man called. "The Big C got its hooks in you again I'm guessin'."

"I'm afraid so," Warren replied as he took a seat and allowed a technician to clean his port. Minutes later a nurse inserted an IV needle and four hours of infusion began. "Any word on Professor Seehausen?" he asked Gordo.

"You ain't heard?" Gordo said as he handed Warren a copy of the Omaha World-Herald. On the front page was an article about a local Creighton University professor's nomination for a Nobel Prize in physics, one Clark Seehausen. His obituary was on page twelve.

"Wow," Warren uttered.

"Not bad for a guy with…what does he have again?"

"Multiple Myeloma."

Gordo snorted. "All those names. Why don't they just call it what it is. Cancer. It's gonna kill you anyway."

"We're still here," Warren said, though his heart wasn't in it.

"Barely. You ever think about writin' your own obituary?"

"Never. How about you?"

"Already done it. Even picked out a picture of myself."

Writing one's own obit began to intrigue Warren. Summarizing your life seemed a daunting task. Year of birth, career, survivors, preferred charities. The date of death, naturally, would have to be filled in by someone else. And then there was the option of a picture. Which one would he choose? How old would he wish to look? He turned to Gordo to ask his advice but the old man was already asleep, likely the result of taking a handful of Oxy's. Sighing, Warren opened his lap and started a Sudoku game marked "extremely difficult." He solved the puzzle just before Dr. McHale showed up. The spry man moved directly to the IV bag hanging above Warren's head. Then, after making note of the type of chemo infusion, he used a stethoscope to examine his only patient's heart and lungs. His questions came last.

"Any belly pain, Warren?" McHale asked.

"No. But my back hurts like hell."

"Any dizziness, double vision, headaches?"

"Nope."

"Good. Now let's hope we get as good a result as we did from the last treatment."

"Alvin, the last go-around tore my guts up."

"But we got what I could've have sworn was a remission. And you can live with a little nausea and weight loss, right Warren?"

There it is, Warren thought, that damned dismissiveness.

"Are you with me Warren?" McHale asked as he wrote orders.

"Sometimes I think you want me dead," Warren spit. His words stopped McHale dead in his tracks.

"What an awful thing to say," McHale said. For once the frenetic man wasn't fidgeting with his bow tie or cleaning his glasses. His expression showed his dejection. Warren could see that his accusation had stung his doctor.

"Sorry Alvin," Warren said in retreat. "It must be the cancer talking."

"I hope so," McHale said. Then, without another word, he left the chemo room. Me and my big mouth, Warren thought.

Weeks passed and Warren's treatments finally ended. Once again his hair fell out and he went back to shaving his scalp. Fatigue had returned as did nausea, the latter fairly well contained by marijuana. Narcotics continued to offer adequate pain relief. By autumn he weighed 175, a far cry from his portly 235 just fifteen months before. It was fortunate that he was retired and that he didn't need to buy smaller business suits. Still he spent a pretty penny on shirts and slacks that fit him. One morning after dressing he happened to hear Gabriela at work in the kitchen. His appetite had not yet returned and he had little taste for the hearty breakfasts she always made. To give himself the best chance of consuming what she would surely put before him Warren smoked some pot in his bedroom. Then he took an Oxy. Somewhere in this stretch of his life he admitted to himself that he was a bonafide drug addict. Pain and gastrointestinal woes were things to control but they were not any longer the reasons he used marijuana and narcotics.

"Buenos dias," Warren called when he walked into the kitchen.

"Good morning Boss," Gabriela returned. "Your vitamins and protein powder are waiting for you."

"Yummy. What's for breakfast?"

"Breakfast burritos. I bought the eggs, veggies and beef at the farmers' market. I made the the tortillas myself."

"Aren't you the nature girl."

"After breakfast we'll start on level #2 yoga."

Warren groaned. Yoga always stirred up his back pain. Sometimes even his pain pills failed to quell it, meaning he had to spend the day lying down. Though he was chronically ill spending the day on the couch felt to him like a waste of time. "I'm going to take Theo for a walk," he told Gabriela as he downed his supplements.

"Fine. Your food will be waiting for you."

Minutes later Theo was in his harness and Warren held the short leash, a design meant to tell the blind dog that his master was close by.

The harness bore a clear message, a sign that read BLIND DOG. These days they covered precisely the same ground each day, taking the right-sided sidewalk to the Methodist Church, crossing the street, then back home with Warren always between his dog and the sparse traffic of the quiet neighborhood. If they met other walkers, especially those with dogs, Warren called out a warning indicating Theo's blindness. By now most neighbors knew of the Great Dane's condition and made sure he wasn't startled. The walk took ten minutes on the dot. When done Warren removed the leash and hung it on a wooden hat tree in the foyer. It was a signal to Theo to head for his food bowl that sat precisely to the left of his wire kennel.

Done with feeding his dog Warren headed back to the kitchen. The marijuana had roused his appetite and he finished one burrito without a problem. Gabriela ate with him, but not before laying out the several vitamins and protein shake for her Boss. "What did your doctor say about your condition?" she asked Warren.

"McHale's exact words were: let's be happy with our even keel." Warren replied.

"What does that mean?"

"The scans still show cancer but it's not in new places."

"I guess that's a good thing. Are you up for another Thanksgiving dinner? It's only a few weeks away."

"Why not. Will Gaby be there?"

"And Edgar."

"Damn."

"Boss, they're engaged."

Warren groaned, muttering, "I know, I know."

"Take your supplements," Gabriela demanded as she cleared the breakfast dishes. As she stood at the sink she had more to say. "Gaby isn't pregnant yet. The poor girl wants a child so badly."

Recalling the last conversation he had with the young Latina, Warren could hear her odd phrase, "going for a pregnancy." He had to wonder if Gaby had availed herself of the services of her place of employment, the Omaha Fertility Center. Gabriela's next words satisfied his curiosity. "She and Edgar are thinking about *in vitro* fertilization," she reported.

"I hear that's exshpensif," Warren said. He realized he had just slurred a word, but hoped Gabriela hadn't noticed. He didn't get his wish. The woman turned toward him with a deep squint on her face. "Expensive," Warren carefully repeated.

"You better not be lying to me, Boss," Gabriela warned.

"I've got cancer in my brain. Give a guy a break."

* * *

Weeks flew by and in no time it was Thanksgiving Day. It was late morning, when on a walk with Theo, Warren saw a shiny car pull into his drive. He knew the make and model instantly. It was a 1957 Chevrolet Impala. The chrome looked new and the paint job, a bright blue, looked professionally done. Edgar got out of the driver's seat. Gaby popped out from the opposite side. She was holding a glass dish covered by aluminum foil and waved to Warren before hustling inside 41 Crestwood. Edgar strolled toward Warren. The sight reminded Warren of how similar the young man was to himself at that age. Those days are over for me, Warren thought.

"Nice ride," Warren called to Edgar.

"It's my first of what I hope to be a collection of vintage cars," Edgar said as he approached. Just then Theo growled and Warren almost lost his grip on the leash. "Whoa!" Edgar yelled.

"Back away, Edgar," Warren warned.

"No problem."

"My dog is blind."

Edgar moved to one side to read what was on the harness. "You need to re-think your signage," he scolded. "From head on you can't know you have a blind dog."

Warren just grunted a reluctant assent. He knew Edgar made a good point but was unwilling to give the guy any credit. "Why was Gaby in such a hurry?" Warren asked.

"She's anxious to put her dessert in the freezer," Edgar explained. "She was on my case the whole way over here to drive faster. I'm lucky I didn't get a ticket."

"You sound annoyed," Warren said, happy to finally be on the offensive.

"That's not the half of it, dude," Edgar muttered.

"Oh?"

"She's constantly on my ass about having a baby. It's driving me nuts. At first it wasn't so bad. She'd take her temperature to pinpoint ovulation and we'd have sex. But now she's talking about some fancy procedure..."

"*In vitro* fertilization," Warren offered.

"That's it. Do you know how expensive that is?"

"I know it's pricy," Warren said. Just then Theo whimpered. "Come on inside, Edgar. I have to kennel my dog and you look like you could use a beer."

"Now you're talking. Lead the way, dude."

A while later the men sat in the den watching an NFL game. Edgar drank a Michelob Ultra, Warren a Sam Adams Octoberfest. Enticing aromas began to waft from the kitchen as the Latinas were hard at work preparing the customary turkey, dressing, yams and cranberry sauce, and spicing up the meal with sweet corn tomalitos and calabacitos. Then, out of the blue, Edgar spouted his comment. "Gaby tells me you have cancer," he said. Warren felt as though his privacy was being violated. But he also considered that Edgar had just shared a detail of his sex life with him.

"That is true, unfortunately," Warren confessed. "I've had three round of chemo and two rounds of radiation."

"Is that a lot?"

"I think it is. But I know an old man who has had continuous treatment for three years."

"How are you faring if you don't mind me asking?"

Warren did mind. The last thing he wanted to think about was his lingering cancer. "If you must know I still have a few sites," he muttered.

"Sorry dude. I was just curious."

Warren's irritation got the best of him causing him to make a rather insulting comment. "For a man your age you talk like a teenager," he fired a Edgar. He was surprised that his words produced no effect on his guest.

"All my fraternity brothers talk like me," Edgar said. "It's a tradition we agreed to honor all of our lives."

"How cute," Warren said. He was trying hard to get under the skin of the financial advisor. He was failing.

Eventually Gabriela called the men to the dining room. To help ensure that he would be able to enjoy the food Warren visited his bedroom for a hit of pot. Unfortunately, he overdid it. When he joined his guests he found, to his chagrin, that Edgar had taken the seat at the head of the table, and because of his marijuana high his words came out garbled. His exact words were, "My chair. Mine."

"Ay-yi-yi," Gabriela exclaimed. "Are you stoned Boss?"

"Stoned?" Edgar exclaimed. "Is there pot in this house? If so I'd like some."

Warren didn't reply. More accurately he couldn't reply. Giving up the attempt to take back his head seat he settled for a place opposite Gaby. Gabriela placed the Thanksgiving turkey in front of him and then sat opposite Edgar. Warren became aware of the recitation of a prayer and when it ended he trained his eyes on Gaby. Perhaps it was the marijuana that had him believe, at that moment, that the young woman was the most beautiful creature he had ever seen. "Boss?" a voice called from his right. "Boss?"

"Hmm?" Warren uttered as he turned his head toward Gabriela.

"Can you carve the turkey?" Gabriela asked.

Of course I can, Warren thought, though no words came out of his mouth. He stood, grabbed the carving knife and a fork, and started in.

"Dude, you're doing that all wrong," Edgar said. Indeed, Warren had cut off one wing. But Edgar's criticism irritated Warren. He plowed on, cutting off the other wing and then started on a leg. As he sawed he pulled on the leg, which suddenly parted from the turkey. The appendage was well buttered and because of his yanking motion he lost grip on the drumstick. The leg flew across the table and landed in Gaby's lap.

"My new dress!" Gaby cried as she lifted the turkey part like she was holding a dead mouse.

Gabriela hurried Gaby off to the kitchen to help her clean her dress. Warren kept at it, cutting at the other leg and then slicing at the breast. Edgar looked on with a grin on his face. At one point he said, "What a completely fucked up mess."

Frustrated, Warren threw down the utensils. His head was swimming and his vision became bleary. Suddenly he had no taste for the plenty that lay before him. And he didn't wish to hear another word from the man on his left. Without a word he left the dining room and made his way to his bed. There, he took an Oxy and stretched out for a nap.

In Warren's dream he sat in the Methodist Church attending a colleague's funeral. To his right was the coffin and peering over its purple lining was a tuft of gray hair. Stu sat to his left but was replaced by the old bare chested Indian man who walked to the coffin and looked in. Warren followed him. Lying in the coffin was himself, Warren Westing. When he woke his bedroom was dark and he truly didn't know, at least for a moment, whether he was dead or alive.

"You're finally awake," Gabriela said at the bedroom door. She moved to the bed and snapped on a lamp. That was when she spotted the amber vial of pain pills. "What are these?" she said as she read the label. "Boss, have you been lying to me? Are you on narcotics?" Warren had nothing to say. He had been found out. He only hoped Gabriela wouldn't leave him. Lying still, he waited for her to say something. He didn't roll toward her but listened to her breathing. A good minute later she left the room, saying, "Tomorrow we're going to have a talk. And tomorrow you're going to tell me who Naomi is."

Warren felt relieved to be alone He used the bathroom, stripped down to his boxer shorts and got into bed. Out of habit he reached for his bottle of pain pills. The bottle was gone. With a sigh he turned off the lamp and tried his best to fall asleep.

XX

The morning after Thanksgiving Warren met with Dr. McHale in the out-patient facilities of UNMC. McHale had the latest test results. He also carried a cool demeanor. "Your mets are remaining stable and there are no new lesions," the doctor advised. "I think we should sit tight for now. Any questions?"

Warren had no trouble understanding why his physician had lost his perkiness. "Alvin, I am truly sorry for my remark that day in the chemo room," he said. "Once again, I apologize."

"And once again I accept your apology," McHale said, though as he spoke he seemed to avert his eyes from his only patient. Warren guessed that though accusing the doctor of wishing him dead was inappropriate at best, the comment was becoming more accurate by the day.

"I need more pain pills," Warren said.

"No problem," McHale said as he pulled out a prescription pad and began writing. Seconds later he handed the script to Warren saying, "I'll have the dates and times of the next round of tests emailed to you. Have a nice month." Then he walked out of the room.

Disappointed that he had failed to win back the friendship of his doctor Warren nevertheless appreciated having an OxyContin prescription in his possession. He headed directly to his Walgreen's pharmacy where he handed his script to the young woman with the bad case of acne. As always, after reading what the prescription called for, she called for the head pharmacist. And as always the suspicious grump insisted on calling Dr. McHale to verify the legitimacy of the document. When Warren finally got his pills he couldn't help leveling a wise crack. "Still listening to Jesus music I see," pointing to the old radio on a back shelf. Indeed, a hymn crackled from the relic.

"That, sir, is none of your concern," the pharmacist said.

"But you don't hesitate to make my pain pills your concern."

"Narcotics are…"

"Yes, I know. But I've been filling my prescriptions here for months. It's time you understand that I need my pills, that Dr. McHale really does write for them, and that I do not sell them on the street. Christ man, get on board."

"How many times to I have to tell you that I find that language offensive."

Warren snickered. "Like I give a damn," he said as he wheeled and walked away. "I'll pay for these up front," he called over his shoulder.

A while later Warren pulled into his driveway. He used the garage entry, stopping along the way to hide his vial of pain pills in his golf bag. He then walked in the kitchen. Gabriela was waiting for him. She sat at the butcher block island counter with her hands folded in front of her. And she was squinting. "Talk time?" Warren joked. Gabriela's expression didn't change.

"I've done some thinking, Boss," Gabriela said as Warren plopped on a stool. "I have to assume you're a narcotics addict by now. This business of using pot for your appetite is probably a lie as well. If I wasn't so implanted in this home and dependent on what you pay me I'd be done with you. But at my age I don't think I could start over. So here," she said as she tossed him the vial of pills she had confiscated the night before. He caught the vial with one hand. "Take your pills. I won't stop you," she said.

Gabriela's concession had a strange impact on Warren. It seemed to him as though she was giving up on him, much like Dr. McHale had make him feel as though he was being dismissed. "But we can still rely on supplements and yoga, right?" he pleaded.

"You're calling the shots now, Boss. I just work here. But I still want to know who this Naomi is."

"She's a friend who has cancer," Warren said. He didn't completely understand why he felt it necessary to withhold the whole truth, but he also didn't understand the complexities of the female mind. A partial truth seemed prudent. "Why do you care?" he asked her.

"It was all those messages she used to leave for you at work. It felt like you two shared a secret."

"Nope. No secrets."

"Hmm."

Just then a loud bang came from the window over the sink. Warren knew what had happened. Rushing outside to the back yard he found a male cardinal lying on the ground. He picked up the bird hoping that the impact against the window hadn't killed it. It was dead. "Enough of this," he whispered. Grabbing the sunflower seed feeder he headed for the rear of the yard. There he hung the feeder on a low tree branch. He knelt and buried the cardinal in a pile of mulch once used by Margie. It had been a while since he thought of her. The memory reminded him that her ashes were still in her walk-in closet. Then he thought of Stu Gottlieb. He missed his best friend. So much death, Warren thought. Then, before standing, he began to cry. He knew he was next.

* * *

A week before Christmas, Warren dressed for an Omaha Symphony fund raiser that Gloria Chase, Stu's widow, had asked him to attend. Standing in his walk-in closet in his boxers, he uncovered a navy blue suit that he had recently purchased. His first look at the suit worried him, as it looked far too small. He reminded himself that the thing was tailored for him. When he put it on he came to grips, once again, with how much weight he had lost.

It was early evening when Warren descended the stairs. After walking and kenneling Theo, he waited in the kitchen for Gabriela, his guest for the event. She appeared wearing the same outfit she wore the day they had dined together in Latino Village. "I know that dress," Warren commented.

"It's my favorite. Is it cold out?"

"There's a breeze. You'll need a coat."

A bit later Warren and Gabriela sat in the Lexus cruising toward the Omaha Civic Auditorium, the site of the fund raiser. In the short time it took to get to the destination a wintry blast of sleet came out of the darkness and covered the area with a thin layer of ice. Warren regretted not wearing a coat over his new suit and hoped the unexpected storm would abate as quickly as it appeared. "The weatherman didn't say anything about this," he complained.

"This is Nebraska, Boss," Gabriela said with a sigh. "Sometimes I wonder what I'm doing here."

"What are you doing here?" Warren asked, chagrined that he didn't know the answer.

"It's a long story, Boss."

"Oh?"

"I'll tell it to you someday. The sleet is letting up. Let's get inside before it returns."

Before climbing out of the car Warren took a pain pill. Gabriela clucked her disapproval but didn't say a word. Warren's first step on the parking lot pavement was a slippery one. As always, he was terrified of falling, acutely aware of how easy it was for a cancerous bone to break. Luckily Gabriela shared his concern and came to his aid with a supporting arm. The walk to the entrance of the auditorium was a slow and careful process, but eventually they arrived at a well lit and salted area. They separated to negotiate a revolving door and reunited in the lobby. Warren took Gabriela's coat and checked it. As he did so he brushed a few icy bits of sleet from his suit and off his bald scalp.

The main hall of the civic center was decorated in rich, even gaudy, Christmas themes. A three-dimensional Santa sat in his sleigh with a large bag of presents and the reindeer seemed to be ready to fly off the stage, this display sitting above empty chairs meant for a promised symphony performance. To the left were tables of warmed food and to the right was a bar. Warren led Gabriela to the booze. His mouth was dry and he craved a cold beer. They found Gloria Chase at the bar sipping on a glass of club soda. She looked good in her black sequined pants suit, or so Warren thought. The outfit did justice to her runner's physique. He wondered how she was bearing up without Stu, hoping she was getting along better than he was. The fact that Gottlieb wasn't at the party deeply saddened him.

"Thank you for coming, Warren," Gloria said when she spotted him, offering a cordial hug and a quick buss on the cheek. She then stepped back and glanced at Gabriela, obviously waiting for an introduction. Warren did the honors, keeping an eye on Gloria's reaction. It was clear to him that she assumed she was looking at the new woman in his life. And in a way she was.

"Well, enjoy yourselves," Gloria said after the introduction. "The drinks and the food are on the house though I will ask you to tip generously. The symphony is going to play in about an hour from now..."

"Set me and my boy up with two Lone Stars," the voice bellowed. The corpulent man at the bar in the Western-style suit, cowboy boots, and white Stetson hat was Billy Bob Richardson. Gar Young stood next to him. Gar had dressed for the occasion, shedding his fatigue jacket for an old corduroy coat and a string tie. His long hair looked as dirty as ever.

"Oh no," Warren muttered. He suddenly felt in need of that drink. "A white wine for you, Gabriela?" he asked as he shuffled toward a bartender.

"Por favor."

Just then Gloria threaded an arm around Warren's, saying, "I want you to meet our biggest donor." Seconds later he was standing in front of the most obnoxious man he had ever met. Gloria's introduction was cut short by another bellow.

"Ain't you the Yankee who was supposed to play golf against me and Gar at Osage Hills?" Billy Bob directed at Warren.

"I'm afraid so," Warren said.

"Where's the Jew?"

Warren stared at the large round red face under the white hat. A rage welled up inside him, his self-control compromised by the narcotic's dampening effect on inhibitions. Without hesitation he reached for an open bottle of red wine on the bar and dumped its contents on Billy Bob's Stetson. Red wine trickled over the hat brim onto the shoulders of the man's suit.

"Gall dang boy!" Billy Bob screamed as he wiped at the wetness. "Have you lost your gall dang mind?"

Warren glanced at Gloria. He guessed she wouldn't be pleased. His was right. Apparently desperate to right things she asked a bartender for a towel and began a feeble attempt at drying the suit. It was hopeless. The wine from the hat brim kept trickling on the shoulders foiling her efforts. Next, Warren looked at Gar Young who had an amused expression on his scarred face. Finally he found Gabriela, who looked shocked. At least she wasn't squinting.

"Do you know how much this here suit set me back?" Billy Bob said to anybody who was listening.

"I'm so sorry, Mr. Richardson," Gloria said.

"It ain't your fault honey. It's this Yankee here."

"His name was Stuart. Stuart Gottlieb," Warren said. He tried to keep his voice steady, trying not to slur his words.

"We're done here," Billy Bob shouted. "C'mon Gar."

As the men walked off, Gloria had words for Warren. "If that man stops donating to the symphony I will have your head," she hissed.

"Stu was your husband, for Chrissakes," Warren protested.

"Stu is gone. I still have my work," Gloria added. She threw the wine soaked towel on the bar and stormed off. Warren ordered a white wine and a beer and stood next to Gabriela as though nothing had transpired.

"That was mean," Gabriela commented.

"I despise that guy," Warren replied.

"I can tell."

"Let's get some food," Warren suggested as he offered Gabriela his arm. She accepted his invitation and threaded her arm around his. The couple made their way through a sizable stylishly dressed crowd to a long table of catered dishes. Warren chose a chicken breast in a mushroom sauce, au gratin potatoes, green beans and a warm roll, way too much food for a guy with cancer. Gabriela went for a thick slice of prime rib that she flavored with a dab of horseradish sauce. They were standing near the food line munching away when Gar Young showed up for a free meal. Notably, his friend Billy Bob Richardson was nowhere to be seen. Warren was surprised when Gar approached him.

"You don't know how many times I wanted to do what you did with that wine," Gar said to Warren. The man ate a chicken leg with his fingers and washed it down with a Lone Star beer.

"Why do you associate with that bastard?" Warren asked.

"Shit man, without him I'd probably be homeless."

"The rumor is you saved his fat ass in Vietnam."

"I don't want to talk about that, man."

Warren gazed at the gaunt figure standing in front of him. Gar still wore the stud earring in his left lobe. His deep facial scar was as prominent as ever. And he reeked of cigarettes. His presence brought Warren an odd memory. "Do you remember what you said about being struck by lightning?"

"What?" Gar asked.

"That day at Osage Hills Country Club. We were in the bar. A thunderstorm had canceled our golf match. I must have ducked at a crash of thunder because you asked me what I was afraid of."

"I don't remember so good."

"You asked me what I thought would happen to me if a bolt of lightning struck me."

"That sounds right."

"You had an answer. You said nothing would happen. I'd just be dead, period. So there was nothing to be afraid of. I'll never forget it."

Gar just smiled. "I'm going outside for a smoke," he said. It was clear to Warren that the conversation was over.

After eating their meals Warren and Gabriela joined a standing crowd to listen to the Omaha symphony play several seasonal pieces, the last of which was a sing-a-long, the familiar "We Wish You a Merry Christmas." Before leaving the civic center Warren wrote a check for $500 and made sure to personally deliver it to the violist Gloria Chase. The money seemed to ease her outrage at his earlier behavior, but he guessed that if he had caused the symphony a financial hardship her friendship would become a thing of the past.

On the way out Warren made a stop in the men's room. Gabriela told him she would wait for him near the coat room. Standing over a urinal he experienced a little unsteadiness. The beer had combined with the Oxycontin to render him a bit tipsy, a state he was growing fond of lately. After washing his hands and inspecting his appearance in a mirror he exited the bathroom and looked around for his companion. As promised she stood near the coat room. And she was talking with Billy Bob. Warren was about ten feet from them when Gabriela slapped the fake cowboy in the face. The blow was so fierce that it echoed through the lobby.

"Gall dang this ain't my day," Billy Bob cried as he walked out of the auditorium.

Joining Gabriela, Warren saw the scowl on her face. "He called me an illegal alien," she growled.

"What an ass hole," Warren said.

"Give me the keys to the Lexus," Gabriela demanded. "I'm driving home." Knowing better than to disagree with the Latina when she was angry, Warren complied.

Once home Warren experienced a degree of exhaustion as never before. Another pain pill lessened the throbbing in his back but sent him directly to bed, groggy and out of energy. It was just after 9p.m. His sleep was fitful and not at all restful. He made a visit to the bathroom around 4 a.m and could not get back to sleep. Tossing and turning, pounding his pillow, changing positions, he finally gave up the effort at the break of day. In another trip to the bathroom he left the door open so Theo could hear the sound of his urination. A deep bark from below made him smile.

A while later, clad in a winter coat and boots, Warren took his blind dog for his morning walk. As always he and Theo covered the same route. On this trip Warren felt chilled. It occurred to him that he might have a fever. Back home he fed Theo, grabbed a bottle of Snapple and headed for his den to watch the morning news. While sitting in his old chair he took his temperature. It was 100.5 degrees. He decided that a call to his physician was in order. But first he took in a bit of local news coverage, a taped interview from the night before. A reporter was talking to Billy Bob Richardson in front of the Omaha Civic Center. Both wore winter coats. "Your donation to the symphony was most generous," the reporter said.

"Always glad to help pardner," Billy Bob drawled. As repulsive as the scene was to Warren it told him his wine assault on the used car salesman hadn't cost the symphony a major donation. Snapping off the TV he called Dr. McHale's exchange. Then, before he knew it, he fell asleep.

It was a recurrent nightmare, one that Warren had suffered since childhood. In this dream he was a boy playing outside on a dirt playground during a grade school recess. The day was hot and he became thirsty. He ran inside the school to the dank basement, the site of the water fountains. Two stained porcelain fountains adhered to a badly chipped painted wall. One didn't work. The other produced a trickle of water too weak to permit a drink. His thirst led him to a stinking bathroom that housed two urinals, a sink, and two toilets. The sink was clogged with wet paper towels. The floor in front of the urinals smelled of urine. Next came the worst part of the dream. He became aware that one of the toilets had overflowed. Excrement began to flow everywhere. He left the bathroom but the foul wet discharge followed him. Before he could find his way out of the basement his shoes became soaked. In seconds he was ankle deep in dark water contaminated with feces. The stench was too awful to bear.

The dream usually involved Warren wading around in the basement looking for a chair or a bench to stand on. This night was different. This night he managed to flee from the stink and find refuge out on the playground. Another departure from the nightmare had the playground change to a grove of birch trees through which flowed a stream. He knew the water was cold and pure. The old Indian was sitting on the bank. Warren sat down next to him. They didn't speak. The bubbling water and the rustling of birch leaves soothed the boy's frayed nerves. Dipping his bare legs in the water he enjoyed a cleansing but the cold water caused him to chill. The chills, it turned out, were very real and they brought him out of his slumber. The pain in his chest and the harsh cough told him something was desperately wrong. Shortness of breath made him sit bolt upright.

"Gabriela," Warren called. His voice was weak and he instantly knew his call for help hadn't reached her. Struggling to his feet he stumbled to the kitchen. He was so cold he thought his body would crack like a dropped chunk of ice. "Gabriela," he rasped again. This time his voice reached her bedroom.

"Ay-yi-yi," Gabriela blurted when she joined Warren in the kitchen. She helped him onto a stool where he slumped forward, his frail torso collapsing on the island counter. "Stay with me, Boss," she said. "I'm calling an ambulance." For Warren the minutes between his sudden illness and his rescue felt like hours. His head rested on an ear, its weight against the hard counter surface. One arm lay next to his face, the other dangled on his lap. His eyes closed as he lingered in semi-consciousness. It was only the painful coughing that kept him awake. When the EMTs arrived he heard their reassuring voices and minutes later found himself strapped on a stretcher. Once in the ambulance his awareness improved with a steady flow of oxygen delivered by a nasal cannula.

"What's my problem?" Warren squeaked as he glanced to his right at a young man in a blue uniform.

"I think you've got pneumonia sir," the man said.

Christ, Warren thought. What next?

XXI

"You're lucky Warren," Dr. McHale said. The diminutive man was standing next to Warren's hospital bed perusing a chart. "You've got pneumococcal pneumonia limited to the right middle lobe. An immuno-compromised patient such as yourself could've found himself in much more desperate straits."

"What now, Alvin?" Warren asked. The fact was he had never felt so sick, not even during the worst of chemotherapy.

"The day you become afebrile is the day I'm sending you home with a visiting nurse and IV antibiotics. I want to minimize your exposure to hospital bacteria."

Warren was too exhausted to ask his doctor to explain his medical mumbo-jumbo. Once again he was placing his trust in McHale, who went on with his plan. "While you're here I'll check your liver and run a couple other scans," the doctor added.

"You do that, Alvin," Warren rasped.

"Hey, don't get snippy with me. I'm the only friend you've got."

"Sorry. I'm just so tired of being sick."

"You've got stage four prostate cancer. What do you expect?"

Warren had no reply. His head fell back on the pillow as he waited for McHale to complete his work. He wondered if there was a stage five to this wretched disease.

"I'll be back at 7 a.m. tomorrow," McHale said after finishing writing orders. With characteristic speed he bounded out of the room. Alone now, Warren glanced to his right. The other bed of the semi-private room was empty but obviously in use. Minutes later an orderly wheel-chaired its occupant to the bedside and an elderly man crawled under the sheets. The man lay on his back with his eyes closed. Warren felt an urge to say hello but didn't want to disturb the old gentleman. Besides, having pneumonia had a way of limiting one's sociability.

Eventually it became time for lunch. Two trays of food were delivered and positioned at the bedsides. The patients swung to sitting postures and surveyed what they were expected to eat. Under covered plates were chicken breasts and beets. To drink were small glasses of milk. Dessert was green jello. As Warren took his first bite of the rubbery chicken he had a good look at the old man. "You're the man in the truck," Warren exclaimed. His words compelled the old Indian gentleman to look his way. The old man's leathery facial skin crinkled in a smile.

"I remember," the old man said. "It was outside that liquor store."

"Somehow it feels like I've known you forever," Warren said.

"How can that be?"

"I haven't a clue."

The old man took a bite of chicken and then a spoonful of green jello. "White man's food," he mumbled. "Hospital jello is always green," he added.

Just then Warren began to cough. He grabbed some tissue paper and caught what he expectorated, a glob of purulent bloody phlegm. "Christ," he cried as he gazed on what had just come out of his body.

"Pneumonia?" the Indian guessed.

"That's what I've been told," Warren said as he returned to his lunch.

"That's what I've got. Maybe that's why we're roommates."

The men finished their meals without exchanging another word. Then the old man curled up on his bed facing away from Warren, who for lack of anything better to do intended to take a nap. But before he fell asleep Gabriela showed up for a visit. Her heavy winter coat was sprinkled with snowflakes. "It's beautiful outside, Boss," she said as she shed her coat and took a seat at the side of his bed.

Lying on his left side, Warren had a limited view of his visitor, having to look between the struts of his bedrail. "I'm feeling better, thank you," he said in weak sarcasm.

"I'm sorry. How are you feeling?"

"Actually I've never felt worse."

"That's saying something."

"You're telling me. So, I assume it's snowing."

Gabriela began brushing the snowflakes out of her hair. "You know, I've been in Nebraska for many years but I cannot get used to the snow."

"Now is a good time to tell me the story of how you ended up in Omaha," Warren said.

Gabriela eased back on a metal chair, crossed her legs, and gazed at the ceiling. "Where to start?" she asked herself.

"Keep your voice down," Warren warned. "I think my roommate is sleeping."

Clearing her throat Gabriela began her tale, her voice soft but steady. "As you know I came to the U.S. when I was 14," she began. "I lived with my aunt and uncle in San Diego while my parents remained in Mexico. The whole idea was to allow me to learn English. I did just that, along with the game of tennis."

"So you've said," Warren commented, remembering that Gabriela was good enough to play in the U.S. Open back in the 70's.

"I met Ernesto, my future husband, when I was still playing professional tennis," Gabriela continued. "He was also a pro. We married when we were both 25 and had a 20 year marriage. No kids but we were happy enough teaching tennis at various clubs in California. As you know Ernesto died from prostate cancer. By then I was getting a bit too old to continue as a tennis instructor, so I attended a junior college and studied law and keyboarding. My sister, Gaby's mother, was living in Omaha and suggested that I move east and join her and our extended family. In 2002 I applied at Sanders, Litchfield & Tannenbaum as a legal secretary. That's when we met."

"I can't believe I didn't know that..." Warren started. A coughing fit seized him. He sat up, both hands over his mouth. As before, a thick bloody mess shot from his lung. "Jesus Christ," he muttered after the spell ended. Gabriela handed him a wad of tissue and he wiped his hands clean. "Disgusting," he added.

Just then an orderly appeared with a wheelchair. After checking Warren's wristband he said, "Time for your CAT scans Mr. Westing." Warren grudgingly complied, lowering the side rail and slipping onto the wheelchair. He dreaded what the scans would reveal.

"Good luck, Boss," Gabriela said.

"What did you say your husband's name was?" Warren asked before being wheeled out of the room.

"Ernesto."

"Ernesto," Warren repeated. During the trip to the radiology department he listed all the Ernies he had heard of in his 66 years. There was Ernie Brooks, a high school acquaintance who played quarterback on his football team. Then there was Tennessee Ernie Ford who had his own TV show in the 50's. Who could forget the famous Cub Ernie Banks? Muppet Ernie qualified for his list. It was then that he called out a question to the orderly who was pushing his wheelchair. "Your name wouldn't be Ernie, would it?"

"I'm afraid not Mr. Westing," the young man said. "Why do you ask?"

"Just killing time, son," Warren said. "Just killing my time."

By the time Warren finished the testing he was beyond exhaustion. During the scanning his fever had spiked. Worse, the pain in his chest grew to a piercing stab that made breathing an agony. Finally back in bed a nurse gave him an Oxycontin and Tylenol, which gradually reduced the fever and pain and allowed him a much needed sleep. When he awoke a food tray sat next to his bed. It was time for supper.

"Your breathing rattled up a storm my friend," the old Indian said. Once again the men were facing one another, both sitting on the edge of their respective beds.

"This pneumonia is worse than chemo," Warren complained as he removed the lid of his food plate His effort caused the cube of green jello to jiggle.

"You have cancer?"

"Unfortunately."

"I'm sorry to hear that." The old man tried cutting his slice of ham but ended up biting off a piece while holding the ham in his fingers. "Just like rubber," he muttered.

At the end of the meal a nicely dressed woman appeared carrying a manila envelope, which she handed to the old man. She explained that the envelope contained his personal items that she was returning to him in preparation for his imminent discharge that evening. The Indian thanked her and she left the room. Reaching into the envelope he produced three pieces of jewelry, two earrings and a necklace all made of silver and turquoise. The sight of the jewelry jarred Warren's memory.

"I know you from somewhere other than the day I ran into you at the liquor store," Warren claimed.

"I don't see how."

Warren took a bite of cold mashed potatoes. "Maybe I'm starting to lose my mind," he muttered.

The old Indian chuckled. "It gets worse with age my friend," he said. Warren guessed that the man wasn't joking.

Just then the old man's physician burst into the room, pulled the curtain closed to have a so-called private conversation with his patient, and began jabbering. Lying back Warren listened to the rapid fire instructions, surprised at how similar the physician's style was to that of Alvin McHale. In minutes, the one sided discussion was over. Warren heard the Indian open his closet and rustle into his clothes. It was then that the old man stuck his head through a crack in the curtain and spoke to Warren.

"My people believe that everything happens for a reason," the Indian said. "We saw each other at the liquor store and we shared a hospital room. That is important to remember and even treasure. I don't know what it means but perhaps we will find out sometime. Peace be with you brother."

Warren stared at the leathery face. It reflected the times the man had endured in his long life. It also showed the very thing the old Indian had wished for him. It showed a quiet peace. The face disappeared behind the curtain, and Warren heard the Indian leave the room. Warren never again saw him in the flesh.

Alone again, Warren played with the controls of his hospital bed, settling on his head resting at about 45 degrees and his knees in a comfortable flexion. He closed his eyes in an attempt to take a nap but found sleep elusive. To pass the time he attempted to name the U.S. presidents, getting as far as Lincoln. He did better remembering the main players on the famous Cincinnati Reds Big Red Machine, the powerful major league baseball team of the 1970s. He went on to a list of his brushes with death. There was the time, as a teenager, he was driving too fast on a gravel road and couldn't slow down fast enough to avoid barreling across a two-lane highway narrowly missing a dump truck. It was his eleventh winter when, while being pulled on his sled behind his father's pickup through the snow- covered streets of Prairie Center, he decided to plow through a snow drift rather than keep to the snow-covered asphalt. After the fun was over he took the time to inspect his path that he had created through the drift and discovered that he had missed a fire hydrant by inches. Once, during an attempt to save a drowning childhood friend, he nearly died as a victim of a double drowning, kicking free of the boy just in time to call for help. That boy lived. There were a few harrowing moments he had experienced in his Lexus, but he couldn't decide if they qualified as brushes with death. He was about to move on to another mental exercise when he recalled the experience that should have terrified him but, at that time, did not. It was his tenth birthday, June 30, 1957. He was in a small shed with his grandfather, the shed where the old man kept his lawnmowers. The place was hot and smelled like oil and dirt. Standing still he watched his grandfather remove the cap of a mower's gas tank and start pouring fuel into the tank. One thing everybody knew about his grandpa was that he was never without a White Owl cigar in his mouth. That day was no exception. Warren couldn't take his eyes off that glowing ash, the end of the cigar hovering directly above the flowing golden fluid that trickled into the gas tank. The truth was so clear to him in that moment. If the ash fell into the tank he would die. He imagined, in that moment, that there would be an explosion and then a fire would incinerate him and his grandfather. The event would turn into a terrible memory for his family. They would speculate for years on how the accident came to pass. No one would know for sure what happened, that a careless old man and his trusting grandson died because of a White Owl cigar.

That ash didn't fall. There was no explosion, no fire, but the memory disturbed Warren more and more with each recollection. Shaking his head in an attempt to rid himself of the image he changed the bed's positions and in so doing clumsily caused the IV needle to jump out of his port. "Shit," he cursed, knowing that he needed the help of a nurse.

"What did you do young man?" the nurse joked when she answered his buzzer. In seconds she had the problem resolved. "Do you need another pain pill?" she asked Warren.

"Sure," Warren answered.

"And a THC?"

"Why not," he said, happy to try some medical marijuana. He knew the pill wasn't as good as the real stuff but there was no way he could smoke in a hospital bed.

Two days later, after spending long, lonely hours alone in his room, Warren was ready for discharge. His chest X-ray was clearing, his scanning was done, and he hadn't had a fever for 24 hours. Dr. McHale made rounds early and when he burst in the room before 7 a.m. he found his patient dressed and ready to go home.

"All right, here's the plan," McHale began. "A visiting nurse will be at your home each day at 8 a.m. sharp with four IV doses of antibiotic. You'll learn how to properly clean your port and insert the IV needle. The antibiotic goes in every six hours. Five days from now you'll get another chest X-ray. If the pneumonia continues to clear I'll switch you to an oral antibiotic that you'll take for another week. Any questions?"

"What did the scans show?"

McHale didn't miss a beat in revealing the very bad news. "There is still metastasis in your brain, liver and spine. And the lesions look larger. I'm sorry Warren."

"God dammit," Warren mumbled. Walking to the single window of his hospital room he looked out at the snow covered buildings of the medical complex. He had a view of the main entrance. There was a giant Christmas tree decorating the circle drive. "I'm losing, aren't I?" he asked McHale.

"I'm afraid so."

"I've done a lot of thinking about dying."

"And?"

"There are times when I'm fine with the idea. There are times when I'm scared shitless."

"Sounds normal to me. Listen, you have to tell me what you want to do from here on out. I'm talking about your cancer."

Warren wheeled around and faced McHale. "From here on out?" Warren shot back. "You've already got me in the grave," he yelled.

Throwing up his hands, McHale headed for the door. "Tell you what. You go home and think about radiation to your brain and more chemo. Call me if you want to proceed. If not I'll arrange hospice and make sure you've got plenty of pain meds."

McHale left the room. Once again Warren was alone. He began

pacing, irritated with his physician for his lack of empathy and feeling the desperation in what he guessed was the last stage of his cancer. He decided on the spot to go ahead with radiation, as he didn't mind being bald and could endure the fatigue. More chemotherapy, though, was another matter. The long hours of infusions and the sickening side effects were perhaps more than he could stand given his weakened state. But first things first. This fucking pneumonia has to go, he thought.

Just then a woman entered the room carrying a large manila envelope that she gave to Warren along with a few pleasant words of farewell. The envelope held his wallet, Rolex and cell phone. He promptly called Gabriela who promised to pick him up at the hospital entrance. After retrieving his winter coat from his closet he headed for the door only to be met by an orderly with a wheel chair.

"How about a ride, Mr. Westing?" the young man said.

"I can walk," Warren protested.

"Sorry. Hospital rules."

Knowing it was silly to resist, Warren accepted the wheelchair ride. He and the orderly were alone in an elevator when he asked his question: "What do you know about Alvin McHale?" Though he didn't have a view of the orderly he could sense his hesitation.

"Well, he's been around a long time," the young man began. "You could say he's 'Old School'."

"What exactly does that mean?"

"He's kind of set in his ways."

"I've got another question for you," Warren directed to the orderly. "What's with this UNMC oncology board?"

Again Warren sensed hesitancy in the young man. "This is just my opinion," the orderly prefaced. "I think the board is just for show, for publicity."

"You're kidding."

"Every staff member is required to allow the board to review their cancer cases to foster treatment recommendations. But no staff member is required to follow those recommendations."

"So the board merely suggests treatments?"

"That's one way of putting it. It looks to the public like cancer is getting top priority at UNMC but basically the final decisions are still in the hands of the private physicians."

The orderly's words had a sobering effect on Warren. The possibility that he was getting treatment that was other than what a board of experts had recommended was, at the very least, disturbing. What was more, his doctor seemed to have been complicit in the deception, the "show" as the young man described it. Sure, McHale had made it clear that the final decision on his patient's therapy was his but had not divulged how closely he had adhered to the board's suggestions. Warren felt deceived and vowed to confront McHale at first opportunity.

Eventually the elevator opened to the busy hospital lobby and Warren was wheeled out the front door to the waiting Lexus. He thanked the orderly for his help and information and climbed in the passenger seat. Gabriela sat behind the wheel. Though the outside temperature read 25 degrees she wasn't wearing a coat. "Aren't you cold?" Warren asked her.

"Hot flashes," was all Gabriela said. It was all Warren needed to know.

The date was December 24. Warren obviously had no opportunity to go Christmas shopping and was pleasantly surprised to find a few wrapped gifts under the tree when he got home. Inviting aromas wafted from the kitchen. Theo expertly navigated from his kennel to the foyer to greet his master. As Warren gave his blind Great Dane a hearty scratch behind the ears and then a belly rub, he felt the tremendous relief in being free from that prison of a hospital with its blinking IV apparatus and green jello.

"Are you hungry, Boss?" Gabriela asked. "I can whip up some eggs and bacon."

"I think I'll wait for whatever you're cooking. It smells wonderful."

"It's a prime rib."

"Nice."

Making his way to his bedroom, Warren decided to shower, washing to wash away all traces of the hospital. Afterwards he had a good look at his body in the full length mirror. It was wasting away, his skin hanging on his bones like a shroud. He didn't bother checking his weight. For an outfit he chose the green V-neck sweater and dark green corduroy slacks. His leather belt didn't have enough notches to hold up his pants so he folded the belt line over once to create an artificial paunch. His real paunch was long gone.

After taking a pain pill Warren joined Gabriela in the dining room.

Two place settings sat at opposite ends of the table and hot dishes lay between them. "Just the two of us?" Warren asked.

"Gaby and Edgar are spending the holidays with his parents in Chicago," Gabriela explained. "My sister flew to Mexico City to be with our father."

Warren didn't say so but he felt grateful to have Gabriela's help and company. It would've been a lonely Christmas without her. "Let's eat. I'm starved," was all he had to offer. He took his traditional seat and reached for the nearest bowl of food, a move that put a scowl on Gabriela's face. Knowing the drill, Warren folded his arms on his lap while she offered a prayer. The moment she finished he began piling mashed potatoes, bacon and broccoli, and two thick slices of medium rare prime rib on his plate. He made sure to cover the meat and potatoes with Gabriela's gravy. Having lived on hospital fare for days, Warren savored the expertly prepared meal despite his chronically dull taste buds. As he ate he knew he had some test results to share with his friend.

"The cancer is growing," Warren told Gabriela.

"That's not good. So, what's in store for you Boss?"

"Umm, this is delicious Gabriela," Warren said as he ate some bacon and broccoli.

"Gracias. So. Your plans?"

"More of the same I suppose, once the pneumonia is gone."

"Do you think you can stand more radiation and chemo?"

Warren didn't answer Gabriela's question. Rather he focused on his meal. As he ate he thought of his hospital roommate, the old Indian gentleman who ate the disgusting hospital food with him. Remembering the remark about the jello always being green, Warren wondered if that was really the case.

After eating, Warren and Gabriela retired to the living room to exchange Christmas gifts. He had nothing for her but she had anticipated that, wrapping a box of chocolates for herself. It was when Warren began unwrapping his gift that he began to feel disoriented, like he was drunk. His vision blurred and then he saw double. He wasn't aware of the moment he lost consciousness. It was the next day, in his hospital bed, that Gabriela described what had happened to him next. He had suffered his first seizure.

XXII

"He's a sick puppy," were the first words Warren heard when he regained consciousness. He was lying on his back on a hospital gurney in the UNMC emergency room. An emergency physician was ending his shift and signing off to his replacement. "Brain mets and pneumonia," the doctor continued.

"What's the primary?" the replacement asked.

"Prostate."

"Who's his oncologist?"

"He doesn't have one."

"What?"

"He's McHale's patient."

"Oh. That explains it."

As for Warren, he felt well though he was terribly confused. The smell and room lighting told him where he was, but he had no idea how he got to the emergency room. He also didn't know why he was there.

"You're awake. That's a good thing," the ER physician said to Warren.

"What happened to me? Why am I here?" Warren asked.

"You had a seizure my friend. The cancer in your brain probably caused it."

"Christ."

"Dr. McHale is on the way in. He's already given the order to admit you."

"I just got out of here," Warren whined.

"Yeah, I know. That's tough luck, especially since this is Christmas Eve."

Knowing he was in for a wait, Warren tried to find a comfortable position on the gurney. His arms and legs ached. Try as he might he he couldn't remember having a seizure. He glanced at the plastic bag of IV medication hanging above him, guessing that he was getting agents to prevent another attack. At long last McHale showed up. "Christmas Eve, Warren?" he joked. "Have some decency."

"This wasn't my idea, Alvin," Warren said.

McHale shed his winter coat, revealing his red bow tie and green buttoned sweater. He took a quick look at the IV bag and grunted his approval. "Fortunately a visiting nurse is already in place," he began. "I'll add these meds to your antibiotics and send you home after a 24 hour observation in our lovely hospital."

"Just one day inside?"

"Unless you have another seizure."

An orderly showed up and Warren was whisked away. He was told he was heading for a Neurology floor but when he entered his room he found it essentially the same as the one he occupied for his pneumonia. He spent a restless night and greeted Christmas morning alone. Gabriela showed up around 9 a.m.

"You're eyes were rolled back in your head and you were foaming at the mouth," Gabriela said as she described the event of the preceding day. "You shook so hard. I thought you were going to die. It was the most frightening thing I've ever seen."

"Funny. I don't remember anything," Warren said, who by now felt in full possession of his faculties. "Anyway the good news is I get to go home today if I don't have another one of…what you saw."

Christmas day passed slowly. Gabriela stayed at Warren's bedside until dark. It was around 9 p.m. when Dr. McHale showed up. He was still in his Christmas garb and carried Warren's chart. "No seizure activity," he rattled off. "That's a good sign. Have you given any thought to more cancer treatment?"

"I'm guessing I should have more brain radiation," Warren said.

"Wise choice. I'll get you started first thing tomorrow."

"I'm undecided about more chemo. I may not be able to bear up."

"Nonsense. You're a little underweight is all."

"Alvin, look at me. I'm skin and bones."

McHale glanced at the chart. "150 pounds. That's not too bad."

"A year and a half ago I weighed 235."

McHale shook his head impatiently. "I remind you that your liver is involved. We've got to keep that in check," he said.

It was then that Warren remembered his promise to himself. "Alvin, I want to ask you something I hope you'll give me a straight answer."

"Fire away," McHale said. He fidgeted with his bow tie, a sign to Warren that his doctor was about to bolt out of the room.

"On several occasions you've mentioned an oncology board," Warren began. What, exactly, is your relationship with this group?"

"The board's job is to review all cases of cancer and recommend treatment. To be honest I usually ignore their recommendations."

"My God. I would assume the board is made up of experts…"

"Look Warren. There is no right way to treat prostate cancer. I've had years of experience with what I consider to be a tried and true methodology. Now if you're dissatisfied for some reason…"

"I'm not dissatisfied. I'm just curious as to what it was that you ignored."

McHale stopped fidgeting and glared at Warren. "Do you trust me?" he asked his one and only patient.

"Of course," Warren replied.

"Then hear this. You've done as well as could be expected with stage four prostate cancer. Sure there are other treatment options out there but I'm not convinced that they would've taken you any farther than what I prescribed for you. That's my opinion and I'm proud to say that it's based on years of experience."

Warren's fell back on his pillow. He felt exhausted. "Fair enough, Alvin," was all he had to say.

Snapping closed the chart McHale headed for the door. "Merry Christmas, Warren," he called. A second later he was gone.

* * *

The next day Warren needed to be at the UNMC radiotherapy department for more radiation. Back home he met a visiting nurse with a pack full of medications meant for intravenous administration. After showing Warren how to clean his port, she taught him how to connect the pre-mixed IV bags to a plastic line which led to a large gauge needle that was to pierce the center of the port. The IV medications, an antibiotic and two drugs to prevent seizures, ended in five days and were replaced by oral meds. On the fifth day the nurse handed him five prescriptions signed by Dr. McHale, a week's worth of antibiotics, a large and refillable supply of seizure meds, and an even larger supply of Oxycontin and medical marijuana. As it turned out Warren didn't bother filling the marijuana prescription. He preferred the real stuff.

It was was the gnawing belly pain that led him to decide to undergo yet another round of chemotherapy. So one cool morning in early March Warren managed to get himself to the UNMC chemo room. He was using a cane now in an attempt to take some stress off his back when he walked.

"Mr. Westing. How are you, sir?" the male nurse called when he spotted Warren. "I've got your favorite chair ready and waiting." Warren was in no mood for levity. Scowling, he plopped in the padded chair, stripped off his shirt to expose his port, and tried his best to prepare for four hours of monotony. In no time a new cancer drug was dripping into his body. He had expected to see Jim Gordon, or Gordo, getting his infusion and asked the nurse about the old man with leukemia.

"Mr. Gordon died last month," the nurse said. Warren sighed and shrugged his shoulders. The Big C is a bear, he thought, a tribute to his chemo pal. It was then that he remembered what Gordo used to do to pass the time while getting chemo. Pulling his vial of OxyContin out of a pants pocket Warren downed four pills. He was asleep in minutes.

Somehow Warren made it through the weeks of treatment. Pain and nausea had been his steady companions but a new malady cropped up. His mental acuity began to wane. Most days felt to him as though they were dreams from which he couldn't escape. When the radiation and chemo stopped his dreaminess persisted. But he received some good news. His cancer had been checked. Dr. McHale warned him not to get his hopes up and Warren knew his doctor spoke the truth.

Winter gave way to Spring and Warren's health steadied. On a sunny Sunday in April Warren sat in his den watching the final round of the Masters golf tournament. Theo lay at his feet. It was around 2 p.m. when Gabriela and Gaby came in from a morning of shopping. Gabriela carried bags of groceries to the kitchen. Gaby approached Warren with a question. "Could I have a minute?" she asked. Always happy to lay his eyes on the lovely young woman, Warren muted the TV and and gestured for her to take a seat.

"You know that Edgar and I are trying to have a baby," Gaby reminded Warren. Truth be told he had forgotten all about the effort but he thought it important to tell a white lie to show some interest.

"Sure I do. And how is it going?" Warren asked.

"Not well. My ovulatory problem has been corrected but Edgar's sperm motility just won't respond to treatment."

"Sorry to hear that."

"Mr. Westing…"

"Warren," he insisted.

"Warren. I'd like your permission to use your sperm." Gaby's request flabbergasted him.

"What? Why for heaven's sake?" Warren sputtered.

"Well Edgar looks like you when you were…younger. And your sperm is still viable. I know because I checked."

Still astounded by the idea, Warren's eyes flitted from the TV screen to Gaby's pretty face and back again. "That means I would be the father…"

"Edgar will be the child's father. He says not being the biological father doesn't bother him."

"Are you sure about that?"

"Very sure."

As hard as he tried Warren couldn't come to grips with Gaby's proposal. But over the last several weeks he had become used to the inability to concentrate. All he could come up with this day was the certainty that he would soon be dead. What the hell, he thought. If it will make Gaby happy.

"Of course you can use my sperm," Warren declared. Gaby smiled broadly and leapt forward to give him a hug. The squeeze hurt his back and made him wince. But he didn't do anything to cut short the embrace. "You're welcome," he whispered in her ear.

A week later Warren got to spend some more time with the attractive Latina, this time at another symphony fund raiser at Gloria Chase's condo. Gloria had invited Warren and a guest and had asked if he knew of anyone else who might make a generous donation. Aware of Edgar's stature at Bank of America, Warren suggested him. As a result Warren found himself at a small gathering at his deceased best friend's condominium with Gabriela, Gaby and her fiancé Edgar. The first thing Warren noticed about the place was how different it looked. Gone was the black leather and chrome furniture. Instead he saw stuffed chairs and sofas all in soft pastels. On the walls were Impressionists' paintings. In a far corner stood a grand piano on which an accomplished pianist rendered classical strains. Gloria Chase welcomed the two couples and had a warning for Warren. "Billy Bob Richardson is here," she told him. "Please restrain yourself."

"I'll steer clear of the jerk," Warren said.

Just then a pretty young blond woman joined Gloria, who introduced her as her younger daughter. Warren recalled being told of the rift between Gloria and her two daughters and could only surmise that at least one daughter had forgiven her mother for divorcing her father, now deceased. Warren spent a few moments trying to remember the story behind the estrangement, but quickly gave up the effort. These days old stories were eluding his memory, a development he found annoying. He feared that someday they would all be out of his reach.

"Warren, this is Alicia," Gloria announced, prompting a polite handshake. He looked at the young face, noting her light blue eyes and pointed nose. She was as tall as her mother but otherwise bore no resemblance to the violist. Her hand felt small and her grip was weak. She wore a T-shirt, jeans and sandals, very underdressed for a symphony fund raiser. Warren guessed the outfit had been an issue between mother and daughter earlier in the day. It was clear who had won out.

In time Warren, Gabriela, Gaby and Edgar melted into the crowd. They all were briefly engaged by members of the Omaha Symphony who expressed thanks for their attendance. A half-hour into the party Warren and the Latinas were holding plates of food. Edgar was standing at the opposite side of the condo talking in earnest with Alicia.

"The man's fiancee is over here," Gabriela complained as she put an hand on Gaby's shoulder.

"Edgar is a flirt," Gaby said. "I've always known that about him."

"Still, it's not right."

Not wishing to get involved in a discussion about Edgar's social skills, Warren carried his plate out to the open balcony. A refreshing breeze was coming off the river. A disheveled man stood facing the Iowa countryside, his stringy hair hanging over a frayed shirt collar. Cigarette smoke circled his head before being carried off in the wind. "We meet again," Warren said as he found a place at the balcony rail next to Gar Young.

"How's it goin' man," Gar returned as he gave Warren a brief glance.

"How did that golf tournament at Osage Hills turn out?" Warren asked.

"We won it."

"I bet your boss crowed about that."

"For weeks. I got tired hearin' about how God made sure we won."

The two men stared out over the mighty Missouri River. At one point Gar offered Warren a cigarette. "Might as well, Warren said. "I've got a bad case of cancer."

Warren had never smoked cigarettes and coughed when he took his first inhalation. Gar chuckled. "I'm supposed to get cancer," he said.

"I don't follow."

"You've heard of Agent Orange?"

"Sure."

"I got exposed in Nam. The shit is supposed to cause cancer." Gar then gestured with his cigarette. "So are these," he laughed. "Guess I'm as good as dead."

"But there's nothing to be afraid of, right?"

Warren's words silenced Gar for a moment. The ragged man ran a hand over his scarred face. Then he started to talk, though he clearly wasn't speaking to Warren. "There were times in Nam when I was plenty scared of dyin'. Once I peed myself. I saw my buddies get shot or blown to bits. I couldn't shake that. I used to imagine a bullet tearing through my chest. It was fuckin' awful. Dyin' of cancer seems like a vacation in comparison."

"I have to disagree," Warren said. "Having cancer is no vacation."

"You're probably right," Gar said. He crushed his cigarette under a heel. "I'm going to get some chow. Nice talkin' with you."

As Gar Young walked off Warren saw the obvious. Suffering, he understood, came in many forms. Gazing out over the great river and farmland, he finished his cigarette. The next day he bought a pack of his own.

XXIII

On the first day of May Warren uncovered his garden pool. He was happy to find that the water was reasonably clear and cold. After wiping the morning dew from the lounge chair he took a seat and prepared his medications. In short order he held an Oxycontin, two capsules meant to circumvent the grim consequences of cancer in his brain, and medical marijuana, the latter present because he had just smoked the last of his pot the evening before. He downed the pills with some Snapple. Then he lit the first cigarette of the day. In just two weeks he was up to a half a pack a day. The cigarette was half consumed when Gabriela walked out of the kitchen onto the back patio. "We used to call those 'cancer sticks'," she joked as she took a seat on a wrought iron chair. She held a mug of coffee. Since retiring her usual outfit was jeans and a cotton blouse. Her heavy hair was still piled high on her head, held in place by a hair pin.

"Cigarettes can't hurt me," Warren claimed. "I'll be dead before they have a chance."

Gabriela grunted. "I wish you could see yourself doing yoga with a cigarette in your mouth," she said. "How about some breakfast?" she added.

"I'm not hungry," Warren said. Truth be told his appetite had been drastically diminished for months. Even marijuana failed to bolster his interest in food.

"You've got to eat, Boss."

"I just can't. Nothing tastes good to me. The last round of chemo must have burned my taste buds for good."

Sighing, Gabriela stood and stretched. "At least you've got a nice day to enjoy," she said. Warren gazed skyward. A large cumulus cloud occupied most of what he could see. Out of habit he looked for a face in the white fluff. In seconds he had it-the profile of an old man with a large nose. An image of an elderly Indian briefly raced through his mind and then suddenly disappeared. Gabriela's voice ended his daydream. "Gaby is pregnant," she told Warren.

The news made Warren sit up. "Did she use my sperm?" he asked.

"She did. You're going to be a daddy."

"Holy shit."

Gabriela sat back down and sipped her coffee. "There's a problem, Boss," she said. "Edgar is being a real pill about her pregnancy."

"I had a feeling that would happen," Warren said. "I trust their wedding is still on."

"I hope so. They put a contract on my home in Latino Village."

Because his back began to ache Warren stretched out on the lounger. It became clear to him that lovely Gaby faced some difficulties in the near future. He could see her arguing with her disapproving husband over any number of topics ranging from a child born of a sperm donor to a home in a neighborhood Edgar may well find uninviting. "Poor Gaby," he whispered.

"Last night you said you wanted to talk to me about taxes," Gabriela said. Her words reminded Warren of an idea that came to him when he read the latest news letter from his former law firm. He carefully extended his legs and then reached under the lounger to pet his ever-present dog. With eyes closed he began to unfold his plan.

"As you know you will inherit my estate," Warren started.

"A generosity I will always be grateful for, Boss."

"There is a step we can take to reduce your state tax regarding your inheritance. We can get married."

"Ay-yi-yi. You are losing your mind."

"I'm serious. We're already living together. There's no reason not to…"

"Boss, I'm an old fashioned girl. Marriage means something to me. And now there is something else that should tell you why we shouldn't get married." Warren instantly understood what Gabriela was thinking.

"I will be the father of your niece's child," Warren droned. "Therefore I shouldn't be her uncle by marriage."

"Correcto."

"Christ. It's always something."

Gabriela finished her coffee and headed for the kitchen, saying, "I've got some cleaning to do. Do you need anything?"

"I could use some more pot."

"I'll make a call. I bet I can arrange home delivery," Gabriela said as she entered the house.

Alone now, Warren turned on his left side and assumed his traditional sleeping position. Though he had been awake only a couple hours he fell into a deep sleep. He dreamt he was a child standing at the head of a flight of stairs. He started to walk down but tripped, sending him airborne. He fell head first, sensing the hard stairs under him and waiting for the painful crash of his body on cruel wooden edges. He grasped for something, anything that would prevent or reduce impact. The fall went on and on. The anticipation of the smashing was terrifying. He held his breath, knowing he couldn't fall forever. Then the dream started over. When he woke the dream had repeated itself many times. But his falling body never hit the stairs.

When Warren's eyes opened the right side of his face was hot and tender. He swung to a sitting position and checked his Rolex. "My God. It's noon," he murmured. You just let yourself be sunburned you moron, he thought. Shuffling from the back patio to the kitchen, he found a note from Gabriela telling him she had gone to the grocery store and to expect a marijuana delivery around noon. Sure enough the front doorbell rang at that very moment. When Warren opened the door he found a brown bag on the welcome mat. Inside was a baggie of pot and a note asking Gabriela to send the money to the usual place. Warren chuckled as he grabbed the bag and turned to Theo who had effortlessly navigated his way to the foyer. "The woman is a pro," Warren said to his blind dog. Theo tilted his giant head to the left in tacit agreement.

Out of habit Warren walked to the refrigerator and surveyed its contents. What he wanted was a beer but he soon found that the only brand available was Michelob Ultra. Chick beer, he thought. Minutes later he was in his Lexus heading to Stogies. Warren walked into his favorite bar and grill just after noon and took a seat at the end of the bar near the rear of the pub. The popular place was filled with a lunch crowd and he had to wait several minutes before placing a order for a locally brewed stout. The brew tasted good but he soon felt full, even bloated. A second pint was out of the question. As he tried to get the bartender's attention to get his bill his eyes strayed to the front door. Two people he recognized walked in. One was Edgar, Gaby's fiancé. The other was Gloria Chase's daughter Alicia. He watched them as they slid into a booth. He had a clear view of the couple but figured the crowd kept him out of their sight. The first unusual thing he noticed was their sitting positions. They did not sit across the table from one another. Instead they sat next to one another. In fact they appeared to nestle and touch in what could only be called a romantic manner. After ordering the couple had a few moments alone. That was when Edgar took Alicia in his arms for a prolonged kiss.

"Holy shit," Warren said. A burly man sitting next to him at the bar heard the epithet, turned to him and then followed his line of sight.

"Well would you look at the lovebirds," the man said as he gazed at the kissers. "Hey you two," he yelled. "Get a room!" After the embrace Edgar looked in the direction of the heckler and flashed a middle finger. "Oh buddy, you just made a big mistake," the man said as he started to get off his bar stool.

"Let me handle this," Warren told the man.

"You?" the man said. "Gramps you look like death warmed over."

"I'll call you if I need you."

The man grinned and returned to his beer. "I'll be right here," he said. Warren put down a ten dollar bill on the bar and made his way to Edgar's booth. There he stood waiting to be recognized. Perhaps because of Warren's wasted appearance it took Edgar several seconds to realize who he was. It was unlikely that Alicia remembered him from just one brief introduction at her mother's condo.

"Hey dude," Edgar finally said to Warren. His tone was less than cordial.

"What the fuck do you think you're doing?" Warren shouted in as stern a voice as he could muster. Alicia huddled against the back wall of the booth. Edgar turned to face Warren in defiance.

"It's really none of your business," Edgar said.

"You're engaged. Gaby is pregnant."

"Yeah. I know all about that."

"So what are you doing with another woman?"

"Look dude, I'm not crazy about becoming a father to another man's kid."

"Gaby said you were behind the idea."

"She tells everybody that. She's lying."

Edgar's words shocked Warren. But lie or no lie Gaby was going to have Warren Westing's child. That made her family. "Now you listen to me ass hole," Warren began. "I'm going to tell Gaby what I've seen here today…"

"You're too late. I already broke off the engagement. There isn't going to be a wedding. And I'm not going to be any sort of a father."

Once again, Warren was utterly surprised by Edgar's words. What was more, he had no fitting response to the young man's brashness. But one idea occurred to him. Turning toward the bar he caught the eye of the guy who had taken exception to Edgar's signed insult. Waving the man over, Warren had one parting remark for Edgar. "I hope this hurts. Dude," he said. Then he headed for the front exit.

When Warren got back home he found Gabriela's Honda in the garage. He also spotted a car he didn't recognize parked on the street. Its owner was crying in Gabriela's arms. The Latinas were in the kitchen, the aunt's strength supporting her heartbroken niece. Warren decided to let the women have their privacy and quietly made his way to the backyard patio. Theo followed him. Because the day was sunny and mild the sliding glass door was open with only a screen door separating the patio from the kitchen. As Warren stretched out of the lounger he could hear parts of the conversation between Gabriela and Gaby. "I wanted this baby so badly," Gaby sobbed. "I should have seen this coming."

"I could kill that weasel," Gabriela said Hearing those words made Warren snicker. He knew she was squinting.

"What am I going to do now?" Gaby cried.

"You've got your family. Things will work out. You'll see."

"Do you think I can stay here for a while?" Gaby asked. "Mama is still mad at me because I work at a fertility clinic. And I don't want to go home because I might run into Edgar." Hearing this got Warren to his feet. When he walked into the kitchen both women looked at him with expectation.

"You can stay in Margie's old room, Gaby," Warren began. "Just give me a few days to have it cleaned and to buy a new bed."

"Thank you, Mr. Westing."

"Warren."

"Thank you Warren. But you don't have to buy a new bed."

A grimace formed on Warren's thin face as the memory of finding his wife dead in her bed surfaced. "Believe me, a new bed is an absolute necessity," he said. He started to explain to Gaby why he felt so strongly about this matter but felt his energy quickly waning. "An absolute necessity," he repeated. Then, because the brief time outside reminded him of his sunburn, he headed for his bedroom for a nap.

XXIV

To accommodate Gaby, Warren paid for a few days' stay at the Doubletree Hotel in downtown Omaha. He also bought a queen-size bed and gave Margie's to Goodwill. Gabriela volunteered to help clean the unused bedroom, and one morning accompanied Warren as he entered the dusty space. They both commented on how stale the room smelled. Gabriela opened a window. Warren moved directly into the walk-in closet. Except for Margie's purse and ashes, and a small step ladder, the closet was empty, the clothing having been donated to Goodwill. He stared at the two items on the top shelf, surprised that the passage of time hadn't somehow made them disappear.

"I need to dust and vacuum," Gabriela declared as she surveyed the place. "I'll be right back," she added as she left the room. Warren assumed she went after cleaning tools and decided, rather impulsively, to move the purse and box of ashes to his room. His decision was loosely based on these things being too personal to be kept in a guest's closet. But his thinking was cloudy these days. His common sense wasn't what it used to be. First he reached for the purse, tipping it toward him. Its contents spilled on his head and shoulders, and the plastic box of Tic-Tacs shattered on the hardwood floor. White candy flew everywhere. "Dammit," he cursed. Figuring the box of ashes would be even harder to manage he grabbed the step ladder that Margie had used to gather things out of her reach, positioned it under the box and climbed to the second rung. Perhaps he should have known that a man in his weakened state had no business climbing even the smallest of ladders, that his balance and strength were likely compromised. But he was in the game now. He had the ball.

The disaster unfolded in just a few seconds. Just as Warren grabbed the box he slipped off the ladder and staggered backward while holding the cardboard container above his head with both hands. He managed to keep on his feet but his back smashed into a wall. The box also hit the wall and fell from his grasp. Tipping forward on the way to the floor, the cardboard lid fell off, the plastic bag of ashes burst open and Margie's remains spewed out filling the closet with a fine gray dust. "Jesus H. Christ," Warren stammered when he got his bearings. "What have I done?"

Just then Gabriela walked in the room with a vacuum cleaner and a duster. "Ay-yi-yi," she exclaimed when she peered in the closet. "Are you okay Boss?"

"Not really," Warren muttered.

"Where did all that dust come from?"

"I spilled Margie."

"What?"

"Margie's ashes."

"Oh no."

"I'm going to need a broom and a dust pan," Warren said as he stared down at the spillage.

"I can vacuum her up," Gabriela joked. Warren glanced at her and saw the smile. Then he began to laugh, snickering at first and gradually breaking into a hearty belly laugh. Gabriela cackled along. It had been a long time since he enjoyed a good hoot. It felt wonderful.

* * *

Three days later Gaby moved into 41 Crestwood. That evening the trio sat in the dining room sharing a pot roast. The Latinas showed equal enthusiasm for the beef and white potatoes and green beans. Warren ate very little. Neither medical marijuana nor the real stuff sparked his appetite these days. But his pain remained under adequate control with narcotics at ever increasing doses. Gabriela had long since given up her campaign to get him to avoid pain pills. She also stopped buying vitamins and protein supplements, and hadn't bothered to get another yoga tape. Warren noticed. He also noticed that Dr. McHale had started calling the latest test results and not scheduling appointments. Warren's sense of isolation was steadily growing. To him it was the worst part of having cancer. To date, though, he had managed to keep up his spirits by reminding himself that he was to be a father. He only needed to stay alive for six months to see his child. "How did your OB-Gyn visit go?" he asked Gaby.

"Very well," Gaby reported. "I had an ultrasound today."

"And?"

"It's a boy."

Gabriela clapped her hands with joy. "Did you hear that Boss? You're going to have a son."

The news elated Warren. "We need to celebrate," he said.

"What did you have in mind Boss?" Gabriela asked.

"I happen to know that Osage Hills Country Club serves an excellent brunch every Sunday. I say we give it a try."

"Are you sure?" Gabriela said. "You and food aren't exactly on good terms these days."

Warren grinned, saying, "I'll take one for the team."

"What does that mean?"

Toying with the small cut of beef on his plate Warren thought on the many times he and his high school football teammates used the expression "Take one for the team." The truth was, he wasn't the best team player. He liked to run the ball and he didn't like contact, hence his preference for end runs. But he knew Gabriela was waiting for his answer. "It means I'll do my best to enjoy the brunch," he said, though as he spoke he doubted he would be able to fake genuine enjoyment

The very next Sunday Warren drove the women to Osage Hills Country Club where they were seated in an elegant dining room. A long buffet table ran along a back wall and was loaded with a variety of foods ranging from quiche to sliced ham. At the end of the buffet stood a chef carving a rack of lamb. Before eating the trio enjoyed a delicate Chardonnay. Warren praised the wine though in fact it tasted to him like cold water. Gabriela gave her niece a stern look when Gaby took a drink of wine. The young pregnant woman had an explanation. "My doctor says I can have one glass once a week," she said. Her words did nothing to take the squint off her aunt's face. Luckily Gabriela moved on.

"As much as I'm happy Edgar isn't in your life, I hated to lose your contract on my home," Gabriela told Gaby.

Gaby's expression turned serious. "I doubt I can get a loan on my own," she said. "But sooner or later my son and I will need a place to live."

"You two can live at 41 Crestwood for as long as you like," Warren said.

"You don't know how comforting that is to hear, Mr. Westing. I mean Warren. I've got a big bill to pay before I can move ahead."

"Which is?"

"The *in vitro* procedure was pretty expensive."

"Don't worry your pretty head about that, Gaby," Warren said. "Your son's father will pay for it."

The Latinas fell silent. A tear streamed down Gaby's cheek. Gabriela's shoulders heaved and a big smile graced her face. Finally she spoke. "Boss you're the most generous man I've ever known," she said.

"Let's just say I've gained a certain perspective on life," Warren said as he smoothed a hand over his bald scalp. Gabriela reached over and ran her hand over the same skin.

"Why don't you let your hair grow back, Boss?" she asked. "You used to have a handsome head of hair."

"It's too late for me, Gabriela. You know that."

"Maybe. Maybe not. No matter what, I'm here for you."

Just then a loud talking jowlish man wearing a white stetson hat sauntered into the dining room. With him were two men in golf attire and one Gar Young who wore a fatigue jacket with its sleeves cut off. "Best grub in Omaha," Billy Bob Richardson told the two men as they sat two tables away from Warren, Gabriela and Gaby. Warren, for one, groaned in disappointment. The last thing he wanted was a loud-mouthed bigot ruining his celebratory lunch.

"Gents, you need to start listenin' to me. Your golf games would get a whole lot better if you let Jesus Christ into your hearts," Billy Bob shouted. The would-be cowboy buttered a dinner roll and bit into it, chewing as he talked on. But his talking ceased the moment he stopped breathing. His face turned fiery red as he struggled for air. Pounding on the table with his fists emphasized his desperation. Billy Bob's face turned blue and his eyes bugged out of his pudgy face. It was apparent to most that a bite of dinner roll was obstructing the man's airway. In a flash Gaby, the registered nurse, leapt into action. She rushed to a position behind Billy Bob, wrapped her arms around his torso and began the Heimlich maneuver. Unfortunately she proved too small to handle the corpulent man. It was then that Gabriela stepped in, replacing her niece in the rescue. All it took was one jerk of her strong arms to force the wad of dough out of Billy Bob's mouth. The sound of his first inhalation echoed off the dining room walls.

"Oh my God," Billy Bob managed to declare between gasps. "I almost died." His two guests stared at him in disbelief. Gar just smiled.

"What do you think of Hispanics now, Billy?" Gar asked. After gaining some composure Billy Bob replaced his fallen white Stetson on his fat head and gazed over at Warren's table where Gaby and Gabriela had returned to their seats. For once the loudmouth was apparently at a loss for words. Notably not a word of thanks left his mouth. Warren noticed.

"I guess Jesus didn't see that coming," Warren directed at Billy Bob. The barb made Gar laugh out loud.

"What are you laughin' at pardner?" Billy Bob shot at his friend.

"I'm laughin' at you man," Gar replied. "You're a joke."

"A joke huh? Well laugh at this joke. You're fired."

"You think I give a shit man? You can take your job and your used cars and shove 'em up your fat ass." Gar took the time to light a cigarette before leaving the room. Billy Bob stormed out of the dining room and his guests followed him. In a short time Warren, Gabriela and Gaby were alone.

"I didn't know you knew the Heimlich maneuver," Warren said to Gabriela.

"There's a lot you don't know about me Boss." Warren had to admit that what she said was true and he wanted so much to remedy that. Suddenly he felt what had lately become an ever more frequent and unwelcome dread. He was running out of time. He looked on as the heroic Latinas calmly took their plates to the country club buffet, both acting as if the day was ordinary, as if they had not just taken part in saving a life. Because he wished to be part of their energy, their spirit, Warren followed suit and lined up behind them. He put a little mashed potatoes and gravy on his plate and asked the chef for a slice of lamb. In time the trio was sitting at their table. Warren took his first bite. It was tasteless, and apparently Gabriela noticed his disappointment. Reaching into her purse she fetched a bottle of Tabasco sauce and handed it to Warren. "Emergency stock," she explained.

The lunch went on, both women eating second helpings. Warren didn't finish his first plate, but the Tabasco sauce helped him eat all of his lamb. Toward the end of the meal Gabriela had a question for her niece. "So Gaby Gomez, what are you going to name your son?" she asked.

The pretty young woman smiled as she put her hand on Warren's forearm. "What's your middle name, Warren?" she asked.

"It's Alvin. Why?"

Gaby's smile widened. "I'm going to name my child Warren Alvin Gomez," she said. Her words stunned Warren. He searched for words of thanks but none came. Not one to cry easily, a tear nevertheless coursed down his cheek. It said everything.

*   *   *

Weeks passed and summer turned into autumn. The odd trio continued to reside at 41 Crestwood, Gaby taking her aunt's advice to stay with her until after the baby was born. Warren's condition slowly but steadily worsened, his weight dwindling, his appetite next to nothing, and his back pain only marginalized by large doses of narcotics. He always used a cane while walking these days but spent most of the day sitting or lying down. Gabriela took over the chore of walking Theo, a change that took the blind giant a while to accept. But the old dog gradually accepted her as his permanent walking companion, perhaps sensing that his owner was too sick to make the trip.

By the end of October Warren's ambulation was limited to short trips within his home. To enhance Warren's mobility, Dr. McHale suggested an electric wheelchair. Warren was taught its use by an enthusiastic physical therapist at UNMC. One day as he was busy learning the ins and outs of the devise in an out-patient facility he was approached by a middle-aged woman in a long white coat. She looked Asian and was very short. Her name was stitched in red cursive over a breast pocket. The letters M.D. were clear to see but her name was very long and difficult to make out. When she spoke her name it came out clipped in a heavy accent. But what got Warren's attention was her large head. It seemed far too big for her body. Her black eyes and red lips against a face covered in makeup made her look like Mrs. Potato Head.

"I'm the chairperson of the UNMC oncology board," the woman told Warren after introducing herself. "I'm well acquainted with your case," she added.

"I guess you should be," Warren commented. "I've had three rounds of treatment."

"My colleagues and I have been very disturbed by Dr. McHale's choices with respect to your care. Frankly, he has used agents that are practically obsolete. He has also ignored other therapeutic modalities that may well have helped you deal with your prostate carcinoma."

"Why are you telling me this?" Warren asked.

"The board wants to make it clear to you that Dr. McHale has turned a deaf ear to our recommendations at every juncture of your therapy…"

"Ah, the old disclaimer. Don't worry Doc. I'm not going to sue you."

"I'd think the fact that you've been denied state-of-the-art treatment would be upsetting to you."

Warren had an answer. "Look lady, my wife and my best friend were given your state-of-the-art treatments and they're both dead. Dr. McHale put off retirement for me. He's made house calls. And I'm still alive."

"Sir, our statistics show…"

"Statistics? I'm a mathematician. Numbers can be juggled to fit conclusions. If you and your board get a kick out of reading medical journals to each other have at it. As for me I'll take friendship over data any time." The strength in Warren's voice surprised him, as it seemed to put the woman back on her heels. In fact Mrs. Potato Head had nothing more to say, simply nodding her head, turning, and walking away. In continued defiance Warren wheeled around and sped forward, weaving in and out of obstacles meant for wheelchair practice. His speed and agility reminded him of running with a football, dodging this way and that to elude tacklers. The last maneuver of the day was an end run. And when he crossed the imaginary goal line he raised his arms in celebration.

*   *   *

Two days later was Halloween. Warren asked Gabriela to join him for his first trip outdoors in his electric wheelchair, which proved to be fortuitous because of the many deep cracks in the old sidewalks of

Dundee, cracks that could have caused the frail man to fall. When the wheelchair lacked the power to make it over a crack Gabriela pushed the chair. Otherwise electric motor was enough to allow Warren a smooth enough ride.

The neighborhood was filled with children in costume and many gawked at Warren as they streamed by. One girl around ten years of age and dressed like Cinderella stopped in front of him to ask a question. "What are you supposed to be?" she asked Warren, who could hear Gabriela's tittering behind him.

"What do you think I am?" Warren asked the girl.

"A zombie?" she ventured. Warren thought carefully about what he must look like. He was bald, his cheeks were hollow, his skin was a pale yellow, and his clothes hung loosely on his emaciated frame. He decided that he filled the bill.

"You're right. I'm a zombie," Warren said. "But I'll never catch you because I can't walk very well."

"Cool," the girl said before she moved on.

"You don't look like a zombie, Boss," Gabriela teased as she gave the wheelchair a shove.

"Sure I do. I'm just not dead yet." Warren's sobering words got no response from Gabriela. As she continued to escort him through the neighborhood he gazed forward searching for his future. Children darted everywhere. They were full of promise. He was only promised the misery of cancer. Still, the Halloween evening was fill with joy and he did his best to fulfill his role of zombie, shouting boos or growling ominously at passing trick-or-treaters. But when the evening wound down and he was wheeled home he reflected on what he had said earlier. I look like the walking dead, he thought. Hell, maybe I'm dead already and don't know it.

That night Warren did something unusual for him. He drank a Jack Daniels on the rocks. In fact, he had two.

XXV

Another Christmas season arrived. Warren felt grateful to see it though he knew it would be his last. Dr. McHale stopped by 41 Crestwood one snowy morning. Warren was still in bed and Gabriela escorted the doctor to his bedside. McHale immediately sorted through the amber vials of medications that sat on a bedside table, grunting his approval as he did so. Though Warren had been in bed since 8p.m. the night before he was still impossibly tired. He struggled to prop himself up on two pillows to converse with his physician. "And how is my only patient," McHale began.

"Dying," Warren said.

"How many OxyContins do you take a day?"

"Eight."

"Yikes. Any headaches or blurred vision?"

"Not yet."

McHale leaned in to have a look at Warren's eyes. "Your sclera are as yellow as butter," the doctor said. Having been exposed to medical jargon for eighteen months Warren knew what his physician meant. The discoloration of the whites of his eyes reflected his failing liver.

"How long do I have Alvin?" Warren asked.

"Maybe a couple of months," McHale said.

"So I might see my son born after all," Warren said to himself. McHale heard the words.

"Your son?" McHale repeated.

Just then Gaby walked in the bedroom carrying a breakfast tray. McHale stared at her protruding belly, and seemed to instantly arrive at his conclusion. "Warren you are an impressive old dog," he said.

"It's not what you think," Warren said.

"Your modesty is admirable," McHale said with a grin on his face. "But back to business. Have you considered hospice?"

"I've got plenty of help right here," Warren said as Gaby placed the tray on his lap.

"I can see that," McHale said. "Well, call me if you change your mind. I probably won't be back."

The last sentence struck Warren particularly hard. The wiry man had been a companion since cancer showed its ugly face. Perhaps his methods weren't as cutting-edge as his colleagues but they had added nearly two years to a life not without its adventures. Warren extended a hand for a shake and Alvin returned the favor. "Thank you for hanging in there with me," Warren said. McHale just nodded and then walked away.

Warren turned his attention to his breakfast, picking at the food as Gaby looked on. He bit at an end of a bacon strip and took one bite of scrambled egg. It was like eating cardboard. "I'll get you some Tabasco sauce," Gaby offered.

"Don't bother," Warren said. "I'm just not hungry. Sit and talk with me." Gaby lowered her mass to the edge of the bed. Warren considered the move to be rather impressive seeing that her body seemed to lack the necessary angularity to sit anywhere. "Our baby is going to be a big one," he started. Gaby smiled as she ran a hand over her pregnancy.

"I can't thank you enough for letting me use your sperm," Gaby said. "I can't tell you how much I wanted a child."

"A woman as attractive as you are shouldn't have any trouble finding a husband," Warren said.

"I need to be careful when it comes to men. Sometimes I don't use good judgement," Gaby said. Her expression turned wistful and a bit sad. Warren wanted to offer some advice but held back. *What do I know about romance,* he thought?

"Are you going to raise our son Catholic?" Warren asked.

"Sure. That is if you don't object."

Warren snickered as he pointed to Gaby's belly. "That child in there is yours alone. I'm in no position to counsel you."

Gaby slid off the bed and waddled to a desk that hugged a back wall. On the desk was a framed photo of Warren Westing, a professional portrait done at the request and expense of the Sanders, Litchfield & Tannenbaum law firm. She picked up the photo and returned to the bed. "May I have this?" she asked Warren.

"Of course," Warren said. "But why in the world…"

"I want to show our son what his father looked like," Gaby said.

Gaby's thoughtfulness rendered Warren speechless. He had experienced just a handful of kind gestures in his life. This, he thought, was one of the best. He took the photo from Gaby and gazed at his 40 year old image. This is the one for my obituary, he decided.

Just then Warren's cell phone rang. The caller ID read Steven Westing. "Shit" Warren cursed. On an impulse he handed his phone to Gaby. "Talk to my brother, would you?" he begged.

Gaby took the phone but she looked puzzled. "What do you want me to say?" she asked.

"Steven is going to want to know if I've dealt with dying. Tell him I've joined a…discussion group on the subject. That should shut him up."

Warren looked on as Gaby talked to his brother, glad that he didn't have to hear the preaching of the minister who claimed to be an expert in end-of-life issues. The brevity of the conversation surprised him. Steven tended to be long-winded. "What did he say?" he asked Gaby after she hung up.

"He said he was just confirming the meaning of his last dream," Gaby said.

"What bullshit," Warren muttered.

"He said your were in a good place, whatever that meant. He said he wouldn't bother you again."

"Well, that's a good thing."

"I guess you two don't get along."

"My mother said we were oil and water."

Gaby sat on the edge of the bed. "Is your mother still alive?" she asked.

"No. She died last year in a nursing home."

"Were you close?"

"Not really. But I visited her once a week for years. We played checkers, watched movies, ate lunch, took walks. Things like that."

"What was wrong with her?"

"I was told she suffered from dementia. But she may have been over-medicated. To this day I regret not taking more of an interest in her care."

"It sounds to me like you were an attentive son."

Warren shifted his weight a little, slightly easing the pain in his back. The word "attentive" made him think of the distance he had kept from Margie and her cancer. He began to wonder if he had also kept a distance from her emotional life, explaining why she had entered into an affair. Then, suddenly, as he gazed at the pregnant lovely young woman a wave of affection swept over him. For the first time in many years he felt like he was part of a family. "You and your aunt have been very good to me," he told Gaby.

"And you have been good to us," Gaby said. Glancing at her belly Warren began to feel an urge, a determination, to lay his eyes on his son.

"What is your due date again?" he asked.

"February 14. Valentine's Day."

"Just under two months," Warren murmured. "I've got to make it." Somehow the pledge bolstered his strength and confidence. Slipping out from under the covers he headed for the bathroom in his silk pajamas. He left his cane at the bedside. Every step sent pain up and down his spine but he persevered until he reached the sink where he supported himself with his arms. He peered into the bathroom mirror and as always was shocked by what he had become. This time, in addition to the wasting, he saw what McHale had mentioned, the unmistakable yellow hue of the whites of his eyes. No liver, no life, he thought. But the son of a bitch has to last two months.

*   *   *

In January a severe winter seized Omaha. The cold weather and icy roads led Gaby to take early maternity leave. Gabriela made fewer trips to the grocery store but made sure to buy extra food on each venture out. Warren's need for medication became problematic, particularly his heavy use of narcotics. His supplies seemed to run out as fast as they were restored, which promised frequent trips to the pharmacy. Luckily the UNMC hospice service offered medication delivery, and Dr. McHale insisted that Warren at least accept this part of the hospital's resource. McHale also explained to Warren the reason for his decrease in mental acuity. Most medications were metabolized by the liver and his liver's abilities were slipping. The pain pills, opiates, were backing up in his system. Grogginess, lack of concentration and frequent naps were to be expected. Indeed, Warren spent more time sleeping than awake.

One cold morning Warren managed to slip into an old sweater, corduroy slacks and leather slippers before facing the day. As usual Gabriela held his arm as he walked down the stairs to his wheelchair. Warren held onto the bannister for dear life, knowing the likely dire consequences of a fall. Fortified with two Oxy's, he headed for his old chair in the den. Gabriela brought him a Snapple. He took one sip. When the doorbell rang an hour later Warren was asleep. Gabriela shook him awake. "You have a visitor Boss," she said. His eyes popped open. Standing before him was Naomi Zycyz.

"Naomi," Warren squeaked. "What in the world…"

"I am visiting Gloria," Naomi said. She was still in her heavy winter coat and wool cap. "I thought I would drop by and see how you are faring."

"May I take your coat, Naomi?" Gabriela offered.

"Not just yet thank you. I need to warm up first."

"Would you like some tea?"

"That would be lovely," Naomi told Gabriela. Warren gazed at the women in his life, one from the past and the other in the present. He was sure Gabriela knew that Naomi was the woman who once left all those messages at work, and he remembered how hard he had once worked to keep his sexual relationship with Naomi a secret. Now it hardly seemed important.

"Have a seat, Naomi," Warren said as he gestured to a chair. "I'd like to do a little catching up." As Gabriela moved off to brew tea Naomi pulled up the padded chair and loosened her coat. The first thing Warren saw was that ugly brown blemish on her neck, a consequence of playing a viola. "So, are you still with the Boston symphony?" he asked.

"I am. I feared the Boston winters but I see Omaha can be just as awful."

It was then that Warren recalled Naomi's colon cancer. "Do you still have that…what is it called?"

"A colostomy bag. Yes I do. And how is your cancer treating you?"

Warren sneered. "Look at me. There's your answer."

The old sex partners had a cordial and lengthy talk touching mostly on old times, the marijuana they enjoyed together in the "Sugar Shack," the delightful way pot brought out the flavor of food, and the inventive ways they physically pleased one another when Warren was ill from chemo. They also talked about the future. Naomi intended to retire soon. Warren bragged about his son who would be entering the world in a month. Near the end of the conversation a poignant moment arose. They were focusing on the future when Naomi said, "This may be the last time we have together."

Warren had been thinking about his end for so long he took the remark in stride, saying, "Everything has an end. Even us."

Finally removing her winter coat, Naomi stood and walked over to Warren. Her height was just a bit greater than Warren's, who was still seated. She placed a gentle kiss on his dry lips. "Thank you for wonderful memories," she whispered. At least that's what Warren thought she said. Her soft heavily accented speech was still difficult for him to understand.

Just then Gabriela returned with a pot of tea and three mugs all balanced on a serving tray. She placed the tray on a coffee table and poured. In no time the trio sat together sipping hot tea. "I feel like I know you," Gabriela directed to the guest. Naomi smiled as her eyes flitted from Warren to Gabriela and back again to Warren.

"You two look very happy," Naomi said. "Are you married?" The question led Gabriela and Warren to look at each other as if one expected the other to offer an answer. Warren's alertness, however, was beginning to flag. He gulped his tea in hopes that the caffeine would keep him awake. Balancing his mug in his lap he rubbed his eyes and shook his head. He didn't feel Gabriela taking his mug from his hand, nor did he know exactly when it was that he nodded off. When he awoke he found himself still in his old chair under a blanket. Naomi was gone.

* * *

In his bed, his laptop braced against his skinny legs, Warren noticed that the date was February 1. Gaby's due date was just 2 weeks away. He checked his e-mail, looking in vain for a personal message from an old college buddy or law associate. The only item of interest was the latest news letter from his old firm of Sanders, Litchfield & Tannenbaum. His work as a tax attorney seemed to him like a distant memory. He wondered if anyone at the firm remembered him, if his spot had been filled by someone younger. He thought back on the years he and his friend Stu Gottlieb shared experiences, not only at work but out on the town. It was hard to accept that they, two hard working, well-dressed attorneys no longer haunted the firm's hallways or Omaha's eateries. How he longed to fart a goodbye to his old chum just one more time.

It was late morning and Warren had slept late. Slipping out of bed he had to steady himself before visiting the bathroom. His pills were waiting for him next to the sink. As he urinated he listened for Theo's bark. Lately his dog had not responded to the sound, and Warren figured his pet's hearing had begun to fail. A dog both blind and deaf would be a challenge. Thankfully he had Gabriela.

As he brushed his teeth Warren stared at this image in the mirror. His head looked like a pool ball, the yellow one. He believed it was the #1 ball but he wasn't certain of that. Out of morbid curiosity he stepped on the digital scale. He weighed 130, more that a hundred pounds less than his pre-diagnosis mass. When he moved to his walk-in closet he donned clothes that just a month before had fit him but now draped on his wasted body. He had stopped buying new duds. It seemed like a waste of money.

The walk down stairs was a slow and careful process. Usually Warren waited for Gabriela's help. This day, for some reason, he felt strong enough to take on the chore by himself. Clutching the bannister rail he placed one foot down on the first step followed by his other foot, and then repeated the process until all twelve steps had been covered. His back ached as he moved and he couldn't wait until he was in his wheelchair. In time he wheeled into the kitchen where he found Gabriela over the stove and Gaby, in all her immensity, sitting at the butcher block island counter. When Gabriela spotted him she shouted her displeasure. "Boss! You know you shouldn't walk down those stairs by yourself." Warren smirked a little. It always tickled him when she squinted.

"How is my son this fine February?" Warren asked Gaby. The young woman ran a hand over her swollen belly and smiled.

"Little Warren Alvin is just about ready to come out," Gaby said.

Warren thought about confessing his impatience regarding the seemingly interminable march to the due date. Each passing day felt longer to him as though hours were added at each sunset. To make matters worse it was obvious that each passing day took time off his life, that his illness eroded him from within and posed a very real threat to his chances of seeing the birth of his son. But he said nothing. After all he was just a sperm donor. The imminent birth was something that belonged to Gaby and not him. "Can't wait," was all Warren said as he accepted a glass of Snapple from Gabriela. The cool drink soothed his parched throat but he had lost the ability to appreciate taste. Dr. McHale had called it a side effect of his medications. To Warren it was just another step in dying.

"I've got to take Gaby to her final ob-gyn check at 1:30," Gabriela advised Warren. "Can I pick up anything for you while I'm out?"

"Cigarettes," Warren answered. Truth be told he wasn't smoking much these days. He had lost the taste for tobacco as well as for food. "Don't buy a carton," he added. "A couple packs should do."

"There's something else," Gabriela said. Staring, Warren searched her face for her mood. To his dismay she looked serious. "Theo didn't eat this morning. And he didn't want to take his walk. I think he's sick," she said. Warren just sat back in his wheelchair and sighed. He knew this day was coming. He had hoped he would be gone before his beloved dog. "Should I make a vet appointment?" she asked.

"I guess you better," Warren muttered. "Tell the vet to call me if it's... bad news."

Hours later, as Warren dozed in his den in front of a muted TV, Gabriela leashed Theo and coaxed the giant through the kitchen, out the garage door and into the back seat of her Honda. Then the Latinas, clad in winter coats, climbed in the car. Gabriela backed it out of the garage onto the shoveled driveway then out on Crestwood St. where she sped away from Dundee toward UNMC. Warren hadn't heard them leave. He was dreaming. Walking the streets of a busy city he headed for a destination, a place he needed to be and would recognize when he got there. But as he walked the city grew more congested, the traffic thicker, the daylight dimmer, the noise louder. Day turned to night and neon signs flashed everywhere. A man sat under a streetlight, his legs crossed in front of him. It was the old Indian. He was shirtless and wore a turquoise and silver necklace with matching earrings. "Vani nasi a ro," the Indian said to Warren as he walked by. Persevering, Warren kept up his pace but could feel himself tiring. He believed his destination was always just around the corner but was always disappointed. The dream lasted the entire length of his nap and when he was awakened by the ringing of his cell phone he was exhausted. Just as he accepted the call he noted that he had been asleep for three hours.

"Mr. Westing?" the voice asked. It was a woman's voice.

"Speaking," Warren said.

"My name is Diane. I'm a vet assistant who helped evaluate your dog Theo."

"Yes?"

"We have bad news. Theo's kidneys have shut down."

Warren's shoulders slumped. He almost dropped the phone. He knew what he would hear next. "We think it best that we put the old guy down," the woman said. "I'm sorry."

"I agree," Warren murmured. "He's had a good life."

"Do you want him cremated?"

"Yes. That would be fine."

The vet assistant talked on about the details and timing of the cremation but Warren had trouble paying attention. Closing his eyes he saw the old Indian man and the city backdrop. He rubbed his eyes in a silly attempt to erase the image. It was only when the woman asked if he had any questions that he forced his eyes open. In the most even tone he could muster, he thanked her and hung up. He laughed at himself when he realized he had heard very little of what she had said.

Barely awake, Warren thought back on the day Theo had joined the family as a puppy. It was during the first year of his marriage to Margie. "You were a good friend, Theo," he whispered. "Just as good as Gottlieb." Wheeling over to his dog's kennel he remembered his decision to deal with Theo's blindness. That was a good decision, he thought. He closed the door to the wire cage with the sad realization that he would never have another dog. But he would have another box of ashes to deal with. As he returned to the den, he vowed be more careful with Theo's remains than he had been with Margie's. He and Gabriela could do without another mess on their hands. Then, as solemn as the moment was, he couldn't help letting out a short laugh at the thought of Gabriela offering to vacuum up Margie. That, he remembered, was some funny shit.

Back in front of the TV, Warren searched for something lighthearted to watch. He settled for the movie "Young Frankenstein." He made it through the entire show before taking more pain pills. Regarding his cancer it was, so far, a pretty good day. He didn't hear the women return because he fell asleep again. He didn't eat a morsel of food despite Gabriela's urging. And when daylight waned he accepted Gabriela's help up the stairs for an early turn in. As usual he wondered if this day would be his last.

XXVI

Warren Alvin Gomez was born on February 19, 2014, weighing in at 7 pounds 12 ounces. He looked nothing like Warren Westing, instead showing a dark complexion, a shock of dark hair and brown eyes. The day Warren first saw his son, the day Gaby stood in front of Warren's wheelchair, pulled back the blue blanket and showed the infant's face to him, the wasted old man swelled with pride. "He has my nose," Warren claimed. Gaby and Gabriela agreed, though he knew they were lying.

Three months sped by. Warren now spent most of the time huddled in his bed or stretched out of the backyard lounge chair next to the garden pool. Luckily, the May weather proved to be warm and mild and he much preferred to be outside during the day. Gaby made sure he spent some time with Little Warren, as the baby came to be called. Gabriela offered Warren a steady stream of food she thought he could handle but was lucky to get her Boss to drink a glass of Snapple. When in his backyard Warren often reached under the lounger to pet Theo, who of course wasn't there. The futile effort made him groan with grief, but the ever present narcotic in his bloodstream insured that his disappointment was short-lived. Furthermore he was beginning to have headaches and to have prolonged periods of double vision. Dr. McHale told him the cancer in the brain was likely expanding but offered no real treatment except to increase the doses of his anti-seizure medications and to wish his patient good luck.

One pleasant afternoon Warren had a visitor. To his delight it was his old lover Naomi Zcycz who was back in Omaha as a guest performer with the local symphony. They reminisced over the wrought iron table near the backyard pool. Though the temperature was just over 80 degrees Naomi wore a light sweater. As always her hair was in a heavy braided pony tail. She drank hot tea. Warren sipped on a glass of his favorite beverage.

Suddenly Warren couldn't hear Naomi's voice. Then his vision went dark. His head fell forward and came to rest on the iron table, his arms dangling in front of him, his body precariously perched on his chair. He felt someone's hand on his shoulder and guessed that Naomi, or perhaps one of the Latinas, was trying to shake him awake. It was then that he lost all awareness of his surroundings, including bodily sensations. He was certain he was dead.

"Vani nasa a ro," the old Indian said. "You did well, my friend."

Warren only heard the words, but he knew who, or what, produced them. He felt like he was dreaming and understood that this dream had no ending. He didn't feel sick, nor did he feel well. Memories simply were not part of the experience, if that was what he was doing, having an experience. Time wasn't passing, he wasn't moving, he lacked a sense of self. To be sure he wasn't who he used to be, but he made no judgement on what he had become, if anything. Everything surrounded him yet nothing was there. Somehow he knew the game was over, that he had finished his end run. He had no feelings about that. He wasn't happy, sad, worried, bored, impatient, or curious. He just was.

THE END

Printed in the United States
By Bookmasters